Dani Atkins was born in Londo... London. She moved to rural Hertfordshire in 1985, where she has lived in a small village ever since with her family. Although Dani has been writing for fun all her life, *Fractured* was her first novel and became an eBook sensation. This is her fourth novel.

Find out more about Dani Atkins:
@AtkinsDani
DaniAtkinsAuthor

Praise for *Our Song*:

'*Our Song* is exceptional, touching and powerful.
Dani Atkins has real talent and has created such unique and
memorable characters. I am a fan for life' **Michelle Russell**

'I'm trying to recover from finishing *Our Song*! I think my husband
was really worried as he came in from work and I was loudly
sobbing my heart out!! Fantastic book about two friends that lost
their way and found immense courage and strength within them to knit
their friendship together again' **Suzy Eales**

'One of the best things I have ever read, I completely fell in love
with this book and have been recommending it to all my friends! A
real weepie, but full of hope too. Amazing' **Hannah Morris**

'A truly poignant story which intertwines the lives of four different
people. Dani's writing captivates the reader from the very beginning,
allowing you to identify with and care about the characters as the plot
develops. A thoroughly enjoyable read' **Rachael Harris**

'Pure escapism ... Dani has a way of writing so that
you see and feel everything. This was a truly captivating
story, impossible to put down' **Louise Jarvis**

'One of the most absorbing books I've read for a very long time. Dani has
a special ability to make you feel like you are part of the story – something
not many writers achieve. She has now made me cry with every book
she's written. It's a story that will stay with me for a long time and I think
it would make the most amazing film' **Michelle Wilson**

'*Our Song* had me hooked from the first page. It is the story of four people and how they have been thrown together by tragedy. Be prepared to cry your heart out' **Patricia Saich**

'I was captivated from page one by the spectrum of emotions this novel provokes, with the twists and turns that fate delivers Ally, Joe, Charlotte and David. As the story cleverly unravels you will become addicted to this page turner and the characters will stay with you long after you have read the last page. An absolute joy to read! I didn't think Dani Atkins could eclipse *Fractured* but she has!' **Helen Nellist**

'Captivating from the first page. An emotional heart-wrenching roller coaster throughout – tissues a must!' **Zoë Braycotton**

'*Our Song* is a beautifully written, powerful and emotive love story that will have you reaching for the tissues, and wanting to get to the end without ever wanting it to finish. I loved, loved, loved it!' **Julie de Mattia**

'A captivating journey through the interweaving lives of Ally, Charlotte, David and Joe, as their story of love, tragedy, reconciliation and hope unfolds and tugs at your heart strings. *Our Song* is one of those rare gems of a story that linger and radiate in your mind long after you have finished the last page. Another masterpiece from Dani' **Denise Kanetti**

'She's done it again! Another masterpiece by Dani Atkins! A put-your-life-on-hold, intoxicatingly addictive read that leaves you in total awe of Dani's ability to convey the complexity of raw human emotion in a way that draws you in, making you feel as if the story were actually happening to you! Amazing!' **Becky Davies**

'We get to know the characters intimately, and then Dani confronts us with incidents no one would wish to face. Having held our hands through all this, she delivers a punch to the stomach with a final heart-wrenching twist. What a brilliant book, and one which I will be thinking about for a long time' **Prue Stopford**

'I was captivated from the beginning, hanging on by my fingernails as the story roller coasted to a tear-jerking conclusion. I was unprepared for the depth of emotions Dani made me feel. A must read' **Nadia Donnelly**

This Love

DANI ATKINS

SIMON &
SCHUSTER

London · New York · Sydney · Toronto · New Delhi

A CBS COMPANY

First published in Great Britain by Simon & Schuster UK Ltd, 2017
A CBS COMPANY

3 5 7 9 10 8 6 4 2

Simon & Schuster UK Ltd
1st Floor
222 Gray's Inn Road
London WC1X 8HB

www.simonandschuster.co.uk

Simon & Schuster Australia, Sydney
Simon & Schuster India, New Delhi

A CIP catalogue record for this book
is available from the British Library

Paperback ISBN: 978-1-4711-4225-3
eBook ISBN: 978-1-4711-4226-0
eAudio ISBN: 978-1-4711-6626-6

Typeset in Bembo by M Rules
Printed and bound by CPI Group (UK) Ltd, Croydon, CR0 4YY

Simon & Schuster UK Ltd are committed to sourcing paper
that is made from wood grown in sustainable forests and support the Forest
Stewardship Council, the leading international forest certification organisation.
Our books displaying the FSC logo are printed on FSC certified paper.

This Love

To Kimberley
Who once found a phoenix in a wine bar

Prologue

It was the handwritten sign on the window that drew me in. If they'd written *'Second-hand'* or *'Used'* I'd have kept on walking. Even the nostalgia of *'Vintage'* wouldn't have stopped me from continuing on down the high street. But they got me with *'Pre-loved'*. I hadn't come out with the intention of shopping for new clothes, but *'Pre-loved'* made me think of abandoned pets, in need of a new and caring owner. It was somewhat worrying how easily I was sucked in by the sign in the charity shop window, given how little money was sitting in my current account. But it was too late to worry about that when the woman behind the counter was already straightening up from whatever task was occupying her at floor level, and turning towards me.

'Can I help you?'

I smiled and pointed at the sign Sellotaped to the window, the letters shadowy and reversed, but still legible. 'Pre-loved designer dresses?'

The woman pointed at a circular dress rack in the far corner of the charity shop. 'Are you looking for anything in particular? We have some lovely evening dresses that have just come in.'

I shook my head and felt the unfamiliar tickle of my hair grazing the base of my neck. It still felt odd that it ended there instead of halfway down my back. 'Actually I'm looking for a plain black dress.'

'Can't beat an LBD,' said the woman, tapping the side of her nose conspiratorially, as though we were members of a secret society, speaking in code. I gave a tepid smile and headed for the dresses. This corner of the charity shop was devoted entirely to clothing, and if it weren't for the sign above the door, you could easily be forgiven for thinking you'd wandered into a rather exclusive and select boutique. It was an affluent area, where the houses were mostly executive, the mummies were yummy, and no one tackled the rugged terrain of the school run without a four-by-four. Even the rejected items in the charity shop felt aspirational.

A surprisingly large section of the rail was devoted entirely to black dresses. The hangers scraped like chalk on a board as I flicked through the garments. Long-sleeved, short-sleeved, winter wear and a gorgeous lightweight fabric that I was pretty sure was pure silk. In the end I found four dresses in my size and pulled them from the rail. The woman behind the counter had been watching me from her sentry point beside the till. 'There are some lovely designer dresses there,' she advised. 'Would you like to try them on?'

'Yes, please,' I said, walking into a small cubicle separated from the rest of the shop by a bright chintzy curtain. It was about the size of a WC closet on an economy plane, which made wriggling out of my jeans and jumper a fairly tricky manoeuvre. After a great deal of hopping around on one leg as I tugged the boots from my feet, I slipped the first dress from its hanger and stepped into the black puddle of fabric. The zip purred up comfortably, although I'd been certain it was going to be too small. I smoothed the material down over my hips, wondering if I would always feel vague surprise when something this size fitted me so well.

I pulled the flowery curtain aside and studied my reflection in the full-length mirror conveniently positioned outside the changing space. The assistant was busy with another customer, allowing me a few moments of privacy as I turned left and right, pulling and tweaking the dress into place. At this point in the proceedings I'd usually do a few practice smiles at my reflection. *Hello, this is me in my new dress. What do you think of it?* Today, somehow, that didn't seem appropriate.

I tried on the dresses in turn, never expecting that each one of them would fit me so well, and look equally good. I examined the four cardboard price tags. They were ridiculously cheap. Even combined, they were still only what I would reasonably expect to pay for a single new dress anywhere else. Feeling comfortable that I'd successfully justified my purchase as a saving, I changed back into my own clothes and approached the counter.

'Do any of them suit you?' asked the assistant politely.

3

'They all do,' I said, 'so it's hard to pick between them. I hadn't expected there'd be so many to choose from.'

The woman looked up and glanced around the shop, checking we were alone. We were, although I hadn't heard the previous customer leave. 'To be perfectly honest, we're *never* short of black dresses.' Her voice dropped to a whisper and she leant a little closer towards me. 'A lot of them have only been worn once. You see, people often buy a new dress to attend a funeral, but somehow they never want to wear it again afterwards.' She straightened up sharply, as though suddenly realising she might just have talked herself out of a sale. 'But I'm sure you're not superstitious about that,' she declared, as though she'd been able to tell that about me after our brief fifteen-minute acquaintance. 'It's not as though the dresses are affected by where they were worn, and it seems so extravagant to discard them after just one wearing.'

I reached into my handbag for my purse, pleased I'd visited the cashpoint earlier that day, even if the money had been intended for my weekly groceries. 'Actually, I haven't got a problem with that at all, because that's why *I'm* looking for a black dress.'

'Oh, for a funeral?' asked the woman, her voice taking on an instantly sombre tone. 'I'm so sorry, my dear.' I pulled out two notes from my purse, anxious to leave before she grew bold enough to probe a little further. 'Which of these were you taking?' she asked, reaching for a used carrier, which boasted the name of a top-end retailer. Even the bags here were upmarket.

'All of them, please,' I said, laying down my money on the glass-topped counter.

'All four?'

'Yes, please.'

I could see the questions dancing in her eyes behind her wing-tipped spectacles. I could see the one that polite decorum prevented her from asking. *'Surely you don't have four funerals to attend? Not four? Surely not?'*

I wondered **how** she'd react if I simply nodded my confirmation. Would she look aghast at the colossal misfortune that must have led to this, or would she blame me for not taking better care of the people around me? I could hardly blame her. Four funerals was indeed excessive.

In a world of miracles, I would never need these clothes. Grief wouldn't be standing like a stalker in the shadows, waiting for the moment to colour everything in grey, again, and again, and again. Perhaps I was being unnecessarily pessimistic. Perhaps *nothing* bad would happen to the people I cared about. Perhaps this time, love would be enough to keep them with me.

Or perhaps it was time I finally grew up.

Chapter 1

I dreamt about the fire again last night. This time I didn't scream. This time there were no feet thundering in panic down the stairs to see what was wrong. This time the only rest I disturbed was my own.

I woke up panting heavily, wrapped up like a burrito in the tangled sweat-dampened sheet. I reached for the clock on the bedside table, knowing I should feel more surprised than I did that the digital read-out registered it was ten minutes past two. Again. For years my subconscious had kept waking me, reminding me, of something that needed absolutely no reminder. I thought I'd finally left those memories in the past, but they'd crackled back into life since the night of the fire. They hadn't gone at all; they were going to be with me forever, just like the small scar the flames had left behind. I turned my arm, and in the moonlight studied the five centimetres of skin above my inner wrist that, until the day I died, would forever be red and thickened. I wasn't the only one who still carried the marks of that night, for he had a scar too, practically identical to mine. That bothered me far more than my own.

I don't light candles any more. If I want atmospheric lighting, I'll dial down a dimmer switch. Halloween pumpkins are always going to make me uneasy, and it has nothing to do with their ghoulish grins or the jaggedly carved teeth. Because that was how it started ... at least, that's what the fire investigators said.

Four Months Earlier

October

I was surprised to have been invited to the party. I stayed for only twenty-seven minutes before wriggling through the mass of bodies jammed in the hallway to reach the front door. Two vampires, one zombie, and a man dressed like Marilyn Monroe (I have no idea why) all tried to stop me from leaving. But to be truthful, I had probably had enough after the first two minutes. The remaining twenty-five were just to be polite.

It's not as though I knew the group of guys in the flat below mine that well. Well, not at all, really. I mean, we exchanged pleasantries in the lift, nodded politely and smiled if we happened to be emptying our mailboxes at the same time, but I knew nothing about them except that they worked somewhere where suits had to be worn, were fond of music with a deep thumping bass that trembled through the ceiling and walls, and filled up the bottle recycling bin in the basement with liver-worrying regularity. I suspected my invitation was more to prevent me from complaining about the noise of the party than anything else. The group reminded me of university students, who hadn't realised that they were now in their mid-twenties and that the partying years were finally coming to a close.

My own party years at university had ended ten years earlier. Now at thirty-one I could look back on those days with a fondness and nostalgia that I don't think I'd felt at the time. The edges of my memories were nicely blurry with age. The best thing I took away from university (aside from a degree in modern languages, which allowed me to earn my living as a translator) was my friendship with Julia. I don't think a single day has passed when I haven't silently thanked the university administrator who'd randomly placed us in adjacent rooms in our first year halls of residence. I remember very little about the Chancellor's speech on that very first day, except for the bit when he told the crowded auditorium that sitting right there in that room were the friends who were going to stay with us for the rest of our lives. His calculations were a slight overestimate. I'd only made *one* friend who I knew would be with me for everything that lay ahead. But sometimes, even if they're travelling on a completely different path than you, one truly exceptional friend is all that you need.

Julia was part of the reason why I hadn't returned to my

home town after graduation. Not that I'd needed a great deal of persuading to stay in our university town and share a flat with her, it's fair to say. Some part of me had always known when I'd packed up my possessions, pulled the Blu-tacked posters from my bedroom walls, and finally cleared out my wardrobe, that the house I'd grown up in would probably never be my permanent address again.

Julia was *definitely* the reason I hadn't declined the party invitation on the night of the fire. 'What else were you planning to do with your Saturday night?'

'Er, watch *Strictly*?' I'd said hopefully, which actually had sounded a great deal more appealing than getting dressed up and making small talk to a group of people I didn't know.

'Sophie Winter, you are *never* going to meet anyone new sitting in and watching television. You're going to be thirty-two next year. Can you hear that deafening tick? That's your biological clock counting down.'

I'd given her an affectionate squeeze, and chosen not to point out that there were still another eleven months to my next birthday. 'Actually, I'm not sure I can hear anything above the sound of your raging hormones,' I said, smiling down at Noah, Julia's second child who also happened to be my two-month-old godson, fast asleep in his Moses basket beside us.

'Hmmm . . .' she agreed, with the kind of satisfied smile that pulled and tangled so many emotions within me. 'I guess I'm just so happy, so content, that I want you to have everything I've got too.'

'You're offering to share Gary with me?' I teased. 'Wow, you really *are* a good friend.'

'No. But I don't want you to give up on the possibility of finding your own Gary. He's out there ... somewhere. He might even be going to this party on Saturday.'

'I doubt it,' I'd said. 'And for the record, you do know a person can still be perfectly happy being single? Life isn't like a game of Snap, where you have to find your other half in order to win, you know.'

Julia had smiled and pushed a long lock of auburn hair behind one ear as she bent to pick up her suddenly grizzling baby. 'It's not meant to be a game of Old Maid either,' she said, trumping me into silence. 'And anyway, you're not, are you?'

'Not what?' I asked inarticulately.

'Perfectly happy.'

I twisted in my chair and looked out of the window at her neatly manicured garden, until I was sure the prickling sensation at the back of my eyes had gone, before turning round to face her. 'No, I'm not. But that's okay. Not every story has to have a happy ending.'

There's something wrong when your best friend worries about you. It makes you feel selfish; it makes you feel guilty. It also makes you agree to go to a party you never wanted to attend in the first place.

As I wriggled my way past the party-goers, a cocktail of odours wafted out of the front door after me like a noxious cloud: alcohol, cigarettes and the distinctive odour of candle smoke. The last was hardly surprising, for I'd spotted at least half a dozen pumpkins, lit from within by flickering red candles, positioned on every flat surface that wasn't already covered with beer bottles.

I took the stairs back up to my attic flat, and was already kicking off my uncomfortably pinching heels as I let myself through the front door. One shoe narrowly missed hitting a small smoke-coloured bundle of fur that launched towards me and began weaving around my ankles. It was only a matter of time before he successfully brought me down with that move, I thought, as I bent and scooped him into my arms. 'Hello, Fred,' I said, burying my face into the thick fur of his neck. 'Did you miss me?' An answering purr thrummed through his body like a motor, which I took as a 'yes'. Fred was the pet I'd always longed for and never got as a child. He was the sounding board for all my decisions, and rarely contradicted my choices, even the poor ones. He was a present for my thirtieth birthday, from me to me, and while Julia might joke it was the first step on a slippery slope to becoming a crazy cat lady, I wasn't worried. The fact that my landlord was willing to turn a blind eye to pets was a deciding factor in moving into the attic flat. *'As long as he doesn't pee on the carpet,'* was his only stipulation. It was a reasonable request of any tenant.

As I went from room to room flicking on lights and drawing the curtains, it felt as though I hadn't left the party at all. Music from oversized speakers still thumped up through the boards beneath my feet, while open windows in the flat below allowed half the street to join in too, should they wish.

I changed into old comfortable pyjamas, made myself a couple of slices of buttered toast, and slipped my feet into a pair of oversized fluffy sheep mules that Julia's daughter Lacey had given me last Christmas. I suppose I was feeling a little down and deflated as I flicked through the channels on the TV before finding the one that showed a never-ending loop of *Friends* episodes. I drew my legs up onto the settee, automatically avoiding the place where one of the springs was just beginning to poke up through the upholstery. Pulling a crocheted afghan over me, I waited until the cat had circled six times before settling on my lap and sat back to watch a group of people who were, as yet, blissfully unaware that one day there might not always be someone who was *'there for you'.*

The noise of the alarm woke me, but I wasn't scared. Well, not to begin with, at least. Years of remembered middle-of-the-night false alarms from my student days had led to a dangerous complacency about that constant beeping sound. I think that's why I wasn't initially concerned when the piercing noise pricked and punctured my sleep like an annoying needle. I sat up and rubbed my eyes blearily, automatically glancing down at my watch, probably to ensure accuracy when I told this story the following day. *'And then, just before midnight, some idiot set off the smoke alarm.'*

I'm not sure how long it took me to work out that the shrill warning claxon wasn't just because someone had burnt their middle-of-the-night toast snack. I know it still hadn't filtered through to me as I padded into the kitchen, to make sure the idiot responsible hadn't actually been me. There was still an awful lot of noise coming from the party below. In fact, it was now quite riotous. I would have thought things would have quietened down a little, but from the shrieks I could hear through the floor below my feet, things were still in full swing. I paused halfway across my tiny kitchen and listened again. They didn't sound like shrieks of laughter or drunken merriment. They sounded like screams. For the first time I noticed that the vague haziness around me might not just be from my sleep-filled eyes. I inhaled deeply and smelt it then. There was something sharp and acrid in the air.

I raced to my front door, the security chain rattling beneath my shaking fingers in my haste to release it. From there I could hear the smoke alarm, the one positioned on the ceiling of the stairwell, screaming out its warning. I opened the door a crack and almost instantly the device in my own flat joined in the chorus. Not that I had needed it to tell me what my eyes could already see. The hallway was filled with smoke. Thick grey belching clouds of it were fluming up the stairwell, occasionally interspersed with lightning flashes of something bright orange. The building was on fire.

I slammed the door shut, but a small opportunistic cloud had squeezed through the opening, making my gasp of terror dissolve into a coughing fit. I had to get out. *Right now.*

There's a question people often ask themselves. *What would you save if your house was on fire?* I now know the answer to that one. Nothing. Not one damn thing. Let the fire have it all. As long as everyone is safely out, the possessions you leave behind for the flames to devour don't matter one little bit.

It took only seconds to find Fred; all I needed to do was follow the peculiar yowling sound I'd never heard him make before. His small body was trembling as I swaddled it into the folds of a thick quilted coat. The bundle jerked and jolted as though it held something possessed, but I gripped it firmly, hoping the fabric was thick enough to resist his thrashing claws until I got us out of there.

I don't know why I ever imagined I'd be able to leave through the front door. It's not as if I'd failed to notice the flames creeping up the stairs like deadly intruders. What did I think – that I could run through them like a stuntman in an action film? Two steps into the shared hall was all it took for me to realise there would be no exit for me that way. I hurriedly retreated to the smoke-filled sanctuary of my flat, slamming the door behind me. But even as I stood panting rabidly beside it, I could see thin white smoke serpents coiling sinuously in through the floor-level gap. Fred had shot from the coat as soon as I put it down, and I hurriedly began ramming the slightly shredded garment under the door, with enough force to rip back several fingernails and not even notice. The smoke continued to meander in, lazily audacious, as though it had all the time in the world to get to me. *No need to hurry here, none at all.* I, on the other hand, had every reason to hurry. I yanked a second coat down from the rack on the wall with such force that the hook flew clean out of the plasterboard. In other circumstances I'm sure I'd have worried about the damage . . . but it didn't even register. The coats offered a temporary barrier, but behind it the smoke was determined. It would find a way in.

I raced back to the lounge, which was the only room that looked out onto the main road. Fire was licking out of the open windows of the flat below. I saw a shape twisting and turning in the flames, and for one dreadful moment I thought it was a person, before I realised it was the billowed-out curtains, flapping and contorting in the air as the blaze consumed the room behind them. The street, three floors below, kept disappearing from view beneath a thick blanket of shifting smoke, like cloud base through a plane window. Through the gaps I saw people streaming from the building. Most of them were running; some didn't stop, even though they were clearly no longer in danger. They raced across the empty road and kept on going, as though the fire was still coming after them. I saw people collapsing to their knees, perhaps in shock, perhaps in gratitude to have made it out alive. Some of them looked like they were throwing up. Bile rose thickly in the back of my throat, and suddenly I felt like joining them.

As my fingers fumbled for the brass sash fastener to open the window, I tried not to think of the row of spiked iron railings that lined the concrete steps leading to the building's basement flat. Because if I stopped to think – even for a second – I would see myself impaled on them, flapping and skewered like a fish on a spear. Jumping could prove to be every bit as lethal as not leaving at all.

I braced my arms against the frame of the lower sash and pushed upwards with all my strength. It didn't move. It scarcely even creaked. It felt as solid as though it had been nailed shut, which it just as well might have been, I realised in horror, as I ran my finger over the thick layer of paint sealing every join. *'The whole flat has just been redecorated,'* I recalled my new landlord declaring proudly when I'd viewed the property two months earlier. That was what had sealed the deal, I remembered. Now the only thing that appeared sealed were the windows . . . and my fate.

I tried several more times to prise it open, without success. Hammering on the glass to get someone's attention was ineffective and totally useless, but I still wasted several vital minutes doing it anyway. There was chaos and confusion on the narrow pavement. No one was going to be able to see me beating against the stuck window this many storeys up. I spun around, surveying the room with terrified eyes, looking for something heavy enough to smash the glass. I kept picking up and discarding totally ridiculous objects, like the TV remote control, the plate my toast had been on, and even a cushion off the settee, before I forced myself to slow down.

Think. Think. Use your brain, said a voice I hadn't heard in quite a while. Panic was making me slow and stupid, and I couldn't afford to be either. *Try another window,* suggested the voice in my head. I nodded, as though the idea had come from someone else.

The kitchen and bathroom windows were protected by thick security rails, which had always reminded me of the bars of a prison cell. It was terrifying to realise that tonight that was *exactly* what they'd become. But the bedroom window looked out onto a side street, and beneath it was a flat roof. *That* would be my way out, I realised, as I ran through the home that was no longer my safe and comfortable haven. It was a smoke-filled Alcatraz and I had very little time left to escape from it.

Some half-forgotten piece of advice prompted me to close the bedroom door. It's funny the things your brain chooses to store away, never once knowing that one day they might actually save your life. Fred was already yowling by the window when I ripped the curtains apart so forcefully I heard material tearing from the hooks. Because of the direction of the wind, there was hardly any smoke outside my window, but being visible from the ground was immaterial – because there was no one there to see me. The focus of everyone's attention was very much on the front of the blazing building.

The narrow street that ran along this side of my flat was always quiet, even in the middle of the day. At this time of night it was as empty as a desert highway. Eyes screwed shut in concentration, I tried to visualise the topography of a place I walked past several times a day without ever really noticing it. Beyond the corner where the wheelie bins lived, there was a lock-up storage room belonging to the laundrette next door. That was the flat roof I was going to have to climb onto, I thought, looking down at the moss-covered square of concrete two floors below me. It looked a great deal further down now that I knew I was going to have to leap onto it.

The idea of jumping was terrifying, but realising I wasn't going to be *able* to do so, was even worse. Had I been a fresh-air fiend, or one of those people who always slept with the window open, I would already know my plan of escape was impossible. My bedroom window didn't open, except for the small fanlight at the top. While feeling smug about how warm and cosy my new bedroom was, why hadn't it occurred to me that in an emergency there could be no escape from this room?

I thumped my hand in frustration on the reinforced glass of the double-glazed unit, looking for a handle in the casement that I knew didn't exist. Panic was creeping through me, at a rate even faster than the encroaching flames were greedily consuming everything in their path. I thrust the fanlight open as far as it would go, which really wasn't that far at all. I could just about get my head through the gap, but there was no way the rest of my body was going to be able to follow. If I'd never eaten a single slice of pizza, if not even one burger had ever passed my lips in the last thirty-one years, it *still* wouldn't have made the blindest bit of difference. No one except a contortionist or a very skinny ten-year-old could have wriggled their way through that narrow opening. Or a cat. A cat could get out that way.

The cool October air on my cheeks was cruelly tantalising. I could feel freedom; I could smell it – even if it was heavily tainted with the odour of smoke and burning timbers. But I just couldn't reach it.

'Help!' I screamed. It was, I realised, the first time I had ever screamed in my adult life. It felt strange, as though I was somehow pretending to be someone in trouble, as though none of this could possibly be real. From the direction of my front door I could hear a weird crackling and popping sound. 'Help! Help! Help!' I bellowed into the night. It turned out that I knew how to do it, after all.

No one came. No one. I kept screaming, hoping that above the noise and chaos at the front of the building, just one pair of ears might tune into my cries. When every light in the building suddenly flickered and went out, plunging me into complete darkness, I screamed again. I ran to the bedroom door, wrenched it open for a second before slamming it shut with a gasp of terror. I now knew the source of the weird noise at my front door. It was alight; the frame and panels were blazing in a halo of bright orange flames, making it look like the portal to hell itself.

Sometimes, even though you know something isn't going to work, you still have to go right on ahead and try it anyway. I picked up the low wooden stool that was beside my dressing table. It was made of oak and the legs felt solid beneath my fingers as I curled them around the wood. I waited until my eyes were fully adjusted to the darkness, putting those moments to good use with a couple of practice swings. When I was as ready as I was ever going to be, I wiped my palms dry on the material of my pyjama legs and swung back the stool, aiming it at the dead centre of the window pane.

I didn't expect it to shatter. I know double-glazed glass doesn't do that. But I thought it might crack, or maybe bow slightly. What I definitely hadn't expected was for the stool to bounce off the glass as though it were a trampoline. The force of the rebound knocked me off my feet. The air at floor level was a little clearer than the rest of the hazily smoke-filled room, but I didn't linger down there long enough to enjoy it. I picked up the fallen stool and swung it again. And again. And again. The glass remained intact, but on the fourth swing the stool exploded in a flying cascade of spindles and splintering wood.

After his undignified treatment with the coat, it was hardly surprising that Fred struggled violently when I picked him up and carried him to the window. He was a house cat. He used an indoor litter tray and had no idea of the dangers posed by the outside world. Except the *real* danger to his life was now *inside* the flat. I turned him around in my hands and looked for a long moment into his terrified green eyes. If this were a *Lassie* film, I'd be telling him to go and fetch help. I'd be instructing him to find someone with a really long ladder to come and rescue me. Timmy was most definitely down the mineshaft right this minute. But this was real life, and the best I could hope for was that only one of us was left imprisoned in the smoke-filled flat. I kissed the cat on the top of his head, then lifted his squirming body up to the small window opening. He teetered for a moment on the narrow sill, glancing back at me as though questioning my judgement. I don't blame him. It suddenly looked like a very long distance to jump. Just as I was about to change my mind, I felt his muscles bunch and stiffen beneath my hands and then he was gone, flying down through the night. I peered down at the roof, convinced I'd see a small grey mangled and twisted body, but he was already gone.

The smoke was getting thicker by the second and despite stuffing whatever I could find along the gap at the foot of the door, I knew I was buying only a few more minutes of air. I thought longingly of my mobile phone, plugged in and charging on my work desk in the lounge. Would it have made any difference if I could have phoned the emergency services to tell them I was trapped up here? As a plan it was probably only marginally better than hoping the cat would alert someone. I swallowed down an unfamiliar cry, which sounded far too hysterical to be laughter.

I saw his car drive past the side street. I saw it slow down almost to a crawl as it approached the burning building. I grabbed the beaded scarf I'd worn that night, and dangled it through the window, like Rapunzel tossing down her hair. The sequins glittered in the light of the street lamp like miniature starbursts. Surely someone would see that. The vehicle paused at the T-junction, then drove off. I slammed my forehead against the glass in frustration, so hard it actually hurt. This was hopeless. It was going to take a miracle for anyone to find me before the fire did.

Then a miracle happened.

Through the gap in the window I heard a throaty roar of an engine as the same car reversed at speed back along the main road, before screeching around the corner and hurtling into the side street. The driver stopped right in the middle of the road and leapt out. He looked to be about my age, or a year or two older. There was only one word to describe the look on his face as his eyes went up to my window and saw me. Horrified.

'Help me!' I cried, my voice breaking into sobs of relief that it was far too early to feel just yet. For a moment I thought he hadn't heard me, because he didn't move, he didn't say anything, he just kept staring up at the window. Finally his head whipped like a tango dancer's as he looked back towards the end of the street, and the main road. He ran two steps towards it, then stopped and shouted up at me.

'Wait there!'

It wasn't as though I had another option, I thought, but I nodded like a lunatic anyway. 'Please hurry. I think the fire's getting closer,' I shouted through the gap.

He was almost at the corner when a loud explosion ripped through the building. I heard glass shattering and people screaming. I don't know what had caused it, or where it had come from, but I suspected that a really, really bad situation had just got even worse. My rescuer clearly thought so too, because he screeched to a halt, rocking on his trainer-clad feet, and came running back towards me. Under any other circumstances I would probably have been in awe of his athleticism as he paused for only a moment and then leapt lithely up onto the lid of one of the industrial bins and then hauled himself up onto the flat roof beside it. He positioned himself directly below me. My head was still sticking out of the window, at a forty-five-degree angle, like a dog on a car journey.

'Can you open the window?' he called up. I'd been prepared to overlook *'Wait there'*, in the heat of the moment, but really ... if it was that simple, wouldn't I have done it already? Was it ungrateful to wish for a rescuer with a better grasp of the situation?

'No, I can't!' I yelled back down at him. I felt bad about the rage suddenly racing through me. It wasn't as though any of this was *his* fault. At least he was trying to help. 'And it's double-glazed; it won't break. I've already tried.'

He frowned and squinted, at either me or the window frame. 'Everything breaks ... eventually,' he declared. He spun around looking for ... I don't know what ... some magical window-shattering device perhaps. Finding nothing, he turned back to me. 'Where did you hit it?' he asked urgently.

I couldn't understand why that was important, but I lifted one hand and pointed to the dead centre of the glass. I looked through it to see him shaking his head at me. 'That's no good. The weakest point is in one of the bottom corners. Try again.'

How had I not known that? I thought, looking down at the man who had suddenly gone from idiot to genius in the space of less than five seconds. 'You'll need something metal and sharp,' he shouted up.

'Like scissors?' It was his turn to look like he was talking to someone intellectually challenged.

'Something heavy.'

I shook my head. I don't know what kind of women he

knew, but clearly they were the type who kept crowbars tucked beneath their mattresses. He said something else then, which I couldn't quite catch, because inexplicably the wall beside me had suddenly begun to make a peculiar sizzling noise. I withdrew my head and stared at the plasterboard in horror. It sounded as though there were snakes trapped in the cavity, or a platoon of miniature chefs stir-frying in there. I saw the blisters appear, without at first realising the danger. Small white bubbles began to bloom in the plaster, popping in seconds, as the molten paint succumbed to the heat inside the walls. I stared in horrified fascination as more and more blister-like sores broke out, as though the wall was in the throes of some terrible disease. As indeed it was.

Beneath my window his voice was shouting up at me. Distracted, I tore my eyes from the wall and finally concentrated on his words.

'An iron. That would do it. The sharp pointed end of an iron.'

My head snapped around so quickly I heard every little bone in my neck crick in protest. There, in the corner of my room, stood the ironing board that I'd forgotten to put away before I left for the party. And sitting squarely in the middle of the board was the small domestic appliance that might, just possibly, get me out of there.

I'd like to say the iron pierced the window at the first swing . . . but that's not how it happened. It took maybe four or five blows before a small hole appeared where the nose of the iron had battered against the glass. It looked like a tiny bullet hole, I thought, as I saw the spider web crazing of the glass all around it. From somewhere down on the flat roof I heard the man cheer before he yelled, 'Hit it again.'

The hole kept getting bigger and bigger until it looked as though a bowling ball had flown through it. A few more swings and suddenly the window simply disappeared in a raining shower of shrapnel shards. I wanted to punch the air in victory, I wanted to cry out in triumph, but just breathing was becoming hard enough to do. With the first pane gone, and the layer of gas cushioned between them dispersed, smashing my way through the second sheet of glass was a piece of cake. I heard the tinkle of falling glass raining down on the flat roof below, and hoped my rescuer hadn't been looking upwards when it happened.

I gripped the edge of the frame and looked down at the man who'd been yelling encouragement at me the whole time. No Juliet had ever stared down from her balcony at Romeo with more gratitude.

'Cover the edge of the frame with something before you climb out,' he advised wisely, and when I saw the jagged shards of glass still embedded around the edge of the frame I was grateful for his advice. To escape from the burning building and then sever my femoral artery on my way out would be a really terrible way for this all to end.

I pulled the duvet from my bed and threw it over the frame. It had only delayed me by a few seconds, but that was all the time it took. It was almost as though the fire had been secretly waiting for me deep within the walls, holding on for just the right moment to still get me. I climbed out through the window and sat gingerly on the edge, smoke billowing around me. I think my rescuer was saying something about lowering myself from the frame, about not just jumping down. But suddenly the wall beside my head exploded like a fiery grenade. I heard the sizzle of my waist-length hair catching alight, felt the heat of it burning against my neck.

I jumped.

Chapter 2

He told me later that I looked like a fiery angel swooping down out of the sky. It was a very romantic way of describing the most frightening moment of my entire life. My hair flew up and around me, like wings with the ends tipped in flames. I executed a very un-angelic landing however, crashing into him as he stood arms outstretched hoping to catch me. That was never going to happen. He made a sound halfway between a grunt and an asthmatic wheeze as I knocked him to the ground and landed squarely on his diaphragm, forcibly expelling the air from his lungs. That I'd made the four-metre jump without breaking a single bone – in either of us – was a miracle in itself. But it wasn't one we had a chance to marvel at, because the very real and immediate danger was my hair.

I know First Aid. I think I even got a badge for it once, way back in my Girl Guide years, but knowing what you're *meant* to do, and actually making your terrified body comply, are two entirely different things. 'Keep still,' my rescuer shouted, as I twisted my head from side to side, instantly making the problem so much worse. With the flat of his hand he pushed me down onto the damp mossy surface of the roof, and began to beat out the flames with his bare hand. There were sizzling sounds and a dreadful smell, which even to this day haunts my nightmares. Some of it was the smell of singed hair, and some of it was the reason why my brave rescuer ended up losing a sizeable patch of skin on his wrist. I raised my own hand and joined him in beating at my blazing hair. You have to work against every instinct in your body when you deliberately place your hand into a flame. Self-preservation and saving my own skin – quite literally saving my own skin – drove me to ignore the pain and keep battering at the fire until it was out. I have absolutely no idea what drove him.

Finally the flames were out. Adrenalin must have been coursing through both of us, so that even though we should have been in agony, neither of us was immediately aware of the burns we'd just sustained. That was still ahead of us.

'Are you alright?' Even though his face was hovering not far above mine, he still had to shout in order to be heard over the very welcome sound of approaching sirens. I nodded up at my rescuer, whose hand was still pinioning me to the roof. 'It's okay,' he reassured. 'Don't cry, you're safe now.'

I opened my mouth to say that I wasn't crying, but then felt the dribble of tears trickling into my ears, so I guessed I was. I tried to speak, but a small choking sound, half word, half cough, was all my smoke-filled throat could manage. His eyes flew upwards when he saw mine grow wide in alarm as I spotted a flurry of flaming particles fluttering through the darkness towards us. They floated silently down from the building, like ignited leaves in a combustible autumn. One larger piece, which I suspected had only recently been my bedroom curtains, wafted lazily downwards. The hand pressed against my breast bone curled into a fist, grabbed a handful of my pyjama top, and used it to haul me up against him. The flaming curtain fabric landed on the exact spot where only a moment earlier my head had been.

'Let's get off this roof,' he said urgently, pulling me to my feet. I followed him fearfully to the edge, my eyes irresistibly drawn to the window above us, where the fire was hungrily devouring all my possessions.

He made the descent from the flat roof look relatively easy, even though I noticed he was cradling his burnt hand protectively against his body. My own injury was now starting to make its presence painfully felt, and I knew – without even trying – that there was no way I was going to be able to hang from the edge of the roof as he'd just done.

'Jump, I'll catch you,' my rescuer said from the shadows somewhere below my feet. It seemed almost ungrateful to remind him how well that had worked out for us the last time. I closed my eyes, scraping an already diminished barrel of bravery. 'I won't let you fall,' he promised. I looked down at the man holding out his one good arm in readiness. 'You have to trust me,' he implored, as I hesitated. A burning timber fell from the building and landed close behind me, showering me with glowing hot embers that stung like a swarm of sand flies. I dropped to a crouch and lowered myself onto the cold damp surface of the roof. He brushed a stray lock of hair back from his forehead and met my frightened expression with one of surely misplaced confidence. 'Keep coming. I've got you,' he encouraged, as I wriggled closer to the edge of the roof . . . and just kept going.

I'm not sure if it was bravery or reflex that allowed him to catch me in both arms, good and injured. The pain from his burn must have been excruciating as I landed on it, but although he winced, his hold on me never faltered. He carried me in his arms towards the end of the road, even though I'm sure I could have walked on my own by then.

'I need some help here!' he bellowed to no one in particular. Shapes came towards us through the darkness and several hands reached out for me. Burly firemen in yellow-trimmed uniforms lifted me from his arms and carried me towards a low flat wall where several other dazed and shocked victims were already sitting. I lost sight of my rescuer in the crowd, as other firefighters led him away from me.

Two fire engines had been summoned to the blaze, and as I watched the four powerful jets of water being directed at the building, it suddenly hit me how unlikely it was that this place would ever be my home again. Ten minutes later, when a section of the roof caved in, I realised I was now officially homeless. I had nothing left except the clothes I was wearing: a pair of penguin-patterned pyjamas and some fluffy sheep-shaped slippers. I didn't even know if Fred had made it out safely, which clearly worried *me* far more than the fireman placing an emergency gel dressing on my burn. The restraining hand he placed on my shoulder was firm, and told me exactly what he thought about my idea of searching for my missing cat.

'If I could just go and look—'

He shook his head. 'I've seen enough cats run out of burning buildings to know that yours is probably a very long way from here right now. Give him time to calm down and he'll come back home.'

He turned to attend to the person sitting next to me, the drama of my missing pet clearly very low down on his list of priorities. I looked up at the charred timbers of the attic roof, silhouetted against the flames like a ribcage of a prehistoric dinosaur. Fred might very well return, as the fireman had predicted, but this burnt-out shell of a building would never be home again for either of us.

I shivered and pulled the edges of the blanket someone had draped around my shoulders closer together. The chill I felt came from somewhere deep within me, and had little to do with the cool October night. There were crowds of people surrounding me, yet I sat on the wall feeling totally alone. I couldn't even see the man who'd saved me from the roof. All around me people were busily talking into their mobile phones, reassuring loved ones they were alright. There were people I should call, but as my own phone was a hundred degrees or so past serviceable use, contacting them would have to wait.

I was placed in one of the first ambulances to leave for the hospital. Thankfully everyone had made it out of the building, and most of the injuries were similar to mine, just minor burns and smoke inhalation. We'd all been incredibly lucky. Just before we drove away, I caught a fleeting glimpse of the man who'd rescued me. He was weaving through the chaotic crowds as though he was looking for something, or someone. Before I had the chance to call out to him, someone slammed the ambulance doors to a close, and slapped sharply on the metal panelling, as though geeing up a reluctant horse. We drove away in a halo of blue flashing lights towards the hospital.

The clipboard on my knee was juddering, as though the waiting room of A&E was inexplicably in the throes of an earthquake. The pen, fixed to the board by a length of string, rolled from side to side and then executed the stationary version of a bungee jump and disappeared. It swung like a pendulum, slapping against my pyjama-clad leg which was jiggling convulsively up and down. Extreme stress was the obvious cause, and I don't think anyone could deny that jumping from a burning building was one of the most stressful things you'd ever have to live through. It was, easily, the second worst night of my life.

I turned my attention back to the form. They weren't hard

questions, but I was struggling to complete them, without having to scribble addendums beside my answers. Name. Okay, that one I had. But address? Did they mean the flat that up until a few hours ago was my home, but now no longer existed? Or should I put down my parents' address, even though it was over two hundred miles away, and I hadn't lived there for twelve years? Or where I was going to live now? Because if *that* was what they wanted to know, then I had absolutely no idea what to write.

Phone number was tricky too. I *had* a number, but the phone it used to live in was probably a blackened, melted version of its former self. Next of kin should be easier to complete, I thought, printing the names of my parents on the dotted line, in letters that looked oddly shaky, and not at all like my usual handwriting. Just as long as the hospital didn't plan on contacting them, of course. Because my pension-age parents were away on the first holiday they'd taken since my dad's heart attack, and for them to receive another bad news telephone call was a risk too high to take.

I stopped writing when a pair of soot-stained trainers came to a stop directly in front of my chair. I lifted my gaze slowly, travelling from his feet up his legs, noting a long jagged tear in the knee of his jeans, then upwards past a shirt that had probably started out the evening as white, but now looked like a 'before' garment in a detergent commercial. It seemed to take me forever before I reached his face, although I'd known who it was from my first glimpse of his Nikes.

'You're here,' he said, sounding hugely relieved. 'I was beginning to think they'd taken you to a different hospital.'

I stared up at the face of the stranger who'd gone out of his way to make sure I survived, and everything I wanted to say to him suddenly locked in my throat. I know how to say 'thank you' in at least six different languages, but none of them could ever adequately express what I owed this man.

'How are you feeling? Have you seen a doctor yet?' I shook my head, noting he was sporting the same temporary dressing on his burn as the one I'd been given by the triage nurse. 'Is there anything I can do for you? Anything you need?' His face looked anxious as he studied me . . . *my fault*; his skin was smeared with dirt . . . *my fault*; his clothing was torn and his arm was burnt . . . *both my fault*. And yet the only thing that appeared to be worrying him was my welfare, not his own. His concern brought about the one reaction I was hoping I'd be able to stave off until I was somewhere far from here, when I was all alone and quiet. I burst into embarrassingly loud tears.

It's wrong to judge people on how they react to the distress of others. Some men just can't cope with women crying; it's how they're wired. Fortunately the man standing in front of me wasn't one of those. He slid smoothly onto the garish orange chair beside me, and gathered me into his arms. He certainly never asked if I was happy being held so intimately by a total stranger, and to be honest I really don't know what my answer would have been if he had. I gratefully buried my face against the solid wall of his body, inhaling smoke, detergent, sweat and some lingering shower gel all impregnated into the fabric of his shirt, and allowed the wide warmth of him to muffle the sound of my tears. There are women who cry delicately and neatly, whose noses never run when they are doing it. Unfortunately I'm not one of them. Finally I raised my head, leaving behind a large damp oval on his shirt. He reached out an arm and hooked up a box of scratchy white NHS tissues from the top of a pile of magazines, and passed them to me.

He didn't rush me. He didn't pester me with questions or fuss; he just waited. 'Better?' he asked eventually, when the bundle of damp tissues in my palm was about the size of a tennis ball.

'Yes. I'm sorry about that ... and your shirt,' I added, looking at the mess my outburst had left behind. 'And your jeans, and—'

'None of that's important,' he reassured.

I shook my head, and caught an unpleasant whiff of singed hair. I picked up a length that earlier tonight had reached down to my waist and now fell far short of my shoulder.

'And that's not important, either,' he added. 'That's the great thing about hair – it grows back.'

I threw the strand to one side, because my hair was nothing, not important at all. 'I don't know how to even begin to thank—'

'Then don't,' he interrupted. His eyes were caramel-coloured, I noted. And if it wasn't such a totally ridiculous question, given everything that had happened that evening,

I would have asked if they were contacts, because I'd never seen anyone with that particular shade before. They were honey, shot with amber and tawny flecks, which ran through his irises like strands of spun sugar.

'I don't even know your name.'

'It's—'

'Ben Stevens,' called out a nurse, consulting a chart in her hand and looking around the assembled patients, like an auctioneer waiting for someone to make the first bid. The man got to his feet, smiled and looked down at me. 'Like she said,' he confirmed quietly, before turning his attention to the waiting nurse. 'Here.' He took a step forward and I saw a brief grimace of pain twist on his face, before he wiped it away with another fleeting smile directed at me.

'I'm Sophie. Sophie Winter,' I said, hesitating for a moment before awkwardly extending my hand towards him. He gripped it in his, but instead of shaking it, he just squeezed it warmly, and that should have felt wrong, and overly intimate, but strangely it didn't.

'I know,' he said softly, before releasing my fingers and walking stiffly towards the nurse.

I didn't realise at first that he'd been waiting for me. I thought it was just coincidence when I finally emerged from the treatment room, my arm swathed in a stiff white bandage, that he was the first person I saw.

'How did you get on?' Ben asked, levering himself away from the wall he'd been leaning against.

I pulled a small face and shrugged. 'Okay, I think. I have to come back to the Burns Unit on . . .' I peered at the appointment card in my hand, 'Tuesday.'

He held up an identical card. 'Likewise.'

I bit my lip, once again overcome with guilt. 'I am *so* sorry you got hurt saving me. You were a real hero tonight, you know. You ought to get some sort of medal, or award or something.'

A strange look passed over his face, and I could tell he wasn't the type of man who wanted or needed that kind of recognition. 'Anyone would have done what I did,' he refuted. 'Absolutely anyone.'

I didn't want to make him uncomfortable, so I said nothing more. We looked at each other a little awkwardly for a moment, and I could feel our brief and unusual encounter drawing to a natural conclusion, and wondered why that felt wrong, like unfinished business.

'Look, I was just about to call a cab to drop me back to my car. Is someone meeting you here, or would you like a lift somewhere? Where are you going now?'

I looked at him blankly, then glanced up at the utilitarian wall clock. It was almost three in the morning. I had no clothes, no money for a cab and nowhere to go, but I was strangely reluctant to confess any of that to this heroic and charming stranger.

'I . . . I'm probably going to call a good friend of mine and see if they can come and get me.'

His phone passed so quickly and seamlessly from his

back pocket into my hand, he could have been a practising magician – or a pickpocket. I was normally good at guessing someone's profession, but he gave away no hints. I could see him in a suit and tie, chairing a board meeting, or working in the open, wearing boots and jeans, his skin weathered by the elements. I needed more clues than just a well-educated voice and a muscular body.

'You can use this to call him . . . or her.' There was a question in his voice, but it wasn't one I felt needed answering.

'Thank you,' I murmured, heading towards a small row of empty seats to make my call. I waited until he'd turned towards a vending machine and begun pressing buttons before switching on his phone. At this hour of the night there was only one person, aside from my parents, who I felt able to disturb. The phone was the same model as mine and I confidently pressed the icons on the screen until the familiar keypad materialised in front of me. My index finger hovered hesitantly, and even before it grazed the screen, I knew this wasn't going to work. I closed my eyes and concentrated like a medium at a séance. I *knew* Julia's number, knew it better than I knew my own. She'd had the same one for years and I spoke to her practically every day. Those eleven numbers should be so deeply embedded in my muscle memory, I should be able to dial them without thinking. Perhaps that was the problem; I was trying too hard. I let my fingers fly over the keypad. The first two wrong numbers did nothing more than grunt and mumble, before hopefully going straight back to sleep.

The third one was downright rude. I'd have explained my circumstances if he'd given me half a chance, but it was impossible to slip an explanation in between the torrent of swear words.

Ben looked horrified when he walked back towards me carrying two polystyrene cups and found me quietly crying again, his phone passing between my hands as though I was learning to juggle, really slowly.

'Did your friend say no?' His eyes were flashing in ready indignation.

'No. It's not that. It's just ...' He leant forward on the hard plastic seat he'd taken on the row opposite me, his body language encouraging. 'It's just ... I can't remember her number. It's gone. Completely gone. I know it, really well, like I know my own name. But when I try to visualise it, it's as though it's fallen out of my memory into a black hole.'

'It's just delayed shock,' Ben advised wisely, leaning forward and retrieving his phone from my hands, before it fell to the floor. 'Give it a moment, think about something else, and it will come back to you.'

I wanted to believe him, and not just because I had nowhere else to go that night, but somehow I wasn't sure. 'Here, have one of these,' Ben offered, passing me one of the cups he'd set down on the table. 'It might be tea or coffee, or possibly some strange new hybrid,' he apologised, handing me the unidentifiable brew. It was hot, and there was more sugar in it than I usually took, but he'd probably done that deliberately.

'What about family? Could you call your parents?' he asked.

I carefully swallowed my mouthful of coffee before answering. I was of an age when a full complement of parents was no longer an automatic assumption. It made me wonder if he thought I was younger than I was. 'They're away on holiday, and hearing about this would only panic them.' I could hear the concern in my voice, and I imagine he could too. 'My dad's not been well . . . this is the kind of thing they should find out about when it's all over and done with.'

'I see.'

We sat in silence, sipping the unpalatable drinks. The A&E had slowly been emptying around us and now, apart from the occasional passing nurse or orderly, we were completely alone.

'So, had you lived in that flat for a long time?'

'No. Fred and I only moved in a couple of months ago.'

'Fred? I thought you were the only one in the flat. Did he manage to get out alright?'

Genuine torment twisted my features and I dug my nails into my palms so hard I left tiny crescent moon indents on my skin. I was determined not to cry in front of him again.

'I threw him out of the window,' I said, my voice small and tight. Ben looked fairly horrified, until I added, 'Fred's my cat.' I watched him carefully, prepared to revise my entire opinion about him depending on what he did or said next.

'Then I'm sure you saved his life,' Ben replied, scoring

a solid ten out of ten for his response. 'Cats are incredibly resilient. If *you* made the jump, I'm sure he did too.'

'I hope so,' I said, my head bowed, allowing what was left of my hair to shield my face from view.

I suspect Ben was trying to sneak up on my subconscious, when he unexpectedly thrust his phone into my hand. 'Feel like trying your friend's number again?' Ten incredibly frustrating minutes later, I knew I was going to have to admit defeat, Julia's number was still mysteriously lost to me.

'Look, this is ridiculous,' I said, finally returning the phone to its rightful owner. 'All I'm doing is just guessing random numbers. You should go and get your car and go home, you really don't need to wait here with me.'

'I don't feel comfortable just leaving you here,' Ben protested.

'Well, you should. You did a good thing tonight, but it doesn't mean you have to keep looking out for me.'

He studied me for a very long moment before replying. 'What if it does?'

I shivered suddenly in the overheated hospital. 'Honestly, I'll be fine. I'm sure you're right, Julia's number will eventually come back to me.' I glanced up at the clock. 'And it'll be morning in another four hours or so. I'll get a cab to their house when it's a more respectable time to turn up at their door wearing just my PJs.'

I liked the way he smiled. It came quickly, as though his lips had a natural inclination to curve upwards. He had a mouth made for smiling. 'Any time's pretty good for that,' he joked, and then looked really pleased at my response. He got to his feet, reached into his pocket for his wallet and a pen and began scribbling something on an old receipt. He passed it to me. 'That's my number. I want you to promise you'll call me if there's anything I can do, or if you need anything . . . a place to crash, a shoulder to cry on, someone to catch you when you leap from tall buildings . . . anything.' His voice trailed away. I unfolded the receipt and saw within it a neatly folded twenty-pound note. The man really was a master of sleight of hand.

'What's this?'

'Taxi money.'

'I can't take this from you.'

'It's not for you, it's for the cab driver,' he reasoned.

'I still can't take it. How will I pay you back?'

'Don't worry about it,' he began, and then, seeing the uncomfortable expression on my face, he quickly amended his reply. 'Give it to charity,' he said. 'Any one you like.' It was a good solution and however much I objected, I had to be realistic. I was going to need fare money.

I got to my feet, certain this would be the last time we'd ever meet. It felt like an appropriate ending. I extended my arm to shake his hand, but somewhere between leaving my side and reaching his, it faltered in the space between us, before dropping back down. Instead I leapt forward and impulsively hugged him tightly. After a slight hesitation, I felt his arms come up around me, holding me against him. It would have been very easy to stay there, feeling safe and protected, but we really had reached the final page of our story. I stepped out of his hold and looked into his uniquely coloured eyes.

'Thank you, Ben. Thank you for everything.'

'Look after yourself, Sophie Winter,' he said, remembering my full name. He turned on his heel and disappeared through the automatic doors into the dark night.

'Are you sure this is where you want me to drop you, love?' asked the cab driver, pulling up as close to my former home as the barriers cordoning it off would allow. I looked through the taxi window at the ruined building. Although the flames had been doused several hours earlier, the orange glow of the street lamps revealed parts of the structure were still smouldering. Grey tendrils of smoke wafted upwards, like the exhaled breath of a sleeping dragon. It made the building look moody and dangerous, as though it couldn't be trusted. Perhaps that's what the men sitting in the two police cars and the small fire truck parked by the kerbside felt too.

'Yes. This is the place,' I confirmed, my voice subdued. I looked up at the blackened walls of my bedroom and the shattered window out of which I'd jumped.

'Nasty fire,' observed the driver, surveying the damage, while I climbed wearily out of his cab and pulled out Ben's twenty-pound note. The driver looked at me as I stood shivering on the pavement, as though seeing me for the first time since I'd jumped into the back of his taxi at the hospital. His eyes took in the soot-stained pyjamas, the bandaged arm and the thick blanket I was holding around my shoulders like a cape.

'This was your place, wasn't it?' he asked, inclining his head towards the corner flat. I nodded sadly and passed him the note through the window. 'Put your money away, love,' he said gently. His face distorted behind sudden big fat salty tears, that refused to disappear no matter how many times I blinked. A garbled message, probably announcing his next fare, crackled through on his radio. He hesitated for a moment, then switched off the unit. 'Why don't you jump back in, and let me drop you somewhere else? It doesn't look like there's anything you can do here now.'

Unexpected kindness, especially when it comes from a total stranger, has a way of felling you. It's neighbours leaving casseroles and pies on your doorstep. It's finding someone's washed your car or mown your lawn, and you have no idea who it was. It's handwritten notes from people you don't know, attached to bunches of flowers left propped up against the kerb.

'That's really very kind of you, but I'll be fine,' I assured the driver, relieved when after a long moment of inner struggle he gave a small helpless shrug and drove away.

It had still felt far too early to turn up at Julia's house, when I'd hastily jumped into the taxi on the hospital forecourt. I'd hurried from A&E with no plan in mind, other than my need to get out of there. I wasn't acting rationally, or thinking clearly, and for a woman who usually plans everything in minute detail, that was really unlike me.

I'd drifted into a light doze on the uncomfortable waiting-room chairs, and then the call had come in announcing the incoming ambulances. Suddenly the quiet department had begun to rev into life around me. Doctors began to emerge from the bank of lifts, yawning widely and rubbing their eyes. The number of nurses suddenly increased, and all around me the air bristled and crackled with anxious anticipation.

'It's a multiple pile-up on the dual carriageway,' answered one of the nurses, when I'd asked what was happening. 'We're not sure yet how many cars or passengers are involved.'

It had never been my intention to leave the cocooned sanctuary of the hospital until morning, but as doctors and nurses began lining up at the doors, awaiting the arrival of the first casualties, I'd slipped past them into the night without stopping to question where I was heading. As I hurried across the tarmac to the taxi, I'd glanced back at the assembled medics. They looked like actors, waiting for their cues, and I had no desire to still be there when someone yelled *'Action'*. When the cab driver had asked 'Where to?' I'd automatically given him the address of my flat, almost as though I'd forgotten it had burnt to the ground several hours before.

It wasn't something I could forget now, I thought, as I gingerly walked up to the barrier in my highly inappropriate bedroom footwear. Two officers were chatting in the first police car, but on noticing me, the one in the passenger seat climbed out of the vehicle.

'Can I help you, miss?' I looked at the implausibly young

officer and suddenly felt old and stupid, and knew the next words to come out of my mouth were only going to compound that.

'I was wondering if by any chance you'd seen a cat around here? He's small and grey and has white fur on his back legs and tail.'

The young policeman looked sympathetic, but strangely not altogether surprised. 'No, I'm sorry. It's like I told the gentleman earlier, he'll probably not come back until things have died down, or until he gets hungry.'

'Gentleman? What gentleman?'

'The guy with the bandage on his arm.' He glanced down at my wrist and then back at my troubled face. 'He has one just like yours. I know you're both worried about your cat, but I'm sure he's safe somewhere. The pair of you really shouldn't be wandering around out here in the cold, not after what you've both been through tonight, you know.'

It didn't take long to find Ben. The streets were quiet once I'd stepped away from the burnt shell of the building, and sound carried easily in the crisp night air. It wasn't difficult to hear his cry slicing through the darkness.

'Here, kitty-kitty. Here, kitty-kitty.' I followed the sound of his voice, padding over a small grassy area and soaking my furry slippers in the process, as I tracked him to a poorly lit alleyway.

'Here, kitty-kitty.'

'No one really says that when they're calling a cat,' I announced as I walked up behind him.

'Jesus!' he yelled, spinning around so suddenly it looked as though he was going to lose his balance. 'You shouldn't go creeping up on people in the dark like that!'

'Sorry,' I apologised.

'What are you doing here, anyway? You're meant to be at the hospital.'

'And you're meant to have gone home,' I countered. My glib rejoinder was ruined a little by the wayward chattering of my teeth.

'You're freezing,' Ben announced, shrugging out of the thick jacket he must have collected from his car before beginning to search for my missing pet. He held it out, and although part of me wanted to decline the invitation of the warm fleece-lined sleeves, the sensible part of my brain wouldn't let me. I slipped my arms gratefully into the garment, allowing the thick fabric and the residual heat from his body to envelop me.

Mindful of my burnt arm, he drew me against him and began to briskly rub his hands up and down my back, as though towelling dry a dog. Somehow, on this very strange night, the normal boundaries of personal space seemed to have completely disappeared.

'You shouldn't be walking around the streets in the middle of the night like this,' he muttered, his voice almost lost in the sound of his hands briskly moving up and down over the jacket.

'And you should?' I countered.

'At least I'm not in my nightie,' he chastised. A totally

ridiculous image of him wearing something pink and flimsy popped into my head and refused to fade away like it should have done.

'I'm okay now,' I said stepping back a little clumsily out of his reach. He didn't argue, but his eyes looked troubled as he watched me huddle deep inside the folds of his oversized jacket. I glanced up and down the dimly lit alleyway. There was a block of garages belonging to an industrial unit, an overflowing rubbish skip, and a row of sheds and outbuildings from the adjacent houses. Basically there were hundreds, maybe even thousands, of places one small scared cat could hide in the darkness. Feeling a little self-conscious, I cupped my hands beside my mouth like a yodeller and called into the night. 'Fred. Fred.'

I stared into the darkness, willing the shadows to transform into a small grey bundle of fur running towards me. We waited in silence for several minutes before Ben gently took my elbow, leading me away. 'Let's try a little further down the road.'

I fell into step beside him, feeling guiltily that I was keeping him from his rest, but at the same time immeasurably glad that I wasn't doing this alone. 'Thank you ... again,' I said quietly, as we stood shoulder to shoulder staring into a small thicket of trees. 'This is really good of you.' Several moments passed before I thought to ask, 'How exactly would you have identified Fred if you'd found him?'

Ben looked a little abashed. 'Yes, well, it wasn't a perfect plan. Fred's not ginger with a torn ear and a nasty temper?'

'No. Why?'

'The first cat I tried to catch was.'

It shouldn't have been funny, and I really shouldn't have laughed, especially when I saw the long scratch the stray had left on his hand. But all my emotions were so close to the surface that any one of them could bubble over with the least encouragement: tears; laughter; anything.

'It'll be easier now you're here,' he admitted.

But it wasn't. I'm not sure how long we'd have continued searching if it hadn't been for the rat. It was the only creature we'd encountered as we walked up and down the empty side streets and alleyways. If there'd been a contest to see who'd jumped the highest when it darted out from beneath a refuse bin, it would have to have gone to a photo finish.

'Ugh, yuck!' I cried, leaping behind Ben and using him as a rodent shield. My hands had latched on to his upper arms, and beneath the cotton of his shirt I could feel the powerful muscles flexing.

'I warn you, if that thing comes back, it's every man for himself,' Ben declared over one shoulder, his eyes fixed on the shadows beneath a van where the rat had disappeared.

I thought for a minute he was joking, but the expression of distaste on his face looked decidedly real. He caught me studying him, and gave a small grin, his eyes still fixed on the van. 'Not so brave and heroic now, huh?' I knew in that moment that I liked this man, and not just because he'd rescued me, and was still looking out for me, long after he could simply have just walked away. No, what I really liked was that he saw nothing wrong in revealing a weakness. I'm sure many people would have been drawn by his attractive face, caramel eyes or toned body. But for me, it was the squeal he'd given when he'd seen the rodent that did it.

I was the one who called time on our search. I was so exhausted I could hardly walk straight, and Ben too looked done in, his pace gradually slowing as we searched the area without success. 'This is never going to work in the dark,' I admitted.

Tellingly, Ben didn't disagree with me. 'What you should do is put up some posters with his photo and your phone number. Maybe even offer a reward.' I wondered then if he'd forgotten the total sum of all my possessions was the clothes I was currently wearing and his borrowed twenty-pound note. Strange as it might sound, I'd almost forgotten it myself as we'd searched the streets together in the dark.

'Look, I don't want this to sound like a sleazy line, or anything. But why don't you come back to my place and we can print something out. At least then, when it's daylight you'll be able to put them up around the neighbourhood.'

There were a great many reasons why I shouldn't even have considered his suggestion. In the cold light of day, I would see it was a reckless – possibly even dangerous – thing to do. No one knew where I was, who I was with, or where I was going – *I* didn't even know. I was pretty certain Julia would probably kill me herself when she found out the risk I'd taken. But that was something I'd worry about later.

There were a great many reasons why I should have politely, but firmly, declined his invitation. Instead, I surprised not only myself, but him too when I said, 'Okay. Good idea,' and allowed him to lead me to his waiting car.

I actually fell asleep on the ride to his house, shocking myself further with my total disregard for my own safety. I deserved to wake up and find we'd arrived at some super-creepy desolate cabin in the woods. In my head I saw it clearly. There'd be an axe propped up on the porch beside an ancient rocking chair, which creaked backward and forward all by itself. There'd definitely be no phone line, or internet, or any means of summoning help.

It was a relief when the car finally came to a stop to dis-cover I was in a perfectly ordinary residential street, and not in a scene lifted straight out of a horror movie. Even so, I still experienced a moment of pure panic when Ben laid his hand on my shoulder and gently shook me awake. My traumatised brain clung on to the refuge of sleep, and as my eyes squinted through the darkness, I had no idea where I was, why I wasn't in my own bed, or who the man beside me could possibly be. Then it all came back, crashing over my head like a wave you hadn't seen coming. I blinked myself fully awake, suddenly remembering it all.

I peered through the windscreen at the three-storey build-ing in front of me. It was large, and if I had to guess an era, I'd have gone for Victorian. It was the type of period build-ing that's frequently converted into flats, and I wondered which floor was his. It turned out they *all* were. I unfolded myself from the front seat of the car, creakily and carefully, like someone twice my age. Everything ached, as though I'd gone crazy on Day One of a new gym membership, and now deeply regretted my enthusiasm. I'm sure Ben noticed me hobbling as I walked beside him across the paved driveway, and although he was too polite to comment, his pace slowed, matching mine.

Automatic security lights flooded the area as we approached a set of arched double doors, which made the front entrance look vaguely ecclesiastical. Perhaps that's why I was expecting a Gothic interior when Ben unlocked the doors and ushered me inside his home. My guess couldn't have been more wrong, I realised, as I scanned the huge open-plan ground floor. That was when the weird feeling of déjà vu hit me, almost before Ben had clicked the door shut behind us. The skin on the back of my neck prickled uncomfortably, and I was back in spooky territory all over again. I most definitely had never set foot in this place before, so why did it all seem so incredibly familiar?

I stepped cautiously into the room, taking it all in. The square footage was vast, like a sleek New York loft apart-ment, mysteriously squirrelled away inside the most unlikely of buildings.

'The previous owner was an architect,' Ben explained, flicking on lights and tossing his house keys onto a small table near the door. Part of me, the part that still thought I was acting recklessly going to a stranger's house in the middle of the night, told me to remember where the keys were. Just in case. The rest of me was still open-mouthed and slightly dazed by his home. The entire rear wall was made of glass, offering a glimpse of a subtly lit wooden deck. The garden beyond was a mystery, although the shadowy sway of large leafy fronds hinted at something far removed from a suburban square lawn with tidy flower beds.

I did a full 360-degree rotation, taking it all in, from the modern lines of the sleek kitchen that flowed seamlessly into the dining area, with a table far too large for one. It seemed unlikely that Ben lived there alone. The thought should have been comforting, yet strangely it wasn't.

Across the gleaming polished wooden floor, were two distinct areas: one housed a large L-shaped settee, beside a modern fireplace set within the wall, while in another part of the room there stood a work station and desk. Here was the computer and printer that I'd come to Ben's home to use.

I could feel him looking at me curiously, and realised however odd it sounded, I was going to have to explain why I'd been staring impolitely at his home. 'This place ... your house ... I know it probably sounds crazy, but I feel like I know it. Like I've been here before.' I pointed towards a corridor leading off from the main room. 'Through there is the master bedroom. And it's got one of those enormous wet room things, hasn't it?'

I expected him to look shocked, but he simply confirmed what I said. 'That's right. Do you want to see?' I shook my head. Checking out his bedroom was one reckless step too far, but my eyes had grown wide in astonishment. *How had I known all of that?*

Ben laughed lightly. 'Don't look so worried. You're not the first person to say that. The house featured in one of those property makeover shows a couple of years ago.' Suddenly everything fell into place and I stopped thinking my traumatic night had somehow turned me psychic. 'Oh, yes,' I cried, clearly relieved. 'I remember now, wasn't the wife injured in some sort of accident?'

'Skiing,' Ben confirmed, crossing to his computer and jabbing at the power switch. The screen blinked obediently into life. 'That's why everything's open-plan, to make it easier for her electric wheelchair. But that's not why I bought it,' he added, glancing over his shoulder at me as he rattled his password into the keyboard. He rolled the chair back from the desk, gesturing for me to sit on the soft leather seat. 'You can't see it now, but the garden is the best feature of this place. That's what sold it for me. Every morning it's like waking up deep within a tropical rainforest.'

He leant over my shoulder and hit a couple more keys. I could smell the smoke of the fire and a pheromone-heavy scent that in romantic novels they'd probably call 'manly', but in real life is usually referred to more prosaically as sweat. My nose twitched like a rabbit, and I was glad he couldn't see.

The pixels on the computer screen rearranged to display the familiar logo of a well-known search engine. 'You're in,'

Ben declared, his mouth so close I could feel the breeze of his words ruffling my hair. 'Why don't I make us both some tea while you get started here?'

I nodded, my fingers already finding their familiar resting place on the keyboard. By the time he came back carrying two steaming mugs, I'd already lifted a couple of recent photographs of Fred from my Facebook page. Ben placed one of the mugs beside my right hand and studied the screen. 'I was wondering where you were going to find a photo.'

I paused in the middle of cropping the image to size, and looked up at him a little sheepishly. 'Okay, yes. I am *that* person, the one who posts pictures of her pet on Facebook. You have my permission to laugh.'

He looked at me, glanced at the screen briefly, and then back at me for a very long moment. 'I'm not laughing.'

I could feel my cheeks beginning to grow warm and turned my attention back to the flier I was creating. Ben leant up against the wall beside the desk watching me, which for some reason made me hit several wrong keys as I typed in a brief description of Fred. I leant back in the chair and read it through carefully, trying not to get emotional as Fred's eyes looked accusingly at me from the screen.

'Don't forget to put something about a reward in there,' Ben reminded.

I pulled a face. 'All I have at the moment is twenty pounds, and technically that's not even mine, it's yours.'

He laughed easily. 'Don't worry about that. I can lend you the money until your finances are up and running again.

If someone finds him, you want them to have a reason to return him.'

'At least he's chipped,' I said with a sigh.

'As in broken?'

'As in micro-chipped,' I explained. I hit the return key and hesitated, before typing in my mobile phone number as the point of contact.

'Why not put mine down too, in case someone finds him before you've got a replacement phone,' Ben suggested.

I bit my lip worriedly. Our connection should already have been broken. What happened earlier that night should have been a single transient moment, and yet every time I thought our association was about to come to an end, something happened that just kept extending it. It made me uncomfortable, and at the same time it made me glad, and I'm really not sure which emotion bothered me most.

When a hundred copies of the flier had been printed and stacked in a neat pile on the desk, there was nothing more to be done until I distributed them around my old neighbourhood. I switched off Ben's computer and went to join him at the wall of glass, which looked out onto his garden.

'What time do you want to go to your friend's house?'

'If we could book a cab for around eight, that would be great,' I suggested tentatively, hoping the money he'd given me earlier would still be enough to cover the fare from here. Wherever *here* was, of course.

Ben had a different plan in mind. 'You don't need a cab, I'll drive you.'

I swallowed nervously. 'You really don't have to. You've already done more than enough for me.'

His eyes met and held mine, and I tried to tell myself it was their unusual coloration that was distracting me, making me lose my train of thought as his gaze refused to release me. With an effort that felt almost physical, I wrenched my eyes from his, feeling too drained to argue. I was too depleted to do anything except agree, which I did, swaying slightly on my feet from exhaustion.

'Why don't you sit down and rest for a while?' Ben suggested reasonably.

I looked at the dining table chairs and then at the settee. There was a lot of white and cream in his home, and a lot of black on me and my clothes. 'What I'd *really* like is to get some of the smell of the smoke off me. Is there somewhere I could freshen up?' I asked tentatively.

So, already in a highly vulnerable situation, what would be the most stupid thing a woman could do in a strange man's house? Voluntarily decide to get naked, that's what.

Hot water rained down on me from the powerful shower jets. The revolting grey-flecked soap bubbles that had trickled down my body from the first two shampoos finally ran clear. But even when I knew my hair was clean and no longer smelled of smoke, it still felt dirty and brittle. I ran my hand down the uneven length of it, and allowed myself a very feminine moment of self-pity that something that had been a part of me for so long had literally gone up in flames in less than a few seconds.

Showering had been surprisingly tricky using just one hand, a problem I hadn't even considered when I'd padded up the open-tread staircase behind Ben.

'The bathroom is over there,' he said, pointing towards one of the doors leading off from the spacious hall. 'Help yourself to toiletries and towels . . . or whatever,' he finished, in a voice that hinted he actually had no idea what women use to look the way they do. 'These two bedrooms are both guest rooms, so feel free to use either of them to change, or lie down, or take a nap.'

I nodded gratefully. 'It's a big house, do you live here alone?'

He hesitated for a moment before replying, and I wondered if my idle curiosity had come across as rude. I ran the sentence through my head again, but could see nothing wrong with it, but then my judgement was seriously sleep-deprived, so who could tell.

'I do. I like having space around me.'

This place certainly had plenty of that, I thought as I looked around the roomy bedroom next to the bathroom. There was a king-size bed – that I *wouldn't* be sleeping on, and enough hanging space in the mirrored wardrobes to easily hold every item of clothing I owned. *Used to own*, I mentally corrected, as the realisation that I now had just one solitary garment to my name came back to me. It was something that had obviously occurred to Ben too.

'I'll see if I can dig out something small enough for you to wear and leave it in here for you – unless you'd prefer to stay in your own things?'

I looked down at my stained and blackened pyjamas, which I doubted would ever be white again, no matter how many wash cycles they went through. 'That would be great, thanks, Ben.' It was the first time I'd used his name, and he smiled slightly when he heard it on my tongue, as though it was a pleasant surprise.

'Are you going to be able to manage in the shower?'

I blinked up at him, wondering if he had really just offered to help me bathe. My right eyebrow rose several centimetres all by itself. He read the expression and laughed, but there was a tinge of embarrassment in the sound.

'I meant with that,' he said, pointing at my bandage.

It was my turn to be embarrassed. *'Not every man you meet will be a scumbag,'* Julia had advised, after my last attempt at dating had ended badly. I hadn't believed her then, but maybe I should. To say I had issues with trust and intimacy would be a huge understatement.

'Sorry,' I said, feeling my face begin to flush. I hadn't blushed this much since I was a teenager. I thought I'd out-grown the habit, but tonight it was back with a vengeance. 'Yes, of course. I hadn't even thought— You're going to need one too,' I said, perfectly aware I was babbling, but I always did when I'd made a fool of myself.

Ben disappeared downstairs, returning with a roll of tape, some scissors and several sturdy plastic bags. Five minutes later we were both sporting matching protective mitts, that made us look more like we were about to enter a boxing ring instead of a shower cubicle. His hands had moved quickly and efficiently, winding the tape round and round my arm. He was surprisingly gentle, more so even than any of the doctors or nurses had been. I looked down at his head bent in concentration over my wrist and felt a jolt of an emotion I didn't recognise running up my arm like an electric current. It's everything that's happened in the last six hours. It's the shock. It's the adrenalin. It's not knowing what's going to happen to me next, I told myself, as I finally stripped off my clothes and stepped into the shower closet. And it *was* all of those things . . . but it was something else too, something new, and unfamiliar. And it scared me.

There was something weirdly disconcerting knowing we were both showering at the same time, but I shied away from probing too closely as to why that should bother me. Ben was downstairs, in his own bathroom. He'd been a perfect gentleman and entirely respectful, but that still hadn't stopped me from looking for a lock on the upstairs bathroom door. There wasn't one.

When I finally emerged, pink and flushed from the shower, I bundled up my dirty pyjamas and secured one huge fluffy towel around me, and draped another around my shoulders. The only bare skin showing, as I crossed the hallway and entered the guest bedroom, was my feet. Ben had clearly been there while I showered, for there was a neatly folded pair of joggers and a T-shirt sitting on the pillow. I snipped the protective bag from my wrist, pleased to discover the crepe bandage was still dry, and then paused with the scissors still in hand to survey my reflection in the wardrobe's mirrored doors. I looked sadly at the scorched, uneven lengths of hair. When I was younger I'd begged my mum to let me have short hair, but she'd always refused, saying my hair was my 'crowning glory'. At school I'd been the only girl who could actually sit on her own hair – an interesting but slightly pointless achievement. Still, old habits die hard, and although I no longer wore it that long as an adult, I still only ever asked for a trim whenever I visited a hairdresser.

Putting a pair of scissors in the hands of someone who isn't in total control of her emotions is never a good idea. The evidence of *just* how bad an idea it was soon scattered on the floor around me. The first snip had definitely been the hardest to make ... after that I was committed to carrying on. I cut savagely, feeling the tickle of cuttings falling onto my bare feet. I kept hacking away, as though my hair was to blame for everything that had happened. I paused mid-snip and glanced in the mirror, and let out a cry of despair. I'd made an even bigger mess out of something that was already disastrous. It looked as though I'd gone to a stylist who used garden shears on their clients' hair.

The noise of feet thundering up the stairs pulled me away from the scarecrow looking back at me in the mirror. 'Are you alright? I heard—' Ben broke off. 'Oh.'

'I think I made it worse.'

His eyes went from me, down to the scattered cuttings

covering the carpet where I stood, and then back up to my face. The fact that he didn't say anything at all spoke volumes. The woman in the mirror, the one having a *really* bad hair day, looked like she was about to cry. Ben glanced down at his bare wrist, as though surprised to find his watch missing. That wasn't the only thing that was absent, I suddenly noticed. He was only half-dressed, and had responded to my cry wearing nothing except a pair of faded jeans. His feet – like mine – were bare, as was his torso, which was taut, muscled and still tanned from wherever he had taken it on holiday. I was suddenly uncomfortably aware of the scarcity of our clothing. Ben, however, seemed far more occupied by my catastrophic haircut.

He glanced at the digital bedside clock. It was quarter to six, and I saw the formation of an idea on his face and watched it crystallise into a decision.

'I have a very good friend who's a hairdresser ... well, she owns her own salon, actually. *And* she's a ridiculously early riser.'

'Ben, we can't. It's stupidly early on a Sunday morning. She's not going to want to sort out this mess at this hour at the weekend.'

He was smiling confidently. 'Yes she will. She really likes a challenge.'

No, she really likes you, an unexpected voice suddenly corrected inside my head. *It's you she likes, not the challenge.* I must have looked a little horrified, as though he too might have heard that inappropriate and random thought.

'Honestly, trust me. I know she won't mind. She'll already be awake, and her flat is above the salon. Why don't I call and ask her?'

I looked once again at my reflection. That I needed expert help to fix the damage wasn't in question. But did I really want Ben's *very good friend* doing it? It was six o'clock on a Sunday morning, and I was fresh out of options.

'Okay. As long as she doesn't mind . . .'

'She truly won't. She's really lovely like that.'

He left me then to go and phone his *really lovely* friend, who wasn't going to say no to him, I already knew that, even before he came back upstairs a couple of minutes later to confirm it.

I dressed hurriedly in his borrowed clothes. Everything was way too big, but I pulled the waist drawstring on the joggers tight enough to relocate a couple of my internal organs, confident that at least the joggers couldn't accidentally slip down. The absence of a bra was uncomfortably obvious through the soft, well-worn fabric of his top, but there wasn't much I could do about that. I would have to ignore my full and bouncing breasts and hope Ben was enough of a gentleman, or so absorbed in his hairdresser girlfriend, that he would do the same.

'Carla's place is only about a ten-minute drive away, so we should still be okay for getting you to your friend's by eight,' Ben assured as he held open the passenger door of his car. It was cold, and the path was covered in a thin sheet of ice crystals, which caught the beam of his headlights when he switched on the engine.

'No luck yet remembering her number?' he asked, pulling off his driveway and onto the empty road.

I'd actually not even tried, but it seemed almost negligent to admit that, so all I said was, 'No. Not yet.'

On the back seat of his car, bound by an elastic band, was the small bundle of fliers, which hopefully would help reunite me with my missing cat. There was nothing else I'd needed to take from Ben's house. There was nothing else I had.

'It's a shame you never got to see this place in daylight,' Ben had lamented when he'd turned off the kitchen lights, and ushered me towards the door. 'The garden is really spectacular.'

I wasn't much into horticulture, and the kindest thing I could ever do to a plant was to decide not to buy it. They lived much longer that way. But there was one thing I was curious about.

'How come the architect sold this house? He'd obviously spent a lot of time and money making this place perfect for his wife. Why did they move?'

Ben had switched off the last light so was just a shadowy shape, whose face I couldn't see, when he replied. The only good thing about that was that he couldn't see my reaction to his words.

'She died,' he stated baldly, totally unaware of the physical effect his words would have on me. And why should he have been? It wasn't a natural reaction, it wasn't normal, but then wasn't that the very definition of a psychosis? 'She died, and he couldn't bear to live here without her.'

It isn't normal to cry when you hear about the death of someone you've never met. But I did it anyway.

Chapter 3

I spent the short drive trying to imagine what Ben's hair-dresser friend Carla, the one who scarcely slept and was *'really lovely'*, would be like. By the time he announced we were 'Almost there', I was pretty sure I had her figured out. She'd be as sharp and trendy as her upmarket salon; she'd have legs that started in the region of her armpits and an edgy haircut. And of course she'd be blonde.

'It's still so early to be calling on someone,' I said, plucking nervously at the hem of his borrowed T-shirt as we drove past a modest parade of shops. Apart from a small bakery on the corner, which was just unlocking its doors, they were all in darkness. 'Are you really sure she won't mind?'

'Absolutely,' Ben assured. 'I know Carla. She'll have been up, dressed and eaten breakfast long before I phoned her.'

It would have been far too impolite to ask him how he knew so much about her early morning habits, but it was hardly a stretch to join up the dots. I could see them together, breakfasting in her modern apartment on glasses of biliously green wheatgrass and something wholesome made from quinoa. She didn't sound like a Corn Flakes kind of a girl.

I couldn't have got it more wrong if I'd tried. As soon as Ben pulled up outside the unlit salon, I began revising my opinion. The shop didn't look glitzy or particularly modern from the outside, and the sign advising that Tuesday was '*Half-price OAP Day*' didn't exactly fit in with the image I'd painted in my head. We got out of the car and Ben drew his mobile from his pocket, while I studied the bright pink fascia with the gold curlicue letters: '*Carla's*'.

'We're here.' He spoke quietly, but with such little background noise it was easy to hear the topnotes of warmth and affection in his voice. I felt like I was eavesdropping.

Ben placed a guiding hand lightly against the small of my back and steered me towards the salon's entrance. In the shadows at the back of the shop I saw a figure emerge. She raised an arm in a cheery and enthusiastic wave, as though signalling a plane in to land. In the reflection of the plate-glass window, I saw Ben wave back. Carla glided across the darkened salon and flicked on the interior lights. They weren't the piercing spotlights I'd imagined, just humble slightly old-fashioned fluorescent strip lights. They flickered for a moment, as though deciding whether or not they could be bothered to work, before flooding the shop in a glaringly bright glow. And the Carla I'd conjured up in my imagination disappeared in a magician's puff of smoke.

The lights weren't the only thing dazzlingly bright in the

shop. The figure walking towards us, dangling a large set of keys from one many-ringed hand, looked more like an exotic Caribbean islander than a suburban hairdresser. Every imaginable colour in the spectrum was represented in her silky kaftan top. The only thing brighter than her garment was the enormous smile the short middle-aged woman gave Ben, before swallowing him up in the folds of fabric for an even bigger hug.

'How are you, my darling?' She pulled back from him, caught sight of his bandaged wrist and her sunny expression clouded and faltered before transforming into one of concern. 'What is this? You never said you'd been hurt.'

'It's nothing,' Ben said dismissively, which I would certainly have disputed, if I wasn't currently struck dumb by the colourful – in every sense of the word – character standing between us.

'And you must be Ben's new friend Sophia,' she cried, turning to me with a huge red-lipsticked smile. I corrected her on the name, but let the misapprehension that Ben and I were friends stand.

'Well, it's a pleasure to meet you, Sophie,' declared Carla, who took me by surprise as she enveloped me in a hug almost as huge as the one she'd given Ben. 'I understand you've had quite a night of it, you poor love.'

My eyes went to Ben's, unsure how to answer, but Ben just smiled at me easily and reassuringly. *Everything here is fine. Relax*, his warm eyes silently instructed.

'So, Ben tells me you might be in need of a little re-style,'

Carla said diplomatically, stepping back and scrutinising the peculiar crow's nest currently masquerading as my hair. She frowned slightly, as though looking at a piece of modern art in a gallery that she didn't quite 'get'. I glanced at my numerous reflected images in the wall of mirrors, and couldn't really blame her.

'It got burnt . . . and then I tried to even it up, but . . .' My voice trailed away. Carla was too professional to say the thing I felt sure she had to be thinking: *'Well, you've made a right bloody mess of that, missy, haven't you?'* She continued to study me for a further minute, and I could feel myself beginning to grow tense as I waited for a low, under-the-breath whistle, the kind plumbers and electricians like to give when the job they've come to estimate turns out to be much bigger than they'd expected. But instead, Carla's eyes just twinkled merrily. 'Nothing there we can't fix up just fine, my love,' she said, reaching for my hand and giving it a warm squeeze. My eyes prickled and I blinked hard several times, because I was done with crying for one night, I really was. Ben had been right: Carla *was* lovely.

'So,' she said, turning her attention to Ben and forcing his focus away from me. 'What we girls don't need is a huge hulking man getting in our way while we get to work. So I suggest you go off and wait in Antonio's for his first batch of buns and Danish to come out of the oven. Tell him I sent you, and he'll probably give you a coffee too,' she said, her hand firmly propelling Ben in the direction of the door.

Carla was a small multicoloured powerhouse, shuffling

him away like a tiny kaftan-wearing locomotive, but she wasn't tall, and Ben looked easily over her head, allowing his eyes to ask the question. *Are you okay? Do you want me to stay?* I shook my head and the smile I gave him in reply was only a little bit wobbly.

Carla watched Ben with an indulgent expression on her face as he pulled the door shut behind him, turned up the collar of his jacket against the cold early-morning wind, and headed towards the bakery. I stole a quick curious look at Carla, wondering at their unlikely friendship. She was almost old enough to be his mother, but somehow I doubted they were related. There were rings on practically every one of her fingers, all except her wedding one. Bracelets jingled at her wrists and long beaded earrings hung from her ear lobes, which were only just visible beneath a red-and-gold-threaded headscarf swathed like a turban around her head. I wondered if she too was having a bad hair day.

Slipping easily into her professional role, Carla ushered me towards the small row of basins at the rear of the shop, keeping up an easy flow of inconsequential chatter. Any moment now she'll be asking me where I'm going for my holiday next year, I thought crazily, and had to bite really hard on my lip not to giggle at the thought. I was so over-tired and overwrought that I really wasn't in control of my emotions at all.

Like a tiny matador, Carla swept a gown around my shoulders, and settled me at the basin. She probably had a team of juniors who usually performed this task for her clients, but she gave no sign that this was beneath her, as she expertly shampooed and towel-dried my hair.

'This is really very kind of you,' I said awkwardly as she settled me onto a seat at one of the styling stations. 'But I feel bad that Ben has disturbed your Sunday morning.'

Her eyes met mine in the mirror, and I found it impossible to look away from the knowing expression in their blue depths. Her brows, I noticed, were darkly pencilled in, as though making a flamboyant statement. They matched the rest of her.

'It's no bother at all. Any friend of Ben's automatically gets the gold star treatment, as far as I'm concerned. He's a great boy, you know. A real diamond, as my old mother would have said.'

I swallowed awkwardly, not sure if Carla was aware that until a few hours ago Ben had been a total stranger to me . . . was *still* a total stranger, come to that. She seemed to think something deeper lay between us, and it felt a little rude to openly correct her. 'After all the help he's given me, it's the least I can do,' she added mysteriously.

It would definitely have been rude to ask her exactly what she meant by that intriguing remark, but the question burned on my lips, begging to be asked, as she picked up her scissors and comb and set to work.

'So have you known Ben for long?' I asked eventually, as the flashing blades snipped and chopped away through my chestnut-coloured hair.

'Oh, for quite a while,' Carla confirmed, which told me

nothing. 'A mutual friend introduced us, and when he heard I was having a few issues with this place,' she waved her hand expansively in the air to indicate her salon, 'he gave me some sound advice and help.' Was Ben a business manager or a financial adviser? I could visualise that, almost. 'And without his help, I doubt my Vegas trip would ever have happened,' Carla continued.

'He's a travel agent?' I hazarded, not sure that I could see that one at all.

Carla laughed prettily, like a woman half her age. 'Oh bless you, sweetheart, no,' she said at last, wiping a tiny tear of amusement from the corner of her eye. 'He's just travelled the world a lot. He helped me book things: the flights and hotels and whatnot. I'd probably still be staring at the brochures and daydreaming about going if it hadn't been for him. Would you like to see my photos?' she asked excitedly, laying down her scissors to rummage in a small drawer at the reception desk. I was a captive audience, so what else could I say except yes? I smiled politely, as I took the bulging wallet of snapshots from her outstretched hand.

As she blow-dried my hair, I leafed through the stack of glossy photographs. There was Carla beside the Las Vegas sign, grinning wildly outside Caesars Palace and the Bellagio, and finally arm-in-arm with a very authentic-looking Elvis. Everywhere looked familiar, although I'd never been to America. The final batch of photographs showed Carla standing precariously close to a sheer drop in the gloriously rugged Grand Canyon. She looked red-faced and elated under a blistering Nevada sun. There was a look of triumph on her face as she faced the camera, executing a jubilant double thumbs-up. On her head was a pair of oversized sunglasses, holding a thick shock of bright red hair back from her face.

Carla switched off the dryer and peered over my shoulder at the photograph in my hands and sighed a little wistfully. 'That was a *very* good day.'

A cool blast of air blew away the lingering desert heat, replacing it with the cold damp morning as Ben returned to the salon, carrying two enormous bags bearing the bakery's logo. The smell of warm baked goods mingled with the scent of hairspray. The two shouldn't have gone together, but oddly they seemed like a perfect blend.

'Are you all done here, or do you need me to walk around the block a few more times?' he asked.

Carla replied with a small tutting noise, as though she found him vaguely annoying. The fact that nothing could be further from the truth shone like a beacon from her eyes as she watched him shrug out of his thick jacket.

'Your timing is perfect. We're all finished up here,' Carla declared, giving my newly cut hair one last professional ruffle with her fingers. It was the shortest I had ever worn it, and for a moment I hardly recognised myself in the mirror's reflection. I turned my head from side to side, experimentally, feeling the unaccustomed tickle as it grazed the back of my neck.

'Obviously, you can grow it long again, but personally I

think it really suits you like this,' Carla confirmed. 'What do you think, Ben?'

I could feel his eyes studying me, as though he was seeing so much more than just a new haircut. 'It looks great. Very . . . er, fetching.'

'I just wish she'd have taken some money for doing it,' I said for about the fifth time after we'd left the salon and begun making our way across town to Julia's house. It was a little after eight o'clock, and although I was more tired than I think I'd ever been in my life, I was also feeling much more positive. Perhaps that was down to Carla's expert assistance, or the three sugary pastries I'd consumed for breakfast. *Surely all dieting rules could legitimately be thrown out the window on the day your home has been destroyed by fire?* No one died in the blaze, my belongings were covered by insurance, and the fliers would help me find Fred. Life would go on. It always did.

We turned into Julia's road and I was just directing Ben where to park, when it happened. Perhaps it was the familiar sight of their modern semi-detached house that triggered the memory, or even the sensible family car parked in the driveway that finally succeeded in unlocking the door in my head? It was a little embarrassing how easily the numbers suddenly tripped off my tongue. There was a sing-song cadence and rhythm to them, which mocked my inability to recall them for the last eight hours. Julia's phone number had mysteriously re-emerged from wherever my troubled brain had hidden it.

'I told you it would come back,' Ben said with an easy smile as he pulled on the hand brake.

'Why didn't you invite him to come in?' asked Julia, who spoke over the top of my reply that I had indeed done that, but Ben had refused, as she exclaimed yet again, 'Oh my God, Sophie, I can't believe your flat burnt down.'

I was seeing it and re-living it all over again through her eyes, and it was terrifying to realise how very easily my life could have been lost the night before ... if it hadn't been for Ben.

'How on earth did you manage to jump out of the window?' Julia asked. 'It's so damn high.' I gave a small shrug. I was good with words, it was how I earned my living, but there were none that could adequately explain that moment of terror when you do something unthinkable, because the alternative is even more horrible. 'You could have broken your leg – or your neck,' she declared dramatically.

'I think I was more likely to have broken Ben's,' I said solemnly, remembering again how I'd used him as a human crash mat to cushion my jump.

'I really wish he'd have come in. I'd liked to have had the chance to thank him for saving my best friend's life,' she declared, plucking a tissue from the box positioned between us on the kitchen table, and blowing her nose noisily several times. I reached across the scratched pine surface when she was done, and squeezed her hand. No words needed to be said; we both understood that.

Gary placed a cup of steaming coffee in front of each of us, not bothering to ask if we wanted a refill. He was a good man; he knew the drill.

Julia smiled gratefully up at him and shook her long auburn hair off her face. It was still unbrushed and bore evidence of its night on her pillow. She was clearly still having trouble processing everything that had happened to me since our conversation yesterday afternoon. 'I just can't believe that while we were here, sleeping and snoring our way through the night, you were going through such an awful experience all by yourself.'

'Not exactly by herself, by the sound of it,' corrected her husband mildly, collecting our dirty cups and taking them to the sink. 'And we weren't *just sleeping*,' he added. 'I personally heroically tackled two very dirty nappies produced by your son,' he said, dropping a swift kiss onto his wife's head. I felt a small smile find a home on my lips, the way it often did when I saw them together. Gary was the perfect antidote for Julia's tendency to be over-dramatic. He knew exactly how to divert her from any potential meltdown, be it impending childbirth or a friend's close shave with death.

'How come he's always *mine* when his nappies are crappy?' Julia asked, perfectly aware that once again her husband had performed his own particular brand of magic. Gary shrugged, as though this was right up there with the greatest mysteries of the universe.

'Beats me.' Moments later he tactfully disappeared from the kitchen, muttering something about 'getting out of our hair', a remark that made me self-consciously reach up and brush my hand against mine's new shortened length. Julia gave me a watery smile and a small nod of approval.

'It looks good. Don't worry about it.' I forced my hand to return to the table. 'So, what happens now?'

'I have absolutely no idea,' I replied, swallowing down a mouthful of hot coffee, hoping the caffeine would do the trick and invigorate the parts of my brain that wanted to go into a deep and catatonic sleep. 'I guess tomorrow I'll speak to the insurance company and find out how I go about making a claim. Perhaps there are some emergency funds they could offer until I get my finances sorted out?'

I saw Julia bite her lip worriedly, and knew her well enough to realise she was already stressing about not being able to help me out with money. 'I don't need anything from you,' I insisted, 'except perhaps a temporary roof over my head?'

'Well, that's obviously a given,' Julia replied automatically, still looking concerned. I reached across the table to grip her hand in both of mine. 'Seriously, Jules, I know you and Gary are down to one income right now, so don't even think about offering me money.' I gave a small sound that was almost a laugh. 'If that was all I needed, I could have taken Ben up on his offer.'

'He offered to lend you money? More than just the cab fare?' Julia's voice was incredulous.

'Uh-huh,' I replied, feeling almost as uncomfortable talking about it with her as I'd done when Ben had broached the subject during the car journey from Carla's.

'It's just a loan, until you get back on your feet,' he'd reasoned, as though offering to lend a total stranger an unspecified amount of cash, with no guarantee of ever getting it back, was an everyday occurrence.

'I can't accept it,' I said, feeling yet another hot blush seeping onto my cheeks. 'I mean . . . thank you for offering, it's really generous of you. But, well, it would feel wrong taking money from you.'

'You make it sound like you'd be stealing it.'

I had looked awkwardly through the windscreen, focusing on anything except the man beside me. 'I don't want you to take this the wrong way, but have you ever spoken to anyone about this weird hero complex of yours?'

He'd looked so startled for a moment that he didn't even notice the traffic lights had turned to green, until he earned himself an angry hoot from the car behind us.

'Is that what you think is wrong with me? That I'm a frustrated super-hero, scouring the town in my mask and cape, on the lookout for young women to rescue?' I was glad there was a note of humour in his voice, because this was an awkward conversation to be having with someone you didn't really know, and I truly didn't want to offend him.

'You've done your bit as a Good Samaritan, and then some,' I assured him. 'I'm always going to be in your debt . . . I already owe you far more than money.'

'Okay. I understand. And I don't want you to feel uncomfortable about any of this, so I'm only going to say this one more time: if you need anything, anything at all, just promise me that you won't be shy about asking.'

'Okay, I promise,' I said. My fingers weren't crossed, I was way too old to play that childish game, but I also knew I had absolutely no intention of keeping my word on that one.

'I won't sleep,' I told Julia.

'Okay,' she replied calmly from somewhere on the staircase below me.

'Truly. I've gone way past it now. I can just power through until tonight.' My assertion was ruined slightly by the sneaky yawn that escaped as I finished speaking.

'Sure you can,' Julia agreed, her voice eerily similar to the one I'd often heard her use when coaxing three-year-old Lacey.

'What I need to do is to get back to the flat. I need to search for Fred.'

'I'll go, while you're lying down – *not sleeping*,' she added pointedly.

'He's not going to come to anyone but me,' I said, my voice beginning to slur slightly with exhaustion as I walked into the master bedroom and saw the invitingly comfortable bed that was practically beckoning to me. Julia crossed to the window and twitched the curtains together, shutting out the grey winter's morning.

'Just lie down and close your eyes. You don't have to sleep,' she reasoned, perfectly aware that once my head hit the pillow I was going to be out like a light.

'Just for half an hour,' I conceded on a mumble, kicking off my grubby slippers and climbing on top of her duvet. It must have been Julia who threw the soft fleecy blanket over me. She must have been the one who flicked off the lights and closed the bedroom door firmly shut. Because it wasn't me, that's for sure. I didn't so much fall asleep, as tumble headlong into it, as though I'd been dropped from a very great height.

Five hours later I padded sheepishly down the stairs. The house was freakishly quiet with no sign of its usual, rather noisy, inhabitants.

'Just going to rest your eyes, huh?' Julia said knowingly as I walked into the open-plan living area.

'You should have woken me,' I said. My voice sounded strange, as though someone had stuffed my mouth with cotton wool balls while I slept, and my throat felt scratchy and sore, presumably from the smoke.

'You needed to sleep,' Julia said, passing me a large mug of tea. I took a grateful mouthful, burnt the roof of my mouth, and didn't even care. 'So where is everyone?' I asked, scanning the clearly empty lower floor.

'Gary's taken the kids to a friend's for the afternoon. So as soon as you've finished your tea, why don't we go and find you something to wear from my extensive pre-pregnancy wardrobe, then we can head out.'

Julia and I had spent our university years practically pooling our wardrobes, and there was a curious feeling of déjà vu as I stood in her bedroom, rummaging through her clothes for something to wear.

'At least you won't have to rush out and buy loads of new things,' she said ruefully as she watched me zip up a pair of indigo skinny jeans. 'I'm still many months away from getting back into most of those, so you might as well get some use out of them.'

I was busy folding up Ben's borrowed clothing, and wondering how on earth I was going to get it back to him, but I paused to give her a quick hug. 'I'd pick Noah over a size ten bottom any day of the week.'

'That's easy for you to say,' grumbled Julia, surveying her reflection in the full-length mirror. For a moment I slipped back through time, to somewhere I tried always to avoid. A time when all I'd wanted to do was hide, from my parents, from my friends, from any of the well-intentioned people who were trying to help me. But the person I wanted to hide from most was myself. Even now, so many years later, it was hard to look back at photographs of that sad overweight teenager. She was someone I hardly recognised, even though the face she wore was mine.

'Oh. My. God, Sophie. There's absolutely nothing left.' Logically, of course, you know what the words 'burnt to the ground' mean, but there's still something gut-wrenchingly shocking in seeing it with your own eyes. Despite a brisklyblowing breeze, the lingering smell of acrid smoke still hung in the air.

I'd started to get nervous when Julia had still been several streets away from the flat. I could feel my pulse racing beneath the crepe bandage on my wrist, and there was a tightness in my chest, which felt like I'd swallowed a large mouthful of something indigestible that wasn't going to shift, no matter how much antacid I took.

There was a crowd of onlookers ringed around the building, pressed up against the barrier, shoulder to shoulder, as though at a rock concert.

'Rubber necks,' Julia muttered angrily, as she climbed out of the car. We'd had to park some distance down the road, and were practically in the exact same spot where Ben's car had stood in the early hours of the morning. I wondered briefly where he was right now. Was he alone in his house, catching up on some well-deserved rest? Or was someone with him, looking after him? A girlfriend, or a fiancée, perhaps?

I linked my arm through Julia's and tugged her gently past the crowds staring at the blackened walls of my former home. There was nothing there to see, nothing left except debris and destruction.

'Let's find that cat of yours,' said Julia, snapping into action and delving into the bag we'd brought with us for the string, scissors and Sellotape we would need to post the fliers I'd created on Ben's computer.

It was Julia who found the first one. We'd separated, hoping to cover more ground by taking opposite sides of the street. But only moments later she had called me back.

I'd trotted across the road to where she stood beside an old gnarled oak tree.

'What?'

Julia said nothing, but stepped to one side to reveal something already nailed onto the roughened bark. I blinked stupidly at the flier, and then looked back at the stack in the crook of my arm.

'Looks like your new friend got here first,' said Julia.

We went down the surrounding roads anyway, to find Fred's face staring at us from practically every tree and lamppost. He was also to be found in virtually every shop window on the high street. While I'd been busy sleeping ... Ben had been busy elsewhere.

'Strange guy, your new pal,' commented Julia, with more than a hint of suspicion in her voice, as we settled back into her car some time later.

'Isn't he, though,' I replied.

I frowned at the small screen, made a couple of minor adjustments, and then looked up. 'Does this sound okay?' Julia stopped folding the pile of tiny baby garments that were still warm from the dryer to give me her full attention. I cleared my throat, as though I was about to recite a soliloquy. 'No need to panic, but I've lost my phone, so if you need to contact me over the next few days, you'll have to reach me on Julia's number. Will explain properly when you get back. Hope you're having a good holiday.'

Julia gave a small shrug. She was both a mother and a

daughter, and saw the situation through different eyes than mine. 'Are you sure it wouldn't be better to just tell them what happened? If either of my two were involved in a life or death situation, I certainly wouldn't want to wait several weeks before hearing about it.'

I moved Julia's phone to one side as Lacey wormed her way across my lap, like a tiny commando on an assault course. 'It's not really the same when they're still too young to go to the bathroom by themselves,' I said lightly, nuzzling my face into the soft skin at the back of Lacey's neck and blowing a giggle-inducing raspberry into her flesh.

'You know your parents better than I do,' Julia said, resuming her laundry folding and not fooling me for a minute that she approved of my decision. But she was right about one thing: I *did* know them, and what was best for them. Julia was just going to have to trust me on this one.

Ten past two in the morning was when everything changed. That was the time when the phone had rung. My parents didn't have mobiles back then, so it was the house phone, trilling sharply on the table in the downstairs hall, that had woken us. I had switched on my bedside lamp, blinking in confusion as I read the time on my digital radio's display.

I heard a door opening at the end of the hallway, and the soft rumble of my father's voice answering my mother's question. I swung my legs out from beneath the duvet, scattering the line of soft cuddly toys from the foot of my bed as though they'd been felled by a giant. I didn't pause to pick them up, just stepped over their fallen plush forms as though they were victims of some dreadful atrocity. But the victims weren't a collection of cuddly toys I'd outgrown years earlier; it was someone much closer to my heart than that.

My room was evidence of the line between child and adult that I currently straddled. Boy band posters on the wall, make-up and jewellery scattered over my dressing table, and soft toys on my bed. I walked to my bedroom door under the unseeing eyes of the boys from McFly, who looked down at me from various locations on the pink-wallpapered walls. My dad was already halfway down the staircase when I stepped into the hall.

'What is it, Daddy? What's wrong? Who's ringing us in the middle of the night?'

My mother answered, not moving from her position in her bedroom doorway. Her hand was gripped tightly onto the door frame, as though she was on a boat in rough seas and was struggling to keep her balance. Her hand looked bony, and old, in a way I'd never noticed before. I always remember that. She tried to summon up a reassuring smile, and failed miserably. 'It's probably just a wrong number. Or maybe it's one of those stupid prank calls,' she said, but her voice was all wrong, and I knew in that moment that she didn't believe what she was saying any more than I did.

I glanced across the hallway at the door next to mine, expecting to see it shut. But it was wide open, the way it had been when I'd gone to bed three hours earlier. The room beyond it was in darkness; the bed not slept in. A coldness went through me, starting in my throat and filling my stomach, as though I'd swallowed an icy drink, way too quickly. I looked back at my mother and saw my own fear reflected in her eyes.

The ringing phone was finally answered. 'Yes. I'm he, I'm him. That's me,' said my father, struggling to sound articulate in a way no man who taught English for a living should ever do.

I turned away from the faces of my parents, more terrified by their expressions than I was by my own racing imagination. I ran to the window, the one that looked out onto our front drive. I saw my father's car, which he'd pulled over as far as he could to one side of the driveway, trying to eke out a little more space. And beside it I saw . . . nothing . . . except for a large Rorschach-style splodge of black on the concrete, clearly visible in the glow from the nearby street lamp. *'That oil stain's never going to come out, is it? It's made a right old mess of the drive.'* When had that argument raged? Last week? The week before? It suddenly seemed very important that I should remember exactly when those words had been spoken. Panic does that to a person; it makes you reach out for inconsequential things to hold on to, while the structure of your world begins to crumble around you. It's strange the things you grab hold of: half remembered arguments, wooden door frames. You try to keep upright, try to stay grounded, but really you're in the pathway of a tornado, that's going to whip the world out from under you either way.

'What are you saying? Can you repeat that? I don't under-stand,' cried my father into the phone. He was shouting, and he *never* shouted.

'Oh God, no,' moaned my mother. Her hand had left the door frame and was now clutching her throat.

'We're on our way.' I heard his words, but I was already running, trying to escape back to the sanctuary of my room, trying to hide, but already knowing it was no use. Nothing was ever going to be the same again.

I got lost twice trying to find the Burns Unit. I hadn't allowed nearly enough time to find a hospital parking space, and in the end I'd reluctantly had to abandon Julia's car in an area where I was pretty certain it could get clamped. And I certainly didn't have any money to pay the seventy-five-pound fine if it did. I gritted my teeth as I trotted down the long and strangely deserted hospital corridor, hoping that the last person who'd given me directions had actually pointed me in the right way (unlike the first two). This could well be the point where the thin rubber band of friendship finally snaps, I thought. I'm living in your house, eating your food, wearing your clothes and sleeping on your sofa, oh and by the way I just got you a whacking great parking fine. Of course Julia and Gary would deny it if I brought up the subject, but even after forty-eight hours, I could see that crashing on their living-room settee was going to get very old, very quickly. As if to confirm it, I felt a sudden sharp twinge in the small of my back. Sleeping on floors, sofas, or anything in fact that wasn't an actual mattress, lost a lot of its charm once you outgrew your twenties.

And then there were the nightmares, creeping back into my life with an unpleasant familiarity, like bumping into the kid who bullied you at a school reunion. I'd woken up screaming in the early hours every single night, my dreams a combination of flames and an ever-ringing telephone. I'd woken the baby each time, who in turn had woken Lacey. It hardly made me an ideal house guest.

I glanced at my watch, still not used to wearing it on the wrong wrist, and saw that I was already ten minutes late for my appointment. I broke into an unaccustomed run and covered the remainder of the corridor at a pace that ensured that when I finally burst through the department's double swing doors, every single person in the waiting area looked up. It was hard to tell if the redness on my cheeks came from embarrassment or my sprint.

Every face turned my way. Only one of them smiled. Ben.

'Hi,' I mouthed, and pointed pantomime-style towards the sign-in desk, where a slightly irritated-looking receptionist was watching me expectantly. Perhaps people didn't usually enter the subdued outpatient department in quite such a dramatic fashion.

'I'm sorry,' I apologised, as I passed her my appointment card. 'I'm afraid I'm a little late.'

She frowned, took my card, and clattered something into her keyboard. 'Take a seat,' she instructed.

I turned back to face the waiting area. There were only

about ten patients in the room. There were loads of free chairs, but there was only one place I could possibly sit. Ben got to his feet as I approached, and I realised how few men bothered to do that any more. The feminist in me wanted to say, *'Why should they?'* but the other Sophie, the one who seldom got to say her piece, found it rather charming.

'I think I'm in trouble already,' I confessed, slightly flustered when Ben greeted me with a swift kiss on the cheek. Was that appropriate? I wondered. We weren't really friends, we were just ... my thoughts petered out as I realised there probably wasn't a word or phrase to adequately describe what we actually were.

'I've been here almost half an hour, and no one's been called in yet,' he reassured me, easing the long length of him into the seat next to mine. 'How are you? How's the arm?'

I looked down at my bandaged wound, and then across at his. They were the reason why, yet again, our paths had crossed. My heart was still beating faster than normal in my chest, which I was putting down entirely to my exertions. It most definitely wasn't due to seeing Ben, because I'd known there was a good chance we'd bump into each other at the hospital. And it definitely wasn't because he looked so much more attractive than I'd allowed myself to remember. That certainly wasn't affecting me at all.

'It's a bit sore, that's all. You?'

'The same, really.' I bit my lip, feeling guilty all over again. 'Thanks for your text, by the way,' he continued. 'There was no need to thank me, though. It was no trouble, and most of the shops were happy to take a poster. Any luck finding him yet?'

I shook my head, and Carla's new haircut swung jauntily from side to side. I quite liked the way it did that. 'No. I've been back several times, but he seems to have totally disappeared. I've phoned rescue shelters and all the vets in the area . . .' My voice trailed away as I realised how little interest any of this was likely to hold for him. He was probably only making polite conversation; it wasn't like he was genuinely concerned. Somewhere between all the pathetic blind dates and failed Tinder meet-ups, I seemed to have forgotten how to hold a normal intelligent adult conversation with a man. No wonder Julia thought I was destined for eternal spinsterhood.

'Can I get you anything from the drinks machine?' Ben offered. 'It might even be palatable this time,' he added as an inducement.

I smiled and shook my head. 'No, I'd better not. They'll probably call us soon,' I said hopefully, looking at the large clock on the wall behind the reception desk.

Ben gave a slightly crooked grin, which was attractive enough to make me forget where we were, and why. 'You don't know much about hospital appointment times, do you?' he said easily.

I gave him my own – considerably less charming – grin in reply. 'Not really. Why, do you?'

Ben looked momentarily uncomfortable, but rearranged his features so quickly I managed to convince myself I must have imagined it. 'Not specifically. But I think we might be here for quite a while yet.'

I think we provided a far more diverting distraction to the other waiting patients than the two-years-out-of-date magazines or the dog-eared editions of *Reader's Digest*. Most of them didn't even try to pretend they weren't listening in as Ben asked me how I was progressing with the painstaking process of reassembling my life, phoenix-style, from the ashes of the fire.

'Well, I've spent enough time on hold with various companies and organisations to know I never want to hear the song *Greensleeves* again for as long as I live.'

Ben laughed openly in the overly quiet room, his head thrown back, his eyes crinkling at the edges, in a totally natural and unselfconscious way. I realised in that moment that he was the kind of person who was extremely comfortable about who he was, and largely unconcerned about drawing attention to himself, or what others might think of him. I, on the other hand, who'd spent so many teenage years trying to perfect the art of being invisible, found such nonchalance completely intriguing.

'And *have* you sorted everything out?'

I shrugged. 'I've made a start. At least everything these days is backed up on a cloud somewhere,' I said, unconsciously glancing out the window as though all my personal data might actually be visible, floating past on a circling cumulus. At least three of the other patients looked with me – *that's* how I knew they were all listening.

'And is it working out okay staying with your friends? Do they have enough room?' I knew he was only making polite conversation, filling in the long boring minutes while we waited to be called, but it was so easy to be fooled into thinking the expression in those warm caramel-coloured eyes was genuine concern.

'Yeah, it's fine. For now, at least,' I said, unconsciously rubbing the small of my back as I thought of the impending discomfort of a third night on Julia's unyielding sofa.

'You do know I have a big house?' Ben said artlessly. My eyebrows rose a little, as did those of a middle-aged woman sitting diagonally opposite me.

'Yeees,' I said, drawing out the word, as though it was made of elastic.

'Well, if things are a little too crowded at your friend's, you're more than welcome to move in with me. You could have the basement.'

The middle-aged lady blinked several times in surprise. I really hoped I didn't do the same, because she had looked comically shocked at the invitation.

'That's really kind of you, Ben, but—'

'You really don't know me from Adam,' Ben completed easily.

Where the hell were all the doctors in this place? Shouldn't some of these patients have been called away for their appointments by now? 'It's not that,' I said, dropping my voice down a notch or two. A couple of the listening patients leant further forward in their seats, clearly unhappy at not being able to hear me properly. 'It's just that I'm obviously going to need a new *permanent* place to live, rather than another temporary stopgap. As soon as my finances are sorted, then I can start looking properly. Julia and Gary's sofa will be fine until then.'

Ben leant back in his seat and nodded, as though that was entirely what he'd expected me to say. A door opened beside the reception desk and three nurses came out, each holding a clipboard.

'Like bloomin' buses,' commented the middle-aged lady, the one who'd seemed very relieved that I'd turned down Ben's invitation. 'You wait here for hours, and then three of them come along at once.'

'Sorry. Tell me again exactly what he said,' asked Julia, sweeping sliced carrots from her chopping board into the casserole dish. They tumbled through the air like tiny orange skydivers. I finished peeling the last of the potatoes, before looking up to meet her eyes.

'Ben said I was welcome to stay in his basement.'

Julia went to work on an onion, her blade slicing through the innocent vegetable as though it had offended her in some way. But I think I was the one who might have done that. 'Just like you read in the newspapers. Pretty young girl goes into some bloke's basement and no one sees her again for about ten years. That kind of thing?'

I tried to hide my smile, but I knew she could see it anyway. 'Yes, Jules,' I said, playing along. 'Exactly like that. Except I don't actually think those guys *ask* the women first if they'd like to move in.' Julia gave me her very best mock-serious look, but I easily defused it. I'd had years of practice. 'I think he only offered me somewhere to lodge in case I was in your way around here, and his place is really huge.'

'Is it?' Julia replied, slamming the cast-iron casserole lid on our evening meal, as though the vegetables might be thinking of trying a daring escape. 'Well, obviously it's up to you, Sophie. But it all sounds more than a little odd, don't you think? I mean, who asks someone to move into their home, knowing she has no way of paying any rent, and not asking for anything in return?'

My eyes softened as I looked at her across the granite worktop. 'A really good friend,' I said reaching over the cool grey surface and squeezing her hand. 'That's who.'

Julia crossed the kitchen to the fridge, drew out a half-full bottle of wine and waggled it at me temptingly. I nodded and reached into the cupboard for glasses. 'Besides,' I said, taking a flute of chilled Sauvignon from her outstretched hand, 'your clothes fit me so much better than his, so I *have* to stay here.'

By mutual consent we moved to the lounge area, curling up at either end of the settee like matching bookends. 'It's a bit cheeky, though, don't you think?' commented Julia, taking a long and satisfying first sip of wine. The baby monitor crackled for a moment and I saw her tense and then relax when there was no ensuing cry. 'I mean, he's got this enormous mansion place, and all you're offered is a dark and dingy basement room.'

*

Ben and I had been called for our appointments at the same time, so it had hardly been surprising to see him return to the waiting room just as I was buttoning up Julia's warm winter coat. It had felt completely natural to leave the department together, and I'd fallen into step beside him, happy to follow his lead down the many identical-looking corridors and stairwells as we headed towards the hospital's main entrance.

'I got so hopelessly lost after I parked the car, but you just made that look embarrassingly easy,' I confessed, after he'd effortlessly taken me to the place where Julia's – fortunately unclamped – car was parked.

'I had a friend who was in here a little while ago, so I got to know the layout when I visited him,' Ben explained, with a casual shrug of his shoulders.

'Navigation is definitely not one of my strong points,' I admitted, extracting Julia's car keys from my bag, and swinging them from my fingers like a pendulum.

'Then remind me never to get you to map-read,' Ben said, as though he and I would be taking a trip together some day, which of course was never going to happen.

'Will do,' I said, extending my hand as though I was going to shake his, before realising how ridiculously formal that would look. My hand fluttered for a moment, like a bird surfing an air current, before reaching up to rest lightly on his shoulder. I think I was aiming for an air kiss, or a brief fly-past of my lips against the side of his face, but my sense of direction let me down again. At the last moment Ben moved his head, and instead of his cheek, my lips inadvertently brushed against the corner of his mouth. I drew back quickly, thought about apologising and then realised it would probably embarrass us both. I saw a twinkle of humour buried deep beneath the gold of his eyes, and realised that actually it would probably only embarrass one of us. He seemed pretty bullet-proof on that score.

'Remember what I said about the basement flat. The offer is open any time you might need it,' he reminded me, chivalrously holding open Julia's car door as I climbed in.

'I don't think staying in someone's dark dingy basement sounds like much fun.' Julia's words snatched me back out of the memory. There was a strangely curious, yet knowing, look in her eyes, as though she'd been able to peer into my thoughts and was unsurprised by what she'd seen there.

'If I remember it correctly, the basement is nothing like that.'

'You've *seen* it?' asked Julia, the wine slopping slightly in her glass as she turned to me in surprise.

'You have too.' Her frown told me she wasn't following me at all. 'On TV. The house was featured on that property show you and Gary are always going on about.'

'Aah,' cried Julia, leaping to her feet and plucking up the remote control. 'We've recorded every series of that. It should still be saved, unless Gary's deleted it.'

It took a surprisingly short amount of time before Ben's front door swung open on the TV screen, and a man who I didn't recognise, the former owner, invited the camera crew into his home. The show followed its usual format, showcasing the finished project and then deconstructing it to reveal how the end result had been achieved.

I saw Julia glance at me anxiously when the footage switched to the architect's wife talking animatedly from her hospital bed about the home her husband was building for her. I bent down, picked up the wine bottle and used the moment to refill both our glasses. When I next looked at the large plasma screen, they were back to talking about kitchen fitments.

The basement flat was featured about halfway through the programme. It was a completely self-contained annexe that the architect had designed for the full-time nurse needed to assist in the care of his wife. Rather than the dark and dingy room Julia had predicted, the basement was surprisingly light and airy, and like the accommodation above it, open-plan in layout.

'I suppose it looks sort of okay,' said Julia grudgingly. 'I can see why you might be tempted.'

I nudged her thigh gently with my foot, feeling suddenly as close to her as I'd done when we'd spent virtually every night in each other's rooms at university, devouring DVD box sets and huge slabs of Cadbury's chocolate with equal pleasure.

'Seriously, not tempted,' I confirmed.

I had to admit the garden that Ben had spoken of looked incredible, and the fact that the architect's wife had been a horticultural expert before her accident made it even more poignant. It was interesting to see that very little of the décor appeared to have altered when the property changed hands. Ben must have bought the house with practically all the furniture included.

'It *is* a nice house,' Julia admitted. 'I can see that. But I still don't want you to move out of here.'

'Neither do I,' I said. And I meant it.

Chapter 4

November

There's a rhyme that always fascinated me when I was a child. It tells how an entire kingdom was lost for *'the want of a nail'*. My own future was decided six days after the night of the fire by something equally whimsical. If I'd bought a goldfish for my birthday instead of a kitten; if Ben hadn't suggested making those posters; if Gary had been prescribed some decent antihistamine medication ... then everything might have ended up differently. Or maybe not.

'Damn it. I don't think that dress *ever* looked that good on me,' said Julia, swaying gently from side to side, with Noah balanced on one hip. She moved with an easy rhythm that looked so natural on her, yet which felt totally alien whenever I tried to soothe my godson that way. I flattened down the soft woollen fabric that clung snugly to my hips and did a critical survey over one shoulder in her bedroom mirror. 'I warn you, Winter, if the next words out of your mouth start with: *"Does my bum ..."* I may have to smother you with one of Noah's nappies.'

I laughed and slipped my feet into black ankle boots. 'I really don't think the size of my backside is going to factor in to the bank's decision of whether or not to give me an emergency loan,' I said, unplugging my replacement phone that had arrived the day before, and checking it was fully charged.

'I've got a low-cut top at the back of the wardrobe that might swing it for you,' offered Julia cheekily.

'Better not. I'll save that one for when I'm applying for a mortgage.' As difficult as the last week had been in all sorts of ways, it would have been so much harder without the support of both Julia and Gary, quietly shoring me up as I began to put the pieces of my life back together again. The younger version of me would have turned away from their help – *had turned away*, I acknowledged sadly, from everyone. Sixteen years older and wiser, I finally knew better than that. And of course, the fire was nothing like the tragedy we'd all lived through back then.

I felt a small stab of guilt at the front door when Julia plucked her car keys from the ceramic bowl where they lived, and handed them to me. 'I can take the bus,' I offered again, but she just shook her head, something Noah seemed to find hysterically funny. I reminded myself to store that little trick away for future use.

'No, it's definitely going to rain,' Julia predicted, looking through the hall window at the angry grey clouds smeared across the sky like a giant's smudged fingerprint. 'And I've got the mother and toddler group coming round for coffee, so you've probably picked a good morning to get out of here.

'I hope it goes well,' Julia said, leaning over to hug me, giving Noah a far too tempting opportunity to grab a handful of my hair in one pudgy little fist. 'Good luck.'

It *did* go well. And two hours later I was sitting in a warm and steamy coffee shop, sheltering from the rain and enjoying a celebratory cappuccino, which I'd actually paid for with money from my own bank account. The cash withdrawal the bank had given me would be enough to tide me over until my new cards arrived. The loan would take a little longer to process, but that was mainly needed to cover a security deposit and rent on a new flat – and I had to *find* one of those first.

My bag silently vibrated against my calf and I reached down to pluck out my phone, certain it would be Julia wondering how my meeting had gone. The number on the screen wasn't hers, although it did look familiar.

'Your number's finally working,' the voice cried, in lieu of a greeting.

'You're my very first call,' I confirmed. I glanced at the time displayed on the phone. 'It switched over about ten minutes ago.'

'Ah, well, that explains it,' he replied. 'Oh, by the way, I should have said, it's Ben here.'

'I know. I recognised your voice,' I said, looking up and catching a glimpse of my reflection in the coffee shop window. There was a silly little smile plastered on my lips, stuck there like the frothy foam from my coffee. And moments later it got even wider.

'I've got some good news . . .'

The rain was falling heavily, and even at full speed the wipers struggled to clear the screen. I drove slowly, my attention split between the impaired view of the rain-washed streets and the Sat Nav display. I didn't recognise the roads, but then I'd been understandably distracted the last time I was there. The house looked familiar though, but that was probably because I'd watched a television programme about it only a few nights earlier. That was something I didn't intend to share with him, because even I could see that my interest looked a little . . . well, stalker-ish.

I leapt from the car so hurriedly, I didn't even bother grabbing my borrowed coat. It was something I regretted when the rain trickled uncomfortably down the back of my neck as I waited for Ben to answer the front door. By the time he did, I was unpleasantly damp and dripping. He stepped back and I performed a cursory swipe of my feet on the mat before following him into the room.

'Where is he?' I asked, the anxiety I'd managed to suppress on the drive now threatening to boil over.

'Over there,' Ben replied, pointing to a large cardboard box, punched through with air holes.

'You've not let him out?' I asked, crossing over to the box, leaving a trail of raindrops on the glossy varnished floor.

'I didn't want to scare him. I thought it was best to wait until you got here.'

I dropped to my knees beside the box, which had begun to jerk and jump on the wooden floor, as though it contained something possessed.

'They said they'd given him water, and thought he'd probably been drinking from puddles on the shed floor. Apparently the roof leaks.' I nodded fiercely, my fingers clumsy and fumbling as I attempted to rip the criss-cross bands of tape from the box lid. 'They were on their way to an animal shelter. It was just pure chance they pulled up beside a tree with a flier on it.'

I was still struggling with the tape, and the occupant of the box, having recognised my voice, was going berserk. 'Hang on, Fred. One more second,' I promised, aware my voice sounded weird. The cardboard box was speckled with drops of water: some came from my dripping hair, but others were from a more embarrassing source. Ben probably thought I was crazy, crying like this over a cat.

'Let me,' Ben said gently, pushing aside my hands and easily ripping the two flaps apart. I saw Fred for a fleeting moment. He appeared greyer than normal – well, more black than grey really – and also considerably thinner, although that had been hard to tell in the seconds between the opening of the box and his spectacular leap from it. He crossed the wooden floor like a grey streak of lightning, and disappeared beneath Ben's settee.

No amount of coaxing could persuade him to come out, so I dropped to my knees, offering Ben a ringside view of my rear end as I groped beneath his settee. Perhaps I ought to ask *him* if it looked big in Julia's dress?

'Why don't we leave him to calm down for a bit?' suggested Ben reasonably, when my efforts to haul Fred out continued to be unsuccessful. 'How about a coffee?' He was already crossing to his kitchen, turning to look back at me, but the next moment he was crashing to the floor, landing so heavily I felt the vibration of his fall reverberate through the boards beneath my knees.

'Oh my God, Ben. Are you okay?' I asked, hurrying to his side.

'Yes, fine,' he said a little brusquely, already drawing himself up into a sitting position. He turned to me and summoned up a reassuring smile. 'It's nothing. I just slipped.'

'It's my fault,' I said guiltily. 'I dripped water all over the floor.'

Ben shrugged my words away, but I felt really bad, especially when I saw him massaging his calf through the denim of his jeans. 'Are you *sure* you didn't hurt your leg?' I asked, biting my lip in concern as he got to his feet, gave a wince he thought I didn't see, and then turned it into a smile.

'No. I'm fine,' he reassured, but there was a definite hesitation in his gait as he continued towards the kitchen.

While Ben made coffee, I insisted on wiping the remaining water from the floor. He found me a cloth and I blotted the boards, retracing the path I'd taken when I'd dripped across the room, although the place where Ben had slipped was already practically dry.

The arty stools at the breakfast bar were quite a challenge if you happened to be wearing a fitted dress. Ben politely looked the other way as I wriggled inelegantly onto the seat, which looked remarkably like a chip basket, but was actually surprisingly comfortable once you were in it.

'I imagine you'll be glad to see the back of me,' I said, my hands cradled around my coffee mug. 'Either I'm crashing down on you from a great height, getting you second-degree burns, or making you fall over. I should come with a hazard warning.'

Ben's shoulders rose expressively. 'Accidents happen.'

I swallowed my mouthful of coffee with difficulty. 'Yes,' I said, and there was a whole chapter of emotions tied up in that single word, none of which I was prepared to share. I never did.

I glanced over at the lounge, still waiting for Fred to emerge. I was strangely torn between wanting him to come out so I could leave, and hoping he'd stay in hiding for a little longer, so I could stay. 'I'm really sorry that I've taken up so much of your time. I must be keeping you from your work . . . or something.' It was a clumsy way of asking what Ben did for a living.

'No, not at all. I'm actually not working anywhere right

now.' He leant back on his stool and stretched, looking totally relaxed and unconcerned that I was so obviously prying. 'This time last year I was a classic workaholic. I had my own company and was doing quite well from it, probably because I lived and breathed work pretty much 24/7.' I glanced around the home he now lived in, and knew that *'doing quite well'* was definitely a modest understatement. 'When a major competitor approached me and wanted to buy me out I resisted at first, but then ... well, it was too good an offer to walk away from. So I sold up, bought this place and decided to take some time off to really think about what I want to do next.'

'Well, good for you,' I said, wondering how it would feel to step out of your old life and embrace a completely new one. It was none of my business, and I didn't know him nearly well enough to ask, but I was certainly curious.

'Sometimes you need to step off the conveyor belt to discover there are more important things in life than just work,' Ben added, his eyes going past me to settle on the tropical fronds swaying in the garden beyond. I wondered if he was thinking of the architect who'd built this home for the woman he loved. 'What I do now is a lot more fulfilling than climbing the corporate ladder ever was.'

I nodded, as though I agreed totally. But as translators rarely scale the dizzying heights of that particular ladder, it just hammered home how little Ben and I had in common.

As though realising this was the right moment to do so, Fred casually sauntered into the kitchen, with a nonchalant swish of his tail, as though our memories of having spent the last half-hour trying to catch him were seriously flawed.

I declined Ben's offer to accompany me to the veterinary surgery, feeling I'd already outstayed my welcome. Fred yowled indignantly when returned to the box and carried to the car. 'Will he keep that up for long?' Ben asked, his eyes glinting with either amusement or sympathy as he positioned the box on the passenger seat.

'Probably,' I said with a resigned sigh. 'So, I guess this is goodbye. *Again.*' We stood on his driveway facing each other, like dancers who'd forgotten the next piece of choreography. 'Well, thank you again for everything you've done for me—' A banshee-like wail came from the car. 'I really am in your debt.'

'You really aren't,' Ben denied, closing the space between us and dipping his head to lightly kiss my cheek. His aftershave tickled my nose and made me want to draw in the smell, the way you do with freshly cut grass. Thankfully I resisted the urge. We both stepped back, acknowledging this was the moment where our acquaintance would finally come to an end. But then I'd thought that before, and been proved wrong.

'I hope he's none the worse for his adventures,' Ben said, as I climbed into the car and clipped my seatbelt in place.

'I'm sure he'll be fine.'

I only hoped the same was true for Ben, because when I glanced back in the rear-view mirror, it looked very much like he was still limping slightly from that fall as he walked back into his house.

'I'm so sorry, Sophie, but he's not going to be able to stay here.' As if Julia's words needed further confirmation, Gary gave another almighty sneeze. His wife picked up a nearby tissue box and passed it to him.

'I'll put him in the utility room,' I said, scooping Fred into my arms. A volley of record-breaking sneezes echoed like the call of a jungle animal as I carried the offender from the room. Obviously I'd known that Gary suffered with allergies, but I'd always thought they were more of the hay fever and house dust variety. I'd never seen him in the throes of a full-blown reaction. It was shocking that less than ten minutes over the threshold, one tiny cat had managed to reduce a six-foot-two, rugby-playing hulk into a snivelling, red-eyed, sneezing wreck.

'Sorry,' I said, returning to the lounge where Julia and Gary had clearly been having some sort of heated exchange, between sneezes, that is.

'Perhaps I could just double up the dosage of my last pills?' Gary suggested gamely, his eyes already beginning to tear up.

My own felt that way too, for an entirely different reason, especially when Julia stepped in firmly. Clearly she had elected to be the 'bad cop'. 'No. They just make you sleepy and it's not safe for you to drive. And it's not as if they work that well anyway.' She turned back to face me, and I knew I'd lost the argument without even saying a word.

'I know how much you love that cat, Soph, but with Gary's allergies, a toddler and a newborn in the house, Fred isn't going to be able to stay here.'

I nodded, perhaps a little too briskly to look entirely natural. 'No. Obviously, I get it. Totally. I'm sorry, I just wasn't thinking.'

I glanced over as an alarming clattering crash came from beyond the closed utility-room door. A tiny betraying muscle twitched beside Julia's right eye and Gary sneezed four times in quick succession.

'I don't think I'll be able to make any other arrangements for tonight,' I said apologetically, glancing at the clock. It was after six, and I'd spent my entire afternoon and most of my money getting Fred checked out at the veterinary surgery, and then buying some essential supplies at the pet superstore on the way home. It simply hadn't occurred to me that he wouldn't be able to stay.

'No, I realise that. That's okay. He can stay in the utility room tonight.'

It was an upgrade on where he'd spent the last six nights, and I really didn't want to sound ungrateful for everything my friends had done for me. Even so, by morning Julia was going to expect me to have found a solution to the problem.

'Perhaps you could put him into a cattery, until your parents get back from their holiday, and then maybe they could have him?' Julia suggested, as I laid the table for dinner and tried to pretend I couldn't hear Fred noisily protesting about his incarceration.

'Please, don't worry about it. I'll figure something out,' I assured her, squeezing her shoulder gently as I went back into the kitchen for the condiments. I pulled the items from the cupboard and saw her looking back at me worriedly.

'We could look online tonight and find one not too far away. Perhaps they have visiting hours, or something,' suggested Julia, clearly feeling horribly guilty. I didn't want to be the one to tell her that catteries weren't like hospitals or prisons. And I certainly didn't want to point out that I couldn't afford the twenty pounds or so a day it was going to cost to keep Fred there indefinitely, because I already knew my parents wouldn't be able to take him. Pointing out all the obstacles and objections was just going to make me look churlish and ungrateful, and I really didn't want to appear that way, especially not with her.

'It wouldn't have been quite so urgent if he'd been found in a week or two, because Gary's going away on business to Toronto. We'd have had a little longer to find somewhere for him.'

A noise, not dissimilar to an ocean liner travelling through fog, reverberated from the region of their bedroom. I don't think I'd ever heard a human being blow their nose quite so loudly. Or repeatedly. Julia was right, of course she was. Even one night was going to be a strain, on everyone and on our friendship. Any longer would be untenable.

I lay awake for a long time after Gary and Julia had gone to bed, finding and rejecting solutions. Eventually all noise from

the utility room had died down. Fred had either escaped –
unlikely, unless he'd learnt how to pick a lock during the last
week – or had finally fallen into an exhausted sleep. I only
wished I could do the same, but the uncomfortable settee and
the even more uncomfortable situation ensured that wasn't
going to happen any time soon.

I pretended to myself that I came to the answer carefully
and slowly, after long and considered deliberation. I pretended to myself that I hadn't known exactly what I was
going to have to do from that very first sneeze. I glanced at
the time on my phone. Half past eleven. Probably too late
to call, I thought, but I scrolled down the directory and
pressed the green phone icon anyway. It rang three times
before being picked up. I didn't bother with any preamble,
or even an explanation. I'd known for hours exactly what I
was going to say.

'Is the offer of your basement flat still open?'

Packing and unpacking are definitely the worst aspects of
moving house. Take those out of the equation, and changing
address is a piece of cake. I'd turned down Julia's offer of a
lift to Ben's, having witnessed the army-like manoeuvres
required to get out of the door with a three-year-old and a
baby in tow. I knew she was still feeling horribly guilty, as
though she'd driven me out of her home, and nothing I could
say would convince her otherwise.

I was in the hall, waiting for my taxi to arrive, when Julia
clumped noisily down the stairs, hauling a heavy suitcase.

'Are you coming with me?' I joked, as she set the large red case down on the floor between us. 'Or running away to join the circus?'

'It's not my bag, it's *yours*,' Julia said, her blue eyes darkened to grey with concern. 'I can't throw you out on the street with nothing to wear.'

I stepped around the case and drew her to me for a hug. 'Listen, you idiot, you're not throwing me out. You and Gary have been brilliant giving me somewhere to stay, but we all knew it was just temporary.'

'Not *this* temporary,' Julia wailed in my ear. It sounded very much as though she was teetering on the edge of tears and if she *was,* it was going to set me off. It didn't seem to take much these days, and unlike her I couldn't blame it on my hormones. 'I've practically thrown my best friend into the arms of a man who wants to lock her up in his basement.'

I laughed, and thankfully a moment later she joined in. 'Okay, so maybe he *is* just a very kind, decent human being, who just happens to have all these spare rooms in his big old house. But we *still* don't know anything about him.'

'To be honest, Jules, I don't think I've known a great deal about *any* of my previous landlords. And I'm only going to be there until I find somewhere permanent; somewhere they let you keep pets.' Julia's mouth twisted, and I instantly regretted my words. With excellent timing, the moment was saved by Lacey who came hurtling out of the lounge and catapulted into her mum's legs, hanging on like a monkey in a hurricane.

I'm not sure who looked most upset when the sound of a taxi pulling up outside the house signalled it was time for me to go. Julia opened the door, letting in a sharp gust of November air that whipped the words from her lips. 'Promise me if you don't like it there, or things don't work out, you'll come back here.'

'What about Gary?'

'We'll put *him* in a cattery.'

A small gasp sounded from the region of her knees. 'Mummy's just being silly,' I reassured a clearly worried Lacey.

'Take the clothes,' Julia urged, nudging the case across the floor towards me. 'Just as a loan until you've built up your own wardrobe again.' She pulled the coat I'd been borrowing down from its hook on the wall and bundled it into my arms. 'And this.'

I shook my head, but I recognised the glittering determination in her eyes. She'd made up her mind. I slipped my arms into the sleeves.

'We're good here, aren't we?' Julia asked hesitantly, as I bent to pick up the suitcase.

'Of course we are.'

'Lunch next week, right?'

The taxi hooted impatiently and I raised my hand as though putting in a bid for a few moments more. 'Absolutely.' I kissed her cheek, suddenly anxious to go. I never had been good with goodbyes, and I'd be seeing her again in just a few days.

I sat in the back of the cab, with Fred in his brand-new carrier on the seat beside me, still unsure if I'd just made the best or worst decision of my life. Only time would tell.

'So, there should be a few things in the fridge,' Ben said, 'and some stuff in the cupboards. I asked the woman who does a little cleaning for me if she'd stock up on some basics for you.'

I opened the door of the tall slimline refrigerator and felt my mouth form a silent letter O. 'How much did you tell her I ate?' I asked, my eyes running over the laden shelves, while mentally trying to calculate if I still had enough cash to reimburse him for all of this. Which reminded me ... 'We didn't discuss on the phone what the rent would be for the flat.'

For a moment Ben looked so totally taken aback, I wondered if he'd already told me and I'd somehow forgotten the conversation.

'Erm, I don't need you to pay me rent.'

I could feel the muscles of my face tightening as I wondered how to put this without causing offence. 'Well, I don't think I would feel right staying here without paying my way,' I said awkwardly. I could feel myself growing warm, and suddenly Julia's black polo-neck jumper seemed like a really bad choice of outfit.

Ben walked away from the kitchen, heading towards the flat's open-plan living space. His stride looked a little stiff, and I wondered if what I'd said had somehow annoyed him.

'I'm not a landlord, Sophie. I'm just offering you a place to live as a friend.'

He wasn't really one of those either, but that would definitely be too uncomfortable an admission to voice out loud. I crossed over to join him on the small two-seater settee, pushing Fred – who'd already made himself comfortably at home – to one side.

'Ben, I don't want you to take this the wrong way, but unless you're willing to take some money towards the rent and basic utilities, I really don't think I'm going to be able to stay here. It just wouldn't be right.'

He shook his head, as though of all the unexpectedly crazy conversations he had ever had with anyone, this had to be the most ludicrous. 'I really didn't think this would be an issue,' he said, still sounding bemused.

I drew in a deep breath and looked at my knees as I spoke. 'Well, I'm afraid it is. I want everything to be . . . you know, above board.'

I looked up and caught his expression of perplexed amusement. 'Were we in danger of being *below board*?'

The flush came back at full pelt, as I realised he was teasing me. At least I hoped it was teasing, because for a moment there it had all sounded a little flirtatious. 'We were,' I declared firmly, making it very clear where we stood by my tone.

'Okay, then,' he said with a sigh. He paused, as though crunching numbers into a calculator, before giving me a figure. 'How would that be?'

I gave a small gulp. I'd asked him to charge me rent, not rob me blind. 'A week?' I said, my voice a very undignified squawk.

Ben's eyebrows rose in earnest. 'A month,' he corrected.

'That's no good,' I said, shaking my head.

'Too high?'

'No. Nowhere near high enough.'

'No wonder people don't like having tenants,' Ben said, his hand absently rubbing across his jaw. I heard the vague scratch of the dark shadowy bristles against his palm and deliberately looked away. 'It clearly causes nothing but aggravation.'

Eventually we managed to agree on a sum that he still thought was far too high, while I knew perfectly well it was only half of what I should be paying him. It was a strange and curious way to begin my stay under his roof.

It was clearly a party. Well, maybe not a party *per se* . . . but it was obviously some sort of social gathering. And there was no reason whatsoever why Ben should have invited or included me in whatever was going on upstairs in the main house. Given how things had turned out the last time I'd been invited to a neighbour's party, it was probably for the best that he hadn't. He was already being more than generous in giving me somewhere to stay. He certainly wasn't responsible for providing me with a social life as well.

Yet with every ring of the doorbell, with every car that

arrived, spilling out its passenger onto the driveway, I felt a little more like a suburban Cinderella, without the chores, of course, because my new flat was immaculately clean and tidy.

I sat on the settee, with Fred asleep on my lap, and tried to resist the urge to look up every time yet another guest arrived. Not that I could see much of the new arrivals, of course. The rear of the flat had full-length French windows, which let in lots of light from the stepped garden beyond. But the window at the front offered only a partially obscured view of the drive. This meant that all I could see of the arrivals were their legs, or more specifically their legs from the knees downward. Playing a game of filling in the missing parts of the picture in my head was a great deal more fun than it probably should have been.

The early evening television programme wasn't holding my attention, but Ben's arriving guests were more than making up for it. His visitors came in a steady stream, most turning up at the door alone. They seemed an eclectic bunch, spanning both gender and age range. The man with the drainpipe leather trousers and the skinny legs had to be young, yet the wearer of the grey flannel pair with the turn-ups walked with the faltering hesitancy of old age. One guest had vivid pink harem pants, and satin shoes that looked authentically Arabian, while another wore thick black tights, bunching slightly on ankles puffy with age, and shuffled past my unseen viewing point whilst leaning heavily on a walking stick. One guest wobbled past my window on spindly red stilettos, while another wore sensible brogues and trousers that were just an inch or so too short in the leg.

It really was none of my business, I told myself, deliberately turning up the volume on the television to tune out the sound of the chatter filtering down through the ceiling above me.

It hadn't taken Ben long to show me around the flat. There was basically just one large living area with a kitchen annexe, a comfortable double bedroom, and a bright modern bathroom. The flat had its own front door, set to the side of the main building, which was accessed down a short flight of stone steps. But the properties were also linked internally. Ben had stood beside a closed door, studying it with a troubled expression on his face. 'This leads upstairs to the main house, but I've only just realised there's no lock on it. Is that a problem?'

'No, not really,' I replied.

Yes, I'd say it is, screamed Julia inside my head.

'Why don't I get a locksmith to come and fit one next week?' Ben suggested.

'Okay. That would be great,' I said.

What's wrong with finding a twenty-four-hour one and getting it sorted today? questioned my inner Julia. I smiled, keeping my lips tightly shut, in case any of my friend's concerns managed to slip their way past me.

After Ben had gone, I'd spent a little time wandering around the comfortably furnished accommodation, opening cupboards and doors and generally familiarising myself with where everything was kept. I found my eyes continually drawn to the door that linked the basement flat to the place where my new unintentional landlord lived. Eventually, without intending to do so, I found myself standing before the panelled doorway, my fingers curled around the brass door handle. Ben had shown me the wooden spiral staircase on the other side of the door, which finished its coiled ascent at a second door that came out in his kitchen. When the basement had been occupied by a full-time carer, this had been a necessary link between the properties. Now propriety dictated that the two homes should be separated, as though two sensible adults couldn't be trusted not to cross the boundary line without the benefit of one of Yale's finest to stop them.

Julia had packed the suitcase she'd given me with the enthusiasm of a holidaymaker taking a flight with no weight restriction. There were enough clothes inside it that shopping could be moved right down on my 'to do' list. It felt strange seeing so many unfamiliar outfits hanging in my wardrobe. They still only took up half of the available space, even though Julia had been more than generous. She must clearly have been imagining a far different life for me than the one she knew perfectly well that I led. There were outfits that I was never going to have occasion to wear. My usual working wardrobe consisted of jeans and jumpers, or – when I just couldn't be bothered – I'd been known to spend the entire day at my desk still in my pyjamas. I tried to remind myself not to do that too often, because even I could see it was the first step on a slippery slope. To combat my inner-hermit tendencies, I made myself venture out of the flat at least once a day, even if it was only to pop out to buy a carton of milk.

The comment my mother had made about my slightly reclusive lifestyle still stung, even though I knew perfectly well that it had come from a place of concern, and not malice. Sometimes I considered inventing a whole fantasy life to relay to them, just to stop them from worrying. I could tell them about the amazing blind date that had led to a new relationship. I could talk about romantic dinners in intimate restaurants, theatre visits, and weekend stays in boutique hotels. I could invent a whole other life for a whole other Sophie. But, at the end of the day, maintaining that fantasy sounded almost as exhausting as living the reality would be . . . so I told them the truth, and tried not to focus on the concern I heard in their voices on our weekly telephone calls.

The soft burr of conversation overhead was even louder when I stood in the kitchen area, breaking eggs into a bowl and chopping up vegetables for my Spanish omelette dinner. I hummed a little tunelessly to myself, as though illustrating to absolutely no one at all how little it bothered me that I was all alone on my first night in a strange place, just below the party-goers' feet. It probably wasn't even a party anyway, I thought. It was probably some boring event, which Ben had known I wouldn't want to attend. (Although how he would have known such a thing I had absolutely no idea.)

He was just saving me from an evening of having to make small talk with people I didn't know, I thought, whisking my eggs with such vigour that small yellow splotches flecked the surface of the gleaming worktop. He'd done me a favour by not asking me, I thought, nodding at the sizzling frying pan, as though the vegetables cooking within it might dispute me on that.

Except it didn't actually sound boring, I had to concede. It actually sounded like it was quite good fun. I could hear the faint sound of music and there was laughter, a lot of laughter. I cocked my head to one side, like a dog tuning into a frequency his owner couldn't quite catch. I jabbed at the remote control, muting the television, and waited. I didn't have to wait long before it came again. I have a good ear – you need to have when you're a linguist – and it was an extremely recognisable laugh. I suddenly knew exactly who had been wearing those harem pants. They were very Carla. Whatever Ben's reasons for not including me in his social gathering that evening, it certainly hadn't been because he'd been worried I wouldn't know anyone.

'Bridget Jones style, or the excruciating thongs?' asked Julia, pulling up Noah's buggy directly in front of a large display of ladies' underwear in the popular high street store.

'Somewhere between the two,' I said, pulling a multipack of briefs down from the rack. After a moment's hesitation I threw in a second set.

Julia eyed the packets sitting in the bottom of the

lobster-net shopping basket, as though she'd like to toss them back where they came from. 'They're not terribly sexy.'

'They don't have to be,' I said, steering her away from the stand before she decided to add a few wispy lace garments to the pile. 'No one is going to see them except me.'

Noah gave a warning grizzle and Julia instinctively rolled his buggy backwards and forwards on the tiled floor. She bent down and tucked the blanket a little more firmly around her wriggling son, then looked up at me with a rueful expression. 'I give us five minutes to get out of here before he starts screaming the place down.' We actually had only three, before Noah expressed – very vocally – exactly what he thought about shopping expeditions.

Tucked away in a back booth of a nearby coffee shop, where Julia could feed him discreetly, we finally had a chance to talk properly. Perhaps shopping with a young baby had been a bit ambitious, but underwear hadn't been the only essential item I'd urgently needed to buy. I'd received several reminder emails from my agency that two translation pieces were fast approaching their deadline, and without a replacement laptop I was going to struggle to meet my commitments. The agency were sympathetic about my circumstances . . . but business was business, after all.

So that morning I'd used up a large chunk of my bank loan purchasing a new laptop and a printer, but annoyingly the models I'd chosen couldn't be delivered for another week. 'You're welcome to come round and use ours,' Julia suggested, lifting a much happier Noah onto her shoulder and patting his back rhythmically. He burped noisily, and then looked around with such a startled expression at the sound that it was hard not to laugh.

'No, it's fine,' I assured her, knowing that there really wasn't anywhere quiet enough in her home to work properly, and not wanting to offend her by actually saying so.

'But you need peace and quiet to work,' she supplied for me. She flashed me a fleeting grin. 'I lived with you for years, remember. I know what you're like.'

'I can always work in a library, until my laptop is delivered.'

We both looked up as a green-uniformed young waitress arrived with our coffees and one hugely oversized triple chocolate muffin, which Julia wasted no time sinking her teeth into. Her eyes practically rolled in ecstasy.

'God, I love breastfeeding. I may do it until he's ten.'

I spluttered on a mouthful of cappuccino. 'Eww, gross. Please don't.'

'Are you sure you don't want some?' she offered, generously pushing the muffin towards me.

'No thanks. Not if I want any of your clothes to still fit me.'

Julia chewed more carefully than she needed to on the muffin, before swallowing mindfully. 'You don't still worry about that, do you? About the weight thing? I mean, I know you don't like talking about it very much ...' She looked a little uncomfortable herself, as though she regretted bringing up one of the few prickly areas we usually gave a very wide berth and avoided. There weren't many people who still remembered that quiet, introspective girl who'd turned up at university, carrying a suitcase, a rucksack and far more excess weight than was healthy for her.

Julia had been there to witness the gradual shedding of many of the issues that had held me down for so very long. The weight was just one of them. Going away to university changes people in countless ways. For me it was more than just an educational experience; it was cathartic. But of course it wasn't a miracle cure. There was still mud on my wings, hampering me from flying. There probably always would be.

My unpacked shopping bags were still where I'd left them on the coffee table. My undrunk cup of tea was still waiting for me on the kitchen worktop, and my unfinished translation pieces were still floating about in the ether, or on a virtual cloud, or wherever it is that documents live when you aren't summoning them to your computer. There were plenty of things I should have been doing; staring into the exotic tropical garden beyond my window wasn't one of them.

The garden had the power to draw and tug me like a tide every time I passed the kitchen window. It was intriguing, mysterious and haunting even more so now I knew the story of the woman who'd designed it. It felt alive and was never static; everything about it constantly moved and swayed, as if unseen spirits were silently weaving in and out of the thick foliage. It was doing that right now, I realised, as I watched two thick-stemmed palms bending and bowing in the wind. Except there *was* no wind today.

It was cold and damp, the way November knew how to be better than practically any other month, but it was also completely still.

I held my breath for so long that when I eventually exhaled, a large section of garden disappeared behind a circle of condensation. It was still slowly clearing away when I saw a pair of heavily booted feet, disappearing into the thick concealing undergrowth. There were so many things I should have done at that point. Things that *wouldn't* have made me cringe with embarrassment the way I found myself doing repeatedly whenever I replayed what happened next. The sensible thing would have been to call Ben's mobile. I'd known from the empty drive that he wasn't home, but I could still have contacted him. Or I could have drawn the blinds, told myself it was none of my business, and walked away. Or if I'd genuinely thought it was an intruder, I should have called the police. Any of those would have been a sensible option. Grabbing a rolling pin from the kitchen drawer, unlocking the French windows and venturing into the garden with the makeshift club in my hand definitely was not.

'Excuse me. Can I help you?' I challenged, speaking to a large clump of foliage where the unknown intruder had last been seen. The bush suddenly erupted into life, as though something – or someone – was about to stampede from it. My heart rate jumped, and I gripped the rolling pin even more firmly in both hands as the undergrowth parted to reveal a young man. He was scruffily dressed, with faded jeans worn so low down on his bony hips I could read the brand name on his boxers. There was something long and shiny glinting in the hand swinging at his side, and I suddenly realised how stupidly reckless I'd been, leaving the safety of my flat.

'Baking, are you?' asked the man, nodding his head towards the rolling pin that I was brandishing like a caveman.

'Are you supposed to be here?' I queried, trying not to sound as though I was suddenly very scared, even though I think both of us could tell from the wobble in my voice that I was.

'Are you?' he challenged right back at me.

'I live here. So I think I'm justified in asking who—'

'Tom! There you are!' came a familiar voice from one of the raised sections of garden above me. 'Sorry I'm late.' I looked down at my booted feet, willing the ground to crack open just enough to swallow me whole. But of course it did no such thing.

Ben came into view, his eyebrows rising comically when he saw me wielding the culinary weapon. The grin he directed at the young man told me all I needed to know: there was only one person who wasn't supposed to be in the garden right then. Me.

'I'm sorry. I know I shouldn't laugh,' said Ben, nudging the tin of biscuits towards the younger man, but keeping his eyes on me.

'No, go ahead. I deserve it,' I said, dipping my head and

then forgetting I no longer had my old and trusted long curtain of hair to hide behind.

'I just don't know what you were going to do with that rolling pin,' said Tom, popping an entire chocolate digestive into his mouth without biting it, or choking. I'd seen a snake do something very similar once on a wildlife documentary. 'I really couldn't tell if she was going to clobber me over the head, or knock up some scones.' I smiled, albeit weakly. This one was going to take some living down. 'You were definitely armed and dangerous,' Ben's young friend concurred, nodding at the wooden rolling pin that now sat like an exhibit in a courtroom trial on Ben's dining-room table.

'I thought you were too,' I said in my defence, looking through the wall of glass and seeing the garden scythe Tom had left propped up against a tree.

As though realising the banter was now beginning to wear thin, Ben turned his attention to the young man. 'Did you get a chance to check out the trees I was talking about? What do you think?'

'It's like I said the other night, if you don't cut a lot of it back, it's going to be a complete mess by the time spring comes around.' The two men exchanged a curious look that I couldn't interpret at all.

'So you're a gardener, Tom,' I said, feeling like the last person to have got the clue in an embarrassingly easy quiz.

I saw Tom's eyes go questioningly to Ben's for an instant before he answered. 'I am. Or well, I was. I'm hoping to get back to it soon . . . but you know how these things go.'

I nodded wisely, although I had absolutely no idea what he was talking about.

'Why don't you have a think about it, and let me know what you want to do when we next get together?' suggested Tom, getting to his feet.

Ben rose too and discreetly passed Tom the solitary crutch that somehow I hadn't even noticed was propped up against the wall. There was something about the younger man's gait that gave it away as he crossed the room; one leg moved differently and a little awkwardly. Tom slipped one arm into the crutch's supporting cuff, and extended the other to me.

'Well, it was very nice meeting you, Sophie. No hard feelings about the mix-up, I hope?'

I shook his hand, acknowledging his manners were a great deal better than mine. 'I'm really sorry about—'

He cut me off. 'Hey, don't worry about it. No harm, no foul.'

Except that wasn't quite true, I thought, as I watched Ben walk with him to the door. There had definitely been harm or foul of some kind to have led to a man as young as Tom losing one of his legs.

When Ben returned from seeing Tom out, he gave my shoulder a fleeting squeeze as he passed my chair. Had he noticed the expression on my face when I'd clocked Tom's disability? Or had I successfully masked my feeling of shock? I hoped so, for I had no desire to explain my reaction to him.

'You okay?' Ben asked lightly.

'I just feel bad . . . for accusing him like that.'

Ben grinned. 'I wouldn't worry about it. Tom will be telling that story in the pub for weeks. And it *was* a perfectly understandable mistake on your part. I really should have warned you someone was going to be walking about in the garden. You could have been wandering around undressed . . . or anything.'

'That might have been less embarrassing than my vigilante Mary Berry response.'

Ben laughed so hard that his eyes actually began to stream. It seemed like a very good moment for me to leave. 'Thank you for the tea, but I really have to be going.' I got to my feet, gathering up the trio of dirty mugs. 'Do you happen to know if there's a public library nearby with computers and internet access?'

Ben's forehead wrinkled. 'I'm not sure. But if it's a computer you need, then feel free to use mine. I'm going out shortly, anyway.'

Both of us glanced towards Ben's desk and work station in the far corner of the room, where I'd made the fliers on the night of the fire. That seemed a great deal longer than just a couple of weeks ago. 'Are you sure?'

Ben was already crossing to his desk, and threw me a glance over his shoulder. 'It's really not a problem. I'm driving a friend to the airport this afternoon, so you'll have the place to yourself.'

*

'So, are you going to have a little ... er, look around while he's out?' Julia was picking her words carefully, but not fooling me for a single moment.

'Snoop, you mean?' I challenged. 'No, my suspicious and frankly morally bankrupt friend, I'm not.' I tried to sound just the right amount of horrified at her suggestion, instead of tempted. 'It would be a complete abuse of Ben's trust.'

I heard Julia sigh disappointedly at the other end of the line. 'I'm only saying it because you're living in such close proximity to a man you know nothing about.'

'Well, the last group of people I lived in close proximity to burnt down the building we shared. I doubt Ben's more dangerous than that.'

'Hmm ...' replied Julia, clearly still in favour of a full Nancy Drew exploration of Ben's home. 'I just think there's something more to his background than he's told you so far ... something seems a little "off". And the internet's no bloody help at all.'

'You haven't *Googled* him?'

'I may have.'

I shook my head, knowing I should call her on this, but understanding it wasn't just idle curiosity on her part. Julia was just trying to protect me, the way she'd always done. 'And ...?'

'And nothing. All I could find was the stuff you already told me about. He had a successful company that got bought out by a big corporation ... blah, blah, blah. Oh, but I *did* find several photos online of him at industry events, with a pretty stunning redhead hanging on to his arm. I think they might have been engaged, or perhaps living together, but I couldn't find any more about it.'

I glanced around the room, already knowing there were no personal photographs on display. Especially none of gorgeous girlfriends; I'd have noticed if there were.

'Apparently she's with someone else now,' Julia added, and there was no accounting for the sudden inexplicable feeling of relief that rushed through me on hearing her words. Part of me wanted to ask Julia for all the details; another part of me knew better than to go there.

'Well, Miss Marple, as fascinating as all this is, I really do have to go now. One of us has to do some real work, you know.'

'This *is* work,' Julia corrected. I heard a soft cooing noise in the background and imagined Noah in her arms, all soft and sleepy from his afternoon nap. 'It's my *job* to look out for you.'

'No, it's not, hon,' I replied. 'Your job is to be my friend.'

'Same difference.'

I achieved far more than I was expecting to do that afternoon, despite two very different distractions. The first was Fred, who was enjoying the liberty of the open door between the house and the basement flat by walking a continual circuit of both homes, stopping only to entwine himself around my ankles as I worked at Ben's desk. The other distraction was unmoving, but just as compelling where it sat folded on the corner of Ben's oak desk.

It had come to light while Ben had once again been setting up the computer for my use. When the screen flickered into life, displaying the familiar software logo, he'd rolled back the upholstered chair from the desk and given a small cry of exclamation. On the black leather seat, rippled in folds vibrant enough to dazzle any eye, was a beautiful multicoloured pashmina. 'Ah, there it is. We looked absolutely everywhere for this the other evening.'

I reached down and plucked up the silky garment. The fabric was vividly coloured, and shot through with strands of gold thread. I'd have been able to guess who it belonged to, even if I couldn't detect her perfume, which I remembered from when she'd stood behind me, restyling my hair.

'Carla thought someone must have picked it up by mistake, but it's not the sort of garment you could easily miss.'

I smiled and ran the pads of my thumbs over the wrap's silky soft weave. 'She left it here the other evening?' It was more of a statement than a question. But whatever it was, something about it made Ben shift uncomfortably on his feet.

'Yes. I had a few friends over . . .' For some reason – and I really couldn't imagine what that might be – there was something about the party that Ben felt awkward about. Perhaps, in hindsight, he felt guilty for not inviting me.

I shook the scarf out like a flag, and began to carefully fold it up into a small neat square. 'She'll be glad to have it back. I believe she bought it on a recent trip,' Ben said. Strangely, he sounded far happier to talk about women's accessories than he was about his guest list.

Every time I paused in my work, I found my eye going to the small folded square. Fred, who'd eventually grown tired of pacing the properties, had repeatedly tried to settle down on it for a snooze, until I turfed him off. Worried that he'd snag the delicate material with his claws, I moved it for safety to my large zip-up tote bag while I worked.

By late afternoon I'd finally completed the most urgent piece of translation. I glanced at my watch as I waited for the pages to print, stacking them with a contract that needed to be signed and posted urgently. The sky was already turning smoky-grey with the descending dusk, but if I was quick I still had time to get to a post office.

I was glad I hadn't protested too strongly about taking Julia's coat, because I needed its warmth when I left the flat and walked, head down, towards the bus stop at the end of the road. Delicate white specks, like a dusting of icing sugar, sprinkled the dark fabric as I walked. The forecast had warned of sleet or possible snow showers, and for once it looked as though they'd got it right.

I had to break into a run to catch the bus, which was just pulling away from the kerb as I approached. I smiled gratefully at the driver, who'd seen me in his mirror and waited. There was a vacant seat beside a window and I slipped into it, clearing a small patch in the steamed-up glass with my gloved hand. I only noticed the fascia because I'd been checking the street names, like a lost tourist, as they flashed past the bus window. Of course the brightly scripted signage was hard to miss, even at speed, but I'd only caught a fleeting glimpse, so I couldn't be entirely sure. It was only when the bus pulled up at a set of traffic lights a few hundred metres down the road, and I saw the bakery where Ben had bought our still-warm-from-the-oven pastries, that I realised where we were. I don't believe in coincidences or omens, but it was definitely weird that the post office I'd randomly chosen from the long list online was practically on the doorstep of Carla's salon.

It was probably the worst time of day to have chosen to join the queue at the counter. Everyone in front of me seemed to have an armful of parcels, or a stack of cards or letters to send. At last a weary-looking clerk beckoned me to the window. I reached into my bag for my purse, which was buried beneath the usual detritus and instead found something soft and unfamiliar. I tugged gently on the fabric, and the woman behind the counter paused in peeling stamps off a sheet to watch as I extracted a length of colourful material from my bag, like a magician performing a trick. I hurriedly stuffed it back into the bag and found my purse.

For a moment I felt horribly guilty, as though I'd been caught shoplifting. I'd slipped Carla's pashmina into my bag to protect it, not steal it, and had completely forgotten it was there. And now, here I was, just a few minutes' walk from where she lived. For someone who refused to believe in omens, it was getting hard to ignore the stacked-up coincidences.

I dropped my stamped envelopes into the post box, and hesitated on the pavement, which was rapidly disappearing under a soft fuzzy coating of white flakes. The snow flurries had decided to upgrade themselves to a full-on mini blizzard, and the sensible thing would definitely have been to head for the covered awning of the bus stop, and get home before the weather worsened. And yet ... I pulled up the collar of my coat, burrowed my chin into the fabric and headed back up the high street, striding into the stinging snow crystals.

'Good gracious, Sophie, is that you under there?'

I shook my head, and a shower of white fell onto my shoulders and all around me, like the world's worst case of dandruff. Carla had been about to close up the shop, and if I'd been just a minute later I would certainly have missed her. The lights in the salon had already been switched off, and her staff had clearly all left for the day. It was only the small glowing light visible from the back office that had prompted me to rap on the door.

Carla ushered me in off the street, ignoring my protests about dripping water and puddles, and slammed the shop door firmly on the blizzard, which seemed determined to come in and join us. She'd undone the buttons of my coat and tugged it from my shoulders before I could even protest that I wasn't intending to stay.

'Nonsense,' she proclaimed, hanging my damp coat up to dry in front of a radiator. 'You at least deserve a cup a tea after braving that awful weather. Come on upstairs to the flat, where we can sit down properly.'

She plucked a warm towel from a nearby folded stack and passed it to me, before disappearing into a narrow passageway at the back of the shop. There was really nothing I could do except follow her.

If I'd thought Carla's wardrobe was colourful, it was nothing compared to the décor of her flat. Every primary colour was represented in the soft furnishings, irrespective of whether or not it clashed terribly with its neighbour. If there was ever an explosion in a paint factory, the end result would probably look a lot like Carla's flat. It should have been jarring and gaudy, but actually it was incredibly warm, bright and welcoming. Much like the woman who had created it.

'Now, do you want me to do that?' Carla asked, hands outstretched to take the towel that I was rubbing vigorously over my soaking-wet hair. I smiled at her, because it was hard in her company to do anything else *except* smile. She was like sunshine embodied into a small, slightly round, five foot two inch package.

'No. Absolutely not – you've finished work for the day. Actually, I'm getting quite good at styling it myself. I've had several compliments on it,' I added, stretching the truth a little, because she was one of those people you just wanted to make happy.

Carla beamed satisfyingly. 'Well of course you have, honey. But it's your pretty face that's getting them for you . . . not my haircut.'

I blushed, because I'd always been a little clumsy receiving flattery, even when it was given so genuinely.

'Well, I'll just put the kettle on, and then you can tell me what on earth possessed you to venture out in this awful weather.' She disappeared into a neat galley kitchen with bright orange units, which would have had me reaching for sunglasses before I'd have been able to make my morning coffee.

'Can I fix you something to eat? Or perhaps you'd like to stay for dinner?'

I shook my head, already feeling guilty for turning up on her doorstep uninvited, without gate-crashing her evening meal as well. 'No, but it's very kind of you to offer. I won't stay long, in case the roads start getting bad.'

Carla nodded and glanced out of her lounge window. The wind was hurling snow at the glass, making it look as though we were at the helm of a spaceship speeding through a star-studded Milky Way. I thought I glimpsed a trace of disappointment in Carla's eyes, but when she turned back to face me her dazzling smile was back in place. That was the first moment when it occurred to me that beneath the colourful façade and good humour, Carla might be lonely.

While Carla made tea, I wandered over to a display unit, which housed an eclectic and intriguing collection of ornaments. There were two beautiful jewelled Venetian masks propped up beside a brightly painted Aboriginal boomerang. Then a little further along, a roughly hewn carving of an African elephant sat beside a picture frame inscribed with the words: *'What happens in Vegas . . .'*

Carla reappeared and passed me a steaming mug. 'You've certainly travelled to some interesting places,' I observed, nodding my head towards the impressive assortment of souvenirs.

Carla's eyes softened as she looked at the mementoes. 'Actually, Las Vegas is the only one I've visited so far. The others are still on my wish list. I've bought the souvenirs to remind me of the places I still want to go to, rather than the places I've already been.' She gave a small self-deprecating chuckle. 'You can buy just about anything on the internet these days.'

I took a large sip of tea, even though it was really far too hot to swallow that quickly. There was something about Carla's admission that made me feel strangely sad. Buying a reminder of a place you'd never even been seemed poignantly touching. Trying to shake off my sudden gloomy mood, I put down my mug and reached for my handbag. 'Actually, the reason why I dropped in on you unannounced was to return this.' I pulled the pashmina from my tote and held it out to her.

'Oh bless you, Sophie. You found my wrap.'

'Well, Ben did actually,' I admitted.

'Well, *you* braved Arctic weather conditions to return it to me,' said Carla warmly. 'What a lovely girl you are. Ben was quite right about you.'

Damn that blush, I thought, already feeling it creeping over my cheeks like a mini bush fire. 'Why? What did he say about me?' I asked, wondering if that odd little squawky voice was actually mine.

Carla's plump shoulders rose so high that they made her long dangly earrings jingle like wind chimes. 'Just that you were very nice,' she said, her eyes twinkling a little with enjoyment. It occurred to me then that Carla would not be above a spot of matchmaking if she thought there was an opportunity. I was still wondering if I wanted to discourage or embrace that idea, when she suddenly excused herself.

'Would you pardon me for a moment, honey? I just want to get a bit more comfortable. Sit down. Make yourself at home,' she urged.

She left the room, pulling concealed pins from her bright red hair as she did. I wasn't prying when I followed her. It was just that Carla had kept up a commentary as she walked from the lounge into her bedroom, and it was hard to hear what she was saying.

'Of course, Ben was taking Franklin to the airport today. Did he get away on time? Oh I do hope he managed to get on the damn plane this time.'

It seemed rude to shout my reply, so I ventured a little closer to her bedroom doorway. I couldn't see Carla, just her reflection in the dressing table's triple mirror, as she withdrew a few more hidden pins from her hair and finally plucked the bright red wig from her head. Beneath the hairpiece she was quite bald, and I took an awkward stumbling step backwards, worried in case she'd thought I was intruding on what was obviously a very private moment.

Silently I crept back into the lounge and collapsed onto a bright red armchair with purple cushions and picked up a nearby hairdressing magazine. Carla reappeared a moment or two later, yet another brightly patterned scarf swathed around her head. I bit my lip, wondering if I was supposed to say anything about what I'd just seen, or completely ignore her noticeable change in appearance. Suddenly the small wooden carving wasn't the only elephant in the room.

It was Carla herself who made it effortlessly easy for me. 'Damn itchiest thing in the entire world, that wig. But what can you do ... people are funny about visiting a hairdresser who has no hair.' She smiled down at me, and I knew then that she'd seen me in the mirror just as I'd seen her. She leant down and gently inverted the hairdressing magazine in my hands, which I'd been attempting to read upside down.

That was the moment when I knew exactly why Ben felt as he did about her. Carla was a very easy lady to love.

The house was in darkness when the taxi delivered me home. The driveway, unmarked by foot or tyre prints, was a thick white blanket almost too pretty and perfect to walk on. The snow had swept up miniature drifts against every window pane, giving them a Dickensian Christmas card appeal. Although Carla had wanted to drive me home, I'd held firm and insisted on calling a cab. The blizzard still showed no sign of letting up, and I preferred to think of Carla safe and warm in her flat when we parted company, not braving the slippery roads behind the wheel of a car because of me.

The journey had taken three times longer than normal

because of the weather. While the driver concentrated on keeping the wheels of our vehicle moving forward in a straight line, my own thoughts and emotions were skidding all over the place. After briefly commenting on the discomfort of her wig, Carla hadn't mentioned her condition again, so I didn't feel that I could either. I remained in the dark as to whether illness, a bizarre fashion statement, or shaving her head for charity were responsible. Of those three options, I really hoped it was the latter one.

What Carla *had* been willing to talk about was Franklin, the friend Ben had driven to the airport that afternoon. 'Worst phobia I've ever seen,' she confided, shaking her head and making a small tutting sound. 'Makes my thing about spiders seem hardly worth mentioning.' She must have noticed my puzzled expression, for she leant closer and dropped her voice a notch, as though to save the absent Franklin from embarrassment. 'Absolutely petrified of flying. He's tried twice before to make this journey to visit his daughter in New Zealand, but so far he's never even made it to the gate. He's not seen her for over ten years, and now with a new grandchild . . . and the way things are, well, you can understand why it's important for him to make this trip. That's why Ben's offered to take him today, for moral support. If anyone can talk Franklin into getting on that plane, it will be Ben.'

'Why's that?'

Carla's blue eyes clouded, and I wondered if somehow I'd offended her with my question. 'Because Ben is one of the calmest and most reassuring people I've ever met. He makes you believe you can conquer anything, whatever it is. A lot of people would be a great deal worse off if Ben hadn't come into their lives.' It was a statement I could hardly argue with, because *I* was one of those people.

Which is why, when Ben said he had a favour to ask a few weeks later, there was no way I was going to refuse him.

Chapter 5

December

'French . . . is that one of the languages you speak?'

'Yes. And German, and I could have a decent stab at Spanish too, if that's any help.'

For the last five minutes Ben had seemed to be teetering on the edge of a decision. Like a diver who keeps walking to the end of the high board and then changing his mind and backing off. There was obviously something he wanted to ask me. What *wasn't* clear was why he was so hesitant about doing so. When eventually the question came, I was none the wiser.

It was almost lunchtime when Ben had knocked lightly on the internal door separating his home from mine. Our paths hadn't crossed for several days, and the first thing I noticed as he walked into my kitchen was the way he was favouring his right leg as he crossed the room.

'Slippery pavement: one. Big hulking six foot two idiot: zero,' he explained with a wry grin.

I laughed and gestured to one of my kitchen chairs, hurriedly scooping the pile of clean underwear on it into the nearby wash basket. Not that I imagined the sight of my lingerie was going to send anyone into a frenzy. It had been an awful long time since I could legitimately claim *that* had happened. I kicked both the random thought and the laundry basket to one side. 'Well, if you're not too busy,' Ben continued, totally oblivious to the sidetrack my brain had travelled down, 'I was wondering if I could possibly commission you . . . or book you . . . or hire you . . . or whatever the correct term is, to do some translation work.'

'No,' I said, leaning forward with my elbows on the table, and smiling warmly at him, which probably jarred with my refusal. 'But you *can* ask me as a favour, from one friend to another, and I'm going to say yes.'

'You don't even know what it is yet,' Ben reasoned. 'I could have a huge job that you've just volunteered to do for nothing.'

I swallowed down a moment of panic, wondering if I'd just talked myself out of next month's rent, which was unfortunate, seeing as he was my landlord. 'It doesn't matter. I owe you.'

Ben shook his head, but there was something sad in his eyes, which I didn't understand at all. 'I have a friend who has a letter he'd like to write. In French.'

I nodded encouragingly. 'Is that all? I can do that for you.'

'I was hoping you'd say that. You see, he's been thinking of sending this letter for quite a while, but he kept putting it off. But now he's finally made up his mind, and I think he really wants to get it organised as soon as possible. He doesn't want to waste any more time. Are you sure you can fit it in?'

There were other assignments I should be working on, but they could probably keep, and the story behind Ben's friend's urgent letter had me intrigued. 'Sure. No problem. Just out of interest, how long has this friend of yours been waiting to send his letter?'

Ben's caramel-coloured eyes rose to meet mine across the tiny table. 'Seventy-two years.'

'Ouch!' I exclaimed, as my tiny hairdresser managed to hit me on the head yet again with her wooden-handled hairbrush.

'Careful, Lacey, don't hurt Auntie Sophie,' chided Julia.

Lacey's huge cornflower-blue eyes looked troubled, until I winked broadly and rubbed my nose teasingly against hers in an Eskimo kiss, which always made her giggle.

'I wouldn't be in such a hurry to do that, if I were you,' warned Julia, disappearing briefly into the utility room. 'Half the nursery is down with colds and the other half keep wiping their noses on the back of their hands.'

'Yuck,' I said, my own nose wrinkling, which made Lacey giggle even harder. She picked up a comb and some bright Barbie-pink glittery hairclips, and went back to styling my hair. Her choice of accessories would definitely have met with Carla's approval.

'Well, I still think it's all a little bit bizarre,' declared Julia, emerging with a laundry basket balanced on her hip bone. 'His friends all sound like caricatures in a wacky comic book strip: the hairdresser with no hair, the gardener without a leg, the traveller who's scared of flying, and the nonagenarian with a broken heart. I mean what does that say about Ben, when he has a group of friends like that?'

She wasn't being serious, but my knee-jerk reaction to defend these people – most of whom I scarcely knew – surprised me. 'I don't know, Jules,' I chipped back. 'You're *my* friend. What does that say about me, exactly?'

Julia looked momentarily taken aback, but then shrugged good-humouredly. 'Okay. I deserved that. Still, doesn't he have any "normal" friends?' She air-quoted the word for emphasis.

This time *I* shrugged. 'I don't know. Does anyone?'

Julia pushed Lacey's small collection of hairbands to one side and perched down on the settee cushions. 'So what time are you going round to meet the old guy?'

'Henry,' I provided, glancing at my watch. 'I'll need to leave soon. But as he lives so close to you, I couldn't resist popping in for a quick restyle and a cuddle,' I declared, scooping Lacey into my arms and burying my face in her soft plump neck. It felt warm and a little clammy. 'Ooh, you feel hot, little one. Are you alright?'

Julia paused mid-fold of the babygrow she was adding

to the small pile beside her, and laid the back of her hand expertly against Lacey's forehead. A frown quickly formed as she withdrew it. 'You *are* hot, chicken. Do you feel alright?'

'My throat hurts,' Lacey declared dramatically, her small hand clutching the offending area as though her voice had just magically been stolen from her. A move she had clearly copied from one of her favourite Disney films.

'Oh dear,' sighed Julia, getting to her feet and heading for the kitchen. 'Calpol for you, my love,' she pronounced. She noticed my expression of concern, and smiled. 'She was bound to come down with something. I just wish she hadn't timed it for when Gary is away.' The baby monitor crackled into life, with Noah's woeful announcement that he'd awoken from his nap. 'What's the betting I don't get much sleep tonight?'

The room was very small and overheated. There was a vague smell of cinnamon in the air, mixed with a basenote of Werther's Originals. It was the smell of grandparents. Even though mine had long since passed away, it still took me back to fondly remembered childhood visits.

I had been walking slowly down his street, searching for elusive house numbers, when the door of a terraced property a short distance away swung open. An elderly man emerged, light reflecting like a starburst off a pair of half-moon NHS glasses, as he squinted in my direction. His sparse snow-white hair was quickly dishevelled by the wind, and the mustard-coloured cardigan covering his stooped shoulders certainly didn't look up to the job of keeping out the December chill. On his feet was a pair of plaid carpet slippers, which were definitely ill-equipped to handle an icy path. With an effort that looked painful, even from fifty metres away, Henry stood up a little taller, holding himself upright against the door frame with a hand clawed by arthritis.

'Are you Sophie?' he asked, taking a tentative step down the path towards me. I instinctively quickened my pace. Slippery pathways and ninety-year-olds looked like a broken hip just waiting to happen.

I smiled broadly. 'Yes, I am,' I said, unlatching the low wrought-iron gate and hurrying up the path to meet him.

'I've been watching out for you, because I didn't want you getting lost.' I instantly felt guilty. While I'd been lingering over that last cup of tea with Julia, Henry had probably been standing like a watchman in his narrow hallway, staring up and down the empty street, waiting for me.

'Come in out of the cold,' he urged, shuffling the short distance down the hallway to his front room. I could have been anyone who'd chosen to answer to the name of Sophie. His trust and vulnerability struck me like two sharp unexpected blows. The hallway was narrow and lined with dark red flocked wallpaper. There were random palm-sized bald patches on the pattern, which looked as though they matched the places where Henry often needed support as he walked. Beside the front door sat a walking frame, its shiny aluminium finish unblemished by use. From the garments draped over it, I suspected Henry might possibly be using it as a coat rack.

'This is very kind of you, giving up your time like this,' he said, his voice a little wheezy from the short walk.

'It's no trouble at all,' I assured him. 'I'm happy to do it.'

He smiled and then paused, as though unsure of what should happen next. I could almost see him searching for the key to access the memory of what you did when receiving visitors. It was clearly a while since he'd had any.

'Shall we sit down?' I suggested, taking the lead.

He looked grateful and nodded, reaching out a hand and lowering himself carefully onto an over-stuffed armchair, beside a two-bar electric fire that was radiating out so much heat it felt like we were in the tropics. I quickly slipped off my coat before I passed out.

'Are you warm enough?' Henry asked, his gnarled hands extended to trap the fire's heat in his twisted fingers.

'Nice and toasty,' I lied, perching on one of the armchairs as far away from the electric heater as I could get. 'Now, Ben has told me that you have a letter you'd like to send to a friend in France?'

Henry glanced up at the mantelpiece, where an old black-and-white photograph of a couple on their wedding day stood in an ornate silver frame. Even with the passage of time I could see the groom in the photograph was Henry. Henry's eyes shifted back to me, and I could see just a hint of guilt in their watery depths.

'That was my Iris. Married for sixty years, we were. These last ten without her have been ... they've been ...' His voice trailed away, but a single tear rumbled down the rough terrain of his wrinkled cheek. Sensing his discomfort I looked around the room, giving him time to compose himself. A cough and a hearty nose blow told me it was safe to turn back.

'The thing is, Iris was a wonderful girl. Knew each other since we were knee-high,' he admitted with a wheezy chuckle. 'She wrote to me all through the war, and those letters meant the world to me, but ... but ...' His voice dropped to a whisper as though the bride in the photograph was listening in to his confession. 'There was this girl, Lucile was her name, she lived not far from Paris, and if her family hadn't taken me in and hidden me in their barn, well ... well, I don't suppose I'd be here now, talking to you.' He looked beyond me, as though the memory of that other time had opened a portal into the past. 'Iris was the one waiting back home for me. Iris was the girl I made a promise to. Iris was the one I married. But Lucile was the girl I never forgot.'

I'd suspected Henry's story would be something like this, but I'd never for a moment thought it would affect me so much. Since the fire, my emotions had undergone a quiet rebellion and refused to be damped down, and had a nasty habit of rearing up and unseating me at unexpected moments. This was one of them. I think both Henry and I were grateful when he suggested 'a cuppa' before we got

151

down to the task of composing a letter to a woman who, for all he knew, might no longer be alive.

Henry's kitchen was scrupulously clean and neat – far tidier than mine, I told him. He looked quietly proud at the compliment. 'Iris liked everything shipshape,' he informed me. 'She wouldn't be happy if I messed things up just because she's gone.' As we waited for the old-fashioned whistling kettle to sing its tune, Henry reached into the cupboard for a willow-patterned plate and then shuffled to a larder, emerging with a packet of biscuits. 'Been saving these for when I have a special visitor,' he announced, his fingers struggling with the unyielding Cellophane.

'Shall I do that?' I offered, reaching out to take the packet from his fumbling hands. I turned it over and saw the 'best before' date was over five years ago. Henry settled a multicoloured knitted cosy over the teapot and glanced over at me, where I stood uncertainly holding the packet of stale biscuits.

'I do love a Bourbon,' Henry admitted, his lips smacking together in anticipation.

'Me too,' I declared, tipping the contents of the packet onto the plate.

There were three things I found surprising that day. One, was that I was in no great hurry to leave Henry's house, even after his letter had been composed, translated and written. It was probably many years since Henry had allowed himself the luxury of re-telling the story of his French love affair, and he had a captive audience in me. It was a romance and a tragedy; a story of sacrifice and true love that could never have a happy ending.

The second surprise was the discovery that even though they may be a little bit on the bendy side, eating stale five-years-out-of-date biscuits is not going to kill you.

But it was the third surprise that shook me most. That was finding Ben patiently waiting for me, when I finally emerged from the over-warm cocoon of Henry's home. Although I was a little slow realising the car pulled up beside the kerb, with its engine quietly ticking over, was his. Darkness and a flurry of sleet had both fallen while I was with Henry, making his pathway doubly treacherous. With my chin tucked into the collar of my coat, my eyes were firmly fixed on my feet, as I picked my way carefully towards the pavement. Sharp needles of sleet stabbed repeatedly against the back of my exposed neck, making me long wistfully for the hair that was now long gone, or a thick woolly scarf.

A car parked directly opposite Henry's home switched on its headlights, and in the twin beams falling sleet danced like dust motes. The car door opened and a tall figure emerged, resting his arms on the roof of his vehicle as he called to me.

'I was beginning to think Henry had kidnapped you.'

I turned so quickly to face him that my very indoor fair-weather boots lost their traction and for a few agonising seconds I felt certain my pinwheeling legs were going to do something on the ice that only Bambi could make look cute. I lurched, skidded and slid before finally grabbing hold of the gatepost for support. By the time I'd got my legs under control once more, Ben had already crossed the road – presumably with the intention of picking me up from the pavement. Thankfully, this time, I didn't need him to rescue me. I gave a nervous laugh, the kind adults do when they've narrowly avoided the sort of tumble most five-year-olds would take in their stride.

'I was about to score you a perfect six,' Ben said with a smile as his hand firmly reached out to grasp my elbow. Through the thick fabric of my coat, I could feel the strength of his grip. Even if I were on sheet ice, there was no way I was falling now.

'What are you doing here?' I asked, probably sounding far less grateful than I was actually feeling, but my heart was still pounding strangely in my chest, which had to be down to my almost-fall. *Didn't it?*

'Apart from waiting for your triple Salchow, you mean?' Ben teased gently. I looked up at him, and in the yellow glow of a nearby street lamp every tiny icy particle that had settled on his hair and eyelashes seemed to glisten and twinkle, like a minute diamond chip. 'I was in the area and remembered you were seeing Henry this afternoon, so I thought the least I could do was hang around and give you a lift back, to say thank you.'

I glanced at my watch. Afternoon had slipped into early evening some time earlier. 'You must have been waiting for ages.' Ben shrugged easily as he held open the gate for me. His warm car beckoned invitingly from the kerb, yet still I hesitated. The lines between us were becoming increasingly blurred and confused. Landlords were supposed to charge you extortionate rent and never fix the washing machine or the leaky toilet when it broke. The kind who saved your life, charged only a peppercorn rent and then threw in an ad hoc taxi service were completely outside of anything I'd ever encountered. But it would have been impossible, and also extremely rude, to have declined Ben's offer of a lift, so I didn't.

What I probably *should* have done was protest a great deal more when he suggested that we stop off on the way back to the house for a pizza dinner. 'Unless, of course, you have plans for this evening?' he asked, turning his head to look at me while waiting for the traffic lights to change.

I fidgeted slightly and was glad when the amber light winked on beneath its red counterpart, pulling his gaze back to the road. My evening plans involved an unfinished translation and the next episode in the box set I was ploughing through. I ran a couple of polite refusals through my head, before I found one I was happy to go with, but before I had the chance to voice it, Ben tipped the scales his way.

'I've actually been a bit concerned about Henry recently. I'm not sure how well he's coping, and it would be great to get your impressions . . . from an outsider's point of view. I suspect this is a tough time of year for him.'

My resolve, already as shaky as a Jenga tower, got one last poke when suddenly every single shop window we drove past hammered home the upcoming holiday season. Twinkling fairy lights on laden Christmas trees, fake snow in pretend drifts and chuckling Santas with impossibly large girths. Sometimes the unrelenting jollity of it all could be more than a little overwhelming. Was that how it was for Henry, as he shuffled around his house, always keeping it tidy, just the way Iris would have wanted?

'I do have some work I should really finish . . .' I laid down my excuse like a poker player who already knows their hand is going to lose.

'You've still got to eat,' reasoned Ben. 'Why don't we have a quick bite and then head back? That way you'll still have time to work later.' There were probably many reasons why I should have declined that invitation. But every single one of them escaped me.

The pizza restaurant was warm and smelled deliciously of molten mozzarella and garlic bread. It was also crowded. We had to wait at the door for five minutes before they could seat us. I glanced around the occupied tables as we waited. It was a Friday evening, date night, which explained why most of the tables held couples. I've always been a people watcher – or just plain nosy – as Julia always said. As we stood in the warm downdraught from the door's heater I glanced from table to table. The hand-holders were clearly on their first dates, as were the girls who were smiling flirtatiously or laughing far too enthusiastically at something that probably wasn't even that funny. I wondered how Ben and I looked to them. Mismatched, probably. But there was nothing wrong with that at all, because unlike practically every other couple in the restaurant, we weren't on a date.

A young waitress with aubergine-coloured hair and a nose piercing led us to a small table near a window, weaving skilfully around the obstacles of other diners and fellow waiters like a practised downhill skier. We paused to allow a waiter carrying an impressive number of pizzas at one time to cross our path. I glanced at a nearby table and felt a jolt of recognition shoot through me. The man, who was leaning forward to hear something his female companion had just said, looked up ... and then looked straight through me. There wasn't even a glimmer of recollection on his face.

Our waitress glanced back over her shoulder and gave us a bright smile. 'Will this be alright?' she asked, already pulling out a chair for me beside the window. The wooden legs scraped against the flagstones like fingernails down a blackboard, setting my teeth on edge even more than the unexpected encounter had done. I bit my lip and glanced around the packed restaurant. There were clearly no other vacant tables, so it surprised me to hear Ben politely ask if there was somewhere else we could be seated.

'I'm sorry. Everything else is taken. We're really busy tonight,' she replied.

'This is fine,' I said, aware that our hesitation was drawing the attention of several nearby diners. I slipped into the seat closest to the window and furthest away from the man I had gone on three dates with – practically a record for me – almost ten months earlier. What did it matter that he had completely failed to recognise me? I probably looked totally different with my new haircut. And I couldn't even remember his name, I told myself, and then resolutely refused to listen to my subconscious chirping silently: *Matthew. His name was Matthew.*

Ben waited until the waitress had passed us the oversized menus and taken his order of a small lager and mine for tap water. My mouth was suddenly incredibly dry, but that always happened whenever I was nervous or uncomfortable. I shifted my chair on the flagstones, putting the table with Matthew and his new companion beyond my field of vision. I raised the menu, which was big enough to hide behind, but some people are blessed with the kind of visual acuity that lets them see what others cannot. Ben was one of those people.

'Who is he?'

I lowered the menu slightly, and peered at him over the top. 'Pardon?'

Ben said nothing but inclined his head in the general direction of the table I most wanted to avoid. I swallowed uncomfortably and looked down. The names of the individual pizzas blurred and danced, refusing to sharpen, no matter how many times I blinked.

'Do you want to wait for another table, or we could leave?' Ben asked. 'Or alternatively, I could just go over and knock him off his chair and be done with it?'

The laugh surprised me, because I hadn't felt it coming. Ben grinned back at me, completely satisfied with my

reaction. He then threw me even further off balance by leaning forward and gently covering my right hand with his. I
hadn't even been aware that I'd been unconsciously fiddling
with the cutlery until his fingers laced around mine and the
knife I'd been toying with fell back onto the serviette.

His eyes were twinkling, but there was also a hint of concern in them as he asked, 'Now, do I need to get the waitress
to remove all the sharp implements from our table, or have
I read this wrong?'

I smiled, and was pleased to see that my vision was now
totally clear, in more ways than one. 'No. I'm fine. I was just
a little . . . surprised, to see someone I recognised. That's all.'

Ben released my fingers and lifted his own menu. My hand
felt cold without his touch and I drew it back onto my lap
before it did something stupid like travelling across the rustic
oak surface to find his again. For several quiet moments Ben
appeared to be considering nothing more challenging than
the merits of Calzone over stone-baked Margherita. But I
wasn't off the hook quite that easily.

'He's an ex, I take it?' He glanced briefly over at Matthew,
who still seemed completely oblivious to the attention he was
generating. I didn't follow his gaze.

'No. I wouldn't call him that. I wouldn't call *anybody* that.
I don't really *do* relationships.'

Ben's menu went all the way down and our waitress,
thinking this was a sign, hopped over exuberantly with
her pad poised to take our order. Ben shook his head and
motioned her away, waiting until she had disappeared back

into the shadows. 'What does that mean exactly? You don't *"do"* relationships?'

I bristled uncomfortably, aware that I had inadvertently opened a door to allow him a glimpse of a room that very few people ever entered. And I really wanted to shut it again, right now, only he had one of his big old size twelve feet in the way, blocking me.

'You know what, Ben. I'm not really comfortable having this conversation. Do you mind if we just drop it?'

There are rules of behaviour. When someone says those words, the other person is meant to immediately back off and start chatting about the latest football scores, or the terrible weather we've been having recently . . . or about absolutely anything at all. Apparently Ben wasn't the kind of person who played by the rule book.

'Why?'

'Why what?' I suspected I could try playing this game for the rest of the evening, but I still wasn't going to win. Something told me he wasn't going to let go easily. For the first time I glimpsed the tenacity and determination of a man who'd clearly been a very successful and focused business-man. The laid-back guy I knew might be superimposed over him, but he was still there.

'Why don't you do relationships any more?' Ben asked, spacing his words out, as though I might be having trouble with their meaning. Of course 'any more' implied that there had once been a time when I *had* been open to letting someone get close, but I chose not to correct him on that. It already felt as though the conversation was whirling around me like an incoming storm, and I was busy battening down the hatches. After a lifetime of practice, I was pretty damn good at it.

'I prefer keeping people at a reasonable distance.' My eyes locked meaningfully on his. If he couldn't hear the words *'Back off now'* being practically screamed at him from their depths, then he wasn't nearly as smart as I'd thought. The caramel of his eyes darkened, making them look like molten sugar, but then he blinked and all I saw in their depths was compassion. Perhaps he'd decided that someone in my past had taken my heart and broken it, and I was quite happy to let him continue with that mistaken conclusion.

'You're sure you don't want me to punch him on the nose? Because it's been a very long time since I had a good reason to deck anyone.'

I glanced over at the man who'd done nothing worse than tell me a truth I really hadn't wanted to hear at the time. I still didn't want to hear it.

'No, not today, Rocky.'

Just before our food arrived, a passing waiter had swooped down to light the solitary candle in the glass holder positioned between Ben and me. The flame flickered into life, and without a single word or conscious decision, we both leant forward and blew it out. I felt the soft breeze of his breath on my face, as he had mine. The innocent moment was suddenly elevated to one of intimacy. Our eyes met, and the strength of the connection born on the night of the fire sputtered strongly into life, like one of those trick candles that are impossible to extinguish.

'Birthday, is it?' the waiter guessed incorrectly. He produced a second match to re-light the candle.

'Actually, if you don't mind, we'd prefer to keep it unlit,' Ben said, laying his hand briefly on the other man's arm. 'We've seen enough flames for a while.'

You'd have thought that following its slightly awkward beginning, I wouldn't be able to relax enough to enjoy the evening, but I did – far more than I'd expected to. Ben was excellent company; his humour was sharp and quick, and his smile easy and charming. Somehow he even managed to make *me* feel more amusing and quick-witted. I rather liked the Sophie I was with him, even though I'd never met her before. But even she could see the red stop lights flashing up a very timely warning. Ben had a unique knack of drawing people towards him. You only had to hear how warmly both Carla and Henry spoke about him to realise how easily his appeal crossed the barriers of age and gender. He was like a practised angler casting out a charismatic fishing line, and I was going to have to swim a great deal harder than I was currently doing to not get tangled up in it.

There was a small tussle when the bill arrived, when Ben categorically refused to let me pay half. 'You gave up your afternoon as a favour to me, and if you insist on splitting the bill, then you're going to have to invoice me for the time you spent translating Henry's letter.' There are battles I wouldn't back down from without a fight, but this wasn't one of them.

I smiled and nudged the saucer with the folded bill further onto his half of the table.

'Thank you,' I said graciously. 'Although I warn you, next time *I'm* picking up the tab.'

Ben's eyebrows rose, and I rapidly rewound the words in my head, wondering why I hadn't realised how presumptuous they had sounded before they came tumbling out of my mouth. *Next time.* Who on earth said there was going to be a next time?

'Deal,' said Ben firmly, getting to his feet and laying down a small pile of notes and effectively closing the subject before I could backtrack my way out of it.

The evening was very much in full swing, and the restaurant was still buzzing with activity and new customers as we began to pick our path towards the door. The route would, as before, take us directly past Matthew's table. Before we got there an excitable group of women, obviously a hen party, jostled laughingly past us. It didn't escape my attention that at least three of them glanced appreciatively at Ben as they passed – including the one wearing the tiara and pink *'Bride-to-Be'* sash. Ben smiled good-naturedly as they bumped into him, their actions pressing us exactly where I didn't want to be, directly behind Matthew's chair. He looked up and obligingly tried to edge out of the way. Luckily I was concealed behind Ben's broad back and Matthew's attention was focused only on him as he looked up. 'Sorry, mate, am I in your way?'

Was it my imagination or did Ben pause for a beat before

replying with words that I knew I'd be dissecting and ana-
lysing for a long time before sleep eventually claimed me
that night.

'No. You really aren't.'

Chapter 6

The first thing that shocked me when I woke up to the sound of my ringing mobile was that it *wasn't* ten past two in the morning. The neon green display on my digital clock told me we wouldn't reach that fated time for over another hour. Not that it stopped my heart from racing in panic as my hands fumbled for my phone, knocking it clumsily off the bedside table so that I had to waste precious seconds hauling it back up by the lead of its charger.

By the time I had the device in my hand, I was already certain the voice at the end of the line would be my mother's. Heart attacks are like earthquakes, they rip the structure and stability from your world. But unlike quakes, it's the aftershock, the *second* heart attack, that you fear the most.

So, for just a moment, when I heard it was Julia's voice at the end of the line and not my parent's, I was overcome with relief. That feeling dissipated almost as quickly as it had arisen when I heard the hitch of her sobs and the naked anxiety paralysing her throat as she struggled to speak.

'I . . . I'm at the hospital.'

The last vestiges of sleep left me in an instant as her words flooded every vein in my body with ice water. My stomach rolled and twisted, and I recognised and understood the origin of the phrase 'sick with fear' all over again.

'What is it? What's happened?'

I had to wait an agonisingly long time before I received my answer, because Julia had begun to cry again, as the words no mother should ever have to think – let alone say – felled her in terror.

'It's Lacey. She's really sick. They're putting her on a ventilator.'

My gasp was loud and raw and echoed harshly in the basement bedroom. 'But . . . but she's just got a cold. She has a sore throat, that's all.'

Julia's moan sounded more lupine than human. 'I don't know . . . I don't understand. I . . . I thought it was croup, but the kettle thing didn't work . . . and then her temperature went so high and her voice was all weird and—'

I cut her off. 'Which hospital? What ward? I'm on my way.'

Julia bravely swallowed down a sob of gratitude long enough to give me the name of the hospital and tell me they were in the Paediatric Intensive Care Unit. We hung up then, neither of us bothering to say goodbye, because this wasn't a normal call, this wasn't a normal night. I swallowed and tasted bile laced with the bitter tang of fear that nothing in Julia's life would *ever* be normal again after today.

It's strange how panic affects you. While one part of you is busy falling to pieces: pulling on socks that don't match; throwing the bra that refuses to fasten across the room in frustration, and shrugging your arms into an inside-out hoodie, a totally separate section is already addressing the practicalities. Calling for a taxi was obviously my first priority, but even before I reached out for my phone, I was already discarding that plan in favour of another. I leapt into the pair of jeans I'd scooped up from the floor like a practised quick-change artist, and was still zipping them up as I undid the door in my kitchen and ran noisily up the wooden staircase to Ben's home. I'd never been more glad than I was at that moment that he'd been slow in arranging for a locksmith to separate our two properties. I flung open the door at the top of the stairs and barrelled into his darkened kitchen.

I hesitated for a moment, getting my bearings in the dark room. Even so, I still managed to collide painfully with the edge of his dining table in the darkness. The dull throb from my hip bone didn't slow me down as I ran in the direction of his bedroom. I'd only ever seen this section of the ground floor on a television programme, but my feet took me exactly where I needed to go.

When I reached his bedroom door, I didn't knock on it. Knocking implies something sedate and controlled, and my assault on the smooth cedar surface was neither of those. I hammered on it, like a panicked claustrophobic trapped in a lift. I was still pounding away when suddenly the wood disappeared and I came extremely close to smacking a very dazed-looking Ben straight in the face. He caught the swinging fist before it made contact, circling my wrist easily with the span of his fingers, and holding me steady when it looked like my legs had forgotten how to keep me upright.

'Your car,' I gasped, with no preamble. 'I need to borrow your car. It's an emergency. Can I have the keys?' I'm not really sure what I expected to happen next. Did I really think he'd simply pass me the fob, without question? Would *anyone* do that? I realised I should have phrased it better, I should have explained properly, but all of that would take time and we were already wasting far too much of it. I wrestled my arm free and tried to inch past him, as though I had every right to push my way into his room and retrieve the keys myself.

'Sophie. Sophie,' Ben said commandingly, lowering his face so close to mine I could feel the warmth of his breath on my lips. 'Slow down. Tell me what's wrong.' His hands were on my shoulders, holding me still as he spoke. I hadn't realised his chest was bare until the moment when I laid my hands flat upon it to free myself. I'm still not sure what – if anything – he was wearing on his lower half, because my eyes were looking nowhere except into his.

'Lacey – Julia's little girl – is really ill. They've got to intu . . . intu . . .'

'Bate?' finished Ben, as though we were in the middle of a crazy nocturnal game of charades.

I nodded fiercely. 'She's not breathing properly. Julia thinks . . . Julia thinks . . .' I dissolved into tears, unable to complete the sentence. I think we both knew perfectly well what Julia was thinking. 'Gary – her husband – is in Canada. So she's all by herself at the hospital. I have to get there. I have to get there *right now.*'

Ben nodded, thankfully understanding the urgency.

'So I can borrow your car?' I asked, my hand already outstretched to take the keys. It was probably the closest I'd ever come to striking another human being in frustration, when he shook his head in reply.

'No. You can't.' Luckily for Ben my reflexes weren't fast, because my hand hadn't even begun to arc when he added: 'You're not getting behind the wheel of a car in this state. *I'll* drive you.' I fell on him in sheer relief, my arms wrapping around his naked upper body without even registering how easy it was to lean on him, and not just physically.

'Finish getting dressed and I'll meet you on the drive in two minutes,' he said, very gently unhooking my clasped hands from behind his back. I looked down at my feet, which wore no shoes, just a pair of mismatched socks. I nodded and headed back down the stairs to the basement at the same breakneck speed with which I'd climbed them less than two minutes earlier. It was only as I raced around my flat, throwing cat biscuits into a bowl and searching beneath the settee for my missing boots that I realised the absence of footwear might not have been what Ben had been referring to when he'd told me to get dressed. Somehow in my haste to wake him to borrow his car, I'd completely overlooked fastening the zip on my hoodie. It was a measure of just how distraught I was that the fact Ben had seen and held me when I was practically topless didn't seem remotely important.

Ben was on the drive before me, busily scraping the windscreen clear of ice. I jumped into the passenger seat as though it was a getaway car. He glanced at me anxiously as he pulled onto the road, and I wasn't surprised by his look of concern. I was sitting upright in my seat, craning forward as though the angle of my body could somehow get us closer to our destination.

'Which hospital am I going to?' he asked, his attention once again on the icy roads. I gave him the name, which coincidentally was the same hospital where we'd both been treated on the night of the fire. Was that really only two months earlier?

I willed every traffic light to stay on green as we approached it, and most of them obligingly did. I was staring so fixedly through the windscreen that I actually had to remind myself to blink. The streets and pavements were frosted with ice, and the darkened foliage of the overhanging trees and bushes looked like it was studded with crystals. The beauty of the night totally escaped me as I dropped my eyes to the car's speedo, willing Ben to press down a little harder with his right foot. Despite my telepathic urgings the gauge remained firmly on the speed limit. It was probably just as well that he hadn't lent me his car, because I very much doubt I'd have been driving so sedately – or safely. But then of course, the people we were rushing to be with weren't known or loved by him. Not the way they were by me.

'Did your friend say exactly what was wrong with her daughter?'

I shook my head, and then realised with his attention fixed on the potentially dangerous roads he'd probably missed that. I tried to make my voice as near normal as it was likely to go, given the circumstances, as I replied. 'I don't know. She really wasn't making much sense. She said something weird about a kettle and then said Lacey wasn't speaking properly ... But if they're putting her on a ventilator, that means she can't breathe on her own, doesn't it?' My hands gripped together in the dip of my lap, so fiercely that the nails left imprints in the skin. Ben took his hand from the wheel and gently released one of mine from its death-lock grip on its partner. His fingers were warm, despite the outside temperature, and the soft brush of his thumb across the hollow of my palm made goosebumps appear down my arms. Every single nerve ending in my body seemed to have been stripped of its usual protective layer. I felt everything; it all had the power to hurt me.

'If she's that poorly, then she's already in the best possible place,' Ben said gently. It was all the comfort that anyone could give me, and I took it readily.

Even though Ben had abided by the speed limit, the empty streets and the lateness of the hour allowed us to reach the hospital in remarkably quick time. Ben swung in off the road and while I was still frantically scanning a signpost with a ridiculous number of arrowhead markers on it, he was already heading off down one of the avenues. At the next mini roundabout I again scanned the illuminated signpost for directions, but Ben had already found the route we needed. He manoeuvred his car down the network of hospital roadways before finally pulling into a car park not far from the entrance to the Paediatric Wing.

'Thank God you were here,' I said, jumping from the car while he was still pulling on the handbrake. 'It would have taken me ages to find the right department.'

'You'd have got here,' he said confidently, crossing in front of his car and placing a supportive arm around my shoulders. Unconsciously I found my head leaning into the warmth of his body, as though it somehow belonged there. I snapped it back upright so fast I'm surprised I didn't pull a muscle.

It probably started when we began to cross the car park. I felt it, as an unpleasant old memory that I was determined to ignore. It was obvious that anyone would feel anxious given the circumstances; it was only natural. I had loved Lacey from the first moment I'd seen her cradled in Julia's arms in the maternity ward, and had fallen even deeper when Julia had passed me the tiny pink-blanketed bundle to hold. Less than an hour into the world and she already had a small squad of people who would lay down their life to protect her. I've never forgotten that moment and I never will.

I will not give in to this, I told myself determinedly as we walked through the automatic doors into the hospital, passing instantly from Antarctica into the Sahara. Perhaps that sudden contrast in temperature was the reason why tiny beads of perspiration suddenly erupted on my forehead like an abrupt attack of acne. Or perhaps not.

There was an unmanned reception desk, but given the rows of empty seats in the brightly lit waiting area and the lateness of the hour, that was hardly a surprise. Did Ben sense a latent reluctance in my stride as he led me towards the bank of lifts? He must have already scanned the wall signs for directions, and his deep voice echoed slightly in the deserted foyer as he said: 'It looks like the Paediatric ICU is on the fifth floor. That's where you said you were meeting your friend, isn't it?'

I nodded dumbly as he pressed the button to summon the lift. I threw a quick furtive glance up at him as we stood shoulder to shoulder waiting for the brushed silver doors to slide open. Already I could feel an uncomfortable tightness in my chest, and my breathing seemed a little more laboured, as though the hospital foyer had been built on a plateau, where the air was somehow thinner.

I almost stumbled getting into the lift, and Ben's hand was immediately at my elbow, supporting me. 'It's going to be all right,' he said reassuringly as the doors hissed to a close and he selected the button with the illuminated number five. The trembling began somewhere between floors two and three. I could feel the shudders running through me, too violent to hide. Ben would have had to be blind not to see them, and he'd already proved himself far too observant where I was concerned. Of course he saw them.

'Sophie, what is it?' His voice was full of concern and somehow that just made it worse. I needed someone to tell me to snap out of it. A sharp slap across the face, that's how they did it in the movies, wasn't it? I wondered how Ben would react if asked him to strike me. Only I couldn't ask him to do anything, because the only sounds coming from my mouth were tiny animal-like gasps of panic.

Ben looked helplessly around our steel enclosure, as though somehow a very small doctor might have snuck in unnoticed; someone who would know how to deal with his suddenly stricken companion. 'Is it the lift?' he asked desperately. 'Are you claustrophobic?'

I shook my head, and felt my vision blur momentarily as sweat trickled into my eyes, like backward tears. In the end he did the only thing he could, which actually was probably the very best course of action he could have taken. He pulled me towards him and wrapped his arms so tightly around me I was held strait-jacket tight against him. He was still holding me like that when the lift doors glided open and we spilled out onto the fifth floor. Everything hit me at once then, the smells of antiseptic and disinfectant, the quiet hush of the hospital and the bitter taste of fear. I wanted to run, and if my legs hadn't felt as though they were constructed from cotton wool, I might just have done so.

Ignoring the sign with the arrow that would take us to the Paediatric Intensive Care Unit, Ben led me into a small darkened day room. He placed his large hands on my shoulders and gently pushed me down onto one of the hessian-covered seats. There was a small water dispenser in one corner of the room, and he left me only long enough to fill a cone-shaped beaker and pass it to me. His fingers remained over mine until he was certain I was capable of holding the cup without spilling water all over me. The ice-cool liquid was reviving, but I could tell the attack was already passing. They always felt like they went on for hours, but the reality was they rarely lasted for more than a couple of minutes. I looked up at Ben, beginning to feel embarrassed, as though he'd caught me performing some intimate private act that no one should ever see. I felt ashamed.

'That was a panic attack, wasn't it?' he asked, dropping down to a crouch so that our faces were at the same level.

I nodded, but kept my eyes down, focusing on my fingers that were gripping my thighs so hard I was going to have bruises. His own hands dropped to my legs and slid beneath my palms to release my hold. There were several reasons why the intimacy of his touch should have made me gasp out loud. It was impossible to determine why I did so then.

'Has this ever happened before?'

I felt as though my whole life was about to unfurl itself before him like a rolled-up carpet. And I instinctively felt myself retreating from him, the way I had done so many times in my past. 'It's just hospitals,' I said, taking a sip of water, not because I needed it, but more to buy me a few more seconds before responding to the comment I knew would be coming next.

'But you weren't like this when we were brought in after the fire. You were okay then.'

I gave a small shrug and got shakily to my feet. Ben rose with me. 'We can talk about this another time,' I said, while knowing that I had absolutely no intention of ever doing so. 'Right now we need to find Julia.' I wiped my hands across my face, as though the panic attack was a stain I needed to erase first. Ben still looked uncertain, but I was already heading for the door. 'Really, Ben, I'm fine now,' I lied as we emerged once again into the corridor. I looked up and saw the sign to the ICU and slammed a heavy steel door on all the memories that were running towards it like a crazed mob. The mental barrier held, and as I pressed the door release on the entrance to the ward and squirted disinfectant onto my palms, I only hoped it would continue to do so, or I was going to be of very little use to Julia.

When you've been friends with someone for as long as I've been with Julia, your shared experiences are like paving stones that mark the path you've travelled together. I knew her better than anyone; she was *my person*. But it was a different Julia waiting for me on the children's ward, one I'd never met before. She was pacing a small section of floor at the far end of the corridor, never straying too far from the two blue doors that led into the ICU. On each circuit she slowed down to stare through a small porthole in the door.

I ran to her, uncaring of the noise my booted feet created

in the middle-of-the-night hush of the hospital ward. The lighting was dim, but it was still bright enough for me to pick out her red-rimmed eyes and strangely aged face before I drew her to me in a hug.

'How is she?'

It took a lot of strength and several moments for Julia to answer. 'They've had to put her in a coma.' *Coma*. The word ricocheted inside my head, echoing off the walls of my memory. 'They have to wait for the swelling in her throat to go down.' Julia gave a bitter laugh that had threads of hysteria woven in it. 'I gave her Calpol for something so serious they have to put you on a machine to breathe for you. What kind of a mother does that make me?'

'You're a *great* mother,' I protested loyally. 'Have you managed to speak to Gary yet?'

She shook her head. 'I've left messages in practically every city in Canada. But I still haven't tracked him down.'

'I'll keep trying, if you like,' I volunteered, pleased to have a job.

Julia nodded and looked so lost and scared that I stepped closer and wrapped my arms tightly around her, much as Ben had done with me, as though his strength had been a baton to pass on. 'And until he gets here, you've got us.'

I was surprised she picked up on the pronoun, but perhaps it was so unusual to hear it coming from my lips that it was always going to sound startling. I followed her curious glance to the entrance of the ward where Ben stood patiently waiting.

'You brought your landlord?' At any other time her words would have made me smile.

'I brought my friend,' I corrected. 'Or rather, he brought me.' It was the first time I realised that Ben had earned the right to that title quite some time ago. As though sensing he was the object of our discussion, Ben slowly levered himself away from the wall he was leaning against and began to make his way towards us.

Introductions were probably unnecessary, but there was something comforting in doing something so very normal on a night when everything else felt wrong. Julia's eyes had filled when Ben held her hand far longer than the etiquette books say you should, and softly expressed his support.

'I'm going to see if I can rustle us up some coffees,' he said, taking just the right amount of command, without being pushy.

'Seems like a good person to have around in a crisis,' Julia observed as soon as Ben was out of earshot.

'He is.'

'I just wish *none* of us had to be here.'

'Ditto that,' I said with feeling.

Any further conversation was cut short then as Julia was summoned for an update on Lacey's condition. She hurried towards the small cluster of medics waiting at her child's bedside while I hovered uncertainly by the door, unsure if I was supposed to follow. There was only one other occupied bed on the ward, around which an incredibly large and very worried Asian family were clustered. In contrast, Julia stood alone beside Lacey. The shackles of the past were holding me prisoner at the doorway, but I gritted my teeth and pulled against them just as the Ward Sister approached, shaking her head regretfully. 'I'm afraid only family members are allowed at the bedside.'

'I *am* family,' I said resolutely, stepping over the threshold and crossing to join my friend before the Sister could rugby tackle me out of there. It was just ten paces to reach Julia's side, but the distance I travelled to get there was immeasurable. Julia knew it, by the way she took my hand and held it firmly in hers, giving and taking support as we listened to the doctors speaking quietly above a backdrop of constantly bleeping machines.

By the time we stepped out of the room I could tell all traces of colour had been bleached from my face. Ben's eyes went straight to mine. *You okay?* they asked. I nodded, strangely taking this new connection between us almost for granted. Ben had managed to rustle up three fairly decent cups of coffee in proper china cups from somewhere. I suspected he'd most likely charmed them out of one of the nurses.

Julia drained her cup long before we did, and it was easy to see how anxious she was to get back to Lacey. 'Sophie, I can't tell you how grateful I am to have you here, but what I really need you to do now is to go home.'

'What? But I've only just got here.'

Julia shook her head. 'Not back to *your* home, hon. Back to mine. I want you to take Noah and look after him until we bring Lacey home.'

'Noah!' I exclaimed, feeling that I should be smacking my head like a cartoon character at having totally failed to notice our party was missing one small four-month-old infant. 'Where is he?'

'The nurses in the next ward are looking after him,' Julia explained. 'But he's not allowed in the ICU and I'd be much happier knowing he was home, in his own cot, with his own things, with someone I trust.' She paused for a beat. 'With someone who loves him,' she added, in case further ammunition was required.

I could see the logic behind her request, but I still didn't want to leave her. 'Then I'll take care of him here, that way no one has to go.'

Julia's jaw tightened, and I knew from old that her mind was already made up. This was the reason she'd summoned me here in the middle of the night. Two children and only one parent – at least until Gary returned. It was really all about the maths.

'I'm still not happy leaving you alone,' I repeated, for possibly the tenth time, some fifteen minutes later. It felt wrong to be holding Noah in my arms while his mother kissed him goodbye. It ought to be the other way around.

'You know where everything is at home. You know his routine. This is the best solution for everyone. Please, Sophie.'

It was an odd feeling leaving the hospital with a set of house keys and a baby that didn't belong to either me or Ben.

'I think it's only fair to warn you,' said Ben, as he unlocked his car and fixed Noah's car seat into position, 'that everything I know about babies could comfortably be written on the back of a postage stamp.'

I smiled wearily and swivelled in the passenger seat to look at the small sleeping infant who was happily unaware of the events shaking his tiny world. 'Just being here is good enough,' I said. Ben gave me the kind of smile that was worth holding on to, and bringing out to examine again when things weren't quite so fraught. For someone who'd never before relied on a man for strength or support – or for anything, come to that – it was very strange how easily I'd let him creep in beneath my guard.

I didn't expect Ben to spend the night with me at Julia's house. I certainly didn't ask him to . . . but then again I didn't put up too much of a protest when he said that he would. 'It just makes more sense, in case you need to get back to the hospital in a hurry.' I stopped halfway across Julia's kitchen, Noah's bottle of warm milk still in my hands as I stared at him wordlessly, realising he was right; the night might very well not have finished throwing emotional grenades at us just yet. I nodded, and tried to look a little less like the terrified teenager who had suddenly woken up from her sixteen-year hibernation.

After Noah had been fed, changed and laid down to sleep, I lingered for a long time beside his cot, watching him gradually lose his battle to stay awake. I was bending low over the cot rail, covering his small kicking legs with a blanket, when I heard the revealing creak of a floorboard in the hall behind me.

I turned slowly, my forefinger pressed to my lips. Ben's shadow fell across the carpet, but he remained on the threshold to the nursery, not venturing further into the room. I could feel his eyes watching me carefully as I turned on the small glowing nightlight, and flicked on the baby monitor. He smiled as I walked on exaggerated tiptoe across the thick pile of the carpet, holding out a hand as I wobbled inelegantly towards him. As his skin touched mine I had a sudden vision of a different house, one I'd never seen before, with a different baby lying in the cot, one with unusual caramel-coloured eyes. The image was so clear and so unbidden that I gasped softly. This time it was Ben who lifted his fingers to his lips, and I found myself wondering when that familiar gesture had suddenly become so sexy.

Where were these thoughts even coming from? I wasn't attracted to Ben, even though he was a very attractive man. My feelings towards him were just those of friendship and gratitude for everything he'd done for me. Weren't they? If they'd changed in any way, shouldn't I at least have been aware of it? And Ben had certainly never given any indication that he was looking for anything more than friendship from me. So the discovery that my subconscious had veered off down an entirely different path was quite a shock. I didn't say a word until we were back in the lounge and the disturbing snapshot of a future that was never going to be had begun to disappear.

'You're very good with him,' Ben commented, moving aside the small bundle of blankets and pillows I had placed on the settee, and sitting down.

'He's a good baby. And staying here after the fire means I know his routine really well. It's about the only good thing to come out of having my home burn to the ground.'

Ben stretched out his long legs, filling all the space between his settee and the one I was perched on. 'Not the only good thing,' he said slowly.

I swallowed so loudly I'm sure he could hear it clear across the room. 'Erm ... do you want a drink ... or something to eat?' I was poised like a runner on the starting blocks, ready to bolt for the sanctuary of the kitchen. But Ben just shook his head and I sank back against the cushions.

'What I was really hoping we could do, is talk.'

I knew instantly what he wanted to talk about, and my eyes flashed down to my watch. 'Look, it's gone three o'clock in the morning. It's a bit late for a chat. Shouldn't we be trying to get some sleep?'

'I'm not tired,' he interjected, cutting across my flimsy objection. 'Are you?'

'No. I still feel too hyped,' I answered honestly. I drew my legs up onto the settee and reached for one of the scatter cushions, drawing it against me like a shield. You didn't need to be a body language expert to recognise the obvious sign of a barricade.

'You had me pretty scared earlier on at the hospital.'

'Sorry,' I murmured, my eyes fixed on the geometric pattern of the cushion held in my clasped hands.

'I didn't know what to do for you; how to help you.'

I raised my head and gave a small sad smile. 'You did alright. There's nothing anyone *can* do, except wait for it to pass. That's the first one I've had in quite a while.'

Ben leaned forward, resting his elbows on his knees. 'What happened, Sophie?'

I shook my head, confused. 'I had a panic attack,' I said, enunciating the words carefully. 'It's no big deal.'

Ben leant even further in, his body becoming a bridge across the space between us. 'Not tonight. I mean what happened to make them start in the first place?'

I pressed back against the settee, an unconscious countermove to his probing. There was a well-rehearsed script for what to say next. But when I opened my mouth, the words wouldn't come. No actor waiting for his prompt could have felt more wrong-footed as I suddenly found myself ad-libbing my way through my explanation. Because Ben deserved better than my usual wallpapered-over version of the truth. Tonight he'd been dragged from his bed in the middle of the night, and had unquestioningly done everything I had asked – for people he didn't even know. He deserved to know why my visit to the hospital had turned me into someone neither of us recognised.

'We haven't really spoken about our families, have we?'

Ben looked totally nonplussed at my apparent change of direction, but went with it. 'No, I guess we haven't.' He paused for a moment before adding, 'Mine live abroad.'

I took a deep breath before joining in our show-and-tell conversation. 'When people ask me if I have any brothers or sisters, I always say that I don't.'

Ben's eyes flickered, and a tiny muscle in his jaw clenched. 'But my mother . . . well, my mother still tells everyone she has *two* children.' I thought I was getting pretty good at reading Ben's facial expressions, but the one he wore right then defeated me. 'We're both right . . . and we're both wrong.'

'What happened?' His voice had dropped to a gruff whisper.

'My brother was killed.'

Ben rocked backwards as though he'd been shot. I guess it had been a pretty brutal way of putting it, but then this wasn't a story I was practised at telling. The false one rolled so much more easily from my lips. 'He was killed by a drunk driver, who ploughed his car into Scott's motorbike at a junction.'

Ben's throat moved up and down and I found myself staring at his Adam's apple, because it was a whole lot easier to look at than the sympathy in his eyes.

'I'm so very sorry.' It's what people always say whenever they hear about a loss, and I never have understood why.

'It's not your fault.'

For the first time since the night we met, Ben looked uncomfortable in my company. Perhaps it *would* have been better if I'd just lied the way I usually did. But I'd started on this road now, and I knew I had to finish. 'His injuries were terrible.' For all my bravado, the next word stuck in my throat. 'Unsurvivable.'

The lounge was lit by only two small table lights, so it was impossible to tell for sure, but Ben's eyes looked to be glittering brightly. His empathy was unexpected, and it made my own eyes fill too.

'Scott was in a coma for three days before they switched off the machine that was breathing for him. I was the only one who wanted them to wait, even though the doctors said that he would never wake up. I couldn't accept that we were all giving up on my big brother. I begged them to wait . . . but I was just a fifteen-year-old kid.'

For a big man Ben could move surprisingly quickly. He switched seats, slipping into the place beside me as though he belonged there. Very gently he gathered me into his arms, holding me as though I was made of fragile china.

'I never went to say goodbye. I couldn't bear to be there when they . . . when they . . .' Most of my last sentence was strangely muffled, for it was spoken into the fabric of Ben's shirt in the hollow of his shoulder. I raised my head and knew the old pain was still as raw and fresh on my face as it had been sixteen years ago. 'I should have gone to say goodbye. I should have told him I loved him.'

'I'm sure he knew that,' Ben said. 'And you were just a child.'

'He was my brother. We were a team . . . and I just left him. And to the day I die I am never going to be alright with that.'

The crying started with a broken sob, like a crack of thunder at the beginning of a storm. It went on for a very long time, and Ben's arms tightened and held me as I cried in a way I hadn't done in years. Eventually, when one shoulder of his shirt was three shades darker than its opposite number, I lifted my head. I looked around for a box of tissues, knowing that in a house with a baby and a three-year-old one wouldn't be far away. Ben reached over to the side table and passed me the box.

'So tonight just brought it all back,' Ben said carefully, as I tried to blow my nose in a way that didn't sound quite so much like a fog horn. I placed a hand on his chest to lever myself away from him, but his lock around me tightened, and I didn't struggle against it, but rested my cheek once again on the large damp patch I had created. '"*Back*" implies it had gone away. But you're right . . . tonight was tough. It was the first time in sixteen years that I'd been in an Intensive Care Unit.'

In a house full of vacant beds it was strange that we both chose to sleep on the settee in the lounge. I must have fallen asleep in Ben's arms, and when Noah's early morning murmurings woke me, I was still there. Only now there were blankets covering me and a pillow had been slipped beneath my head. Ben looked nowhere near as comfortable, scrunched up into the corner of the settee to give me the lion share of the space. Noah's call became a little more insistent and I gently eased myself from beneath the unfamiliar weight of Ben's arm which was resting heavily against the curve of my waist. It was a very long time since I'd woken up with a man beside me, and I was very grateful that Ben was so exhausted that he didn't stir as I wriggled myself free and went to attend to my godson.

Fifteen minutes later, with a changed and hungry infant in my arms, I returned and found Ben already in the kitchen, stirring two cups of coffee. 'White with one sugar, right?' he checked, crossing to the fridge for the milk. He was walking a little stiffly and was absently rubbing his right leg.

'I'm sorry, Ben, you must have been really uncomfortable on the settee.'

He shrugged. 'I've slept in worse places, although possibly not with anyone noisier.' I felt my face flush warmly, but that could just as easily have been because I was finding it very hard to tear my eyes away from Ben's hand that was still rhythmically kneading the muscles in his thigh.

'Oh God, did I snore?'

'A little,' he said, thankfully done with the impromptu massage. 'And you spoke a couple of times, but don't worry, none of it made any sense.'

'And *that's* why I never spend the night with anyone,' I said lightly.

'Is it?' His question wasn't joking at all; it was serious. This was suddenly far too intense a conversation for half past six in the morning.

I spun around and reached into the fridge for one of the bottles Julia kept stockpiled within it. 'Didn't use any of this for our coffee, did you?' I asked, knowing the question would shatter the intensity of the moment.

'No. Should I have?'

'Only if you prefer breast milk in your espresso,' I said with a grin.

He laughed and the awkward moment was gone. For now.

Julia phoned a little later, shortly after Ben had gone back to his home to shower and grab us both some clean clothes. Lacey was showing small signs of improvement from the illness they had now identified as epiglottitis, Julia said, her voice cautiously hopeful. There was no hiding the relief in her tone when she told me she'd finally spoken to Gary, who was hopefully right now somewhere over the Atlantic on his way back home.

'Are you sure you can manage until one of us can relieve you?' Julia asked in concern.

Noah was the last thing she should be worrying about, so perhaps I over-egged my reply a little. 'Of course we can. Noah was so good last night. He didn't even wake us up until gone six this morning.'

'Okay, I'm going to blip straight over that "*we*" and "*us*", but you can be sure we'll be returning to them as soon as things get back to normal again.'

'Just give Lacey a big kiss from me and let me know if you want me to come up to the hospital.'

'To be honest I'd prefer it if you stayed at home with him.' She paused, and then added, '"*Him*" meaning Noah, in case you were wondering.'

I smiled into my phone. 'Just look after yourself. And try

not to worry.' It was an easy instruction to give, and one I knew from experience she wouldn't be able to follow.

Things didn't really start to feel better until much later in the afternoon. When Ben had returned from the house, I'd sent him straight back out to the hospital with a small bag for Julia, containing a change of clothes and some basic toiletries. The text I received from her contained two comments. *'They're talking about taking Lacey off the ventilator later today.'* Which was exactly what I'd been hoping to hear. Her second comment: *'I rather like your new man friend'* was exactly what I had not.

I wasn't in the room when Gary returned, and the first thing his red-rimmed travel-sore eyes saw was a strange man sitting in his lounge. 'Is one of us in the wrong house?' he asked.

I dropped the laundry basket I was carrying in from the utility room and rushed to envelop him in an enormous hug. His arms went around me, and I knew he was holding on for longer than he would normally do in order to compose himself.

'Julia texted to say Lacey's off the machine,' I whispered into his neck.

He nodded fiercely. 'Yeah, I know. I just spoke to her from the taxi.'

'Can I give you a lift to the hospital?' Ben asked, getting to his feet and holding out his hand to Gary, who I noted looked a great deal older than he'd done just one week before.

'No, thanks. I want to have our car there.' He shook Ben's

hand, and nodded abstractedly. 'Who the hell are you, by the way?'

'This is Ben,' I introduced rapidly, knowing that any further explanation would be instantly forgotten. There was a very good chance Gary wouldn't even remember his name by the time he left the room.

As I expected, Gary refused anything to eat or drink, or even the chance to change out of his travel clothes. The pull to be with his wife and daughter was just too strong.

'You *can* stay until this evening, can't you?' he asked, collecting his car keys from the bowl where they lived. 'My mother is travelling down on the train from Glasgow, and she'll be coming straight from the station to take over with Noah.'

I'd met Gary's mother several times over the years. She was a very tiny, but capable, no-nonsense former nurse, who – if I'm totally honest – scared me with her unstoppable efficiency. *'Every time she visits she insists on ironing all my tea towels,'* I remember Julia once telling me. *'Who on earth does that?'*

'You know, I'm happy to stay on looking after Noah for as long as you want. If your mum wants to go to the hospital, I'm happy to stay another night.'

Gary was too tired to worry about whether his reply might sound a little ungrateful. 'No, that's fine, Sophie. You've done more than enough for us already. But you know what it's like at times like this. This is when it's all about the family pulling together.'

He didn't mean to wound me with his words, I know that. And he probably didn't even realise that he'd done so, not even when Ben laid a hand on my shoulder and squeezed it subtly in comfort.

It was hard keeping my eyes open on the drive back home. Ben, who had to be just as sleep-deprived as me, fortunately showed no signs of it as he slipped behind the wheel of the car. I'd felt strangely torn leaving Noah in his grandmother's undeniably capable hands. She'd handled the changeover briskly, as though she was still a nurse taking over from the day shift, scribbling down illegible notes on a small pad she'd pulled from her handbag.

'Oh this wee man and me will be just fine,' she had assured us, following us to the front door like a small Scottish whirlwind that seemed determined to blow us out of the house.

'Were we just dismissed?' Ben asked, his hand resting naturally in the small of my back as he led me to his parked car.

'I rather think we were,' I said, swallowing a huge yawn.

Ben had switched on the radio and the car filled with the soft sounds of jazz. His choice of music met with my approval. It was yet another thing about this man that I liked. Somehow, while I was looking the other way, Ben had found a crack in the wall I had built so carefully around myself. And I don't think he had the smallest clue that he'd done so. I could feel a soft smile forming as I watched his fingers absently tapping out the rhythm of a song on the steering wheel. Was this the right moment to open the door of the vault just a little, or should I keep it tightly shut, as usual? I took a deep breath, like a diver on a high board, and jumped.

'What scares you in life, Ben?'

He took his eyes off the road for a brief second. 'Clowns,' he said decisively. 'Bloody terrifying, aren't they?'

My smile was slow. 'No, I mean what *really* scares you?'

This time the look that he gave me was much longer, and lasted until the traffic lights had once more turned green. 'I take it you mean more than hairy-legged spiders or my last tax return?' I nodded. 'I don't know. I'd have to think about it. What scares *you*?' He'd flipped the question, as I had always known he would.

'What happened last night.' My answer had come straight back, swooping through the darkened car like a bat. 'Losing someone else I care about to sickness or injury, *that's* the thing that terrifies me more than anything. I guess you could say I have a real phobia about it.'

'That must be difficult to deal with. I mean it's not something that you have any control over.'

'Apart from limiting the headcount of people I worry about, there's not much else I can do. And even though I know it's not rational to feel like this, that doesn't mean I can stop it. I see death everywhere.'

'I'm guessing you don't mean in a *Sixth Sense* kind of a way?'

'It's always there, the fear. Like a glimmer at the edge of your vision. Worrying about it is exhausting,' I admitted on a sigh, 'but I can't seem to stop doing it. It's there when

I close my eyes, and it's there when I wake up again.' This time I did laugh, but there was no real humour in it. 'It's the nightmare that just keeps on giving.'

'Don't take this the wrong way,' Ben began awkwardly, 'but—'

I interrupted, to save him the embarrassment of completing his sentence. 'Have I ever seen a counsellor or a therapist? Yes. Several. But this is harder to shake off than just being too scared to board a plane, or worrying about the spider scuttling across the ceiling. Those things won't kill you; the thing I have a phobia about, will.'

'You can't shut yourself off from living, for fear that one day you'll lose someone you love. It's pointless.'

I gave a wry smile. 'No kidding, Sherlock.'

'So stop doing it.'

I sighed and reached for the radio control to turn up the volume. Confession time was over. 'Easier said than done. I've had sixteen years of practice, so I'm pretty good at it by now.'

Chapter 7

It isn't running away if you tell people in advance that you're going, I justified to my reflection the following morning as I brushed my teeth. I dropped my toothbrush onto the small pile of toiletries in my sponge bag and caught sight of the dark smudgy circles beneath my eyes. I should have slept deeply, but I'd caught only stolen slices of rest through the long night, punctured by disjointed and disturbed dreams. Many of them, not surprisingly, involved hospitals in some way, although the patient in the iron-framed bed was neither Lacey, nor even Scott … it was always my dad. After the third occasion of being jolted wide awake with a feeling of impending dread, I stopped fighting my subconscious and made my decision. I wanted – no, needed – to see my family, and I didn't want to wait the couple of weeks until Christmas.

I threw clothes randomly into my overnight bag and poured out my third cup of coffee as I waited for the clock to read a suitable time for paying someone an unexpected early morning visit, to ask for yet another favour. I turned the radio on loudly to drown out the voice in my head that kept warning me Ben's friendship and tolerance were in danger of being stretched like an elastic band to breaking point if I wasn't careful.

The basement flat was well insulated, but sound still travelled between the properties, so it was easy to tell when he was up and moving around. I rubbed distractedly at my forehead as I climbed the wooden treads between Ben's home and mine. My restless night had left me with a sickly headache, and the amount of caffeine I'd fuelled it with had made it turn really ugly.

This time at least I didn't go barging straight into his kitchen, but waited for him to answer my knock.

'Good morning, Sophie,' he said with an easy smile, holding open the door and gesturing for me to follow him, as though finding his troublesome tenant on his doorstep yet again wasn't peculiar at all. He was dressed for a different climate, or a different season. His jeans were fraying around the hem and the faded grey T-shirt looked old and comfortable. His feet were bare and his hair still dripped droplets of water from his shower. He looked like he'd just got back from the beach, or from surfing, or from some other healthy outdoorsy pursuit, I thought as I followed him into the kitchen.

'Coffee?' he asked, picking up the glass pot and waving it enticingly.

'Not for me,' I said, as he poured himself a generous mug. 'I'm sorry for disturbing you like this—'

'I'm kind of getting used to it,' he teased. 'So where are we dashing off to today?'

I bit my lip guiltily, knowing that I deserved that. I *had* been using him like my own private limousine service. That definitely had to stop, I told myself sternly. 'Actually, I *am* going away for a night or two, but the favour I wanted to ask was if you'd be able to feed Fred for me while I'm gone.'

Ben looked less than delighted with my request.

'Obviously, if it's too much trouble, I could take him with me, but—'

'It's no trouble.'

'Are you sure? Because you didn't exactly look keen just then.'

'Maybe that's because I was disappointed you were going away? It's going to be awfully dull here without you.' His eyes crinkled as he spoke. He was teasing me. Obviously, he was. And at my age I should be able to deflect that type of comment as easily as lobbing back a tennis ball. Except I wasn't any good at sport, and apparently I was even worse at banter – if that's what we were doing here.

'Erm, I've written down instructions for what he eats,' I said, pulling a folded handwritten sheet from the pocket of my jeans. 'And there's an enormous bag of cat food on my kitchen worktop.' Ben reached out to take the list and somehow our fingers grazed. I jolted visibly, as though the paper was electrified.

'So where are you going?' Ben asked, his eyes lifting from

our hands to my face. Damn it, he *had* noticed the way I'd jerked my hand back.

'Home,' I answered.

'To Cotterham?'

My head flew up in surprise. Had I told him that was where my parents lived? I couldn't remember doing so, and if I *had* mentioned it in passing, how on earth had he managed to remember it?

'Yes,' I said, still a little puzzled. 'I think what Gary said yesterday about family must have been playing on my mind all night. I woke up this morning knowing I had to go back,' I pulled a small face, 'and also with a colossal headache.' Ben's eyes were instantly sympathetic. 'Actually, you don't have any paracetamols or anything, do you? I haven't got around to replacing stuff like that yet since the fire.'

'Sure,' Ben said. 'I've probably got a spare packet in my bathroom cabinet. I'll just get—' He broke off, already half off his stool, when his mobile phone interrupted him from the other side of the kitchen. He changed direction, swerving to get the ringing phone, while pointing and pantomiming towards his bathroom, signalling that I should retrieve the medication while he retrieved the call.

It felt strange walking through his bedroom, even though he'd just given me permission to do so. The duvet was thrown back, crumpled, as though he'd just stepped out from beneath it, and the pillow on the right-hand side of the bed still bore the visible indent of his head. My preference was always to sleep on the left-hand side, and that thought had no business whatsoever occurring to me as I walked past the foot of his bed.

Perhaps it really was just as well I was going away for a couple of days. That should give me enough time to corral all of these errant thoughts and put them back where they belonged. The borders between fact and fantasy were starting to get uncomfortably blurry and I needed a cold dousing of reality before I became more of a stalker than a lodger.

Of course rifling through Ben's bathroom cabinet was probably not the best way of illustrating this new resolve, I realised as I opened the two double-mirrored doors and stared at the neatly lined-up contents. The lower shelf was filled with the expected toiletries, and I successfully stopped my inner prowler from touching anything, although my nose twitched like a rabbit's as it recognised several aromas that my brain had already labelled as '*Ben*'.

The top shelf was where he kept his medicines, and while they might be accessible to someone of his height, they were just out of reach of my groping fingers. I could see a packet of branded painkillers tucked into the far corner. I leant a little further over the deep porcelain basin, until my fingertips lightly brushed against the edge of the box. They were only millimetres out of reach, and as I waggled my fingers trying to dislodge them, a small brown bottle of pills fell from its position on the shelf. It tumbled noisily into the empty basin, rolling like a ball in a roulette wheel before coming to a stop, its label half obscured. I reached for the bottle to replace it. I saw Ben's name and the date printed on the prescription label, and I'd really like to think that I would have respected his privacy enough not to look at the name of the medication, but I never got the chance to find out. A tall dark shape suddenly appeared in the mirror behind me and in one swift movement he had picked up the bottle of pills and replaced them on the top shelf, label facing inwards.

'Let me get these for you,' Ben said, reaching for the pain-killers and passing me the packet. There was something in his eyes that I had never seen there before. I couldn't name it for sure, but it looked an awful lot like disappointment, and all at once I felt about six inches tall. No wonder I hadn't been able to reach the damn shelf.

'So she's going to be okay is she, Julia's little girl?' asked my dad as he stowed my bag in the back of his car.

'Yes, thank God. Julia said she's already struggling to keep her in bed.'

'They bounce back quickly at that age.'

I looked at him from beneath my lashes as he eased himself into the seat beside me and reached for his seatbelt. We shared a look, just a brief one, but it said a lot.

Much of the twenty-minute drive from the station to my old home was taken up with Dad's amusing anecdotes about their recent holiday. I listened, but with only half my attention. The rest was busy doing a silent summary of his health. Not breathless from climbing the short flight of stairs to the station car park; cheeks tanned from his weeks under the Caribbean sun; hands wrinkled and liver-spotted, but relaxed as they gripped the wheel. As I ticked each item off my unofficial checklist, I felt the tight spool of concern I'd wrapped around me begin to loosen slightly.

'So, it wasn't possible to move back into your old place after that fire in the flat downstairs?'

I hid the guilty look on my face by pretending to study the familiar scenery flashing past my side window. I'd opted for a 'need-to-know' version of the truth of what had actually happened on the night of the fire. There was no need to concern my ageing parents with how close they'd come to living through a second tragedy. But I was going to have to keep my wits about me to make sure I didn't trip up and stumble over my own story.

'No. The fire caused too much damage.' *That*, at least, was no lie.

'But you like this new place you've found?'

'Very much,' I replied. Again, with total honesty. 'Ben, whose house it is, has been really supportive and helpful.'

My dad nodded, and this seemed like as good a moment as any to broach the question I'd been toying with for the entire train journey. 'Dad, would you or mum have any objection if I invited him to join us for a couple of days over Christmas?'

My father's thick grey eyebrows rose upwards, which was hardly unexpected. 'Well ... no. Although I have to say, I'm quite surprised. You've never brought a boy back home before.' There were good reasons for that, but this wasn't the time to go into them. More urgent was the need to make sure no one had got hold of the wrong end of this particular stick. 'Dad, Ben isn't a "*boy*", he's a successful businessman in his thirties. But more importantly he and I aren't … aren't … a thing,' I finished lamely. Translators are good at finding words; it's what we do. But the ones to adequately explain what Ben and I were – if we were anything at all – were beyond me.

'Ben is just a friend,' I confirmed, my voice low with quiet emphasis. 'And when he happened to mention the other day that his family live abroad, I thought inviting him down for Christmas was a charitable thing to do.'

I was quite pleased with that explanation. My mother busied herself, almost to the point of obsession, with many local charities. It was her chosen method of coping. We'd each found our own.

I should have known my answer wouldn't be a one-size-fits-all solution. 'Charitable, huh?' questioned my dad, with a small chuckle I don't remember having heard for a very long time. I realised then that it wasn't going to make any difference what I said about my friendship with Ben. My dad had already written his own version.

'Well, I have no objections if you want to ask him.' He took one hand from the wheel and lightly squeezed my forearm. 'I've been waiting a long time for you to bring a lad back home.'

I sighed, blowing out the air from my lungs in a long steady stream. Dad looked at me and winked, and I smiled back weakly. He was doing that thing that always used to drive me crazy; he was pretending that it was only a matter of time before I found the 'right one' and settled down. And I was doing that thing where I pretended that, of course, this was still entirely possible; that the scars of the past had faded enough not to damage us any more. We played a lot of games like that in my family.

'He'd have to sleep on the sofa bed in the den though, you know that, don't you?' I nodded, my eyes heavy with understanding. Whatever he believed about my relationship with Ben, my father's comment had nothing to do with propriety. My parents lived in a spacious three-bedroom house, but one room was forever off limits to guests.

'I'm sure he'd be perfectly fine with that − *if* he comes anyway. Christmas is only two weeks away and he's probably already made arrangements with friends or someone ... he has a lot of friends.'

The sound of the television playing to its sleeping audience of one floated up the treads of the staircase behind me. My dad's head had nodded forward almost as soon as the opening credits for the afternoon quiz show had begun. I'd seen hypnotists take longer to put people to sleep.

I'd politely declined my mum's offer to accompany her to her book group meeting. 'I really ought to go, because this month's title was my suggestion,' she'd explained. 'If we'd known earlier that you were coming ...' I heard the lightly sprinkled hint of criticism seasoning her words. I let it go, because there was no point coming back to see them and then getting wound up over the small things.

'You go and enjoy your meeting. Why don't I make us dinner while you're out?' I suggested.

Mum picked up her car keys and the paperback that was positioned in readiness by her handbag. She turned to go and then at the last moment came back and gave me a quick and unexpected hug. We weren't a family of huggers, and by the time I had got over my surprise and brought my arms around her, she was already stepping back, leaving just a lingering cloud of the favourite perfume she'd worn for years. In my basement flat there was a new bottle of it waiting to be wrapped and placed beneath the small artificial Christmas tree that would soon be set up in the front room. The thought made a tiny frown appear between my brows, knowing that beneath that same tree there would be a solitary present that would still be sitting there when twelfth night came around and the tree was dismantled. Did I really want to expose my family's eccentricities to Ben? What would he make of them . . . or of us?

It had begun on the very first year our Christmas table had been set for three places instead of four. One of us should probably have said something then, but it all felt too raw and painful. You don't disturb a wound when it is trying to heal. So we stayed silent as my otherwise-perfectly-rational mother continued to buy Scott a Christmas jumper, long after he had no further need of clothing. Still, I don't think either my dad or I had expected this peculiar practice to continue for as long as it had.

I only challenged her about it once, and her tearful reply

that she couldn't bear to leave him out practically broke my heart. The final destruction of that organ came just a week or so later when I saw the jumper in a local charity-shop window. I never could decide what was worse: my mum sorrowfully *un*wrapping the parcel and giving it away, or keeping it hidden for the son who was never coming back home to wear it.

There were four doors leading off the upstairs hallway. Only one of them was shut. I walked slowly towards it and pressed down on the handle. The room should have smelled musty or stale, but the air was fresh, for the door was opened frequently. Far too frequently. I slipped through the gap and closed the door firmly behind me. There was always a moment, even after all these years, when the shock of it still managed to rock me enough to make my footsteps falter. Knowing that he'd never again stand in this room, never again yell at me to get out, I thought with a broken laugh, still had the power to fell me. I crossed to the bed and lowered myself onto one corner.

'Hello, Scott,' I whispered to the empty room.

Hi, Sophie, came my brother's imagined reply.

All three of us came in here, but always alone. We never spoke of it. It was private, like a confessional booth, where the sin we were guilty of was living on, when he had not. This was the place where my parents and I felt closest to him. This was the place where I still heard his voice. The place where the posters on the wall reminded us of his love of heavy metal music, where the shelf of sporting trophies was testimony to his prowess with a ball, where the propped-up electric guitar – the one he'd never learned to

205

play – reminded us of a lifetime of unfulfilled ambitions. I looked at them all, although I'd seen them so many times before they were always with me, burnt like a laser on the retina of my eyes whenever I said his name.

It was the mirror that always drew my eye though. I turned my head towards it, not seeing the reflection of a woman who had now left her twenties behind, but seeing instead the younger version of her, laughing with her brother, as he pushed the ticket for the music festival beneath the edge of the mirror, slipping it beneath the strip of photo-booth images of the two of them. The fifteen-year-old girl was smiling broadly into the camera in each of the four photographs, while the boy beside her pulled silly faces, stuck out his tongue or waggled his fingers behind her head like rabbit's ears.

I closed my eyes and was back on that summer night. *'They're never going to agree to you going to that festival in Germany, you know. Not with those guys.'*

'They don't have to agree. I'm almost eighteen. I don't need their permission, or to have them choose my mates for me. Thanks for lending me the money from your savings account by the way, Soph. You're the best.'

'Just don't tell the rents where you got it from, or they'll kill me as well as you.'

The room swum a little as the memory floated back to me from the past. Had I really said those words, just days before he would be lying on a cold, hard mortuary slab?

'I'll pay you back, just as soon as I get a summer job,' Scott had promised.

'When I figure out how to do the maths, I'm adding interest too,'
I had said laughingly.

I got to my feet, and touched the curling edges of
the unused festival ticket. Sunlight from the adjacent
window had faded the print. The date was now almost
illegible. In another sixteen years would it still be here, a
yellowed square of card, the words invisible, the memory
indestructible?

Would he have argued with my parents that night if
that ticket had never been bought? Was he concentrating
as much as he should have been on his driving, or were
the heated words still going round in his head? They were
impossible questions to answer. And there was one more
that refused to remain silent no matter how many times I
came to this place. If I'd never lent Scott the money ... if
he'd never been able to buy that ticket, would he still be
alive now?

My mum didn't mention my possible Christmas guest until
the following morning, when my dad was out buying his
daily newspaper. Our local paperboy had been rendered
summarily redundant after my father's heart attack. Now
nothing high in saturates got to live in their fridge, and there
were swimming pool and gym timetables held by magnets
to its door. Exercise and eating healthily hadn't saved her
son, but my mum was almost fanatical that no one else was
going to die on her watch. The constant vigil must have been
exhausting, and I could see it in the fantail of lines bordering

her eyes that got just a little bit deeper, a little bit longer, each time I visited.

I was reaching for the jar of marmalade when her gaze fell on the small section of skin on my wrist just visible beneath the cuff of my jumper.

'What's that?' Hurriedly I pulled down on the sleeve, covering up the scar that I already knew she wasn't going to allow me to hide. 'Is that a burn, Sophie?'

I considered lying for a moment. Wouldn't it be easier to just say I did it with an iron? After all, an iron *had* been involved . . . in a way.

'It's nothing, Mum. Don't worry about it.'

Ignoring my words, she reached for my hand, holding it in hers, like she used to decades earlier whenever we crossed the road. Very gently she turned it over and eased back the ribbing by my wrist. The burn wasn't ugly or painful any more, but it was obvious that it was a recent injury. She remained quiet for a very long time, just studying the mark on my arm. When she eventually raised her head, I was surprised to see her eyes were bright with tears.

'Oh Sophie,' she said sadly. 'You should have said something. Why didn't you tell us?'

I shrugged, feeling like a teenager all over again. 'It's no biggie,' I said, realising even my language had reverted back to vocabulary I hadn't used for a very long time.

'If you got injured, then it most certainly is,' she refuted firmly.

'It could have been so much worse if Ben hadn't come along when he did.'

'That's the man who owns the flat you live in?'

I nodded.

'The one you want to invite here for Christmas?'

I gulped and felt my last mouthful of toast shift uncomfortably somewhere in the depths of my stomach. Dad had said he'd find the right moment to ask her, and I had really hoped he wouldn't locate it until I was already on the train and heading home.

'Well, okay then. I'd really like to meet this young man.'

Oh my God. What had I done?

The entire house was in darkness when I returned, which was unusual, but I was too anxious to get in out of the cold to even notice whether Ben's car was parked in the driveway. I could hear Fred's noisy greeting on the other side of the door as my frozen fingers fumbled to insert my key in the lock. I heaved a huge sigh of relief as I hoisted my bag over the step and hurriedly shut out the cold December night.

As I bent down to pick up the mail, I fleetingly scratched the space between Fred's ears. 'Yes, I'm pleased to see you too,' I said in response to his ecstatic purring, which couldn't have been more enthusiastic if I'd been gone for a month instead of just one night. But it *did* feel good to be back, I acknowledged, and much more like 'coming home' than returning to the attic flat had ever done. Now all I wanted was to turn up the heating, change into my comfiest pyjamas, and fix myself something to eat.

Straightening up in the darkness I reached out to turn on the hall light. Despite flicking the switch up and down several times, giving the dead bulb ample opportunity to change its mind, it didn't work.

'Terrific,' I muttered, heading towards the inky blackness of the kitchen, and managing to spectacularly trip over my own bag and bump into several pieces of furniture on the way. 'And I bet I don't have a spare bulb.' My hand groped along the wall until I found the next light switch, and it was only when that too failed to work that I realised the problem was more serious than just one defunct bulb. Even the garden, which was normally subtly lit with blue and green spotlights, was in total darkness.

Fred wound around my ankles, oblivious that only one of us was currently able to see where we were going. I pulled my mobile from my pocket, switched on its torch and cautiously followed the thin pencil beam of light across the kitchen. I had no idea if this was a power cut or a blown fuse, but either way the fuse box was situated in Ben's section of the house and not mine.

I strained my ears in the darkness, trying to work out if the creaking sounds overhead were someone walking on the floor above me, or just the house settling down for the night.

'Stay here,' I commanded the cat, unable to see if he was complying as I opened the door to the staircase and climbed up to the upper storey by the light from my phone. At the top of the flight I opened the door and called out Ben's name, shining my torch into the centre of his kitchen as I walked in. Another, much stronger, beam hit me straight in the face, momentarily blinding me.

'Ben? Is that you?' I asked stupidly.

'Yes,' answered his disembodied voice. 'Hang on a minute, Sophie. Let me get to the fuse box and try the trip switch. Don't move.'

I switched off my own torch and waited. Sounds of something being dropped and a swear word I'd never heard him say before punctured the darkness. I smiled, even though no one could see me. I was still grinning like an idiot when the lights came on and I found myself facing not an empty room as I'd expected, but one that was filled with people.

If this were a film, this would be the moment when they'd all spring to their feet and shout out *'Surprise!'*, but obviously no one did. A circle of faces were trained towards me, as though I was a stagehand who'd accidentally walked on in the middle of a performance. It was just beginning to feel awkward, when a voice I recognised broke the silence.

'Sophie! How lovely to see you again.' Carla got to her feet, dazzling in an outfit of peacock blue and silver. I almost didn't recognise her beneath the blunt-fringed, jet-black, Cleopatra-style wig.

'How are you, Carla?' I asked, walking gratefully into her outstretched arms to receive an enveloping hug. The warmth of her embrace took some of the chill off the awkwardness of barging into a room of strangers. Except, now that I'd had a chance to look around, I realised that they weren't *all* strangers.

Henry inclined his head with a nod of acknowledgement. 'Hello, young lady.'

And from the depths of a leather armchair, I heard another voice ask teasingly, 'What? No weapons this time, Sophie?' I smiled weakly at Tom, who grinned back broadly before biting into an enormous slice of pizza.

'I think that's fixed it,' announced Ben as he rejoined his guests. 'Let me know, Sophie, if anything downstairs still isn't working.'

It began to sink in that I had disturbed Ben's party when it was in full swing. There were quite a few empty bottles of wine on the kitchen worktop, beside a stack of takeaway boxes big enough to accommodate pizzas the size of bicycle wheels. The smell of molten cheese and garlic bread hung like a small delicious cloud over the assembled group of friends, and I prayed my stomach wouldn't growl noisily and embarrass me.

'Oh, great, thank you,' I said, slow to realise that I was being dismissed. I glanced over and caught a disapproving look on Carla's face, which she didn't bother trying to hide. Several of the other guests shifted a little uncomfortably in their seats, suddenly finding the grain on the wooden floor quite fascinating.

'I didn't know if you were coming back tonight or in the morning,' said Ben conversationally. It was impossible not to be aware of the hand that he'd placed in the small of my back, gently shepherding me towards the doorway. 'Anyway, I fed the cat earlier,' he added.

'Oh, is this *your* cat?' asked an elderly female voice. Ben's smile looked a little strained as we both turned to see that Fred, ever the opportunist, had followed me up the stairs and was now happily ensconced on the lap of a very small white-haired woman with the brightest blue eyes I'd ever seen. Her bony fingers were lovingly stroking Fred down the length of his back, and he was clearly revelling in the attention.

'What a handsome fellow he is,' she declared. 'I *do* miss the company of a cat. Perhaps he could stay up here for a while?'

Ben looked genuinely anguished. This was surely the moment when that invitation should have been extended to the human gatecrasher as well as the feline one? The awkward silence wasn't mine to fill, but I did so anyway.

'Yes, of course. Just send him back downstairs when he starts annoying you,' I said to Ben, who looked uncomfortable but unbending. 'Well, it was nice meeting all of you,' I said to the room in general, before heading back to the basement flat where the irony of my parting words hit me like a brick. Because I hadn't been introduced to any of Ben's guests. I hadn't met them . . . because he hadn't wanted me to.

The knocking on the door was persistent and annoying. I hit the Save key on my laptop and padded across the floor to answer it, my mind still on the complexities of the translation piece I was working on. As soon as the door was open, a clipboard and a pen were thrust through the gap. A burly man wearing a thick anorak and a slightly irritated expression stood before me.

'I have a tree for you.' I blinked at him, wondering if I could possibly have misheard. I'd been sent flowers before, once or twice, but never an entire tree.

'I beg your pardon?'

The man sighed deeply. 'A tree. A spruce, to be precise. The order's in the name of . . .' He drew the clipboard back towards him and read an illegible scribble in one of the boxes. 'Stevens.'

'Ah, okay. You want the *main* entrance,' I explained, already starting to ease the door to a close. The man halted it with an upraised hand, sounding far more cranky than I felt was necessary.

'Listen, love, I've been ringing the bell for ten minutes and there's no answer. I've got a whole lorry full of deliveries. Can't you just sign for the tree? I'll leave it up on the drive.'

It was getting cold standing in the open doorway, and I really did need to get back to the translation, so I took the pen he was waggling somewhere in the region of my nose, and signed for the delivery. I returned to my work, and forgot all about it until my phone pinged some time later to alert me to a message. It was from Ben.

'Do you know anything about the giant redwood blocking the driveway?'

I didn't waste time replying. I just leapt up, thrust my arms into a jacket hanging by the door, and rushed outside. All I could see of Ben was his head and shoulders as he walked up and down the length of an extremely long and dense fir tree that was lying horizontally across his driveway.

'Oh,' was all I said, guilt already making me feel uncomfortably warm. Parked on the pavement outside the house, its hazards rhythmically flashing, was Ben's car. It was lucky he'd not driven straight into the tree.

'I think I've possibly got the one they should have delivered to Trafalgar Square,' he said with a wry smile. With him on one side of the tree and me on the other, it was a bit like conducting a conversation from the depths of a maze.

'Oh dear. I think this might be partly my fault,' I said, sounding agonised. 'I signed for the tree without examining it. I'm guessing this wasn't the size you ordered?'

He shrugged, at least I think he did. It wasn't easy to see with the thick branches obscuring my view. 'Well, I asked for a small to medium one ... just as well I didn't go for large, I guess.'

I had to admit Ben seemed to be taking the mix-up really well. I wondered what it took to make him angry or riled. He always seemed so Zen about everything.

'Well, there's not much I can do about it now. I doubt we'll be able to lift this between us. I'll give Tom a ring later and see if he can help.' It didn't seem my place to point out that Tom's physical limitations might make him even less useful than me when it came to lifting an enormous tree.

'Well, I was planning on going for a walk later anyway,'

Ben declared, glancing upwards at the grey clouds that were colliding like dirty candyfloss in the sky. 'But I think I might as well go now. Do you feel like joining me?'

I looked back at my flat, where the translation piece was waiting, daring me to turn him down. 'Actually, yes. I could probably do with the fresh air. Let me grab a warmer coat.'

However, when I emerged from the flat a few moments later I realised that crossing over from my side of the tree to Ben's wasn't exactly going to be an easy manoeuvre.

'Do you think you can climb over?'

I gave a small expressive shrug. 'Let's see, shall we?'

Ben stepped forward to part some of the denser branches, showing me the way. With some inelegant scrabbling I managed to climb over and through the ones on my side of the tree.

'I thought you said you used to be a tomboy, that you were *always* climbing trees,' he observed from the other side of the obstacle.

'I was. But that was twenty years ago. And somehow it's much easier when they're still vertical,' I declared, finally getting one leg over the prickly trunk. Ben's hand reached through the remaining foliage and I extended my own to grasp it. A watery shaft of winter sunlight suddenly broke through the grey clouds and shone down like a torch on his inner wrist, highlighting the scar from his burn. When I gave him my hand, my own scar aligned with his, like two halves of a broken talisman. He tightened his grip and pulled me smoothly towards him. Neither of us said a word. His hold on me had been firm and strong, and had brought us face to face, closer in proximity than we'd ever been before. I could feel the heat of his breath on my lips and had an almost irresistible urge to eliminate the small remaining space between us. For the first time in longer than I could remember, I really wanted to be kissed. But not just by anyone, by Ben.

I let him lead the way, happy to walk beside him in companionable silence as we headed down a forest pathway that led to a large area of parkland. Ben held back some of the overhanging branches that were at face level, and when the rubber soles of my Converse trainers slipped on the damp terrain, he took my hand and somehow forgot to release it, and somehow I forgot to remind him.

'So, do you always order such an enormous Christmas tree?' I asked eventually, as we walked side by side beneath an aisle of trees, whose branches linked over our heads like ancient lace.

'No. But then I've not actually been in the UK for the last few years at Christmas. My girlfriend—' He shook his head as though he couldn't believe he'd made the verbal slip. 'My *ex*-girlfriend and I used to go skiing every holiday season.'

It was the first time he had ever mentioned the beautiful redhead, who – obviously – I hadn't been able to resist searching for online. Holly. It was an easy name to remember at this time of year, but I doubted I'd have forgotten it, whatever the season.

'Do you ski, Sophie?'

I laughed. 'I'd be the one being stretchered off the mountain on the first day of the holiday.'

He squeezed my fingers in his, and our connection felt so much more than just bones and skin joined together. 'Me too, I suspect now.'

It was an odd remark, but I didn't have a chance to ask what he meant by it, because there was clearly something that he wanted to talk about. I could see it in the slightly ill-at-ease expression in his eyes.

'It was Carla who berated me yesterday about not having any Christmas decorations in the house. She was good friends with the previous owners and I'm falling short of the festive mark, or so she said.'

We walked on for a minute in silence, before he drew out the rest of his admission, the one that was making him look so uncomfortable. 'Actually, that wasn't the only thing Carla took me to task on. She was very disappointed with the way I hustled you back into the basement last night.'

'You didn't hustle,' I said, knowing full well that we were both aware that that was *exactly* what he'd done.

'She made it sound like I was banishing you down there with six white mice and a pumpkin.'

I turned my face to hide my smile, knowing how easy it was to see the colourfully eccentric Carla as my fairy godmother. Of course that would make Ben Prince Charming, which was a role he could so very easily play. Seeing me as Cinderella, the princess-to-be, was the only piece of miscasting in that scenario, as far as I could tell.

'I wasn't trying to deliberately exclude you—' Ben shook his head in almost instant contradiction. 'No. That's a lie, I *was* trying to keep you from meeting them, but not because I was trying to leave you out . . . it was because I was trying to protect you.'

His explanation was so unexpected that my steps faltered for a moment. 'Why? Are your friends dangerous in some way?'

Ben gave a sound that fell a little short of being a laugh. 'No. Well, not in the way that you mean, anyway. Perhaps I ought to explain more fully.'

'Might be an idea.'

He drew in a deep breath, and I could tell that what he was about to say had already been rehearsed several times in his head before this delivery. That didn't bode well.

'All of the people in this group have known each other for a long time, much longer than they've known me. I suppose you could say I "inherited" them when I bought the house.'

'Like sitting tenants?' I asked, my frown indicating that I still had no idea what he was talking about.

'The group used to meet up in the house regularly, when the architect and his wife lived there. In fact, the reason that any of them got together in the first place was due to the architect's wife, Maria.'

'The woman who was injured in the accident?'

'That's right.'

'The woman who died?'

Ben bit his lip and I could see the doubt written all over

his face. He clearly didn't know if telling this story had been a good idea after all, but he was too far into it to stop now.

'The friends I had round last night – and they *are* my friends now – they all have something in common. Something I'm not sure you would feel comfortable being around.'

Did it suddenly get a degree or two colder in the park, or had some part of me already made the connection? Faces were spinning through my head like an FBI database. Men, women, young, old … what was the connection? Then overlaying that came another set of images: Carla's exotic headwear, her wigs, Tom's crutch propped up in the corner of Ben's kitchen, and who knew how many other clues that I simply hadn't picked up on.

'They're all sick, aren't they? Every one of your group of friends is sick.'

Ben shook his head sadly. I thought I was ready to hear his answer, but I wasn't, not at all.

'No, Sophie. They're all dying.'

Chapter 8

I might as well not have bothered returning to that translation piece, because I certainly couldn't concentrate on anything as mundane as past participles or the subjunctive tense that afternoon. How did Ben cope with that kind of knowledge? How can you look at a group of your friends and know that soon you are going to lose every single one of them? And there's nothing you can do to stop it?

'How did you get involved with them, and ... *why?*' A sudden, truly horrible, possibility occurred to me almost as soon as the question had left my lips. My eyes widened in shock, and instinctively I tried to tug my hand free of Ben's grasp. Only he wouldn't let me.

'I'm fine, Sophie. And for the most part, so are all the people who you met the other night.'

'Except that they're not,' I contradicted, my voice tight. Ben ignored that, and paused before answering, as a group of three children and a dog ran past us, laughing and carefree.

They wove around us and ducked through the forest, heading in the direction of a large lake just visible through the trees. I shivered suddenly, as though a goose had walked over my grave . . . not just one, but a whole flock of them.

'I met a few of the group when I was viewing the house one time,' continued Ben, when we had the path to ourselves once again. 'Adam – Maria's husband – had kept the meetings going, even after his wife was gone. It must have been important to her, so perhaps continuing with it was his way of keeping her close.'

I nodded. I could understand that. 'But what does any of that have to do with *you*? Surely no one expected you to let them carry on meeting at the house after it was sold?' It was a reasonable question, but I know I didn't imagine the disappointment I saw in Ben's eyes when I voiced it.

'No one *expected* me to do that . . . I offered. I was new to the area and didn't know anyone, but when I was introduced to Carla, and then Tom, I felt . . . I don't know . . . inspired by them, I suppose. I'd sold my business, broken up with my girlfriend and moved hundreds of miles away from everyone I knew, but these people who were facing so much uncertainty had a far more positive outlook on living than I did. It felt good being around them. It still does. Believe me, I get more out of this thing than they do. They've taught me a lot.'

If they had, I really hoped it wasn't a lesson he wanted to pass on, because my knee-jerk reaction was to run from this situation and this place, every bit as fast as those three children had just done.

'So, what happens at these meetings at your house?' In my head I could see memorials being planned, hymns being chosen, and debates over the merits of what type of casket to go for. Ben could see from my expression that I still didn't get it.

'Nothing *"happens"*. They get together, they chat, they eat pizza and drink beer. They tell jokes, and talk about their families, and they make plans. They just ... *live*.'

Ben was speaking in a language I simply couldn't understand, despite my chosen profession. He stopped walking and gently placed both hands on my shoulders, turning me to face him, allowing those warm caramel eyes to look straight into mine. 'Sophie, we're *all* going to die ... eventually. No one can alter that. It's what you do before that happens that counts. No one should be remembered for how they died. But how you lived ... well, that's something that shouldn't ever be forgotten.'

He'd spoken of other things for the rest of our walk, but my memory of those topics disappeared, like a goldfish circling a bowl. All I could see was a bleak and lonely future for Ben. What would he do when everyone he had befriended was gone? Was I the only person he knew who wasn't living under a death sentence? That just couldn't be healthy, could it?

Perhaps that was what prompted me to pass on the invitation that I'd practically turned down earlier that day when Julia had phoned and extended it.

'I don't think that's Ben's kind of thing,' I'd told her hesitantly, when she'd put forward her suggestion.

'What? Eating isn't his kind of thing? Doesn't *everyone* eat dinner?'

I'd sighed, and almost given in then without any token resistance. Julia was capable of spotting one of my barricades from half a mile away and knew just how to barrel through them. 'Look, don't worry,' she continued, her voice cajoling, the way you'd try to tempt a wild creature to come just that little bit closer. 'I promise I won't say anything embarrassing or mention how couple-y you two seemed the other day. I can be discreet, when required. But seriously, Soph, Ben did a really nice thing the night Lacey was taken into hospital – well, you both did actually. And inviting you round for dinner gives Gary and me the perfect chance to thank you properly.'

'Can I think about it and get back to you?' I'd asked, already wondering how to make this all go away without offending anyone. So, when we arrived back at the house after our walk, I think I surprised myself more than I did Ben when I found Julia's invitation unexpectedly tripping off my tongue.

'I'd love to,' he accepted, so readily that all the excuses I was prepared to offer as get-out clauses were suddenly made redundant. 'It will be good to meet your friends properly, in a less stressful situation.' I smiled weakly, knowing that an evening trying to avoid Julia's matchmaking landmines was likely to be way more stressful than almost everything we'd already been through together.

*

It wasn't a date, so it didn't really matter if my hair went right or not. But I was very pleased that it did. It wasn't a date, so I didn't need to buy that new top, but it had called out to me when I'd tried to walk past the shop window, and had refused to be quiet until it somehow ended up wrapped in tissue paper, at the bottom of a carrier bag hooked over my arm. It wasn't a date, but I sprayed perfume on my pulse, which was racing just a little too fast, and smoothed red-tinged gloss over my lips that trembled slightly under the sweep of my brush.

It wasn't a date, but I dashed to the door in my kitchen in response to Ben's light knock, like an overexcited teenager. The teenager I'd actually never been, I thought sadly, as I opened the door and saw not Ben, but two enormous plush toys. I knew he had to be there, somewhere, hiding behind the huge bottle-neck dolphin or the cute cuddly tiger. The animals came in first, and Ben followed.

'They look ... big,' I finished lamely. Ben had mentioned that he intended to buy Lacey a get-well gift, which had struck me as a lovely gesture. I just hadn't expected the present was going to be larger than its recipient.

'Well ... one of them is for the baby,' he explained, a small frown of concern clouding his features at my reaction. 'Are they not suitable?'

Something warm and unexpected unfurled deep inside me at his uncertainty. The image of him wandering the aisles of the toy shop, carefully choosing the gifts, made me smile, and I had no real idea why.

'They're absolutely perfect. The kids are going to go crazy

for them.' That much at least was true, especially Lacey. 'And Gary keeps talking about needing to build an extension,' I teased, 'so this is probably just the push he needs to give them somewhere to live.'

Ben grinned. 'I did warn you that I don't know much about children.' He stopped abruptly as though his tongue had been about to run away from him, then shook his head, as though reckless was the new sensible. 'But I do know one thing . . .' He paused just long enough to ensure I was compelled to look up as I waited for him to complete his sentence. 'You look really lovely tonight.' The words hung in the air between us, totally inappropriate between landlord and tenant, and only slightly less so between friends. They were words that surely should only be spoken when something more tangible existed between two people?

'Was that a little too much?' he asked, his voice and expression showing he was willing to back-pedal, if that was what I wanted.

I shook my head, feeling the fullness of my styled hair sway and brush against my cheeks, as though I was in a commercial. 'No. That was . . . nice,' I said, crossing the room to hide my blush as I collected my own more modest gifts for our hosts: a bottle of wine and a bunch of flowers.

We placed the toys Ben had bought on the back seat of the car, and spent much of the journey counting the number of motorists who did a massive double-take at our oversized travelling companions. That was something that I'd been slow to realise about Ben. There was an unexpected lightness and ready humour that sprang from him, like an underground stream that was determined to find its way to the surface. If my default setting was a degree of negativity and a tendency to live in the shadows, his was the exact opposite. Did that make us compatible, or completely mismatched? I was still pondering that one when my old friend opened her front door and ushered us inside.

Lacey, who was still running around in her pyjamas, adored her gift. What three-year-old wouldn't? Her arms could scarcely meet around the blue-grey fur of the dolphin, as she looked up shyly at the man who'd given it to her and mumbled her thanks.

'That is really generous of you, Ben,' Julia declared, reaching up and kissing him lightly on the cheek in greeting. *I* didn't even do that, I thought, and wondered where that unexpected territorial feeling had come from. Especially as I had no valid claim on either the emotion or the man.

'So, Ben, Sophie tells us you've retired,' said Gary, actually misquoting what I'd told them about the man sitting beside me at their dining table. 'You're going to have to tell me how a bloke as young as you has managed to pull that one off. Because this one,' he nodded affectionately towards his wife, 'is going to have me slogging away until I'm well into my eighties.'

Ben took a small sip of the one glass of wine he had allowed himself. 'Actually I'm more on a hiatus, rather than in retirement. I didn't want to rush into anything after I sold my company, so I suppose you could say I'm taking a gap year, of sorts, to figure out which direction I'm going in next.'

'I wish I could have one of those. Or maybe *two* gap years. So I can come back when everyone in the house is properly toilet-trained.' Julia's eyes twinkled mischievously. 'That includes you too,' she teased her husband. Amid the laughter I felt a tiny frisson of envy twist inside me, the way it sometimes did when I realised that so much of Julia's life – even the bits she laughingly complained about – was probably always going to be out of my reach.

Ben said something low and amusing that I totally missed, but which made everyone laugh, so I joined in, my eyes meeting his over the candles Julia had placed on the table. Perhaps he misread the look in my eyes through the flames, for his hand moved across the table and briefly squeezed mine in support. Even though it wasn't the candles that were troubling me, I still smiled warmly at him, liking the way he always seemed to be looking out for me. I glanced across the table and saw that Julia was also smiling – so widely I could practically count her teeth. I should probably be grateful that she wasn't punching the air and cheering.

It was all going well, far too well. It had been years since I'd spent an evening as part of a foursome – probably not since my student days. I'd certainly never introduced Julia and Gary to any of the transient dates who'd briefly travelled in and out of my life. So spending a relaxed evening chatting companionably and laughing should have felt new and strange, but actually it just felt comfortable, familiar, and remarkably easy.

Julia was keeping to her word and had restrained from probing into Ben's past, although I could see the effort to do so was like an impossible itch she was simply dying to scratch. It was actually Gary who ventured into the area I'd mentally cordoned off with the type of tape forensic teams use to protect a crime scene. He'd clearly not been paying attention during the briefing session I'm sure Julia had held before we arrived.

Taking a sip of wine, he cleared his throat, like the father-of-the-bride at a wedding, right before his speech. 'Seriously, guys, I just want to say how much it meant knowing that you were both here for Jules when Lacey got sick.'

'Glad to have been able to help,' said Ben.

'And, I also want to say that I couldn't be happier that Sophie has found someone like you. She said you were one of the good guys, and now that I've met you, I can see what she means.'

He extended his hand to Ben, who after a moment of surprised hesitation, returned the handshake. I looked around the table for a serviette or a handy cushion, anything to gag Gary with, and from the way she was tugging on his sleeve, it looked like Julia felt the same way.

'What?' he said, genuinely unaware he'd done anything wrong. 'I'm just saying that Sophie deserves the kind of guy you can count on in a crisis, and what Ben did for us, and the way he's there for all his sick friends—'

I got to my feet so quickly that I almost extinguished the candles. I reached blindly for some plates and the serving dishes. 'I'll just get some of these in the dishwasher,' I mumbled, heading at speed towards the kitchen.

'It must be hard, though, knowing there's so little you can do to help them,' I heard Gary continue blithely, still unaware the ground he was standing on was my mental quicksand.

'Actually, there's a surprising amount that can be done. I—'

I turned the tap on to full force, drowning out Ben's reply and splashing most of the worktop with water. I busily rinsed dishes that didn't need rinsing, and noisily loaded everything I could lay my hands on into the dishwasher, until the conversation in the adjacent room was a muted rumble of sounds, rather than discernible words.

I waited for longer than I thought was necessary for the topic to be exhausted, setting Julia's coffee maker into action, and pulling cups from the cupboard and milk from the fridge. Even so, when I had no option but to return to the others, the conversation was, unfortunately, still in progress.

'That's a really wonderful thing. What a satisfying project to be involved with,' declared Gary, who seemed totally oblivious of the death ray glare I gave him as I slipped back into my chair. 'You know, Ben, if there's ever anything you think I could help with . . . well, I'd be happy to do that.'

'Thank you. I'll keep it in mind,' said Ben quietly, turning his head and giving me the kind of look that told me he knew exactly how uncomfortable I was feeling. Once again his hand reached out for mine. This time he didn't let it go.

'You knew about this, didn't you, Soph?' Gary asked, so guilelessly that for a moment I actually felt a little bit sorry for him, because Julia was definitely going to kill him after we'd gone home. 'You knew about the bucket list that Ben helps his sick friends with?'

My eyes flew sideways to Ben's, and in them there was so much understanding that I suddenly wanted to cry. 'No,' I said, my voice hushed, as though I was speaking in a holy place. 'Actually, I didn't know.'

'Well, I think it's just fantastic. It must be so rewarding helping them achieve their final ambitions.'

It felt as though Gary had reached deep into my chest, grappled around for my heart, and then ripped it clean out of me. Julia laid her hand firmly on her husband's forearm, and dug her fingers so deeply into the flesh, she left tiny half-moon crescents behind. 'Ow,' he said, in a hurt tone.

Julia gave him no further opportunity to speak. 'Why don't you take Ben out into the garage and show him the classic sports car you're rebuilding?' She said it brightly, in a breezy sing-song voice, but it was pretty obvious to anyone who knew her that it was more of a command than a suggestion.

Ben released my hand and got to his feet. 'I'd love to see that,' he said with a degree of enthusiasm that made me wonder. He'd certainly never expressed any particular interest in the restoration of classic cars before.

Easily derailed, Gary rose too. 'I've still got a long way to go, but I picked up some fantastic genuine parts the other day that . . .'

Julia said nothing until both men had disappeared out of the back door and were headed towards the garage. 'I will kill him. Slowly and painfully. You have my word on it.'

I shook my head, and somehow managed to find a smile. 'He means well.'

'Oh yeah,' said Julia, putting her arms around me and giving me a long hard hug. 'I know he does. It's just that sometimes he forgets there are certain things that you don't like talking about.' She picked up the two empty bottles of wine from the table. 'This probably didn't help his memory either,' she said ruefully.

I gathered up some more items from the table and followed her into the kitchen. 'For what it's worth, despite the huge size twelve foot my husband managed to ram into his mouth, I actually think he was bang on the money about one thing.'

'What do you mean?'

'Ben likes you. *Really* likes you.'

I shook my head and scraped rubbish into the bin with far more concentration than it required. 'He's just a good friend,' was the reply I eventually summoned up in response.

'It's more than that. But guys have liked you before – why wouldn't they? You're lovely.'

'You're biased.'

Julia smiled and poured us both a cup of coffee. 'Maybe

I am. But I'm also smart enough to know that things are different this time.'

'In what way?'

A small smile played around her full lips and the excitement in her eyes made her look just like her daughter had done when she'd seen the dolphin earlier that evening. 'Because this time, my relationship-shy friend, this time *you* like him back. You just don't know it yet.'

The men came back then, both wiping oil-smeared hands on torn-off pieces of kitchen towel, so the answer they interrupted me from giving remained only in my head, which was probably the very best place for it. *'Actually, I do know. I've known for a while now. And frankly, it scares the crap out of me.'*

'I like your friends.' Ben was the first to break the silence in the car. The darkened interior was already warm, with the dashboard heater blowing full blast, yet his words made me glow warmly. The fact that Julia and Gary *were* lovely wasn't anything I could legitimately claim credit for, but his words still felt like a compliment.

'They're great, aren't they?' I agreed. 'I don't know what I'd do without them.'

I winced and bit my lower lip at my thoughtlessness. Ben had good friends too, a whole bunch of them. Except, unlike me, he was going to *have* to learn how to do without every single one of them. I couldn't even begin to imagine how that would feel. Did helping them achieve their final ambitions make it easier to accept losing them? It was a question I knew I was unlikely ever to ask.

When Ben eventually pulled his car onto the drive, and I saw the dressed Christmas tree for the first time, I could feel my eyes widening in surprise. It had disappeared from the driveway several days ago and was now relocated in his front room, lit with what looked like thousands of tiny twinkling white lights. Ben followed my gaze through the windscreen. 'Yeah, I know. It *does* look a bit like Santa's grotto in there. But it took Tom and a couple of his mates so long to help me get it inside, I didn't have the heart to tell them it was just too damn big to stay.'

I got slowly out of the car, my attention still on the sparkling tree, but not so much that I wasn't aware of the soft pressure of Ben's hand when it came to rest companionably on my shoulder. I felt a strong – almost feline – urge to lower my face and rub my cheek against his fingers, which I would seriously regret giving in to – so I didn't.

'Want to come in and see how it looks up close?'

It was getting late, and my own front door was less than ten metres away from where we stood, but suddenly I wasn't ready for the evening to end. And maybe neither was Ben.

'Wow. It looks even bigger now it's upright,' I declared, walking up to the gigantic spruce.

'Uh huh,' replied Ben, struggling not to laugh at the line, which admittedly had sounded like it belonged in a tacky comedy film.

I laughed to cover my embarrassment. 'I mean—'

'I know what you mean,' Ben cut in smoothly, his eyes still twinkling with amusement as he crossed the room to the kitchen, pausing to switch on a couple of table lamps as he went. He opened one of the cupboards, revealing an array of bottles that would rival any bar. It was a reminder of how often he played host, but I stopped that particular thought, because I knew where it would take me, and I really didn't want to go there.

'Brandy?' he asked, lifting an amber-coloured bottle from the shelf. It wasn't what I usually drank, but then none of this was what I usually did. I sighed softly and it sounded like the wind, subtly changing direction. For the first time in a very long while I knew that I wanted things to be different, I just didn't know how to make it happen.

I took the heavy crystal brandy balloon from Ben's outstretched hand, and followed him over to the fireplace. He flicked a switch and the gas flames jumped up and danced obediently to his command. There were many seats to choose from, but I dropped down to my knees onto the thick sheepskin rug in front of the fire. Ben followed my lead, sitting opposite me with his back resting against a settee. Music had been playing softly when he'd let us in. 'I never like coming back to a silent house, it always feels unwelcoming,' he explained, picking up the remote control and turning down the volume of the haunting jazz saxophone playing from concealed speakers.

'Perhaps you should get a cat. They're a cure-all for silence and loneliness.'

Ben's eyes looked darker in this light as they met mine over the rim of his glass. I dropped my gaze, studying the swirling brandy in my own balloon so intently it looked like I'd lost something in there.

'Are *you* lonely, Sophie?'

His question side-swiped me and I stalled my answer by taking a large mouthful of brandy. It was a ploy that didn't end well, as the fiery liquid burnt a pathway down my throat, making me cough like a teenager sneaking alcohol. Ben shifted towards me, gently removing the glass from my hand, and patting my back, in a way that would probably have been totally ineffective if I was *actually* choking, but it felt nice anyway.

Streaming eyes looked up at him when eventually the spasm had passed.

'Do you need some water?'

I shook my head, feeling a little embarrassed. The hand was still positioned somewhere between my shoulder blades, his fingers resting just above the low scooped-out back of my new top. It was hard to concentrate on anything with them there.

'You never answered my question.'

'Everyone feels lonely now and again,' I said, aware I was hiding behind the generalisation. 'Being alone doesn't make you lonely, but being in a crowd doesn't safeguard against it either.'

Ben nodded slowly, as though my words revealed a truth he had already uncovered. I shifted slightly on the thick fur of the rug and felt his hand drop away. The Christmas tree lights were running in a mesmerising sequence, each LED bulb chasing the one beside it in a never-ending game of tag.

'It's so pretty,' I said, unconsciously breathing in deeply to inhale the foresty scent of pine which filled the room. 'I'd forgotten how a real tree smells.'

'You don't have one at home?'

My eyes clouded, because I remembered the trees of my childhood. I remembered walking down endless rows of them in the garden centre, while our parents argued good-humouredly about which one was too big to fit in the lounge, while Scott and I waited impatiently for them to buy a tree – any tree – so that the fun of decorating it could begin. That was always our job. I could close my eyes and see it so clearly, sitting on his shoulders to reach the upper branches, like we were at a rock concert, except no self-respecting rocker would wear a silly Santa hat. I remember Scott wobbling as I reached up to place the star on the topmost branch and then collapsing into hysterical laughter as he dropped me onto the sofa cushions, declaring in the way that only a brother could, *'Definitely no more mince pies for you, you big lump.'* There was irony there, because in those days I was still as thin as a rake.

I snapped back to the present, shutting the memories back in the box where they belonged. 'No. We have an artificial tree, a tinsel one,' I said sadly.

The memory had led me, almost organically, to the question that I'd put off asking him ever since my return from my parents' house. I still didn't know whether it was the right thing to do, or whether I should continue as I'd done all of my adult life, keeping the sectors of my world totally separate.

The question came out almost of its own volition, as though it had grown impatient with waiting to be asked. 'Ben, what are your plans for Christmas? I mean, I know it's very short notice and you've probably already made arrangements and everything, and I totally understand that, especially as some of your friends might—'

'I'd love to.'

I sat up straighter, blinking in surprise like an owl. 'Huh?'

'I'd love to spend Christmas with you and your family,' he elaborated with a smile.

'He's going to be fine,' Ben reassured as we drove away from the neat little maisonette. 'Your biggest problem is probably going to be persuading him to ever come back.'

'I know,' I said, smiling weakly as I twisted in my car seat and looked back at the house, where Fred was most likely still comfortably cradled in Alice's arms, purring contentedly at the unexpected upgrade in his lodgings. A mix-up at the cattery had put my Christmas plans in jeopardy, and the shot of instant relief I'd felt had been like adrenalin into a vein. It was telling that my first reaction was to feel that I'd somehow dodged a bullet – even though I was the one who'd pulled the trigger.

When Ben had come up with an obvious solution to the problem, in the form of Alice – who clearly adored cats – I should have felt grateful. Instead I just felt rattled that the opportunity to rescind my invitation had slipped through my fingers.

'It was like I was about to get pardoned, and then at the last minute someone discovered the electric chair was working after all.'

Julia laughed at the other end of the phone. 'You're the only person I know who could possibly come up with that comparison. This was *your* idea in the first place, remember?'

'It was a bad one,' I said mulishly.

She had been listening to me reversing backwards and forwards over my decision for days, and had obviously decided the time had come for some tough love. 'Speaking as one of the few people you've invited home over the last sixteen years, I'm going to have to disagree with you on this one. I actually believe this is *exactly* what you – and your parents – need. Ben's visit will be like opening a window in a musty room.' My mother, who was borderline obsessive when it came to housework, wouldn't have liked that analogy, but I knew what Julia meant. And in a little over four hours, traffic permitting, I would find out if she was right . . . one way or another.

My reluctance to ever become involved with anyone had left a great many gaps in my life. Gaps that I hadn't even realised existed until now. For instance, I'd never gone away with a man, I thought, marvelling at the novelty of seeing my case propped up next to Ben's in the boot of his car. He caught me staring at the two cases with a curious expression on my face.

'Have you forgotten to pack something?' he guessed, way off beam.

'Erm, I'm not sure,' I lied, because telling him what I was *really* thinking was out of the question.

'We can always stop at the services on the way, and you can pick up whatever it is you're missing.'

I smiled up at him before slamming the boot to a close. Somehow I seriously doubted whether the Moto shop would be able to supply me with sixteen years of lost opportunities. Ben paused before starting the engine, patiently waiting for me to buckle up. The only other person I'd known who'd been that safety-conscious had been my driving instructor – and probably with very good reason.

'I'm still happy to share the driving, if you'd like,' I offered once again, fully expecting him to decline, as he'd done earlier.

'If I get tired, I'll let you know,' he replied. I smiled, wondering if he was a nervous passenger (he didn't seem the type), was precious about his car (he *definitely* didn't seem the type), or just preferred – quite literally – to be in the driving seat.

I shrugged easily. 'Well, just let me know if you change your mind. The roads outside Cotterham can be a bit of a nightmare if you're not familiar with them, especially if it's dark by the time we get there.'

Ben gave me a quick glance, and I wondered if I'd some-how bruised his ego. The only time I could ever remember seeing Gary get prickly with Julia was when she'd decided to criticise his driving. Somehow, though, I didn't think that was behind the look on Ben's face as he returned his attention to the road.

'Not that I don't feel safe with you,' I felt the need to add on a rush. 'Because I absolutely do. Completely safe.'

He looked back to me, and I was relieved to see the light of amusement dancing in his eyes, like tiny fireflies. No damage had been done here. 'I'm very glad to hear it,' Ben replied, his voice low and as mysterious to fathom as a purr.

Perhaps he didn't trust me with his car, but I *was* in charge of the music for our journey. Given that it was the day before Christmas Eve, he really shouldn't have been surprised when I pulled a Christmas CD I'd borrowed from Julia out of my bag.

'Just as long as you don't expect me to sing along,' he warned with a good-natured grin, as I extracted the classic jazz album from the player and replaced it with the cheesy Christmas one.

'I'm afraid I may well do,' I said with a solemn nod, which earned me a deep throaty laugh.

'I think this is going to feel like a very long journey,' Ben predicted, his voice attempting to sound dire. It had *already* been a long journey to get to this point, but I didn't think that was what he'd meant at all.

We stopped once at the services, for coffee and to stretch our legs. I'd noticed Ben had been flexing his tiredly as we drove, but admitting my attention had been focused on his thigh seemed more than a bit pervy, so I made no comment when I saw him walking a little stiffly as we crossed the car park. Practically every vehicle we passed was loaded up like a sleigh with presents, and Ben's own back seat was no exception. His box of glossy red parcels, decorated with shiny silver ribbon and bows, had made my own supermarket-paper-wrapped gifts look a little sad. There was also a box of fine wines and a delicate orchid he'd bought as 'extras' for my parents. His generosity meant I was already worrying that the book on the history of jazz that I'd felt so delighted to have found for him was starting to feel inadequate.

And that wasn't the only thing I was concerned about. Every time I tried to imagine how it would feel to see Ben sitting at our family Christmas table, in the chair that had remained vacant for so many years, the bundle of tension in the pit of my stomach stirred like a sleeping dragon. This was yet another life experience I had no knowledge of. Did everyone get this nervous when they introduced someone they liked to their family? And wasn't it just about the most ridiculous thing in the world that I'd reached the age of thirty-one before asking myself that question?

When we emerged from the services the first strands of darkness were already pencilling in the edges of the sky, changing the picture from day to night.

'I don't think we're going to get there before dark,' I predicted with a worried frown, a fact that was quickly confirmed by the voice of the radio announcer, with her report of a jack-knifed lorry and hours of potential delays. Ben gave a helpless shrug, and only looked concerned when

I reached for my phone and began to text, my fingers flying over the screen.

'Ever since Scott's accident, they worry whenever there's a delay. It's something I'm always conscious of.'

Ben looked instantly contrite. 'Of course. I'm sorry, I wasn't thinking. Naturally they would worry.'

Several minutes later my frustration had grown. 'I still have absolutely no signal.'

'Here, try mine,' Ben offered, passing me his phone, which I couldn't help notice was warm from where it had been resting against his hip. I dialled my parents' number and held the phone against my cheek, touching him by proxy.

There was no answer on the home phone, but it was possible they were out buying last-minute holiday provisions. The signal kept dropping in and out, and as the traffic jam we were now stuck in was practically stationary, I knew my message was going to have to wait.

'Hang on to it,' offered Ben as I went to pass him his phone. 'One of them is bound to pick up a signal sooner or later.'

I used my phone rather than Ben's, because his was unfairly booby-trapped. I'd seen the contact name '*Holly*' when I was trying to message from his handset, and although I was pleased that my fingers had respected his privacy and stayed away from the string of old messages, my eyes had taken a sneaky glance at the last date contact had been made, and then really wished they hadn't. Serves you right for looking, I told myself waspishly. And anyway, why *shouldn't* Ben be in contact with his ex-girlfriend? Clearly there was a lot of history between them, while he and I had absolutely none. But the prospect of creating some had been glimmering in the distance, like a candle promising a welcome in a place I'd never been before. So it was understandably crushing to realise that *Holly Whoever-She-Was* was perhaps not quite as 'ex' as I would have preferred her to be.

There are many things that you're not meant to do on a road trip. Blow up petrol tankers, as though you were starring in *Thelma & Louise*; eat hard-boiled eggs – for a great many reasons; and fall asleep when you're meant to be navigating. I was guilty of the last transgression. In my defence, the car *was* extremely warm, the headrest comfortable, and the CD – now on its fifth or six cycle – had practically hypnotised me into a Yuletide stupor. Sleep was a bandit, waiting to ambush me the moment my lids fluttered to a close, and it was an easy victory.

I woke up with a start of guilt, realising by the thrum of the road beneath our tyres that we were finally free of the motorway traffic jam. I was slumped a little in the passenger seat and quickly wriggled upright, horrified when I saw the clock had moved on an entire hour since the last time I'd said a word.

'I'm so sorry, Ben. You should have woken me. I didn't mean to—' I broke off from my apology as a very familiar church flashed past my window. It was the one I'd visited

many times throughout my life, and was less than five minutes' drive from my family home.

'How did you know how to get us here?' I asked, twisting
in my seat to verify my surroundings. Yes, there was the park
I used to play in, and a little further up ahead was the football
ground where I'd spent countless Sunday mornings, proudly
cheering on my older brother and his team. 'I didn't give you
my address, did I?' I asked, knowing without a shadow of a
doubt that I had not.

'No,' replied Ben, looking a little uncomfortable at the
sudden inquisition he was facing.

'Then how did you know how to get us here?'

Ben picked up his phone, with its map screen still displayed. 'Cotterham isn't as tricky to negotiate as you made
it sound. I just took a chance on which side of the town I
wanted. The odds were fifty-fifty. I was just about to wake
you up actually, for the final directions.'

Something was a little off in his tone. It was just a little too
smooth, as though he'd practised this explanation in his head
before trying it out for real. Ben clicked on the indicator and
pulled over to the kerb.

'Is something wrong, Sophie?'

I could see him quite clearly beneath the orange light of
the street lamp that we'd pulled up beside. So what if he'd
taken a lucky guess and had just happened to have got it
right? That wasn't so strange really, was it? Blaming him for
having a good sense of direction seemed like a very bad way
to start our Christmas holiday.

I smiled, and it almost reached my eyes. I was still half asleep, I told myself. Still in that state where dream logic seems more valid than the waking variety. It was a good enough explanation to go with, but I already knew the truth went deeper than that. I was still looking suspiciously for the flaws to reveal themselves in Ben. He was just too nice, too perfect. I was still waiting for the other shoe to drop, and hoping all the time that it wouldn't crush both me and my hopes underfoot when it inevitably did.

That my parents were struggling with this unfamiliar territory almost as much as I was quickly became apparent. I'd certainly never heard my dad discuss motorways and link roads in such depth before, but he managed to extract a fifteen-minute conversation on the topic when we first arrived. Almost seamlessly my mother took over with a dialogue that meandered from free-range turkeys and somehow – and I truly have no idea how – to the poorly written, but racy, bestseller her book club was currently reading. Road pollution to soft porn all within thirty minutes of Ben's arrival. I threw him a look of apology across my parents' lounge, wondering if he was already regretting accepting my invitation. To be fair, I could see no evidence of it in his eyes. To say the entire Winter family was nervous was a huge understatement.

I don't think I drew in a single clear breath until after my parents had bidden us goodnight, apologising as they did so for retiring so early. I felt the tension leaving me, like air escaping an inflatable, as I heard their slow trudging steps climbing the stairs. I waited until I was positive they were out of earshot before turning to Ben in apology.

'I'm so sorry.'

Ben looked genuinely baffled. 'What for?'

'For the atmosphere, for all the questions, for every conversation that began with the name *"Scott"*. Perhaps I ought to have warned you about the way things are.'

Ben rose from the armchair beside the fire and squeezed into the space beside me on the old but comfortable two-seater sofa. 'Sophie, everything was fine. Yes, your parents talk about your brother quite a bit – but that's only natural. And they both seem very nice. In fact, they're exactly as I'd expected them to be. I knew I'd like them.'

'And why was that?'

'Because this family and these people are where *you* came from,' was Ben's quietly spoken reply, which effectively stole all other thoughts from my head for several moments.

I leant back against the sofa cushions and closed my eyes, suddenly exhausted, as I listened to the familiar sounds of the house I'd grown up in reintroduce themselves. I was drifting, hearing the tuneless whistle of the wind blowing down the chimney, when Ben's words brought me back with a jump.

'Where are you?'

I blinked sleepily, about to apologise for being almost as bad at hosting as I was at navigating, when I saw him scanning the room from left to right, sweeping over the objects within it like a security camera. My own eyes followed in his wake, still not understanding his question.

'Where are you in this room?' asked Ben, his scrutiny of our surroundings done, as his attention swept back to me. I didn't need to look any further at the collection of precious mementoes to know what he was talking about. 'The pictures on the mantelpiece, the walls and the shelves, they're all of your brother, not you.'

I straightened in my seat, suddenly defensive. 'That's not true. I'm in loads of them.'

Ben's eyes flashed briefly to the line of assorted photo frames. 'Not that many. And never on your own.'

'Perhaps I'm just not that photogenic,' I batted back, a little more sharply than I intended.

Ben's hand came out, so unexpectedly that I think I actually gasped quietly when his fingers rested beneath my chin and gently lifted it. 'That's just not true,' he corrected.

I wasn't sure how I felt about those words, or those fingers, but before I had a chance to examine my reaction they were both gone. His hand gestured towards a glass-fronted display cabinet. 'Every trophy in there, every single one, is your brother's. Why is that?'

'I guess it's because I never played football.' It was a glib attempt to inject some much-needed humour into a conversation that suddenly felt as though it was spiralling out of my control.

Ben shook his head sadly. 'Don't do that. Don't let them make you invisible.'

My eyes were stinging uncomfortably, but I was determined not to cry. 'It's not them – well, it's not *just* them. It was me, too. We all wanted – no, *needed* – to keep as much of Scott around us as possible. *I* was the one who took down my piano certificates and the other photographs, not my parents.'

Ben's eyes were sad and also a little bit angry. 'But they didn't stop you. And they should have.'

We were making up the sofa bed in the den, a name that made the room sound far cosier than it actually was, when Ben picked up on something I thought had slipped under his radar.

'So, how come you've never mentioned that you play the piano?'

I thumped the pillow a couple of times, flattening the feathers inside it, and then flipped it over, attacking the ones on the other side as though they'd annoyed me in some way.

'Played,' I corrected.

'You don't do it any more?'

I looked over to the wall, where a large bookcase now stood in the spot where once an upright piano had been positioned. If you looked very closely, and the light was just right, you could still see the vague outline of its shape in the faded pattern of the carpet. 'We sold the piano.'

'Why?' Ben asked, executing a highly efficient hospital-corner fold, before tucking the sheet and blanket beneath the mattress. I wondered where he'd learnt to do that; the glamorous ex-girlfriend didn't look the precision bed-making type. Perhaps Ben had been an army cadet, I pondered, realising I could easily fill a dozen notebooks with all the things I *didn't* know about him.

'I guess I outgrew my love of playing,' I said, which told only half the story. Ben's expression said he didn't need to ask exactly *when* in my life that had happened, because he'd already worked out the answer.

I bent down and tweaked the covers on his bed, smoothing the blankets flat, and tried not to allow my thoughts to stray to the body that would shortly be lying beneath them. My own room was directly above his, and I knew there'd be plenty of time for me to think about that while lying awake in my own bed.

Chapter 9

It had been a long time since I'd heard the sound of a male voice raised in laughter with my mum's: a voice that wasn't my father's, that is. It made me pause in the hallway outside the kitchen, with a slight stomach-lurching feeling, the kind you get when you go to step on a stair that doesn't exist. I shook my head, which already felt muzzy and thick from sleeping clean through my alarm. Leaving Ben to deal with my parents – who he'd really only just met – was inexcusably rude, but when I opened the kitchen door and saw him happily seated at the table, devouring thick slices of hot buttery toast and marmalade, most of my guilt disappeared.

'Good morning, sleepy head,' greeted my mum. There was a pink flush on her cheeks and cheeriness in her tone that I struggled to recognise as belonging to her at all. Ben's smile was warm and there was a decided twinkle in his eyes as they silently messaged mine over the rim of his mug of tea. Somehow, while I slept, he seemed to have added yet another conquest to his curious senior-citizen fan club. How did he *do* that, I wondered, slipping into the chair he had pulled out for me. Was every single person who met him equally charmed? Perhaps I shouldn't be so surprised that I was so drawn to him after all ... clearly *everyone* was.

'You and I have a busy day ahead,' advised Ben, watching me shake Corn Flakes into a bowl. 'We've got a turkey to pick up, an order to collect from a farm shop and a guided tour to squeeze in before it gets dark.'

I glanced out through the kitchen window. The skies were already dark, but that was due to the thick clouds that hung like a platform across the sky. They held a promise of snow, and bookmakers everywhere were probably already regretting the odds they'd given against a white Christmas.

'I volunteered us,' Ben added unnecessarily. 'But I'm not sure your mum thinks we're up to the task.'

'Oh you,' said my mother, sounding so much like someone I've never met before, my spoonful of cereal stopped halfway to my mouth. Was she actually blushing? Oh my God, she really was. Had Ben slipped something into her tea?

I shook my head, wondering what kind of alternative universe I'd accidentally woken up in. 'Guided tour?' I asked, picking the least innocuous question to pose, rather than the one I really wanted to ask: *'What the hell have you done with my real mother?'*

'I want to see the town you grew up in.'

'Really?'

'Yes. I want to see where you went to school, the park you

played in, where you learnt to ride a bike,' he glanced across the kitchen to check my mother wasn't listening, 'where you went on your very first date and had your first kiss.'

I swallowed slowly and leant a little closer towards him across the breakfast dishes. 'Some of those experiences were a good deal more memorable than others,' I confessed on a low whisper.

His interest was piqued, the way I knew it would be. 'And are there any that you'd particularly like to revisit?'

I got to my feet and began collecting up the dirty crockery. My hair fell forward, hiding an unfamiliar mischievous grin from anyone but him. 'I couldn't possibly say.'

He was laughing softly as I began to load the dishwasher. Forget the mystery of what he'd done with my mother ... what had he done to *me*? Because even I didn't recognise myself in the teasing woman, who was enjoying the unaccustomed banter and was looking forward to the day ahead far more than anything in a very long time.

The turkey was making its last journey ever, in the boot of Ben's car, and we'd carried two laden boxes of fruit and vegetables from the busy farm shop that would definitely be enough for Christmas – even if the holiday season was suddenly extended until the end of January.

'She still shops as though she's feeding a ravenous teenage boy,' I remarked, wondering yet again why so many of my family's habits were locked up in a time warp belonging to the past.

'Phew, for a minute I thought *I* was responsible for this mammoth shop.'

'Well, that might also be part of the reason.' I dug my hands deeper into the pockets of the old sheepskin jacket I'd found at the back of my wardrobe. 'But that doesn't mean you were supposed to pick up the bill.'

Ben's nose wrinkled, and I suddenly caught a glimpse of the boy he must once have been. Or perhaps a peek of the son he might one day father. The thought made me shiver unexpectedly. 'Hmm ... you saw that, did you?'

''Fraid so. And there's no way *that* isn't going to be repaid.' There was a mischievous twinkle in his eyes as he took hold of my arm and tucked it firmly under one of his. 'Tell you what, I saw they had a café in the back of the farm shop. Why don't you buy us both a fancy coffee and we'll call it quits?'

The café was a bright modern extension on the back of the converted barn, which was now a farm shop. Floor-to-ceiling walls of glass covered two sides of the building, which offered amazing views out over rolling countryside. My eyes went to the windows, as they'd always done, checking to see if the neighbouring herd of cows were still cheekily pushing their noses up against the mesh fence. They were.

A young harried waitress approached us almost at a run. It looked like we weren't the only shoppers who'd decided to reward themselves with a coffee and cake treat that morning. My eyes scanned the large room, filled with light oak tables that perfectly matched the exposed beams and roof supports, scoping for a vacant table.

'There's one over there in the corner,' I said, spotting the only empty table in the whole cafe. Old habits die hard.

'Oh, yes. Thanks,' said the girl, flustered that I'd done her job for her. But then, of course, I *had* been doing her job, when she was probably still only a baby.

Ben smiled widely as we took our seats beside the window. Despite the darkening skies, it was still a very impressive view. 'This is really nice,' he declared, reaching for the menu. 'So what do you recommend?'

'The scones here are amazing.'

'Scones it is,' he agreed, happily repeating our choice to the middle-aged woman who arrived to take our order a few moments later. I didn't need to read the badge pinned to her ample chest to know her name.

'English breakfast tea, or would you prefer—?' She stopped comically halfway through the question, her eyes widening in astonishment. 'Sophie? Sophie Winter? Is that you?'

My hand went automatically to my new haircut, although I knew that wasn't the most drastic change in my appearance since we'd last met. She put down her pad and pen and enveloped me in a hug so prolonged, several nearby customers looked our way and smiled.

'Hello, Marjorie,' I said, genuinely pleased to see her again. 'How are you?' My old boss stepped back, her head still shaking slightly in disbelief.

'Oh my goodness, sweetheart. I hardly recognised you. It's been *such* a long time.'

I nodded in acknowledgement. 'Probably not since I left for university.'

'And just look at you. You look so different from when you were my number one Saturday girl. There's hardly anything of you any more.'

I'm not sure I deserved the title or the compliment, although admittedly I was probably several dress sizes smaller than I'd been when I worked there. I was very aware of Ben quietly watching our reunion, and hurriedly introduced them.

'Very nice to meet you, Ben,' Marjorie said warmly, shaking the hand he had politely extended. 'So are you Sophie's young man?' she asked, in that please–ground–open–up–and–swallow–me–now way I'd quite forgotten she had.

I looked over at Ben, totally floored by what should have been a perfectly straightforward 'No' reply. Ben stepped in smoothly to save my embarrassment. 'I think I'm probably a little too old to be called anyone's "*young*" anything,' he joked. It was a good response, and Marjorie was still chuckling over it as she went off to fill our order.

'So you play the piano *and* you used to be a waitress,' Ben declared, like an archaeologist who'd just made a fascinating discovery. 'This is turning out to be a very illuminating visit.'

'Well, everyone's got a skeleton or two rattling away in their closet, haven't they?'

For the first time that day, a fleeting look of sadness passed behind the golden caramel of Ben's eyes. Was he thinking of his ex-girlfriend? This time last year she'd probably been by his side, skiing down a mountain slope in St. Moritz or Klosters or some other expensive resort I was never likely to visit. 'It's just that my skeleton was a little more "well-padded" back in the day.'

Ben's expression softened, and I was suddenly aware of his eyes travelling over my body, in a way I don't think I'd ever seen them do before. 'I think I'd have quite liked to see a more ... curvaceous you.'

'I doubt it,' I said, surprised that my voice still sounded bitter as I remembered that black period of my past, and what had caused it. 'They call it comfort eating. Apparently it's fairly common after a bereavement.' I sighed sadly, and fiddled with the upturned teacup on its mismatched floral saucer. 'Only I didn't gain comfort, just weight.'

'This was after Scott's accident?' Ben probed gently.

'After his death,' I corrected, because I never had been able to see the point in hiding behind a euphemism.

'I'm so sorry you went through such an awful time back then,' said Ben, his hand reaching across the table to hold mine. I looked down at it, wondering if Marjorie was secretly watching us from behind the counter, thinking it meant something else altogether. 'I really wish I'd known you back then. I'd have liked to have been able to help take some of that pain away.'

'No one could have done that.'

Ben nodded, and he looked so moved that I felt it was my job to lighten the dark mood I'd dragged us both down into.

'But the good thing is that you *did* come along just when I needed you. And I remain very glad that you did.'

'Me too, Sophie. And now that I'm here, you might as well know that I've no plans of going anywhere else until you're thoroughly fed up with having me around, and send me packing.'

Long ropes of coloured lights were strung from the surrounding trees, and every so often delicious wafts of hot mulled wine floated over the heads of the assembled singers. It had been years since I'd last attended the late-night carol concert on the town common, although some of my earliest and best memories centred around this local tradition. I'd forgotten how much I'd always loved the Dickensian atmosphere, with friends, family and neighbours gathered together beside a twinkling Christmas tree, everyone holding lanterns, and linking arms and generally looking like we'd all stepped straight out of a traditional Christmas card. Attending the concert was yet another door that we'd quietly closed after losing Scott.

But tonight, with Ben at my side, I was glad that I'd come. I looked up at him, and despite the ankle-deep snow on the ground and the crisp night air that threatened there was more still to come, I felt warm. Ben's lips were moving soundlessly, his eyes following the words on the carol sheet, but I was the only one close enough to know he was only pretending to sing. My own mouth curled into a smile. One day, I vowed, I would persuade him to sing to me, just to find out if his voice really was as awful as he claimed. He looked up and caught me watching him and gave an almost imperceptible wink before silently belting out the carol's familiar chorus.

I hadn't really been surprised when my parents had chosen not to accompany us. My years of living away from home had given me the benefit of anonymity, but for them it was so much harder. Events like this were an ordeal that they'd sooner not put themselves through and I could hardly blame them for that. It's a difficult time of year to act as though you're 'joyful and triumphant', when you're really not.

Embarrassingly *Silent Night* had made me a little teary, and while I was still pretending I had something in my eye, Ben gently pressed a folded tissue into my palm and pulled me firmly against his side. *Was that the moment? Was that when it happened? Perhaps.*

After the concert people were milling around in small clusters, not wanting the magic of the evening to end, or perhaps just waiting until the mulled wine ran out. Ben had carried our plastic beakers over to one of the trees covered in fairy lights, and we stood beneath its boughs, drinking in both the atmosphere and the fragrant beverage.

'To the best Christmas Eve I've had in years,' Ben said, nudging his cup against mine in a toast.

'When you've holidayed at some of the fanciest ski resorts in the world, that's quite a claim.'

'It's not about the location,' he declared, his voice dropping to little more than a whisper as he leant closer. 'It's about who you're with.' For a crazy moment I thought he was going to kiss me, right there on the common with half of the town standing around as spectators. Instead he teased a single lock of hair that had blown across my eyes back into place with his finger. Long after his hand was gone I could still feel the route of his touch against my temple. *Was that the moment?*

When the town clock chimed half past eleven, I was genuinely surprised. The evening, like the day that had preceded it, had flown by far too quickly and I didn't want it to be over. As parking near the common was limited, we'd left Ben's car at home, and after seeing the long snaking queue waiting for a taxi, I suggested that we walk.

'I know it's cold, but it's not that far.'

Ben happily agreed, and I told myself that perhaps he too didn't want this day to come to an end. I turned up the collar of my sheepskin jacket to keep out the first intrepid snowflakes that were beginning to fall as we headed away from the common. Our route home took us past a small copse which was bordered by a narrow footpath. It was somewhere I can remember Scott warning me never to walk alone. *'Just phone if you ever get stuck in town, it doesn't matter what time it is. Never, ever, walk there by yourself. Promise.'* Many older brothers are overprotective, but Scott had practically turned it into an art form. Would he have approved of the man walking behind me, stepping in my snowy footprints as I led us home? Would *any* man ever have been good enough for his baby sister? I wondered. I was still asking myself impossible questions when Ben's small cry of surprise came from behind me. I spun on my heel, almost losing my balance on the slippery path, to see ... no one at all. Ben was no longer there.

'Ben? Ben?' The pathway was unlit and it was practically impossible to see anything. 'Ben?' This time there was a tiny thread of panic in my voice, as a thousand Christmas ghost stories, all of which seemed to involve a headless horseman, suddenly came to mind.

'Down here,' said his voice, from somewhere to the left of the path, at the base of a sloping grassy bank. Except, of course, the bank wasn't grassy at all right now, it was covered in snow and looked more like a miniature ski jump.

I pulled my phone from my pocket and by the light of its torch I pointed it in the direction of his voice. The beam of light found him, lying on his back on the grass, a track of disturbed snow showing his passage from the pathway. I raked the spotlight over him, panicked that he'd hurt himself. The beam swept up to his face, which bore an unreadable expression, but it didn't seem to be one of pain. Nevertheless, 'Are you hurt?' was my first question.

He shook his head, and somewhere along the way the strange look on his face disappeared, leaving only a rueful smile. 'Just what did they put in that mulled wine?'

I knew two small beakers of fruit-flavoured alcoholic beverage weren't responsible, but perhaps *I* was. 'I should have warned you the path was getting slippery,' I said, feeling guilty. Ben still hadn't risen to his feet, and I was starting to worry that, despite his assurances, he actually *had* injured himself in the fall. 'Can you get up?'

His mouth opened and then closed again on a smile. 'I might need a hand,' he said unexpectedly. I let my bag drop from my shoulder and immediately slithered down the slope to reach him. I was pretty certain he was unhurt at that point, but when he held out his hand for assistance, I unhesitatingly gripped it and braced myself to lever him up. But the moment his fingers curled around mine, *he* was the one who pulled, taking me unexpectedly off my feet to land with a soft *whumph* on the snow, making it billow up all around us like a powder puff.

'Very funny,' I said, wondering if the urge to grab a handful of snow and thrust it down the back of his jacket was too childish to consider.

'I thought I'd revisit the experience of having you land on me, from a more manageable height this time,' he teased.

I pushed playfully at his shoulder, far more off-balance mentally than I was physically. 'I was worried you were really hurt.'

'Sorry,' he said, sounding contrite. He hesitated for a moment and bit his lip, with an unfamiliar expression of uncertainty on his face. 'It just seemed too good an opportunity.'

'For what?'

Ben paused, his head slightly cocked to one side, as though he was waiting for something. Perhaps he *was* hurt. Perhaps he'd hit his head, because he was certainly acting very strangely.

'Ben . . .? Too good an opportunity for what?' I repeated.

From the distant common the first chime rang clearly across the cold night sky, signalling Christmas morning. It was the cue he'd obviously been waiting for. 'If this is going to be the Christmas I never want to forget, I wanted it to start just right.'

And then his mouth wasn't talking any more. It was on mine, and it tasted of wine, and snow and cold and bizarrely it tasted of coming home. The kiss lasted far longer than the clock tower chimes did, and we were both a little breathless when we finally pulled apart.

'I told myself I wasn't going to do that, that it was too soon, and that we didn't need this kind of complication in our lives,' he confided in the dark.

'You told yourself all that?'

'I did.'

I wondered if he could tell from my voice that I was smiling. 'So what happened?'

His arms tightened around my back as he pulled me towards him again. 'I also told myself I was an idiot if I missed this chance.'

And then he kissed me again. And *that's* when I finally knew the answer to the question I'd been silently asking myself. *That* was the moment when I knew I was falling in love for the very first time.

I studied Ben as we sat around the Christmas tree the following morning, trying to see if his face bore the same signs that mine did: those of a person who'd spent a disproportionate amount of time re-living those minutes in the snow over and over again. His eyes looked bright and clear, and despite a night on our seriously ancient sofa bed, he looked well rested. I smiled at him over the top of my obligatory glass of sherry, feeling a warm flush flood my cheeks when he smiled back in a way I convinced myself said so much more than just *'Good morning'*.

The house was redolent with the smell of roasting turkey, and King's College Choir were dutifully going through their repertoire from the speakers in the lounge, when I'd descended the stairs. The aromas and sounds of the season were all very familiar, but everything within me felt new and different. I'd seen it on my face as I quickly applied a coat of mascara and ran some gloss over my lips; lips which I swear I could still taste him upon. I should have set my alarm, I told myself, as I pushed open the door to the lounge and found Ben deep in conversation with my parents, because now I'd lost the chance to speak to him before the rituals of the day swept us up in a rollercoaster of activity. But if we'd *had* a moment of privacy, what would I have said to him? Had what happened the night before been just a spur-of-the-moment romantic impulse, or did it mean something more? At thirty-one I should have enough experience to know the answers to those questions, but I simply didn't have a clue.

'Merry Christmas!' had been Ben's greeting, as he got to his feet and kissed my cheek, in a totally appropriate 'great-aunt' kind of a kiss. A small flickering flame extinguished in my heart, only to be rekindled again as his fingers grazed and lingered against my palm before he returned to his seat. It was subtle and fleeting, but it told me everything I was hoping to hear.

'There was a time you'd *never* have been late down on Christmas morning,' declared my dad. 'You and Scott used to . . .' He stopped, like an actor who'd just corpsed in front of a full house, and spent a moment or two awkwardly clearing his throat.

My mother's smile was far too bright, far too wide, and I saw her eye unconsciously flash to a single parcel almost buried beneath the back of the tree. I didn't need to read the silver foil gift tag to know who it was for.

'So, presents!' I declared brightly, sounding frighteningly like a presenter on a children's television programme. 'Shall we do presents?'

I like Christmas. I like the tradition of it all. As a family we held on to every old ritual from the past, changing nothing, afraid to let go of even one tiny element in case yet another memory of Scott faded away. But this year we were in new territory, re-writing the present and perhaps even looking forwards instead of backwards. All because of Ben. I looked up, and for just one fleeting moment I could imagine Scott watching us, leaning up against the wall in that old familiar stance of his, one leg raised, the sole of his shoe planted flat against the floral patterned wallpaper. Only this time that boot would leave no mark. He'd have been a little older than Ben by now, if the accident hadn't taken him from us, but the

Scott of my memory, the one smiling slightly as he watched us from across the room, was seventeen, with a familiar devilish glint in his eyes. He never aged, he never changed; death had made him immortal. I blinked, and he was gone.

'And this is for you and Ted,' Ben declared, pulling a large flat gift from the bag beside him.

'Oh Ben, you shouldn't have,' said my mother, knowing exactly what she was meant to say. Then she pulled off the ribbon to reveal the gift within the shiny red paper, and didn't know what to say at all. And frankly neither did I. For a start I had absolutely no idea when the photograph in the silver frame had been taken.

'What a lovely picture of you,' my mother declared. 'When was this taken, Sophie?'

I gave a puzzled shrug. 'I have absolutely no idea. Ben?' I batted the question on to the man who'd secretly photographed me, and wondered if I should find that disturbing, in a stalker kind of way, or just sweet.

Ben's answer was relaxed and believable, and suddenly I remembered exactly the day the photograph must have been taken. Winter sunlight had been slanting down through the tropical plants in his garden and believing I was the only one at home, I'd slipped out and walked among the shadowy fronds, emerging into a ray of sunlight, which lit my upturned face like a spotlight. That was the moment he'd caught with his camera.

'I was actually photographing some of the trees for Tom – my gardener,' he explained. 'So getting this shot was an unexpected bonus.' His mouth curved into a smile as he looked over at my parents. 'I felt sure you'd like a copy of it too.'

Too? Did that mean that he'd kept a print for himself? Why? And even more telling, how did I feel about that?

'I shall have to find a special place to put it,' declared my mother, already beginning to re-wrap the frame in its gift paper.

I saw a tiny muscle tighten on Ben's jaw, and I sent him a silent telepathic message. *It's okay. Don't say anything. Let it go.* But as it happened, Ben didn't have to say a word. My dad got silently out of his chair and took the heavy silver frame from my mum's hands. With quiet purpose he removed two of Scott's photographs from the middle of the mantelpiece and put the one of me in their place. He stepped back and gave a small nod. 'That's where it should go,' he declared, his voice oddly gruff. My mother's eyes were over-bright, but she didn't object, just bobbed her head in quick and silent agreement.

It was a small thing, and a huge thing, and it made me wonder if the man I'd brought into our home had any idea how much he was slowly beginning to change us all.

When everyone's collection of socks, slippers and toiletries had been restocked for another year, my parents eventually disappeared into the kitchen, politely but firmly refusing all offers of help. It was the first time Ben and I had been alone since the kiss, and I was suddenly nervous. The jazz book I'd given him had been received with much more enthusiasm than it probably warranted, but he hadn't given me a gift in return. Until now. Waiting until he was sure we were alone, Ben reached into the bag beside him and extracted one last present. He held it out to me, and for some reason I found my fingers were shaking when I took it.

I recognised the name on the jeweller's box, recognised it from advertisements at the front of glossy magazines, not from ever having ventured into one of their stores. The wrapping paper fluttered to my feet as I paused with my fingers on the sprung lid of the box.

'I love it, Ben,' I said softly, blue eyes looking into caramel ones, and knowing I should be playing things far more cool than I was. But I just couldn't help myself.

'You don't even know what it is yet.'

'I don't have to,' I said with certainty, 'I already love it.' And with that I allowed the sprung lid to jump open to reveal his gift to me, a beautiful silver bracelet lying on a black velvet bed. I carefully lifted it out, allowing it to dangle across my palm like a tiny silver serpent. The solitary charm spun and twirled in the light, making me smile. When I looked up at Ben, his own lips were mimicking mine, but in his eyes was a glimmer of uncertainty.

'It's perfect,' I breathed.

'That's pretty,' declared my mum, coming in with a tray of canapés and stopping to admire the delicate bracelet. 'What an unusual charm,' she declared, her head dipping to better see the tiny silver object, occupying the first link of the bracelet. 'I can't quite make out what it is . . .'

'It's an iron, Mum,' I said quietly, my eyes and Ben's sharing a moment that belonged to us and the night we had first met. The night when he had first begun to save me, never knowing that it was something he was going to continue doing, over and over again. 'It's an iron.'

'All things considered, I think that went really well.'

'You do?' I questioned, turning as far as my seatbelt would allow to look at Ben. 'Even when they accidentally called you Scott three – or was it four – times? And the unopened present beneath the tree and . . . and everything?' I waved my hand expressively to encompass the general weirdness of my home life.

'Families are imperfect,' Ben declared. 'That doesn't make them dysfunctional.'

I sighed. 'Just a little closer to normal would be nice.'

'Normal is boring. When things are at their worst, people are at their best.'

'I think you may have stolen that line from a film.'

Ben grinned. 'Very possibly.'

Stolen or not, he was probably in an excellent position to judge. A great many of his friends were surely going through the very worst time they'd known, and yet outwardly they appeared more engaged with life than people who couldn't hear their own clock silently ticking away. It was an interesting idea, and one I'd never really explored before. *Did losing you, Scott, make me a better person?* I shook my head sadly. I really didn't think so.

As we travelled through the familiar streets of my home town, I found my fingers unconsciously straying to the tiny silver iron, which bounced gently against the scar on my inner wrist. I hadn't removed the bracelet for almost two days, not since the moment Ben had fastened it around my wrist, his head bowed low in concentration as his large fingers battled with the tiny clasp. He'd been slow to release my hand when the bracelet was eventually fastened, his finger running along the length of empty links. 'Perhaps we can fill these up over time, with some new memories?' he'd asked, his voice unusually hesitant.

I looked down at the links trying to imagine a collection of memories I had yet to make. Something warm and hopeful found a place inside me, and started very slowly to grow.

'I'd like that.'

I was lost in a daydream, fascinated by the direction we were unexpectedly taking, so much so, that I failed to notice the *actual* direction we were taking. I glanced up and saw a busy crossroads a short distance ahead, and every warm feeling inside me was instantly annihilated. I never came this way. I would drive twenty minutes or more in the opposite direction to avoid this section of road, but obviously Ben had no idea of that. I'd seen the newspaper photographs on the day after the accident. I'd seen the car slewed across the road, its metal panels mangled and twisted. And, over fifty metres away, at the place where it had finally finished its deadly skid, was Scott's prized possession – his motorbike – or what was left of it. Driving past the spot where my brother's future had been taken from him felt as disrespectful as picnicking on a grave. I could see from the solid row of cars queued up behind us that it was too late to ask Ben to turn back. My hand automatically gripped the door handle, as though escape was possible, although obviously it was not. Ben made a small sound, which might have been a curse at another driver, except for the worried expression on his face when he saw the torment on mine. How he'd realised the significance of this place without me ever having to say it out loud remained a mystery. Perhaps this fledgling connection between us bound us emotionally in ways I couldn't even begin to guess at. Ben lifted one hand from the wheel to hold mine. His other hand, steering the car, was so tightly clenched I could see the white of bone showing through at his knuckles. He looked appalled at his thoughtlessness, but really, how *would* he have known how I was going to react? How I always react?

'Close your eyes, Sophie,' he said quietly. 'I'll tell you when you can open them again.'

I did as he said, never seeing the place where vehicle and bike had met so disastrously. I knew we must be well past the junction, but he still hadn't told me to open my eyes, so I stayed in the darkness, anchored to this time and place only by his hand on mine. I felt the vehicle slow to a stop and heard the quiet click as the engine was switched off.

'Open your eyes,' he quietly instructed. I had no idea where we were, or where he had parked, because I wasn't looking anywhere except directly into his face, which was so close I could feel our breath mingling as his mouth moved towards mine. His lips were a tender graze, testing my response. Someone groaned, I think it was me, and then his lips weren't asking a question, they were leading, and I was happy to follow wherever his kiss would take me. There would be no more getting lost; it would be impossible not to find a way forward as long as he kept kissing me and holding me as though he never wanted to let me go. I was miles from the place where I lived . . . but finally, I had found my way home.

Chapter 10

'Are you sure you won't change your mind?'

I shook my head, looking up at Ben's house and quietly marvelling at how much had changed between us in the three days since we'd driven from this place.

'You might find you'd enjoy it,' he said, his voice gently cajoling.

'The thing is, I *always* spend the day after Boxing Day with Julia and Gary. And I've got the children presents. And Julia is expecting me.'

They were all good excuses, valid excuses, but they weren't the reason why I had no intention of joining Ben for the karaoke party he was hosting that evening for his friends.

'Karaoke?' I'd questioned incredulously. 'But I thought you said you don't sing. Ever.'

Ben had grinned ruefully. 'Trust me, I won't be torturing anyone's eardrums with my efforts. The party is really for Simon, anyway.'

'Simon?' I questioned, already knowing that I probably didn't want to hear why this out-of-character activity would be taking place at Ben's house that evening.

Ben had taken his eyes from the road for a moment, checking the temperature of the water before continuing. 'Simon's dreamt of being a singer his whole life – and he's got a terrific voice. But he's never been able to get past crippling stage fright. But among friends, with people he trusts, I reckon we can manage to persuade him to pick up the mic.'

'Oh.' My voice was small and cautious, instinctively knowing there was more of Simon's story to come.

'He's going in for major surgery in a couple of days, and the odds . . .' Ben's voice faded away and a sad expression settled over his features. 'Well, they're not the best. So tonight is all about him.'

Of course I was moved by Simon's tale – who wouldn't be? But compassion alone wasn't going to make me change my mind. If anything it strengthened my resolve to keep as much distance as I could between myself and Ben's group of unfortunate friends. I think he understood how I felt, for he'd gently squeezed my hand and hadn't pushed me further.

'I'm sorry, but I can't come . . . I can't . . . you see, there's Julia and she'll have—'

'I understand.'

'And she'll have bought food and—'

'I understand.'

'And Lacey and Noah, they'd be so disappointed if—'

'I understand, Sophie. I do.'

And when I looked into his eyes, it didn't surprise me at all to see that he really did. Ben took my hand, the one with the bracelet, and lifted it to his lips, kissing the clenched fist I hadn't even known I'd formed. 'I know this is hard for you, Sophie, and I'm not going to push you. But my friends are just regular people – regardless of their medical history. They're just trying to make the best of the rotten hand life has dealt them, and enjoy the time that they have left. Isn't that all any of us can do?'

'I know it seems like I'm being irrational and perhaps – one day– I can get past how this makes me feel. But not right now. It feels too soon.'

Coward, whispered my dead brother in my ear, so loudly that I started at the sound of his voice in my head. *Don't keeping running, Sophie. Don't run away from this one.*

'Maybe . . . one day,' I repeated to both the living and the dead man in the car. 'Just give me time. There's no hurry, is there?'

Ben looked a little sad, and I guessed my answer must have disappointed him, although his words were kind. 'No, there's no hurry. Take all the time that you need.'

I stayed far longer than I should have done at Julia and Gary's house, pretending not to notice their poorly disguised surreptitious yawns, or the furtive glances at watches and phones. Short of coming downstairs wearing pyjamas and dressing gowns, there wasn't much more my friends could have done to get me to leave. I was bordering on outstaying my welcome before I finally acknowledged I could delay my return no longer.

It was ridiculous how nervous I felt as the cab approached the house, and frankly ludicrous that I instructed the driver to pull up on the opposite side of the road, where I knew my arrival would be hidden from view by the thick overhanging trees. What sensible grown woman feels the need to skulk in the shadows like a thief, hoping to sneak into her own home unseen? One with unresolved issues that should probably have been faced and dealt with many years earlier, clearly.

At least I didn't have to worry about the noise of my return alerting anyone, because there was no risk of the quiet crunch of gravel beneath my feet being heard above the throbbing beat of the karaoke machine. I could have walked up the drive banging a drum and blowing a trumpet and no one would have been any the wiser. Except, perhaps, for the silhouetted figure I glimpsed at one of the upstairs windows. It could have been anyone: a lost guest looking for the bathroom; or someone collecting their coat. There was no reason to think it was Ben, looking out for me. Yet my heart was hammering an unfamiliar tempo when I let myself into the basement flat. I stood in the dark hallway, my eyes drawn to the door that connected our homes, expecting at any moment to hear Ben's knock, inviting me to join them.

But it never came, and I was glad about that, I told myself, as I quickly undressed and slid beneath my thick duvet, whose tog level wasn't quite high enough to muffle the sounds filtering through the ceiling above me. A small sound, somewhere between a sob and a laugh, burst from me, as not just one, but many voices suddenly joined together in the karaoke classic. I buried my head beneath the pillows, yet still the lyrics of the familiar song found and taunted me, as the voices above belted out a declaration that defied both truth and logic: '*I will survive.*'

'I have a fridge full of leftover party food.' It was an enticing invitation to a woman whose own fridge held a mouldy piece of cheese, two shrivelled tomatoes and half a tin of cat food. 'And there are also an awful lot of half-full bottles of wine that I'm going to need some help with later.'

I returned the smile that was radiating down from his attractive face, wanting so badly to reach up and let my fingers explore the sloping contour of his cheek and the curve of his jaw that it took a conscious effort to keep my arm at my side.

'I missed you last night,' he said, taking one small step towards me, and then pausing to gauge my reaction. Within me it felt like an explosion in a fireworks factory; tiny unexpected fire-flares were going off everywhere. Every nerve ending felt alive and also alarmingly out of my control. Sensing no resistance, Ben's arms reached out to me, his broad hands resting on either side of my waist, like a ballet dancer about to perform a lift.

'You're an optimist,' I said, wondering why my voice suddenly sounded so husky and low.

His answer was similarly throaty. 'Because I'm hoping that you want to kiss me every bit as much as I want to kiss you.'

My head was spinning, making coherent conversation difficult and something I knew I was soon going to be incapable of maintaining. 'No, about the wine. You said half-full, but I'd have called them half-empty. We're so different.'

Ben looked unconcerned and not so easily side-tracked. 'You never answered my question.' I swallowed nervously. 'I really want to kiss you right now, Sophie Winter.' His eyes were on my lips, and I could feel them already tingling in anticipation. Everything felt warm and bathed in red: his mouth; my mouth; my blush; the heat in his eyes.

I shook my head, flicking back my hair, and it was only when the flying strands grazed both his cheek and mine that I realised how close we were standing. He hadn't shaved yet, it was still quite early on the morning after his party, and I really liked that he'd prioritised knocking on my door before anything else.

'I like the differences between us,' Ben said softly, pulling me all the way towards him, closing every gap; soft body curves pressing up against firm and muscular plateaux. 'They make things interesting.'

A bristle-covered cheek brushed against one that was soft and smooth. Warm caramel eyes melted the glacier blue of mine. His arms felt strong and firm around me, making my own seem fragile in comparison as they reached up to lock behind his neck.

'Good morning,' he breathed, his words brushing my lips. 'Have I said that yet?'

I couldn't have formed a reply if my life had depended on it. What had he said about hoping that I wanted to kiss him? I couldn't think about anything else. It was like I was drunk, or addicted after just one small taste of something I should be far more cautious about sampling. I'd never been reckless; I'd never done wild or impulsive. Was I too old to start now, or had I just been waiting for this moment, and this man, to finally begin to live?

It was an intriguing question, but I never got around to discovering the answer, because then Ben kissed me and the world tilted and readjusted to a new and wonderful kind of normal.

Everything about the next four days involved Ben. It was as though thirty-one years of fierce independence, and telling myself there was a danger in closeness, was a religion practised by an entirely different Sophie Winter. This new version of me thought nothing of happily spending every waking moment by Ben's side.

We scrambled eggs in my kitchen, and then ate them in his. We went out for long walks, leaving through my front door and returning through his. It was as though our lives were no longer separate at all. Of course a small worried voice kept whispering to me that it wasn't going to last. We were marooned in those curious days between Christmas and New Year, where time seems oddly suspended. A pocket oasis when work and day-to-day mundaneness are laid aside, as life assumes a temporary lassitude that won't fade away until the calendar page turns over to January. But until that happened I was willing to be swept away on a tide of feelings that were so new and so full of promise, they were filling my head with thoughts of an entirely different kind of new year.

Chapter 11

January

I was curled up against Ben on the settee. It was New Year's Day, and it felt like the last day of a holiday you really didn't want to come back from. We were both sleepy, having stayed up many hours beyond the moment when one year slipped into the next. I don't think either of us had wanted the night to come to an end.

When midnight drew closer, Ben had produced a bottle of champagne and two glass flutes, and armed with a warm blanket we'd ventured out into the chilly December night to see in the New Year and watch the fireworks. He'd taken my hand and led me through a winding path among the tropical trees and plants in his garden, veering down a trail almost concealed by overhanging fronds, which I'd failed to notice on my earlier explorations. The foliage was so dense I doubted that we'd even be able to see a patch of the inky-black sky. But the garden, like the man who owned it, had secrets I had yet to uncover.

Ben's pace slowed and he looked at me over his shoulder. 'Close your eyes,' he instructed. The ground was slippery and glazed with frost, and both of us had slipped and skidded on the pathway, but I still did as he asked. Because I trusted him. Totally. And I still don't think he fully realised what a huge deal that was for me.

'Still got them closed?' Ben asked, coming to a complete stop and placing his hands on my shoulders. My lips parted to answer him, but he stole my words away with an unexpected kiss, which turned into something a whole lot deeper and more lingering than perhaps he'd intended.

His voice was a little unsteady when we broke apart. 'Alright, you can open them now.' At first all I saw were the lights, scores of tea-lights, bathing the area in a shimmering glow. In the depths of the rainforest garden, a hidden oasis had been created. There was a small sunken deck, within which was set a curved bench, buried beneath a deep layer of soft cushions. In a satellite orbiting the deck, Ben had laid a circle of glass jars, each holding a flickering tea-light.

'I figured candles were alright, as long as we're out in the open,' he said, moving to stand behind me and sliding his arms around my waist to pull me back against him. He'd gone to so much effort to create this magical space, it would have been ungrateful to point out that a ring of flames in a highly combustible wooded area might not be the wisest of decisions. But despite my recurrent nightmares about the fire, I felt no fear now. Because I was with Ben. For the first time in my adult life, I knew what it was like to feel totally safe.

I swivelled in his arms and tilted my face upwards. It was normally the only invitation he needed. But not this time. Instead his arms tightened around me, holding me close, as though there was a danger that I might disappear at any moment. His eyes were shadowed by a sad, almost regretful expression that scared me. My fingers wove through the thick hair at the nape of his neck, and brought his head down to receive my kiss. His eyes closed as our lips touched, but the memory of the expression I'd seen within them stayed with me.

We waited for the fireworks from the nearby display, nicely warmed by an efficient outdoor heater and the bottle of champagne. Ben had tucked the thick tartan blanket around us, and we'd snuggled cosily beneath it, waiting for the midnight chimes to ring. It was the closest we'd come to being in a bed together, because despite the undeniable heat between us, we'd yet to cross that final bridge.

The last four evenings had ended with Ben kissing me lingeringly by the entrance to my basement flat. But even when I left the door open and had turned back to look at him, with an expression on my face that even a blind man could have read, he'd still made no move to follow me. He was the one holding back, not me, and I didn't know why. Admittedly it had been a while for me, but not so long that I couldn't recognise the signs that he wanted me. When we parted at my door, both of us were trembling and breathless, and his body pressed tightly against mine kept very few secrets. I could only think he believed I wasn't ready to take things to the next level. But in truth I was so ready, it was practically embarrassing.

I've celebrated New Year's Eve in many different ways, but I already knew that years from now, as a little old lady with white hair and a failing memory, this night would still be with me. This is the one I would always remember.

My head had found a perfect hollow to nestle in at Ben's shoulder, and when my arm snaked around his waist beneath the blanket, I felt the warmth of his contented sigh ruffle my hair. We never did settle our dispute about whether to toast on the first strike of the clock or the twelfth. We still don't know the correct lyrics of *Auld Lang Syne* – or what they mean. And when the first rocket shot out over the black velvet sky, neither of us saw it. It was the best New Year's Eve that we never saw arrive, for Ben had murmured something about 'not being able to wait' and then his mouth was on mine, as he pushed me gently back upon the cushions.

It seemed like a very long time later when he reluctantly lifted the weight of his body from mine. My eyes were unfocused, still blind to everything but him. Despite the crisp night air and the falling temperature, the areas of skin he'd exposed with his searching fingers felt hot and scorched.

'Not here, not now.' Ben's voice held an ache, as though he couldn't believe he was actually saying those words. He tilted my face up to his, his fingers resting beneath my chin. 'Not yet,' he amended, squeezing the promise past his over-zealous conscience.

He held out a hand to help me up, and I took a long moment before placing my own within it. I never saw him drop the tiny charm onto my palm, but I felt its small sharp edges the second he withdrew his hand. My fingers unfurled slowly, like a flower blossoming in time-lapse photography, before opening to reveal the gleaming silver charm resting against my life line, like an omen. It was a tiny sterling silver replica of the bottle of champagne we had just drunk.

'I wanted you to have something for your bracelet to mark this evening. So you'd always remember it.'

I clipped the tiny memento onto the next empty link and held out my wrist so we could both see the two milestones swinging side by side on the chain.

'I won't ever forget,' I said, my voice reverent, as though I was praying. I turned to look at him. 'I love ... it.' I don't know if he heard the missed beat, the second when I hovered dangerously close to saying *'you'* instead of *'it'*. It was too soon and far too fast, and there was no way I could possibly be sure of those feelings yet. But the urge to tell him burnt my throat as I swallowed down the words that I knew I wouldn't be able to hold back much longer.

'So, resolutions. Have you made any?' Ben's question was unexpected, chiefly because he'd been so quiet during the last hour of the old black-and-white film I'd been watching on TV I was almost certain he was asleep.

'No,' I said, yawning widely as I stretched out my legs from where they'd been curled beneath me on the settee. 'To be honest, I don't believe in them.'

Ben's smile was warm. 'Actually, they're really a thing, and I'm pretty sure that making at least *one* is mandatory.'

I reached for the remote and muted the television. 'Really?' I parried, well aware I was being teased. 'So, what are yours, then? Have you made any?'

'Perhaps,' he said mysteriously.

'I suppose you're not going to tell me what they are, in case they don't come true.'

He pulled me towards him and kissed my forehead. 'I think you might be confusing them with wishes.'

I sighed and then smiled. 'Well, they don't come true either.' His eyes met mine and they held a silent conversation where they argued over my last statement. His won. 'Okay, they don't *usually* come true,' I conceded.

Ben was quiet for so long, I thought the subject was closed, but then he reached for my hand, lacing his fingers through mine. 'Perhaps this might be a good year to make one. Maybe a small one,' he suggested.

I lifted my eyes and looked at him, knowing that we weren't talking about losing weight, or joining a gym, or improving my finances. I knew exactly what he was hoping from me: that I'd stop running away from the thing that scared me most.

You bloody well should, taunted the voice of Scott in my head.

'You want me to be more involved with your group of friends, don't you?' My voice was suddenly small, suddenly fifteen all over again.

'I think it would be good place to start.'

Stop messing around, Sophie. Just say yes or you're going to screw this one up too. Imaginary Scott was getting far more vocal with his opinions these days, I couldn't help but notice.

'Maybe, I could give it a try,' I said hesitantly.

'I think that would be really great,' said Ben.

About fucking time, added Scott.

She was already dressed in her warm winter coat and hat when we pulled up outside her home. I saw her through the front window, hurrying to the door, anxious not to keep us waiting. Not that I'd have minded a delay – or even a postponement – I thought, as I watched Ben walk up the drive and greet a much-more-flustered-than-usual-looking Alice with a kiss on the cheek. He waited far more patiently than I knew I would have been able to do as she carefully locked, checked, and then re-checked that the house was secure. Finally Alice looked up at him, gave a small, determined nod and tucked her hand into the waiting crook of his arm.

Ben had been clever in choosing this as the first task for me to become involved in. He knew that I already liked Alice, and was grateful for her help in looking after Fred. He knew I felt in some way obliged to her, and that this request would be hard to turn down.

'All she's looking for is closure, I think,' Ben had said, after putting forward his proposal.

'She wants to have tea with a friend she hasn't seen in over sixty years? *That's* her bucket list wish?'

Ben had reached across my kitchen table, moving aside our lunch plates, to take both my hands in his, as though raising the topic had suddenly made me a flight risk.

'It is,' he confirmed, his eyes watchful as they studied my face.

'Tea?' I queried again, shaking my head as I tried to put myself in the place of an eighty-year-old woman who'd fallen out with her best friend over six decades earlier. 'For a bucket list wish, for a thing you *really* want to do before ... before ... you know ...' My voice petered away. 'It just seems a little tame, that's all.'

'Well, it's not all about scaling Kilimanjaro, or seeing the Pyramids, or surfing on Bondi Beach.' He saw my raised eyebrows. 'Tom,' he supplied, answering my unasked question. 'Although I think that one is probably on hold now until after his next surgery.'

I took a long sip from my glass of water, as though the

discomfort I felt was a bad taste that could be washed away or diluted. Which of course it couldn't.

'All Alice wants is the chance to put an end to the bad feeling between her and Gladys. I guess you could say she's putting her house in order.'

I got a little clumsily to my feet and began to stack our dirty plates. He knew how uncomfortable I felt whenever the conversation touched upon the qualifying entry requirement for his group of friends.

'But don't you think that with Alice's weak heart, she shouldn't be putting herself under this kind of strain? It could be too stressful for her. It could be dangerous for her health.'

'It's going to be scones and muffins and cucumber sand-wiches. It doesn't sound too high-octane to me,' said Ben reasonably, getting to his feet, and putting an arm around my shoulders. I leant into him and felt some of the tension begin to ease, as though there was something physical within him that could neutralise my anxiety.

'Alice just wants someone to go along with her, for sup-port, and although I *could* go – and will do, if you really don't feel you're ready for this yet – I think that having a man there will put a different complexion on their reunion. I'm sure both Alice and Gladys will be far more comfortable if the third party is a woman, someone with a more delicate touch.' He endorsed his words by lifting my hand to his mouth and gently kissing the sensitive skin of my fingertips before allowing his tongue to trail slowly down to the hollow of my palm.

'You don't fight fair,' I said, groaning quietly as he set off a chain reaction within me. 'How am I supposed to say no to you when you're doing that?'

He pulled me closer towards him, his eyes focusing on my lips. 'I haven't even got started yet,' he said huskily.

I said yes and it wasn't because of Ben's kiss, or its unique powers of persuasion. I said yes because it felt like the right thing to do. Alice was old and frail. If this was the one thing that remained unresolved for her; if this was what she really wanted and needed to do, then I'd help her fulfil her wish for a reconciliation with her friend. After all, how difficult could afternoon tea with two octogenarians actually be?

Alice climbed into the back of the car, and after a moment of hesitation, I unfastened my seatbelt and threw a quick glance in Ben's direction. 'I think I might join you back there, if that's okay with you, Alice?' I said. Ben smiled, and his eyes were warm as he gave a small, almost imperceptible nod.

Alice was nervous, that much was obvious by the way she kept putting down and then picking up her handbag, as though it was in danger of being snatched away the moment she dropped her guard. She fumbled with the seatbelt, which I gently took from her thin gnarled fingers and clicked into place. She'd slid into the car on a wave of lily-of-the-valley perfume and an excess of hairspray, and I could see from the thick layer of powder coating her wrinkled cheeks and the bright red lipstick on her lips that she had made a concerted effort with her appearance.

'Gladys was always the looker,' she said, when I commented on how nice she looked. 'The boys used to buzz all around her like bees on a honey pot.' She reached for my forearm and drew me a little closer, although I was sure Ben could still hear us from the front seat of the car. 'Well-endowed, she was, which probably had a lot to do with it too. Whereas I was as flat as a pancake.'

I saw Ben's lips twitching in the rear-view mirror and bit my own to stop them smiling. 'Well, we're all lovely in different ways.'

Alice gave a small tight smile and reached again for her handbag as though it might somehow have gone astray in the last thirty seconds.

'So when did you and Gladys first become friends?'

'Before we could even crawl,' replied Alice. 'Her family lived in the house opposite ours and our mothers were great pals. They were determined we'd be friends even before we were born. And so we were. And because neither of us had any siblings, we grew even closer. Do you have any brothers or sisters, my dear?'

My eyes went to Ben's once more in the mirror, only now his weren't twinkling in amusement. 'I ... I did,' I said in a voice that sounded just like it does when I have a really bad cold; all rough and husky. 'But he died when I was a teenager.'

Neither Alice nor Ben could possibly know that even that admission was a huge step for me to have taken. *At last,* crowed Scott's voice in my head. *I was getting thoroughly pissed off with not existing, you know.*

'Oh, that's sad,' said Alice, with the equanimity of someone who has loved and lost a great many friends and family over the years. It was the occupational hazard of outliving everyone you knew. It made her desire to reach out to Gladys all the more understandable.

'So if you and Gladys were such close friends, what happened? Why did the two of you fall out? Or is that something you'd rather not share?'

Alice gave an old lady laugh, patted her bag, reassured to find it still at her side, and then gave a wistful sigh. 'Oh mercy me, I don't mind talking about it, not after all these years. It'll probably crop up at some point during our tea anyway.' She smiled nostalgically and looked out of the window for a moment before turning back to face me. 'What could two twenty-year-old girls possibly fall out about? It was over a boy, of course.'

Ben's eyes and attention were on the road, but mine were fixed firmly on Alice. 'Vince was his name, and he could have had any girl in the dance hall that night, but it was me he asked.' Almost an entire lifetime later, the memory of that moment still shone brightly in Alice's eyes. 'I knew right then that he was the boy for me.' Alice paused and looked down at the third finger on her left hand, where no ring had ever lived. Her story would have no fairy-tale ending.

'What happened?' I prompted gently.

'Gladys,' Alice replied simply, as though the answer was obvious. 'She'd been away for a while, but she knew all about

Vince from my letters.' Alice reached for her handbag and absently began to fiddle with its clasp. She looked up and her voice was almost matter-of-fact. 'There's no bigger fool than one who can't see what's going on right under their nose, is there?'

'They fell in love?' My voice was little more than a whisper.

'Bless you, Sophie, I'm still not sure if Gladys even *liked* him. She just couldn't bear that I had something she didn't. So she set her cap at him, fluttered those big brown eyes and before I knew it he was holding *her* hand and not mine.'

It seemed like an appropriate moment for me to take Alice's hand, holding it so tightly the crepe-paper skin concertinaed into a ridge of folds. 'You deserved someone better than that,' I said softly, and was rewarded with a kindly look.

'You're a sweet girl for trying to make me feel better, but I got over Vince a long time ago. Although maybe not quite as quickly as Gladys did,' she added with a small disapproving sound. 'Even before she heard about his death, Gladys had got herself a new beau.'

'We never spoke to each other after the night I caught her kissing my man.' Alice's hand fluttered to her chest at the memory, and I threw Ben a panicked glance in the mirror as I tried to remember everything I'd ever learnt about CPR. But Alice had an inner core of steel beneath the candyfloss exterior.

'Perhaps neither of us would have ended up with him. But all I know is that I lost not only my boyfriend but also my best friend on that night, and now I'd like the chance to say goodbye to her properly, before it's too late.'

'And you can,' said Ben manoeuvring into a parking space opposite a small village green. 'Because we're here.'

Alice sat up straighter in her seat, spine and resolve equally unbending as her eyes travelled to the tiny village tea shop that she'd chosen for the reunion. 'Are you sure you'll be alright out here?' she asked, looking flustered all over again now that we'd reached our destination.

'I'll be fine,' assured Ben. 'You girls take all the time that you need.'

The surroundings were picture-postcard perfect and quintessentially British. There was even a family of ducks who waddled from their pond to greet us as I took Alice's arm and assisted her across the grass towards the small Tudor tea shop. It was only mid-afternoon, but lights shone out warmly through its mullioned windows. The doorway was low, more Alice's height than mine, and I had to duck down to avoid the overhead beams that crisscrossed above our heads. The interior was cosy and warm, made more so by a huge blazing fire roaring in an inglenook fireplace tall enough to stand in.

'Shall I take your coat,' I offered, but Alice didn't appear to hear me, for her attention was riveted on a table at the rear of the tea shop, where an elderly woman sat waiting. Alice set off, at a pace a good deal quicker than she'd employed when we'd crossed the green. 'There she is,' she confirmed, her mouth rearranging into something like a smile. It made me realise she hadn't been at all sure whether Gladys would show up.

I hurried to keep up with her as she made a purposeful beeline towards her former best friend. The woman at the table looked up as we approached. The hair, dyed to the colour of late autumn leaves, made her look at least a decade younger than Alice, and the soft wool of her twinset jumper looked expensive.

'She married well, or so I heard,' Alice had informed us earlier. 'More than once, I believe.'

The evidence of that glinted in the diamond rings on Gladys's fingers as she beckoned us over. Alice's pace slowed as we approached the table, which was already set with a brown earthenware teapot and a plate of assorted cakes. I didn't know about Alice, but my own mouth was suddenly dry with nerves, and I eyed the pitcher of iced water on the table longingly.

'Hello, Alice. Long time no see.' Alice's hand went to her throat, and I panicked yet again, wondering how long it would take me to find her pills in the depths of her bag, if this all proved too much for an elderly lady with a heart condition. 'You're looking well,' continued Gladys, her eyes switching from her former friend to me. 'And is this your granddaughter?'

She clearly didn't know that Alice had found no other love after Vince. 'I'm just a friend,' I corrected, when Alice had yet to find her voice. 'Alice never married,' I added, wondering if the other woman could hear the unspoken censure in my voice. Gladys looked a little discomforted, but not as much as I thought she should have done.

'Oh well, it's not for everyone,' she said, dismissing the lifetime of memories she'd stolen from Alice with a single sweeping statement.

I moved a little closer to Alice's side, bunching my fingers into the thick fabric of her coat. 'Alice, would you like to sit down?' She shook her head, but didn't look my way; her eyes were fixed only on her former friend.

'Let me take your coat,' I offered again. 'It's awfully warm in here,' I added, already feeling a trickle of perspiration making its way lazily down my spine. The fire beside us crackled in the grate, as a log disintegrated with a small pop and a shower of embers.

Alice was warm too, I could see that from the tiny beads of perspiration jewelled on her powder-caked upper lip. I reached over and poured her a glass of water, but she ignored it, even when I placed it on the table directly in front of her. Perhaps that was my first mistake.

'Why don't the two of you sit down,' urged Gladys, waving to two vacant chairs. 'We've a lot of catching up to do.'

I went to pull out one of the high-backed chairs, but stopped when I saw Alice had made no move to do the same. My eyes darted between the two women, watching an unspoken conversation that had waited sixty years to take place. The pair of them caught me by surprise; for there was no discussion, no preamble.

'Vince wasn't good enough for you. You should probably thank me for showing you that,' said Gladys, her bright pink lips, which clashed shockingly with her hair, drawn into a tight line. Suddenly I really wished Ben was the one standing by Alice's side. He'd know what to do or say to calm things down. Me, I was hovering dangerously close to saying something fairly unforgivable to an OAP.

I don't know if Gladys's words were the final straw, or whether Alice had always known exactly how this reunion would end. There was a determination and a glint in her eyes as she reached for the glass of water I'd poured her. *Thirsty. Please just be thirsty*, I found myself thinking fervently. Alice lifted the glass, and for a moment it still could have gone either way, and then sixty years of waiting tipped the scales, and the water was no longer in the glass, but airborne and heading in a small cascading jet towards Gladys.

'Bitch,' said Alice, almost pleasantly. It was the first and last thing she said to the woman she'd come here to see. I felt every head in the tea shop turn our way and a collective gasp like a Mexican wave passed from table to table.

'We should probably leave now,' said Alice, turning to me with the sweetest little old lady smile I had ever seen. I didn't need telling twice. I threw one brief glance back at Gladys who looked suitably stunned as the water dripped slowly down her still-well-endowed chest. At least Alice hadn't gone for her face.

I shook my head helplessly at the other octogenarian, not sure which of them was the victim here. I mouthed a 'Sorry'

I'm not sure I meant, and then marched Alice as fast as I could towards the door. The cold January air hit my face like a slap as we left the tea shop and headed towards Ben's waiting car.

I saw him look up in concern at our approach and make as though to get out of the car, but I signalled at him urgently to stay put. I have no idea what must have been going through his head as we hurried across the green, for I was too busy casting fearful looks over my shoulder for angry tea shop staff. I opened the rear door, and Alice climbed into the car with a nimbleness that defied her years. I jumped in beside her.

'Drive!' I urged Ben, even before I'd pulled the door to a close.

Ben would have made a rubbish getaway driver, because he was far too slow in his response. 'What's wrong? What's happened?'

'Just drive,' I repeated urgently.

Beside me Alice smiled beatifically. 'Thank you,' she said to both of us. 'I really *do* feel so much better now.'

'Tell it to me again,' pleaded Julia, still wiping the tears from the edge of her eyes.

'Three times is enough,' I said primly.

Julia shook her head wonderingly. 'You certainly never said getting involved with Ben's friends was going to be this entertaining.'

'For you, maybe,' I said, although it was hard to refrain from smiling every time I thought back to the previous week. I looked around the coffee shop where Julia and I had met for lunch. No one was launching their cappuccinos at anyone, no sixty-year-old feuds were being settled, no feisty OAPs were slugging it out in the corner. It was a little dull.

'So is that it now? Was that your first and last involvement with his friends?' I lifted my cup to my lips and saw the glint of silver catch my eye. There were three charms on my bracelet now, and my eyes focused on the newest addition, a tiny piano, as I answered.

'Not exactly. I'm sort of helping someone else now.'

Three days after Alice had settled her old score in dramatic fashion, Ben had knocked on my door in the middle of the afternoon. I'd needed very little persuasion to abandon the singularly dull translation I was working on to join him for a tea break.

'I have doughnuts,' was his opening gambit as I unlatched my door to find him leaning up against the jamb.

'Is that a medical condition, or do you mean the confectionery?'

Ben's lips twitched, and inside I felt a small happy glow. He liked my sense of humour, and I liked the fact that recently I seemed to have rediscovered that I had one after a very long absence.

'Shall we go upstairs?' suggested Ben, holding out his hand to me. I have something I want to show you.'

'Intriguing,' I murmured as I allowed him to lead me

up the wooden staircase. And it definitely was: intriguing, bewildering and totally unexpected.

It was impossible not to notice it as soon as we entered his section of the house. The wood was glossy and black, and reflected like a mirror in the wintery afternoon sunlight. And it was large, easily taking up an entire corner of the room.

'It's a piano,' I said, as though he might possibly not have noticed the sizeable baby grand instrument that had suddenly taken up residence in his lounge.

Ben released my hand, and thrust his own into the pockets of his jeans. He rocked on his heels and for a moment looking like an overgrown schoolboy who wasn't sure how much trouble he might be in.

'It is,' he confirmed.

'But you don't play,' I added, in case he might possibly have forgotten that rather important consideration before purchasing an instrument which undoubtedly had cost many thousands of pounds.

'No, I don't,' he said, crossing over to the piano and running his hand along its raised lid, as though petting a thoroughbred. 'But you do. Or rather you did.'

'You bought this for me?' My voice was incredulous, but deep down, hadn't I suspected this the moment I entered the room?

'Well, in a way, I suppose I did. But that corner of the room was looking very bare, so I needed to put something there anyway.'

'Most people would have gone for a pot plant,' I said under my breath as I tentatively allowed my fingers to hover over ebony and ivory. It had been half a lifetime since I'd played, and I wasn't sure how ready I was for Ben to prise open yet another door that had been nailed shut for a very long time.

Hesitantly I lowered my fingers and a familiar chord throbbed melodically from the instrument. It was a very different sound from the one our old piano had produced; the piano I'd begged my parents to get rid of. Almost without realising how I got there, I found myself sitting on the piano stool, my fingers flexing and straightening before descending with a little more confidence on the milky white perfection of the keys.

'I'm not going to be very good, not after all these years,' I said.

'I'm practically tone deaf anyway,' he said with a shrug. 'So it'll all sound great to me.'

'So now Ben has you moonlighting as a piano teacher?' asked Julia, scrutinising the bill, before I pulled it towards me and reached for my purse. 'I've got this today,' I said, dropping notes and coins onto the china saucer. 'And I don't think teaching one guy a piece to play for his wife qualifies me as a bona fide teacher.'

'And this bloke . . . is he sick too?'

I shook my head, as an image of Charlie, my one and only pupil, came to mind. A builder by trade; thick broad neck; ruddy complexion and muscular tattooed forearms.

He certainly didn't *look* like the type of man with a burning desire to learn the hauntingly delicate *Für Elise*.

'No, it's his wife who's sick. She's the classical music fan, not him. He strikes me as more of a heavy metal kind of guy.' Julia giggled as she bent over the stroller, and tucked one of Noah's tiny hands back beneath his blanket. 'She's always wanted him to go to concerts with her, but he never has. She has no idea there's going to be an unscheduled addition to the programme at the one she's attending next month.' Julia was looking at me, and it was almost impossible to read her expression. 'Ben knows one of the organisers,' I explained.

Julia straightened, and at first I thought the concerned look on her face was for Charlie's wife Jacqueline, whose illness had already confined her to a wheelchair. But I was wrong.

'Don't you think this is all happening a little too fast?'

'Oh my God, you have to be joking. Every time Charlie plays it sounds like Fred's caught his tail in the door. It'll be a miracle if he learns it in time.'

Julia shook her head, and long auburn strands flew left and right like maypole streamers. 'I'm not talking about them. I mean you . . . or more specifically you and Ben, and how everything you do suddenly seems to be tied up with him. I mean, the guy bought you a bloody piano, for Christ's sake!'

'It fills an empty corner in his room,' I said lamely, repeating Ben's own excuse. It sounded no more believable coming from my lips than it had from his.

Julia reached for my hand. 'I'm just worried about you. I don't want you to get hurt. You and Ben seem to have gone from nought to sixty in a very short space of time, and now he's buying you pianos and jewellery and you're practically living together.'

'Hardly,' I muttered, feeling my cheeks begin to prickle with an unbidden warmth.

'Yes, well apart from the sex,' she said darkly, as though I needed to be reminded of that omission.

'Sorry, do you want to say that a bit louder? I don't think the couple by the window heard you properly.'

Julia managed to look contrite and righteous at the same time, which was quite an achievement. 'I just think it might be time to apply the brakes a little, that's all,' she ended, softening her words with a gentle squeeze of my arm.

'You spent years – literally years – nagging me to get out and meet someone, to stop closing myself off from my emotions, and now that I'm finally doing what you said, you want me to back off? I thought you were happy for me?' I said, almost accusingly. 'I thought you *liked* Ben.'

'I do like him. I really do. I just don't see why everything has to happen so fast. Would it really hurt if you just asked him to slow things down a little? I mean, it's not like there's any reason you have to rush, is there?'

The house was in darkness, which was odd because his car was still on the drive. I don't know what instinct made me turn to his front door instead of mine. He took so long answering the ringing of the bell that I began to think I was mistaken, and that he *was* out after all.

I was on the verge of heading back around the front of the building to my own flat when his door swung open. There was no light coming from the ground floor; the outside security lamp provided the only illumination, but it was bright enough to tell me that I'd had good reason to be worried. Ben looked awful. There was a grey pallor to his complexion and his eyes looked shadowed and haunted. He was holding on to the edge of the door as though he needed its support to stay upright. He looked vulnerable, and it wasn't a look I had ever seen on him before.

'What's wrong? Are you ill?' It was a natural first response; how could I know the truth was so much worse? My anxious question replaced the pain in his eyes with something even more troubled.

'I'm fine,' he said, which was clearly a lie. Even his voice sounded in pain, as though the words were scoring his throat on their way out.

Without waiting to be invited in – because I had a strong suspicion that might not happen – I squeezed past him, shutting the front door firmly behind me. It was only when I was certain I couldn't be easily evicted that I turned to him once more. 'What is it, Ben? Something is obviously wrong.'

For a second I thought he was going to deny it again, but then he shook his head. 'I . . . I've had some bad news.'

People talk about their blood running cold. Obviously that doesn't actually happen. I'm sure my O negative was flowing very nicely through my veins at 98.6 degrees, but it felt like ice water flooding through me.

'You look like you need to sit down,' I said, and I certainly felt like *I* needed to. I'm not really sure who was helping who as we crossed the room and ended up on the settee, side by side but not touching. It was almost as though he was deliberately withdrawing from me, and I suddenly felt frightened all over again.

'What sort of news?' Was that my voice? It sounded like a child's, a frightened child's, and suddenly I heard that echo from the past, the conversation that featured so frequently in my 2 a.m. nightmares.

'What do you mean, Scott's been hurt in an accident? Daddy? What kind of an accident? He's going to be alright, isn't he ... isn't he?'

I shook my head, but it was a real effort to focus, because I was too much in my own personal nightmare to realise I was now in the middle of a brand-new one.

'It's about Tom,' said Ben, his words so close to cracking that I could practically hear the tiny fissures in his voice.

'Tom? Gardener Tom?'

Ben nodded and his eyes slowly closed. And that's when I knew. And yet the words, when they came, still tore into me like bullets. 'He died on the operating table this afternoon.'

Arms came around bodies, his or mine, I couldn't tell. Someone sobbed, and I'm pretty sure that was me, because the tears that ran down his cheeks were totally silent.

'But he was fine the other day. He was teasing me about that stupid rolling pin again.'

Ben nodded, and averted his gaze, looking out at the

garden that held so much of Tom it surely couldn't have helped him. 'He didn't tell anyone about the surgery – well, only his family, obviously. He didn't want anyone to make a fuss. But he must have known how serious things were, because he'd left word with his father to phone me if anything should happen.' Ben paused as though he was reliving that phone conversation. 'He called two hours ago.'

'But he was going to surf on Bondi Beach,' I said stupidly. He showed me some YouTube clips of guys with artificial limbs doing it. He said he was going to make it happen.' My voice was practically an accusation, blaming Tom for making me believe that there was hope, when all the time he'd probably known the chances were so slim they were practically non-existent.

'He never stopped hoping he'd achieve that,' said Ben sadly, 'but I think he knew it was already too late.'

I cried for longer than Ben did, although his grief was deeper than mine. Despite the difference in their ages, Tom had been a close friend. I shuddered at how quickly my brain had automatically adjusted Tom, and everything he was and ever had been, into the past tense.

'His dad's going to let me know when the funeral is taking place. Apparently Tom had told him he'd like me to give a eulogy.' Ben shook his head, and for the first time I saw that below the thin veneer containing his grief there was a fierce broiling anger. 'It's just such a fucking waste. He had everything ahead of him. He was so damn young.'

I closed my eyes and a kaleidoscope of images filled the

space behind them: All of them featured Scott and Tom and their stolen futures.

It wasn't how I had imagined it happening, it certainly wasn't how I'd secretly fantasised it would be, but when Ben and I found ourselves in each other's arms in his bed that night, I still don't know who was comforting who. 'Will you stay?' he'd asked. It was very late, and we'd sat in the dark for hours, in that horrible period of suspended animation after new grief has exploded your reality, like a senselessly thrown grenade. 'I'm not sure I'm up for being alone tonight,' he'd said, and my heart broke all over again at the look on his face.

'Of course I'll stay.'

His room smelled of him; his sheets held him trapped deep within the woven cloth, he was subtly impregnated into the feathery depths of his pillows. Every inhaled breath was of Ben. It was just how I had imagined it would be, and nothing at all like I had ever dreamt.

He'd got to his feet, a little shakily – or so I thought – and held out his hand to me. I'd placed my own in it, trusting him, the way I'd done for the last three months since the night he'd saved my life. Tonight it was my turn to be strong, to be there for him, and I was determined not to let him down. We walked through the darkened house to his room, and I'm glad neither of us reached for a light switch to destroy the black velvet cocoon. He led me with confidence through the lower ground of his home, only faltering when we crossed the threshold to his room, as though suddenly realising where we were and the implications it held. His eyes met mine, and in the moonlight slicing through the window I saw the realisation and uncertainty slowly dawn.

'Sophie, I didn't— This wasn't what I— We don't have to—' He shook his head as though the words he needed had suddenly been erased from his vocabulary. 'I don't want you to be here if you don't want to be,' he said, his voice a whisper, as though the shadows were eavesdropping on his confession.

This was my time to rescue him. I crossed the small distance between us and gently kissed his mouth. 'I'm exactly where I want to be. Where I *need* to be,' I added. In case he needed further assurance of that, I reached for the zipper on my dress. The noise of its tiny metal teeth sounded too loud in the quiet of his bedroom. The dress fell in a soft pool of wool at my feet, and I kicked it away as I stepped out of my shoes. I stood before him in my underwear, filled with a confidence and certainty that I'd never felt before. Ben's eyes never flickered, never once dropped below my face. Continuing to take the initiative, I slowly began to undress him. I began with the buttons of his shirt, my fingers moving smoothly as though we had performed this unfamiliar ritual a thousand times before. I lost momentum only once, when I reached the waistband of his jeans to tug the shirt free. When both sides of the garment were hanging loose, I bunched the fabric in my hands and drew him towards me, gently kissing the broad muscled wall of his chest, then each shoulder in turn as I eased the shirt off him. My mouth was soft and tender as it grazed his skin, its mission to dampen the pain, rather than incite a fire. I think Ben understood that.

I struggled a little with his belt, but he didn't intervene or try to help me, and eventually I eased the reluctant prong free from its hole. The narrow band of leather slithered like a lazy snake through its loops as I pulled it free and lobbed it into one corner of the room. Our clothes ended up everywhere, as though they'd been torn from our bodies in a hurricane, and yet the exact opposite was true. The whole process felt slow, measured and unhurried. When the fastening of his jeans was undone, I began to ease down the zip, already aware of his body's response to my touch. That was when Ben's hands had briefly covered mine, taking over. I nodded in understanding and withdrew my hands as he stepped free of the denim garment, and tossed it somewhere into the darkness.

As though this was my room and not his, I moved to the bed, threw back the covers and slipped beneath them. I held one corner of the duvet up, inviting him in. The moon momentarily disappeared behind a cloud, so I could see nothing, but I felt the pressure on the mattress beside me when he joined me. Then his arms reached out for me and I went into them without hesitation. We kissed lingeringly ... and then stopped just before we crossed the line there would be no return from. We spoke for hours, often making very little sense ... and then fell silent. Ben's hands held me, stroking my back, caressing the angle of my hip and the curve of my spine, but his fingers never dipped below the flimsy lace of my underwear. Deep within me a small gnawing ache for him growled like a hungry animal, but I ignored it, because I understood tonight wasn't about finding that kind of relief. This was so much bigger than that. Sex could be transient. Sex could be meaningless and easily forgotten. But this night, when we bared not our bodies but our souls, was going to stay with me until the day I died.

Chapter 12

'I'm really sorry. You do understand, don't you?'

'Of course I do,' Ben assured. 'I always knew it was a lot to ask.'

'I'm sorry,' I said again, just in case he'd somehow missed the last couple of hundred times I'd said it since he'd asked me to go with him to Tom's funeral. I'd felt bad refusing him in the quiet shared intimacy of his bed when he'd first asked me, then even worse when he'd repeated the request a couple of days later, when writing Tom's eulogy. He hadn't asked me again after that, although that hadn't stopped me from apologising.

It had been a strange and confusing week. Spending the night together had left us in a new place, bringing us closer, and yet my inability to stand beside Ben at the funeral had also driven an invisible wedge between us. In a Venn diagram of us, my refusal had placed me very much in the outer circle. To share Ben's life, to be part of his world in the way I now realised I wanted, I was going to have to fully accept his involvement with his group of friends, and what was inevitably going to happen to them. It was a much bigger 'ask' than just going to afternoon tea, or teaching someone to play the piano. And attending a funeral – any funeral – still felt like one step too far for me to travel.

Ben said that he understood, and I really think he did. He wasn't angry with me. But I sure as hell was.

I studied him closely on the morning of the funeral. Dressed in a black suit and tie he looked like a totally different man to the one who'd held me in his arms; who could make me laugh, and who'd touched and woken my frozen heart. It felt shameful and inappropriate that I found the sight of him in his formal attire so incredibly sexy. It was probably a look his previous girlfriend, the unfortunately gorgeous Holly, had seen many times when Ben had still been a successful businessman. We had both dated the same – but an entirely different – man. Would Holly have gone with him to the funeral? The question popped into my head before I had the chance to censor it, and refused to disappear as I prepared the toast and coffee that I was sure Ben would have no appetite for.

He'd been preoccupied all week with the eulogy, but he hadn't read it to me or asked for my opinion. I guess I'd lost the right to hear the words he'd so carefully penned when I'd turned down the opportunity to go with him.

Ben took two mouthfuls of the coffee I'd made, but ignored the plate of buttered toast. I wasn't surprised. He glanced at his watch many times, and repeatedly checked in his pocket for the typed words he'd spent so many hours working on since Tom's death. We'd not shared a bed again after that first night, and part of me couldn't help wondering if that still would have been true if I'd been brave enough to stand beside him.

Julia understood – or at least she said she did. 'He *does* know that you've not attended *anyone's* funeral since Scott's?' she asked, loyally on my side, even though I suspected she thought my side was in the wrong here. She wasn't the only one who held that opinion; *I* thought I was in the wrong too ... I just didn't know how to overcome my phobia to fix it.

One last glance at his expensive wristwatch and Ben replaced the almost full coffee mug back onto the worktop. 'I should go. I don't want to be late.' There was still plenty of time, but I completely understood his need to leave; I only hoped he understood mine to stay.

I kissed him, trying to infuse one last apology into the touch of my lips against his. He held me tightly, and I could feel the slow and steady throb of his heart through the black fabric of his jacket.

'I hope it goes ... well ...' My voice trailed away. I'd been to just one funeral in my entire life, and it had devastated me. Perhaps if I'd attended a few more I could appreciate how they could also be a celebration of a long and fulfilled life.

But that concept made no sense to me, for I knew only about the other end of the spectrum. I was pretty sure Tom's funeral would feel every bit as tragic as Scott's had done.

The house had seemed unbearably quiet after Ben had finally picked up his car keys and driven away. I couldn't stay in his section of the building, because I felt his unspoken disappointment hanging in the air. So I retreated to my basement flat and tried to busy myself. Work would have been impossible, so I didn't even bother to attempt any, but instead cleaned the kitchen until every surface shone and reflected my remorseful face back at me like a mirror. I wiped work-tops and scrubbed floors, as though my guilt was a stain I could somehow wash away. Even Fred looked at me balefully as I busied myself with domestic drudgery, as though I was serving a penance. His emerald eyes blinked in judgement, and I swear I saw blame in his feline stare.

I stood in my impeccably clean shower cubicle, letting the water run cold as it pummelled the skin of my back. *The back he'd stroked.* And pounded against my parted lips. *The lips he'd kissed.* Trickled through my fingers . . . *The fingers of the hand he'd held.* The hand that should be holding his right now.

I leapt from the shower, already running as I grabbed a towel and raced across the floor, leaving a trail of sodden footprints all the way to the bedroom. I threw open the wardrobe doors and reached for the glossy carrier bag I had tucked far into its depths just two weeks earlier. I'd felt proud of myself when I'd bought the dresses. I felt I was finally moving in the right direction. But it had been so much easier buying something to wear for a funeral when no one had actually died. When reality had slapped me around the face, my first instinct had been the same as it had always been: to run away and hide.

I threw a frantic glance at the clock. And now I would *have* to run, if I wanted to make it to Tom's funeral in time.

Sometimes the Fates conspire to make everything go against you. And other times they just decide to give you a break. So when I pulled the first black dress out of the bag, it wasn't the crumpled mess I was expecting it to be. The pair of black tights my groping fingers yanked from the drawer didn't have a single snag or ladder on them. The comb I dragged through my wet hair was all it needed for me to look perfectly presentable. Even the gods in charge of transport were looking down kindly on me. The random cab company I phoned happened to have a driver who'd just dropped off a fare in the street next to mine. The car was at the kerb waiting for me even before I'd slipped my feet into my shoes and grabbed my bag. I gave the driver the name of the church and asked him to hurry all in a single breath as I jumped into the back seat. My desperation to attend this funeral was strangely almost as great as my previous desperation had been to avoid it.

It was a weekday and mid-morning, and the roads were thankfully quiet. What should have been a forty-minute drive was pared down to just over thirty. I'd tried to keep my brain in neutral during the half-hour journey, because I didn't want to give it a chance to conjure up a last-minute reason to change my decision.

The road outside the church was busy. A collection of cars in a spectrum of colours lined both sides of the street. The palette only changed to black when you got closer to the entrance.

'Don't think I'll be able to get us much nearer than this,' my driver apologised, pulling up at the first available gap. His fare was already folded up within my tightly clenched palm, considerably more mangled now than it had been at the start of the journey. I passed him the note through the window, anxious for him to be gone before I changed my mind and leapt back into the vehicle.

'Thank you. Keep the change,' I said, already hurrying to catch up with a cluster of black-clothed stragglers disappearing into the church. I walked quickly, head down, my gaze fixed on my black shoes, which appeared vaguely sepia-tinged through the polarised lenses of my sunglasses. I wasn't used to wearing them on an overcast February day, but the oversized frames offered a different type of protection, one that had nothing to do with UV rays.

My pace faltered slightly when I heard the slow rumbling approach of a small procession of vehicles. It was a perfectly natural reflex to look back over my shoulder. It was the reaction that followed, the one when I saw the funeral cortège, which was my own unique knee-jerk response. A strange sound, like the moan of the wind, escaped from me as the vehicles crawled sedately past. The floral tribute practically filled the window of the lead vehicle. One word, three letters, fashioned out of red and white blooms. '*SON*.' It was practically identical to one my own parents had picked out sixteen years earlier.

The car directly behind the hearse glided to a stop. This would be the vehicle reserved for immediate family members. My eyes closed and I could smell again the leather seats of the funeral limousine, even though it had been sixteen years since I'd sat where Tom's family were now sitting. I heard the echo of the undertaker's voice, his impassive professional demeanour cracking to reveal the human beneath it, as I'd stumbled on leaving the car. '*Are you okay, love?*' he'd asked, reaching out to grip my elbow to steady me. Behind me my parents were clinging to each other, like shipwreck survivors. But the person *I'd* always leant on, my sibling partner in crime, was no longer there. He was travelling in a different car, lying on a bed of quilted white satin. Never again would his hand be there for me. A recklessly driven vehicle had seen to that.

Wrenching myself out of the past and back to the present, felt like an actual physical challenge. Walking into the darkened church was another. I paused for a moment by the open double doors, while my senses went into overdrive, absorbing it all. The heady aroma of flowers hit me like an assault. They were everywhere I looked, but not the traditional roses, carnations and lilies. There were no cut blooms at all in the church, but instead an array of pots housing bushes and tiny flowering trees. I learnt later that Tom, who'd spent his life nurturing plants, had wanted none to be cut for his funeral; everything was to be replanted to grow again. I cried a lot when Ben told me that.

The church was packed, and I knew that much later Tom's family would be pleased that so many people had come to bid their son goodbye. I also knew that when they entered the church and were led to their seats, their eyes would be blind to the crowds. I couldn't see Ben, but I was sure he would be somewhere near the front of the church. That was fine, I thought, as I squeezed into a vacant space at the end of one of the back pews. The stranger beside me obligingly inched along to give me some more space. Her eyes were red and a damp tissue was already clutched in her hand. I nodded sympathetically but immediately felt like a fraud and an imposter. I looked at the rows of black-clothed people. They were all here for one man, while I was here for another. I hoped Tom would understand and forgive me. I heard again an echo of his chuckling laughter, as he managed to reference our crazy rolling pin introduction one more time. Tears began to roll silently down my cheeks. Perhaps I *was* there for Tom after all.

I picked up the order of service and ran my finger over Ben's name, as though trying to telepathically message him that I was there. *Turn around and you'll see me.* Bizarrely one head *did* turn around, and a pair of eyes went instantly to mine. But they weren't Ben's; they were Carla's. Of course I'd known it had to be her, long before she'd turned in her seat. In a sea of black and grey she was wearing the most vibrant brightly patterned floral dress and matching headscarf I had ever seen. I thought I heard someone behind me tut disapprovingly, and instantly I bristled, because I knew *exactly* what had prompted Carla to choose that particular outfit; she was paying her own personal homage to Tom.

Not that Tom's funeral was likely to be traditional, because I'd already identified the strains of an Aerosmith song playing as we waited for the service to begin. Near the altar two enlarged photographs of Tom were positioned on easels. In one he was bare-chested and bronzed from the sun, working in a garden, one booted foot planted firmly upon the blade of his spade. The other photograph was a little harder to look at. It showed Tom in a hospital bed. You would have expected your eye to go to the shortened leg, which ended in a heavy swathe of bandages. But what actually drew you most was his irrepressible grin and the can of lager held up high, as he toasted whoever was behind the camera. That was Tom.

I didn't want to look at the two empty trestle stands beside the photographs, knowing what would soon be placed upon them. Far better to look at the last unexpected item propped up against the pulpit. The brightly painted surfboard should have looked out of place in a church, but because it spoke so strongly of hope and faith and belief in a better future, I could think of no better place for it to be.

Aerosmith fell silent, and everyone got to their feet. I could tell from the shuffle of movement behind me that the party of pall-bearers was about to carry Tom past his family and friends for one final goodbye. Panic, so acidic it tasted like bile, threatened to choke me. My stomach clenched, in a way that reminded me of every bout of food poisoning I'd ever had – only about ten times worse. For a horrible moment I thought I might actually be sick … and then Ben turned around.

The first expression on his face was shock – leaving mere surprise a million miles behind. His eyes briefly slid past me, and I knew he was watching the approach of the coffin. My hands were fastened on the back of the wooden pew in front of me, holding on so tightly I could see the white outline of each knuckle bone. But then Ben's eyes were back on my face, and there was a softening and warmth in them; they burnt with an emotion he'd never shown before. I can't lip read, and he was too far away for me to be certain, but I thought I saw his lips mouth out the words 'thank you.' My hands relaxed, my stomach untied the knots it had twisted itself in, and the roar of blood in my ears died away. His eyes held mine for one last look before he turned to face the front once more, his attention rightly on the proceedings and the man he'd come here to honour.

I wasn't the only person to cry at Ben's eulogy. Tissues emerged from handbags and pockets all around me, as he sketched out a verbal portrait of a brave young man who'd refused to let a terminal illness define his final months. It should have felt wrong laughing at the anecdotes Ben had included in his speech, but strangely it didn't. This was the speech he might have written as Tom's best man, for the wedding he would never have. It could have been the one he entertained friends and family with at Tom's thirtieth, fortieth or even fiftieth birthday parties, if he'd ever reached those milestones. It might have been the one a much older Ben got to his feet to give at Tom's retirement party. But life had erased all the moments Tom should have taken for granted, and written an entirely different ending to his story.

'You came . . .' There was still a note in his voice that revealed he hadn't ever expected that I would.

'I did.'

'What made you change your mind?'

I tried out several answers in my head:

'Because it was the right thing to do.' No. Too easy, and also a bit of a cop-out.

'Because I'd really liked Tom.' I had liked him. A lot. But in all honesty, that wasn't what had driven me to overcome my crippling fear.

'Because you needed me to be here.' A nice sentiment, but again not entirely true. Ben would have delivered his eulogy with equal feeling and compassion whether I'd been there to hear it or not.

'Because I'm in love with you, and I want to stand beside you through every important moment in your life, good or bad.' That one at least was totally true, and also far too dangerous to reveal. Because I still had no real proof that Ben felt the same way about me.

Bloody hell, sis, are you really that dumb? Scott's profanity in a church didn't surprise me – he never had been particularly religious. I focused on the caramel of Ben's eyes and tried not to let my long-dead brother's voice derail my train of thought. It didn't surprise me at all that Scott wasn't done yet. *This man loves you, surely you know that by now? What else does he have to do to prove it? Hire a plane and have it written across the sky? Take out a full-page ad? Risk his life to save you? Oh wait, hang on a minute, I think he might have—*

'You. I came because of you. Because I wanted to see you looking at me the way you're looking at me right now. Like you're proud of me.'

'I *am* proud of you. I know this couldn't have been easy.'

I looked around the church. Carla was over near the doors, talking to Henry. Alice was sitting to one side, chatting to Charlie and his wife. And dotted around among the assembled strangers were several other faces I recognised from Ben's get-togethers. People I had yet to be introduced to; people I was no longer afraid to meet.

'It wasn't as hard as I imagined,' I admitted honestly. 'I'm among friends.'

The look he gave me was worthy of bottling up and keeping somewhere safe for a very long time, so I could take it out and examine it again and again and again.

Ben pulled me briefly against his side. 'I want to go and say something to Tom's family before they leave for the churchyard. Would you prefer to stay here?'

I moved imperceptibly closer to him. He was my shield,

strong and protective. No one who had known me, even fleetingly, during the past sixteen years would have been able to believe the words coming out of my mouth. I could hardly believe them myself. 'No. I'll come with you. I'd like to pay my respects.'

Hallelujah, imaginary Scott cheered in mocking praise, which still managed to sound a little like a blasphemy.

Of course, it was harrowing looking at their grief-stricken faces and trying to avoid seeing a mirror image of my own family's pain. But I was still glad that I'd gone to speak to them. Tom's mother gripped my hands and said how grateful she was that I'd come, and how much it meant to her, even though I knew she had absolutely no idea who I was. But that didn't matter.

At his parents' request, only a small number of Tom's close friends and immediate family were accompanying them to the churchyard. As I didn't fall into either category, I whispered discreetly in Ben's ear that I was going to slip away and make my own way home. His eyes clouded, and I could tell he was already worrying about me returning to an empty house after the funeral. Would he always do that, I wondered? Would he always look into the distance, like an expert driver, assessing every possible hazard that might be lying in wait on the road ahead of me?

'I'll be fine,' I assured him. Ben gently kissed the edge of my mouth as we stood outside the church, waiting for the last of the mourners to leave. To be perfectly truthful, I was glad to have a legitimate excuse not to be part of the final proceedings. Standing beside a newly dug grave, watching Tom's coffin being lowered into the ground, was possibly one step too far into this new version of my future.

'I'm not sure how late I'm going to be. I think everyone is going back to a relative's house afterwards.'

'It's okay. Don't rush or feel you have to leave early because of me. I'll be at home waiting for you.'

The wind whipped up suddenly, blowing strands of my hair across my face. His fingers reached up to brush them back before mine could. 'I like how that sounds,' he said, his voice low.

'Me too.'

I saw her even before I got out of the cab. Or to be more precise, I saw her *car*, a gleaming black Mercedes which was positioned squarely across the entrance to Ben's drive, totally blocking all access. I was distracted as I fumbled in my purse for the fare money, my attention at first on the unfamiliar car, then travelling beyond it, to where a woman was standing directly in front of Ben's ground-floor window, her hands cupped beside her eyes in an attempt to cut out the glare as she peered into his home.

I bristled, even before I knew who she was. There was something brazen in the intrusion; even though it wasn't my home, it felt like a violation of privacy. Of course, in hindsight I acknowledged that I would *never* have liked her, whatever she'd been doing.

Her coat was bright red. It should have clashed dreadfully with her hair, but somehow it just enhanced it, making the flowing Titian strands gleam like burnished copper.

'Can I help you?' I called out, long before I was close enough for her to have heard me. The words came out a little tighter, a little less courteous, the second time they passed my lips. Logically I couldn't possibly know who she was yet. Except I already did. Because that's what life did to you, when everything was going well ... it threw a large destructive spanner into the works.

Holly was beautiful. Even more so than the internet photographs had led me to believe. Every feature scored its own perfect ten out of ten. Combined, the mathematical computation made me feel dowdy and drab, and that had nothing to do with the fact that I was dressed head to toe in black, while she looked like an exotic fiery bird of paradise.

There was no apology in her eyes as she looked at me. Not even a trace of embarrassment at having been caught peering into her ex-lover's property. 'This *is* Ben Stevens' house, isn't it?' Her voice was mellow, and not the squawk I'd been hoping for, which it should have been if there was any justice in the world. It spoke of a privileged life, one of private schools, lacrosse matches and Saturday mornings at the pony club.

To be honest I was a little appalled by my sudden bad manners, which I could only put down to feeling inexplicably threatened. But perhaps I had it all wrong. I forced a smile up from somewhere, and plastered it across my face.

'Yes. Ben lives here.' *And so do I,* I really wanted to add, but that would have been petty and also misleading. I added *'unnecessarily territorial'* to my list of new and unattractive character traits I didn't know I had. I'd be peeing all around the perimeter like Fred if I didn't rein it in right now.

'Good. I thought this was the address he'd given me.'

Her words were like a swinging scythe. They caught me in my mid-section, with a pain so sharp I wouldn't have been surprised to see an actual wound where they had landed. I had assumed – incorrectly assumed, obviously – that there was no contact between them now. I'd thought that when they'd broken up and Ben had moved here, all communication had dwindled and finally stopped altogether. But clearly that was just my hopeful imagination joining up the dots and coming up with a picture I preferred, rather than the actual truth.

'Do you happen to know if Ben is at home?'

'No. He's out.' I could have expanded. I could have said he was at the funeral of a close friend, but for some reason I wanted to keep that information from her, because she had nothing to do with Tom. Or maybe she did. Suddenly I felt like I was stepping down from an amusement park roller-coaster, and had no idea which way was up. 'I don't think he's coming back until quite late,' I added, in an attempt to be helpful. *Helpful? Really?* questioned my inner conscience.

'Oh fuck it, that's so annoying,' Holly said. The profanity slid easily from her lip-glossed mouth, making me think she probably used that word a lot. Great, now I was turning into a prude too. 'I really wanted to see him today, and

I've had such a long drive. Perhaps I should have phoned first.' *You reckon?* 'Except I'd really wanted to surprise him.' She frowned, and even that didn't make her look any less attractive. 'I really don't think I can hang around here all day waiting.'

I tried not to look disproportionately pleased, and effectively masked my small smile of relief, which faded away as she added, 'Unless I rearrange my plans and go home tomorrow.'

The words Ben and I had exchanged by the church and the unspoken promise they contained were fast dissolving. To be fair, I don't think either of us had anticipated including his former girlfriend in our evening plans.

'Perhaps I could give him a message for you?' I volunteered, trying to be helpful, but only because I suddenly wanted her to be somewhere else, far, far away. There was something about her being there that had set every inner warning bell ringing like crazy in my head. And I didn't know why. That was the moment when it happened; when a strong gust of wind swirled around us ... and suddenly everything changed. The two sides of Holly's coat blew apart, revealing an expensive-looking sheath dress that clung to her full breasts, and just as snugly hugged the unmistakable baby bump.

Her hand went to her swollen belly, perhaps unconsciously, but somehow I didn't think so. 'Actually, don't take this the wrong way, but what I need to speak to Ben about is sort of private.'

I realised then how little Ben had ever spoken about his former relationship. I didn't know exactly when they'd broken up, or why, or if they'd seen each other since he'd moved to his new home. I was trying very hard not to jump to conclusions, because inevitably they took you somewhere you didn't want to go. But the evidence was starting to pile up, and for the first time I wondered if I'd been the biggest kind of fool. A very pregnant woman turns up on the doorstep of her former lover, with something personal she needs to tell him. Two and two doesn't always make four . . . except sometimes it very obviously does.

'Are you one of Ben's neighbours?'

'In a manner of speaking,' I said, wondering why I was already backing away from revealing I was something more in his life than that. Perhaps it was because suddenly I was no longer sure that I was. 'I live in the basement flat,' I added.

Holly looked at me with greater interest, and I tried not to flinch under the raking scrutiny from her emerald eyes, which I noticed were the same shade as my cat's. I could see she was doing her own mental arithmetic, adding up the facts as she saw them and trying to work out my place in the equation. *Good luck with that*, I thought, wondering why the voice speaking in my head suddenly sounded so full of defeat.

'Oh, that's great,' said Holly. 'I don't suppose I could use your loo, could I? This baby's been playing football with my bladder for the last twenty minutes of my journey.'

That was far more information than I needed, but her

request left me with no option but to let the last woman I ever wanted to have anything to do with into my home. 'Er, yes of course,' I said. 'The front door is just around here.'

I directed her to my bathroom and she disappeared speedily towards it. I hovered uncertainly as I waited for her to emerge, fighting – and ultimately losing – a battle with common decency and good manners.

'Thanks for that,' Holly said. 'No one warns you pregnancy makes you practically incontinent, do they?' she asked.

'I wouldn't know,' I said, my voice as tightly wound as cotton around a reel. 'I don't have children.'

Holly nodded as though I'd just confirmed her private suspicion, and I was left wondering if she was just making innocent small talk, or being deliberately disingenuous.

'Can I offer you something to drink?'

Holly smiled, as though she'd known I would have to ask. She slipped off her coat and took a seat at the small table I'd shared so many times with Ben. It felt as though I was witnessing the theft of my own future, and there wasn't a single thing I could do to stop it.

'Would you like tea or coffee?' I asked, my smile so forced, it was making my cheeks ache.

'You wouldn't have any green tea, by any chance?'

The innocent question stung me like a hornet. My cupboard held only the variety favoured by builders, but Ben drank green tea. There was a box of it in his kitchen. Suddenly I realised that *I* was the outsider here, not her. She and Ben had history, a shared past. It was all too easy to see them, sipping their green tea, holidaying in fancy locations, and living a life that I had no business coveting.

'Ben has some upstairs. I'll just get it,' I said, suddenly anxious to put some distance between us. The smell of her perfume was filling my kitchen, and the knowing look in her clear green eyes was frankly a little too hard to stomach. I headed towards the door that led upstairs – the one we hadn't bothered closing since we'd spent the night together – and raced so fast up the wooden treads it probably looked as though I was being chased.

I lingered for as long as I could in Ben's kitchen, waiting until I was sure my face would betray none of the very unattractive thoughts and emotions flooding through me. Holly was still at my table when I returned, but something was in her hands, something dark and soft. I'd completely forgotten Ben had left a jumper hanging over the back of one of my chairs. She ran her hand over the soft cashmere of the garment, as though stroking a pet.

'I bought him this,' she said simply. And the words told me that I had lost, even before the battle had begun. 'So you and Ben are . . .?' She left the question hanging.

I turned awkwardly and dropped tea bags into the waiting mugs, buying myself time. 'We're . . . we're . . .' *What were we?* I had no idea. 'It's complicated.'

'I can't say I'm surprised he's found somebody. I always thought he would after we broke up.'

I poured boiling water into the mugs, with the deliberation of someone performing intricate surgery.

'I don't mind admitting you're a much better and braver person than me,' Holly declared. I turned slowly around. As much as I wanted to agree with her on that score, I had absolutely no idea what she was talking about.

Her hands went to her bump, while mine tightened into anxious fists. 'It's ironic really; the whole reason we broke up was because I couldn't face a future of being tied down and having to care for someone 24/7.' She looked down at her belly, and shrugged. 'And now look what's happened. That's exactly what I'm going to be doing. I guess you never know what life's going to throw at you, do you?'

Forget about understanding life and its meaning, I was having more than enough trouble just following the conversation. Was *that* the reason Ben and Holly had broken up? Had Ben wanted to have a child and she hadn't? And if the child she was now carrying *was* his, how would that affect his feelings . . . for Holly . . . for me . . .?

'How *is* Ben these days?' Holly asked, throwing me off balance by the sudden intensity of her question. 'I haven't seen him in ages.'

I couldn't stop my eyes dropping down to the evidence that said surely it couldn't have been much longer than six months, at the most. Her eyes followed the path mine had taken, and after a moment of looking totally blank, she began to laugh. 'Oh my God. Did you think this is his? That this is Ben's baby?'

I could feel my cheeks changing to the colour of her hair as I nodded dumbly.

'This is *Justin's*,' she said, patting the baby bump. As I had no idea who the hell Justin was, that didn't really clarify anything. 'He's my fiancé,' Holly added, and just like that I suddenly liked her a great deal more. It was a fleeting emotion, one that was soon to be totally destroyed. 'That's why I came here today, to tell Ben about the baby. It seemed only fair that he should hear it from me first, especially after the way *he* was so open about everything.' She gave a small shudder. 'Thank God this baby isn't Ben's, given his situation.'

'Situation?'

'Because of what's going on with him now.'

I felt slow and stupid; the country bumpkin in a room full of intellectuals. 'I'm sorry, I don't know what you're talking about.'

This time it was Holly's turn to look confused, and then just a little bit horrified. 'Oh my God. You and he are involved, and *he hasn't told you*?'

'Told me what?' My voice was tight with panic. I was a rabbit in the headlights, staring at the car that was about to run me over.

Holly bit her lip, and it was the first time in the brief period I had been in her company that she looked less than confident. 'Shit. You probably don't want to be hearing this from me . . . but Ben has MND.'

I misheard, prolonging the agony for a further few seconds, extending the time before the guillotine came crashing down, splicing my life in two. 'Ben has a what?'

Holly sat up straighter in her seat, looking uncomfortable

as she shook her head. 'M.N.D.,' she said, carefully enunciating each letter. 'Motor neurone disease. It's a—'

'I know what it is,' I interrupted, my voice thick and
rough.

'I can't believe he hasn't told you.'

I looked up, but it was hard to see her because she kept
shimmering like a mirage behind the tears that were filling
my eyes.

'Neither can I.'

'Were you *ever* going to tell me?' I'd thought of many opening remarks over the last eight hours, but that was the one
I kept coming back to and in the end, the one I went with.

Ben looked weary and drained, and some small part of me
was already saying I was doing this all wrong, but the box
was open now, and it was impossible to bundle the truth back
inside it. He paused and carefully shut the front door behind
him. His eyes did a quick and surprisingly efficient assessment
of the situation and my mood. I saw in that moment the kind
of businessman he had been: quick and decisive when trou-
bleshooting, not wasting precious time or effort on bullshit.
His gaze slid from my face to the open laptop in front of me,
with the page on MND clearly displayed. His eyebrows rose
a fraction when they fell on the small brown bottle of pills
that I'd taken from his medicine cupboard. At best, I'd risked
his disappointment by invading his privacy to find them. At
worst, I'd risked his anger.

He reached for the bottle, as though it was an exhibit in a

trial, and gave a long sad sigh. And that was the worse reaction of all, because it sounded like something ending.

My guilt at rifling through his possessions hadn't stood a chance when pitted against my driving need to disprove everything Holly had said. Even though a part of me already knew she'd been telling the truth. The pills had just confirmed it. With hindsight, every trip, every stumble, every fall I'd witnessed now became part of a picture I'd been too blind to see.

Ben didn't say, *'I don't know what you're talking about,'* and for that I was grateful. If he lied to me now it would all be over. The only thing left to tether us together was honesty. Without that we had nothing.

'How did you find out?'

'Holly came looking for you today. *She* told me.'

This time he *did* look shocked, but nowhere near as much as I had done every single minute since his ex-girlfriend had delivered her devastating news, and then decided to make a very hasty departure. Ben took off his coat and threw it onto the settee, his eyes never leaving my face.

'Why didn't you tell me, Ben, that you were sick? Why didn't you tell me what this disease was doing to you?'

He flinched, as though the prognosis was something he'd never considered before, and yet I knew from Holly that wasn't true. Ben had known for a very long time what the future had in store for him. He'd shared that information with her ... but not with me.

'Because for the first time in two years, I found myself

unable to accept it – all over again. I thought I'd made peace with what was happening to me. I'd moved on from "*Why me?*" to "*Why* not *me?*". And then you came along and I was right back where I started again. In denial. I *know* I should have told you. I've told you a thousand times in my head, but somehow the words never make it past my lips.' He ran his hand distractedly through his hair, which made him look unspeakably vulnerable and lost, and I wanted more than anything to run to him, to pull him into my arms and tell him everything was going to be alright, but the fear was back, keeping me prisoner on my chair.

'Sit down,' I said, as though this was my house and not his. Ben pulled out the chair beside me, and the nearness of him, the warm smell of him, the vitality of him, was like an assault on my senses. How could he be dying, when everything about him felt so alive?

Ben's eyes flickered briefly to my laptop screen, and then to the ruled pad on the table beside me, covered with my illegible scrawled notes and questions. They looked like the work of a madwoman, and so far removed from my usual meticulous note-taking, I wondered if sometime in the past eight hours I *had* lost a tiny piece of my mind. It had probably splintered away right after my heart cracked in two.

Ben's hands were resting on the table, but they didn't reach for mine. 'I didn't want you to have to face any of this, Sophie. I never intended for anyone to have to go through this with me.' As he spoke, Ben's eyes flew to the screen, seeing the words but not reading them. I had a feeling he was probably familiar with the site. 'After I was diagnosed, I sold my business, settled my finances and put my house in order. Then I came here to live.' He gave a humourless laugh and corrected himself. 'Then I came here to *die*. And I was okay with that.' I made a sound like an animal in a trap. 'I just wasn't expecting to find the one thing that would upset all of those plans.' His voice sounded broken as he continued. 'This was never meant to have happened. I never meant to hurt you. I never wanted to cause you more pain, but I couldn't stop myself from falling in love with you.'

He shimmered before me. There were two Bens, and then four, and then a whole roomful of them. It was the first time he'd said that he loved me, but it wasn't meant to be like this. None of it was meant to be like this. He turned, I turned, and suddenly I was in his arms and he was holding me tighter than I'd ever been held in my life.

'How long have you known?' My question was whispered into his shoulder.

'A while.'

I pulled out of his hold, so I could see his face. 'How long? How long exactly?'

His eyes dropped to the pad beside me, and I knew where his gaze had come to rest. It was on the words I'd ringed so many times I'd scored deep gouges in the paper. Six words that held my future bound within them: '*Life expectancy two to five years*'.

'The symptoms started about three years ago, but I ignored them for a long time.'

We both looked down at the pad as the worst sum I had ever had to calculate gave me its unthinkable answer.

'Have you had a second opinion? Because just one diagnosis from one doctor doesn't mean—'

'Sophie, please,' Ben begged, folding me back into his arms. 'Stop. Don't do this. I've seen people, plenty of people ... enough people.' His voice suddenly sounded weary and sad. It was a middle-of-the-night, giving-up voice, and I didn't recognise it as his at all. 'I've had consultations, they've done tests and then more tests. I've seen doctors, specialists ... quacks. I've done it all. They all say the same thing. It is what it is.'

'But there've been breakthroughs in research – there was one just recently that—' He tried to silence me with a kiss, but I wouldn't let him. 'And they've raised a load of money with that ice bucket challenge. *I did that*,' I added, as though my participation should have bought immunity for everyone I cared about.

'They *will* find a cure,' said Ben softly. 'I'm sure of it. But they might not find it in time for me.'

I shook my head so violently I could hear the crackle of my neck bones protesting. Ben placed his hands on either side of my head, immobilising me, so he could look deep into my eyes. 'I need you to do something for me now. Something very important.'

I knew what was coming and tried once again to move my head, but he held it steady within his strong grip. 'I need you to leave. Leave now. Tonight. Go downstairs, pack up your stuff and go.'

I thought my heart was already broken, but apparently there's no limit to how many times it can shatter over and over again. 'You have to leave, Sophie. You have to walk away ... because I know I sure as hell can't. Staying with me will destroy you.'

'And so will leaving,' I added, my voice breaking.

Chapter 13

'Oh Christ, that sucks. Poor Ben.'

I nodded, and took a long sip of Chardonnay, which totally failed to wash down the lump in my throat. I couldn't remember the last time Julia and I had cracked open a bottle of wine in the middle of the morning. Perhaps not since the day we got the results of our Finals. Although that had been a time of celebration, and today was the exact opposite. She'd reached for the bottle and two glasses before I was even halfway through telling her about Ben, and I hadn't stopped her.

'So what happens now?'

'He wants me to leave.'

'And what do you want?

'I want none of this to be true,' I said, reaching for a nearby box of tissues. Julia kept considerately silent while I cried quietly for several minutes.

'Sorry,' I said eventually as she pulled me into her arms,

the way she did with Lacey after she'd taken a tumble. And that was exactly how I felt, as though I was hurtling head first into a bottomless chasm.

'I guess this explains a lot: Ben's friends and his involvement with that bucket list thing.'

I nodded, remembering Ben's explanation. *'Someone at the hospital told me about the support group Maria had set up shortly before I moved here. I went a few of times, and realised it was something I wanted to be part of. Everyone there understood. We were all in the same boat. Then when Adam put the house on the market, it made perfect sense to buy it.'* Ben's eyes had met mine with an intensity it was hard to pull away from. *'The place was already set up for someone in a wheelchair.'*

'But you're not *in a wheelchair, Ben.'*

'Not yet,' he had replied quietly.

'Ben just seems so damn accepting about the whole thing,' I said, putting my wine glass down so forcefully I'm surprised it didn't crack.

'Well, for him this isn't breaking news, is it? He's had years to accept what is going to happen, and plan for it – you've just had hours. Did either of you manage to get any sleep at all last night?'

I shook my head, knowing I probably looked as terrible as I felt. Hours of talking had got us absolutely nowhere. His disease was like a maze we couldn't escape from.

'Do the doctors know how long Ben's got before things get . . . bad?' Julia's question dragged me back to the present, her words stinging like a hundred tiny paper cuts. I shook my head, already knowing the answer: that no two cases were the same. I'd spent hours the day before staring at screen after screen of facts, as though studying for an exam I'd never wanted to take. I'd learnt a lot during my dangerously informative internet session. But only the bleakest of facts appeared to have stuck. Facts Ben was well aware of, for he'd used them like weapons to drive me away.

'*Little by little, this disease will take me down. Everything I have, everything I am, is slowly going to disappear, piece by piece. It's going to be ugly, it's going to be upsetting and it's going to destroy not just my life, but also the life of anyone around me. I can't outrun it, I can't escape it. But I can protect the people I care about.*' Ben was almost in tears as he took my face gently in his hands. '*I can protect you.*'

Except he couldn't. Because I'd already read too much to be able to deny that what he was saying was true. The unfairness of it all made me want to scream, to beat my fists in frustration against the ground like a toddler in a tantrum. I wanted to yell at someone, to blame someone, but there was no one who could stop this. We were standing in the path of an inescapable tsunami. He wanted me to run from it while I still could, but I wanted to stay beside him to face it. Whatever we did, it was hopeless. We were going to drown either way.

'I think Ben might be right,' Julia said, picking her words cautiously, well aware she was charging straight into a conversational minefield. 'He knows what happened to Scott and how it affected you. And how you are about hospitals and sickness. I think he cares too much about you to screw you up again.'

'It's already too late to just walk away. Would *you*, if it was happening to Gary?'

She looked startled that I'd made that comparison. 'Gary and I are married. We've made a commitment to be with each other . . . in sickness and health, and all that.' Her eyes were suddenly watchful, unsure how I'd react to her words.

'No ceremony, no piece of paper, no big church wedding could make me more determined to be with Ben as he goes through this.'

Julia was motionless for a very long moment, studying me, and then a slow sad smile of acknowledgement crept over her face. 'Then what are you doing here? Go to him. Don't let him push you away. Take whatever time he has left and make every second of it count.'

It had all sounded so very simple in Julia's front room, but a lot harder to accomplish in reality. For a start it didn't look as though Ben was back from his hospital appointment yet, so all the clever arguments of persuasion that I'd been practising on the bus were probably going to have gone clean out of my head by the time we got to speak.

I let myself into the flat, and instantly sniffed the air like a dog picking up a scent. Something smelled different. I threw my coat over the back of a chair, and walked cautiously through my home, unable to shake off a feeling of indefinable 'wrongness'.

'Hello?' I called out, feeling stupid when the only answering cry was a feline one. Fred wound hopefully around my ankles, always ready for his next meal. I shooed him away, and with a deepening frown of concern I pushed open first the bedroom door, and then the one to the bathroom. Both rooms were empty.

Perhaps lack of sleep was making me crazy, I thought, as my eyes scanned the open-plan living area. There was clearly no one in the flat with me, but I still couldn't shake the feeling that there had been. It was the rug that confirmed it. The brightly patterned Mexican floor covering was in the wrong place. It was now at least a metre away from where it had been when I'd left to visit Julia several hours earlier.

Had Ben come down here looking for me? I had no idea how long his hospital appointments took, which was hardly a surprise, because until yesterday I hadn't even known that he had any. No wonder he knew his way so well around the various buildings and outpatient departments, I realised, as yet another tiny piece of the puzzle clicked into place. It was a startling thought, but it wasn't that which brought me to an abrupt halt.

I should have trusted my instincts. I should have listened more closely to my inner Goldilocks, because someone had definitely been in my flat. Not that I had any need to call the police, for the intruder hadn't taken a single thing with them. But they *had* left something behind. I was breathing faster, each exhalation ratcheting up my agitation as I walked slowly towards the door that led to Ben's part of the house. It hadn't been closed in over a week, but it was now firmly shut and sported a brand new heavy-duty lock. The gun-metal finish of the clunky mechanism had been sunk into the smooth oak of the door jamb. It looked like an affront on the wood. Ben had finally got around to calling out a locksmith.

I stared at the lock, my anger rising at everything it represented. He was shutting me out – in the most literal sense of the word – from his life. I spun on my heel and stomped into the kitchen, my eyes darting left and right. They fell on one of the drawers, and I yanked it open with such force that every single utensil within it jumped, before settling back into place on a jangling percussion of discordant notes. My hand reached into the back of the drawer and curled around the object I was looking for. Two voices, practically in unison, spoke in my head. *Really?* queried Scott. *You don't want to stop and think this through?* While the second voice was definitely laughing as it urged me onward. *That's my girl,* crowed Tom. *Go for it.*

I firmly gripped the rolling pin, bouncing it lightly in the palm of my hand, like a thug in a gangster movie, as I walked back to the door. I'd like to think there was a small voice of sanity that at least tried to stop me. I didn't want to believe that thirty-one years of law-abiding behaviour could so easily disappear under a wave of mindless vandalism. Except it wasn't mindless, it was a well-thought-out and considered reaction to something I found unacceptable.

It's still vandalism, said Scott. *In fact it's—*

I never heard what Scott thought that it was, for I lifted the rolling pin high above my head and swung it down with all my strength upon the lock. I have no idea how burglars manage to gain entry so easily. It took at least six blows before I successfully smashed the lock, and another four before I'd made a big enough mess of the door to ensure another one wouldn't be easily fitted.

My face was red and damp from my efforts as I gave a final grunt of satisfaction and yanked open the now thoroughly destroyed door. The gasp I gave drew every last ounce of breath I had left from my lungs. Ben was beyond the door, leaning patiently against the wall, his arms crossed, with a very sanguine expression on his face for someone who'd just stood by and watched his property being destroyed. We looked at each other for a long moment. He broke the silence first.

'Having some trouble with the lock?'

I glanced at what was left of it, hanging uselessly from the architrave, and then down at the rolling pin in my hands. It was impossible to read his features and I had no idea if he was as mad at me as he probably deserved to be. He looked at my handiwork and then back at me. 'That cost me one hundred and fifteen pounds,' he said equably.

'You can take it out of my security deposit,' I replied, knowing we were both perfectly aware that I'd never left one. 'You can't shut me out, Ben,' I said, my voice sounding decidedly wobbly.

He was still hiding his feelings as he looked once more at the smashed lock. 'Apparently not.'

The rolling pin fell from my fingers and clattered noisily at my feet. He glanced down at it, and that was the first moment I realised that he wasn't angry, well, not about the door at least. 'I have to say, I feel far more comfortable now you've got rid of that.'

Pent-up emotions can only be held back for so long, and mine were already straining against every last flimsy restraint. Like a dam in a flood, they burst open on my sob. And then I was in his arms, and he was kissing my face, my eyes, and my lips, even while I was still crying.

'I'm not going to walk away, Ben. I won't. You can't come into my life and change it – change me – and then expect me to let you go like that.'

The kissing stopped and he looked at me sadly. 'At some point, you're going to have to let me go.'

As much as I didn't want to acknowledge it, I wasn't stupid. 'I know that. But please, Ben, not yet. Please don't make me go.'

His answer was to gather me even more tightly against him, until I wasn't sure if the pounding heartbeat I could feel resonating between us was his or mine, or whether our hearts had somehow managed to sync themselves in perfect rhythm for the time we had left.

We were both practically falling asleep at the table. A wakeful night, coupled with the emotional trauma, had turned me into a zombie, barely able to lift the spoon out of my soup bowl. Our matching red-rimmed eyes made us look like a pair of vampires. Even my lips felt tired, as I struggled to make them work.

'What made you change your mind?'

Ben leant back in his chair, his bowl and plate pushed carelessly to one side. 'Probably when I realised I was never going to be able to change yours.'

It was such a U-turn from his determination to face his condition alone, that something about his answer didn't quite ring true. I realised that for the time being at least, my inner lie-detector was going to be on high alert. 'There's more to it than that, isn't there?'

There was a grudging admiration in his eyes as he slowly nodded. 'Perhaps,' was all he said.

I reached for his hand, so clumsy with exhaustion that I almost knocked over my glass of water before lacing his fingers between mine. 'Tell me. What is it? After everything that's happened in the last twenty-four hours, I need you to promise there'll be no more secrets between us.'

Ben said nothing, as though considering my proposition, but it wasn't up for discussion. It had to be total honesty from here on in. That was the deal-breaker.

He nodded slowly and I realised that thankfully, he got that. 'I don't want you to get excited about this.'

I felt so shattered I didn't think I could summon up enough energy to get out of my chair, much less leap from it with excitement. 'About what?'

'These things take place all the time, and mostly they come to nothing at all.'

'What things?'

'Just don't get your hopes up, because I'm not going to.'

'Ben, if you don't tell me what you're going on about, I shall have to kill you myself, long before this bloody illness gets a chance. What are you talking about?'

He was trying hard not to smile, but a small one escaped him anyway. 'They've decided to put me on an experimental drug trial. I found out today that I qualified for it.'

For someone who thought they couldn't move at all, I was out of my chair with astonishing speed and racing around the table to throw my arms around him.

'I knew you'd overreact,' he said, gently unfurling my arms from around his neck.

'I'm not,' I protested. 'Well, maybe I am a little. But bloody hell, this is *wonderful* news. What sort of drug is it? What do they hope it will do? When will they know if it's working?'

Ben shook his head at the sudden irrepressible grin that I couldn't keep off my face. 'There's a folder upstairs with all the information, you can read it later.'

I nodded emphatically, loving this new full–disclosure I was suddenly allowed. Ben pulled me gently down onto his lap, and I curled myself against him like a tiny marsupial. 'These trials happen all the time, Sophie. And mostly they come to nothing. I might not even be on the drug at all; they might have put me on the placebo.'

I wasn't prepared to let a single negative thought intrude

on what was the only spark of hope that I could see on the horizon. 'But they might not have. You said yourself they'll find a cure one day. Why not now? Why not with this drug?' I kissed the side of his neck and his fingers gently stroked my hair. 'At least it's something. It's something we can hope about, isn't it?'

'It is,' he agreed.

We slept together that night, for the first time since Tom died. It wasn't a euphemism, because that was literally all we did. Sleep. I don't think either of us would have been capable of instigating or sustaining anything more than that. This time we shared my bed, instead of his. I can't even remember climbing out of my clothes, and it was almost a surprise to feel the warmth of his naked body behind me as he drew me back against him.

I wriggled backwards and his body responded, but my own was a traitor sabotaging the moment. My eyes refused to stay open and my limbs felt like lead. Ben folded his arms even more securely around me and whispered into my ear, 'Go to sleep.' And as though I was obeying a hypnotist's command, I did.

'I have a surprise.'

The voice sounded remarkably tangible, if it was indeed coming from my dream. I felt the mattress dip beside me and heard the soft clink of ceramic on wood as a mug was set down on my bedside table.

I opened one eye and was amazed to see it was already fully light. I forced the second eye to join in, and saw that Ben was dressed – well, partially dressed anyway – in a pair of softly faded jeans. His hair was damp from the shower, and I could hear the distant strains of music playing on the kitchen radio. My sleep must have been more like a coma, for I hadn't heard a thing.

'Although,' Ben continued, as though I wasn't semi-comatose and largely incapable of coherent speech, 'it's now occurred to me that I probably should have waited and checked with you first. Plus, I don't even know if you *like* surprises.'

'Uhh?' That was all I could manage.

I forced my eyes to open wider and saw that Ben was grinning. He looked about ten years old, if you were able to disregard the dark stubble on his cheeks, that is. 'Not a morning person, then?' he teased.

I rubbed my eyes, which felt unattractively gritty, and pushed my hair – which probably looked like an abandoned bird's nest – off my face. 'Not so much,' I mumbled, reaching for the mug and the much-needed caffeine hit. It helped, a bit.

'I shall have to remember that,' Ben replied, which made me smile, mid-sip, because of all it implied. I wanted a life-time of mornings ahead of us. Two years' worth was going to be hard to settle for, now I knew that more might be possible. His warning not to get my hopes up about the drug trial might as well not have been given. For a pessimist I was being astonishingly 'glass-half-full'.

The coffee was beginning to kick in. 'What sort of a surprise?' I asked dubiously. The day before had been full of them, and none could be described as remotely pleasant. I wasn't sure I was ready to face any more.

Ben was already on my wavelength. 'The nice kind.'

He took a sip from his own drink and I tried not to stare at the movement of muscles in his arms, shoulders and back as he replaced his mug next to mine. Semi-clothed, Ben was a very distracting, although pleasant sight to wake up to.

'It was actually something *you* said last night that made me think of it.' He looked at me encouragingly, as though that should be enough for me to work out what he meant.

'I'm going to need more than that.'

Ben got to his feet, and I found the change of view equally appealing. There was a dark shadow of soft hair on his chest, that arrowed down very interestingly before disappearing into the waistband of his jeans. Jerking my eyes back to his face was a real effort.

'It was when we were talking about the bucket list wishes that I help out with, and you asked what was on *my* list.'

Amazingly I blushed, just as I'd done when the subject had come up the night before.

'Well, there is one thing I'd like to tick off.' His voice had lowered. *'It's something I've been thinking about and having the kind of dreams about that I thought I'd outgrown a very long time ago.'* My embarrassment, which I admit was a little ridiculous for a woman of my age, seemed to charm him. *'But I'm hoping that we can scratch that off the list before too much longer.'*

The question had been there in his eyes, and my answer had been in mine.

But when I'd asked if there was anything else he wanted to do, anything a little less PG, or somewhere he wanted to visit, Ben had just shrugged. *'There's nowhere I really want to be except right here.'* It had been exactly what I'd wanted to hear. Except now it looked as though he had revised that answer overnight.

'There's a place we regularly went to on holiday when I was a kid. It's in a pretty remote section of the Welsh coastline. I've often thought about going back there.'

'You should do it,' I said, tugging the duvet up a little higher to cover my breasts, which felt very exposed in the sheer bra I'd slept in.

'I was hoping you'd say that, because I found the place online and made a couple of calls while you slept, and we could go there for a few days.'

Just how early had Ben got up? 'We should definitely do that,' I agreed. 'When did you have in mind?'

'Today,' he said, his face widening into a broad grin. We were chalk and cheese. He was brave, I was fearful; he was an optimist, and I wasn't; he was impulsive, and I planned and scheduled every detail of my life. It was as though we were at a fork in the road where Ben was 'now' and Sophie was 'then'. All at once I knew which path I wanted to travel.

'Okay,' I said impulsively. 'Just get out of here so I can have a shower and we can be on our way.'

*

It was a long journey, but we didn't share the driving, and I better understood now why not. For as long as he could, Ben wanted to drive. Of course, it could just as easily have been because he'd seen me trying to park on the couple of occasions when I'd borrowed his car.

It had been remarkably easy to drop everything on impulse and decide to take a break. It made me realise it was one of the advantages of being self-employed that I rarely exploited. Ben actually looked a little shocked when I admitted that this would be the first holiday – mini or otherwise – that I'd taken in years. I spent a millisecond or two wondering how many times he and Holly had gone away together, before dismissing her from my thoughts.

In a last-minute pang of conscience I threw my laptop into my bag, in case the urge to work proved too great to resist. But when I walked towards Ben, who looked happy and relaxed as he waited for me beside the open car door, I knew for certain it wasn't coming out of its case.

We didn't speak of his illness at all during the journey, and that was fine with me, because we'd talked about practically nothing else the day before. Instead we chatted about childhood holidays, and for once I found I could speak about Scott without automatically re-living the dreadful night when we'd lost him. Ben had no brothers or sisters, and perhaps that was why he asked so many questions about mine. Or maybe he was cleverly making me re-examine my past and realise that there were a thousand memories that I could revisit without having to feel sad.

We stopped for lunch in a small pub, and although I noticed Ben limping slightly as he got out of the car, I said nothing. If he wanted a nurse in his life he'd have hired one, and the thoughts I was having as he slid his arm around my waist and pulled me against him would have got me struck off any nursing register. I had deliberately not asked Ben very much about the cottage he'd rented for us. All I knew was that it was remote, set practically on the beach, and that it had an open fireplace so big you could stand inside it. I wasn't sure if that would be as true for thirty-two-year-old Ben as it had been for his twelve-year-old self, but I was happy to wait to find out.

It was already starting to get dark when Ben pulled off the main road and took a detour down a narrow lane. 'There's not much in the way of shops or restaurants near the cottage. It's pretty isolated.' He sounded worried, as though that might bother me, but I just smiled widely. It sounded idyllic. 'If I remember rightly, there's a fairly large store not far from here, so we can stop there and pick up some basic provisions.'

A few minutes later Ben swung into the car park of the convenience store. There was a solitary vehicle parked in an area reserved for staff, but apart from that ours was the only car in sight. He switched off the engine and we both stared through the windscreen at the small shop.

'Is this it?' I asked, peering through the late-afternoon light at the small shop front.

'I swear this place used to be bigger,' Ben said, reaching

for my hand and leading me across the tarmac towards the entrance.

'Things always seem smaller when you get older,' I said, and then laughed when I saw the twinkle of amusement in his eyes. We were both still laughing as we walked into the shop and an old-fashioned bell clanged above our heads.

Ben carried the basket, and I threw boxes and packets haphazardly into it, as though we were staying there for weeks instead of just days. We laughed a lot as we walked up and down the aisles, although I have no idea what about. It's not as if grocery shopping is exactly amusing, but with Ben it seemed like fun. When we weren't laughing, or teasing each other, Ben would steal an unexpected kiss. 'White bread or wholemeal?' was answered with his lips covering mine. 'Whatever you prefer.'

I could see a middle-aged woman sitting behind an old-fashioned cash register watching us as we shopped, with an indulgent smile on her face. When we eventually approached the till we had two fully laden baskets – neither of which Ben would allow me to carry.

'Are you staying nearby?' the assistant asked conversationally as she began ringing up our goods. It was the first time in years I had seen anyone do it that way, rather than swiping a barcode.

Ben gave the name of the location of the cottage, and the woman nodded. 'It's a lovely spot, although a bit quiet and remote at this time of year.'

Ben slipped his arm around my waist and gave me a gentle

squeeze. 'That sounds perfect,' he said, giving me a quick flash of a smile that made my knees go a little strange.

'Newlyweds, are you?' asked the woman. I was wearing gloves, so there was no ring on my finger to prove or disprove her assumption. On the counter beside her was an open paperback that she'd been reading when we arrived. It was a they-all-lived-happily-ever-after type of love story, and I suspected she'd privately spun her own romantic tale about Ben and me.

'Yes, we are. It's our honeymoon,' said Ben, and I thought for a moment that he was teasing her, or me, but then I saw the look in his eyes and I realised that he was actually being serious. A whole herd of butterflies moved into my stomach, and refused to settle down.

'Well, then, you must have this . . . on the house,' said the woman warmly, slipping a bottle of cheap sparkling white wine into the carrier bags along with our groceries.

Ben thanked her warmly while I was too busy blushing, just like the bride she believed that I was.

It was just as well Ben had a good memory and an even better sense of direction, because the Sat Nav didn't even recognise that the narrow dusty track we turned down existed. Tall grasses grew impudently in the middle of the road, and gradually the dirt around them became grittier with sand.

'Almost there,' Ben assured confidently, taking one hand from the wheel to squeeze mine. The lane was narrow and twisty, barely wide enough for the car, but there was no worry of oncoming traffic, for the cottage was the only property it served. After one last sharp turn, Ben's headlights picked up the silhouette of a single-storey, wooden-clad residence, positioned so close to the edge of the beach it almost looked as though it had been washed up by the tide.

Even before we'd come to a stop, I already knew that I loved it. It was quaint, and quirky, and looked more like a drawing in a child's fairy-tale book than somewhere real people could live. It faced the beach, and had two shallow steps leading down from a planked deck to a tiny garden that was more sand than grass. Several struts on the picket fence surrounding the cottage were askew or missing. Yet even that looked welcoming, like a broad grin from a mouth of unfortunately neglected teeth.

The wind, heavy with grains of sand, stung my cheeks as soon as I stepped out of the car. I burrowed my chin into the collar of my coat to escape its abrasive caress. The window frames hadn't found it so easy to avoid, and curling tendrils of peeling paint hung from every sill, like feathers after a pillow fight.

'The owner did say something about it being a little "weather worn",' said Ben apologetically, as he came to stand beside me, an arm going around my shoulders. 'I'm guessing they don't have many out-of-season visitors.'

I turned and slid my arms around his waist beneath his open jacket, loving the warmth and solidness of him.

'It's not quite how I remembered it,' admitted Ben. 'It seems—'

'Smaller?' I suggested.

'I was going to say shabbier,' he corrected, looking over the top of my head at the cottage. 'We could always try and find a hotel somewhere, if you don't like it.'

'Absolutely not. I think it's wonderful.' I swivelled to face the vast expanse of beach and the rapidly incoming tide, which was only just visible in the fading light. 'And look, we've practically got a private beach and our very own ocean.'

He squeezed me tightly and kissed the top of my head. 'I think it's actually a sea, but I get your point. As long as you're sure it's okay?'

It was sweet how concerned Ben was that everything should be absolutely perfect. He clearly didn't realise that he could have brought me to a derelict hovel, and I'd have been just as enthusiastic. He lowered his head and placed a soft kiss on my lips, and his mouth tasted of salt from the sea spray, and even that felt exciting and different.

'Just who is this new optimistic Sophie Winter?' Ben teased, his teeth gently nipping on my lower lip. I shivered, and it wasn't because I felt cold.

'I have absolutely no idea,' I replied honestly. 'But I really rather like her.'

Ben insisted on carrying in both of our cases, although I did manage to wrest one of the heavy grocery bags from his arms. After a moment's reluctance he passed it over, and I got a sudden glimpse of how hard the future would be for him, when he *had* to accept his limitations. He wouldn't find it easy conceding to the mutiny of his muscles, when they one day refused to obey his commands. But perhaps this new drug could stop that from happening. *Don't pin all your hopes on a miracle, Sophie,* warned Scott silently. I shook my head in irritation, dismissing his words as if they were an annoyingly buzzing insect. Scott had no business being here. These days were Ben's and mine, and nothing was going to spoil them.

The lower floor of the cottage was basically just one large room, with a small but perfectly adequate kitchen at one end. The furniture was mostly wooden and rustic, making the whole place look a little like a pioneer's cabin. A vibrant Aztec-patterned throw covered one large settee, and I could already imagine us lying on it together, our bodies curled around each other. The room was dominated by the fireplace Ben had remembered so well, and I was pleased to see a generous pile of logs stacked up on one side of the huge inglenook.

'At least we won't be cold,' I said, shivering a little in the cool February air that had followed us in from the beach.

'Let me give you the grand tour of the place, and then I'll light a fire,' Ben promised. We dumped the groceries in the kitchen and I put my hand in his as he led me towards a narrow corridor. 'The bathroom's at the end of the hallway, but I'll show you the bedrooms first.' I nodded, as a weird fluttery sensation shimmied inside me. I was embarrassingly aware of the sudden dampness of my palms, and really hoped Ben hadn't noticed.

'This is the smallest bedroom,' he said, coming to a halt in front of a cottage-style batten door. 'It's the one I used to sleep in when I was a child.' I smiled, but my sudden nervousness made it look unnatural, as though it didn't quite fit my mouth. Ben took my other hand in his and his eyes looked concerned. 'It's the room I will happily sleep in again, if you don't feel ready for ... anything more,' he said softly.

My eyes widened, and I was already shaking my head as he reached for the black iron latch. 'I'd be perfectly comfortable in here,' he assured, pressing down on the handle and allowing the door to swing open to reveal a hot water tank, an ironing board, and a floor mop.

I'm not sure which of us laughed first, but once we started it was hard to stop. By the time I brushed away the escaping tears from the corner of my eye, his mistake had evaporated all the awkwardness away.

'Are you sure? Because it looks a little cramped to me,' I replied, still chuckling. It had been a long time since I'd laughed so long and hard at something that probably didn't deserve it.

Ben pulled me towards him, and suddenly the reason to be fearful, to hold back, was gone as though it had never been. 'In my defence, it *has* been a very long time since I was here.' The fact that he'd never brought Holly to this place was just one more reason to love it.

The next door *was* the second bedroom, and although I knew without a single doubt or hesitation that no one would be occupying it during our stay, I still looked with interest at the room where a much younger Ben had once slept.

The room held a solitary single bed which was positioned beneath the window, and through the undrawn curtains I could see the white foam of every incoming wave. I squinted into the darkness, trying to conjure up the ghost of the boy he'd been, small freckled nose pressed firmly up against the window. 'I used to sit there for hours watching the sea, probably dreaming about being a pirate,' Ben confided, as though he'd somehow read my thoughts. He was standing behind me, and I leant back against him as his arms locked around my waist.

'Were you lonely here, without other children to play with?' My own childhood holidays were a tapestry of memories, with Scott firmly woven into each one.

I felt his shrug rather than saw it. 'It was all I knew, and I was happy with my own company. I was still a good and well-behaved kid when we used to come here.'

There was something in his voice and his words that alerted my radar. He spoke of his childhood so infrequently I'd had to join up my own dots to form the picture. All I knew for certain was that things had been difficult for Ben and his mum when his father had walked out on them following an affair. One night, after a few too many glasses of wine, he'd confessed that he'd 'gone a little wild' for a time as a teenager, before turning his life back around. But when I'd asked him about it, he'd clammed up, and I was the last person in the world to press on a door that someone wanted to stay shut.

The master bedroom was spacious. The wooden-clad walls were whitewashed, as were the floorboards, and everywhere you looked there were reminders of our proximity to the sea. Enormous conch shells and unusually shaped pieces of driftwood were scattered around the room, as though one day, when no one had been paying attention, the tide had simply washed them in through the window. The sound of the sea, whistling its maritime melody, was even louder in here, and I wondered what it would feel like to go to sleep with its constant murmur in the background. I guessed I wouldn't have to wait too much longer before I found out. I gave a little shiver, which happily Ben mistook.

'We need to warm this place up,' he said, rubbing his large hands briskly up and down my arms, as though my circulation needed assistance, when in fact nothing could be further from the truth. The blood was literally racing through every vein and capillary as I imagined us lying side-by-side on the one piece of furniture my eyes kept returning to. The wooden frame of the large double bed was painted a soft sky blue, and a bright patchwork quilt made the bed look even more inviting. I thought again of Ben telling the shop assistant that we were on our honeymoon, and felt the beginnings of a blush warm my cheeks.

'Well, I don't know about you, but I'm absolutely *starving*. Why don't I make a start on dinner?' I sounded too bubbly, too cheery, as though I was auditioning for the role of 'very excitable person' in a play. And I was a shoo-in to get it.

By the time I'd chopped vegetables for the pasta sauce and finally worked out how to turn on the cooker, I'd managed to calm down. It was just the anticipation that was making me jittery, I thought, as I threw salad ingredients into a bowl. Anticipation and excitement, I acknowledged, aware that my hand holding the glass to clink it lightly against Ben's was trembling slightly. The wine rose and fell, mimicking the swell of the waves crashing on the beach outside.

The cottage had heated up quickly once the fire was lit, so I'd been able to discard my thick jumper and was comfortably warm wearing just a shirt and jeans. Ben had also removed his warmer clothing, and joined me at the small dining table in faded jeans and a form-fitting black T-shirt. He was a master of relaxed and easy-going conversation, and after two glasses from our gifted bottle of wine, I finally felt more at ease.

I washed up sloppily, all too aware of the man standing beside me, who somehow managed to look more attractive than ever while wielding a tea towel. I spent far longer than I needed to straightening up the perfectly tidy kitchen, and wiping down the already spotless worktops. When the kitchen was clean enough to conduct surgical procedures, I eventually laid down my cloth.

Ben had placed some fresh logs on top of the flames, and when I finally crossed the room to join him by the fire, they were popping and crackling. And so was I. Very deliberately,

Ben reached over and removed the wine glass from my hand, placing it on a nearby side table. It collided lightly with the lamp, as though making a toast, and it was only then that I realised that Ben was nervous too. Although possibly for an entirely different reason.

He stepped towards me, his hand reaching out and gently cupping my cheek. 'I would love nothing more than to make this feel like a proper honeymoon night,' he said, his voice low and husky. 'What I want to do now is pick you up in my arms and carry you into the bedroom.' My pulse quickened, and I realised that even his voice had the power to turn me on more than any other man had ever been able to do. 'Except I have a horrible vision of us ending up in a tangle of limbs on the floor.' I almost smiled, because I thought he was joking until I looked into his eyes and saw genuine regret. 'It's just one other thing this illness has stolen from me.'

I reached for his free hand and brought it up to my lips, kissing the back of his fingers. 'I don't need those kind of theatrics . . . I just need you.' It was the first time I had admitted it, and he only had to look into my eyes to see how true it was.

'I need you too. More than I should. More than I'm capable of stopping.' Ben's mouth was so close to mine that I couldn't tell if the warmth on my lips was from his breath or mine. 'I don't want to disappoint you tonight.' His voice sounded sad, and I hated the disease that made him feel this way. Hated it like the enemy that it was, trying to come between us. 'It's been a while, for me,' confessed Ben. 'I've not been with anyone since I was diagnosed. 'I'm not exactly sure if—'

I silenced his words with a kiss. 'Then it's about time we found out.' His mouth and tongue were warm and slow as they met with mine, but his eyes were alive with desire when they finally opened and looked at me.

'So this is just in the name of scientific research?' His words were so low it was hard to distinguish them from a throaty growl.

'Absolutely,' I said, my own voice breathy with longing.

Ben took my hand and gently began drawing me towards the bedroom.

It was slow and beautiful. He undressed me as though I was made of glass, and I certainly felt I could shatter into a million pieces as he ran his hands tenderly over my naked body. His own clothes came off far quicker. The bed sheets were cold, stealing the breath from me as he gently pushed me down upon them, his kiss never stopping, even as his hands travelled up from my ribcage to find and caress my breasts. And then nothing was cold; everything was on fire. It burnt slowly, making sure everything combustible within me was alight. And when my legs parted beneath him and we were finally one, everything was ablaze. We'd met in flames on a night long ago, and with the sound of the sea as our soundtrack, we rode together through an entirely different type of inferno.

*

He stood by the window, naked, the reflected moonlight turning his skin to alabaster.

'Ben?'

He turned, and was just a second too slow to hide the look of sadness in his eyes.

'Is something wrong?'

He shook his head. 'Go back to sleep.'

My eyes were heavy, and it would have been easy to do as he said. By morning I wouldn't even be sure if this conversation had happened at all. I threw back the covers, gasping at the coolness of the air in the room, and came to stand behind him, linking my arms around his taut flat stomach. I knew he could feel the softness of my breasts pressed against him from his sharply indrawn breath.

'Is everything alright?' I whispered into the skin of his back.

It was a ridiculous question, because clearly everything wasn't. For an awful moment I wondered if he regretted having taken our relationship to this next level and then he reached for me, tugging me around until I was in his arms. There were tears glinting in his eyes, and I loved the way he didn't try to brush them back or dismiss their presence.

'I love you, Sophie. I am always going to love you.'

Let me remember this moment, this perfect moment, I pleaded to a God I hadn't believed in for a very long time. *I won't mind remembering all the horrible ones from the past, or those that have yet to come. Just let me keep this one.*

'I love you too,' I said, my words a vow and a prayer that I'd never stop believing in.

We woke slowly to the squawking of gulls. Grey morning light cast peculiar shadows on the walls, and for a moment I couldn't remember where I was, and then my brain did a rapid assessment. Warm breath fanning the back of my neck; a pair of legs bent behind mine in perfect tessellation; one large hard cupping my breast . . . its fingers seeking and finding the nipple that was already awake and ready for his touch. I knew *exactly* where I was. I was where I always wanted to be.

The need for food eventually dragged us out of bed, and the temperature of the room made us reach for the clothes that were scattered in a telling circle all around it. 'I'm going to have to keep that fire going day and night,' Ben said, looking at the hearth where just a few glowing red embers remained. 'That way we won't need to bother with all these unnecessary layers.' His hand slid easily up beneath my untucked shirt and found my boob. My bra was still MIA, and I was actually rather pleased not to have found it. Pleased for a good ten minutes or so, before I reluctantly pushed him away.

'Breakfast,' I said, trying to sound as though I was scolding him, while the heat from my eyes revealed my true feelings.

I've always been more of a bowl of Corn Flakes or a slice of toast person, but I devoured the eggs, bacon and sausages I cooked with almost embarrassing gusto. 'I'm going to have to do an awful lot of exercise while we're here if I still want to fit into these jeans,' I said, pushing back from the table with a satisfied smile on my face.

'Funny you should say that, because that's just what I had in mind,' Ben teased, with a devilish glint in his eyes.

I dropped my eyes as though suddenly shy, and then lifted them to meet his and the message I sent him made him groan softly. I smiled and reached for the dirty plates.

'Leave those. I'll do them and light us a fire. Why don't you go and have a shower and then perhaps afterwards we could go for a walk on the beach?'

I glanced out of the window. The wind was blowing fiercely and droplets of rain were already splattering against the glass. It looked cold, it looked like February, and it looked like winter, but all I saw was warmth and blue skies.

'That sounds perfect.'

I half hoped Ben would join me in the shower cubicle. I'd already assessed it for size and suitability while smoothing the foaming gel all over me. It was something I'd seen in films, and read about in countless books, but I'd never yet experienced it. I smiled to myself beneath the hot droplets of water raining down on my head. You could say it featured on my own personal bucket list. My fingers turned a little prune-like and the hot water was beginning to cool before I acknowledged that my secret fantasy was going to have to wait for another time.

By the time I'd dressed in the warmest clothes I'd brought

with me and dried my hair, Ben had already got the fire blazing once more. I had a cheeky sentence planned in my head,
about what he'd missed by not joining me in the shower,
but I never got to say it. He rose slowly from his position at
the hearth, and when he turned to face me, the cut was the
first thing I saw. It wasn't deep, and had probably stopped
bleeding a little while ago. The bruise that went with it was
already a grey smudgy thumbprint on his forehead. Ben's
eyes went to mine, and I could see he was watchfully waiting
for my reaction. Out of nowhere we were suddenly at a very
important moment.

He'd fallen before and he would fall again, I knew that.
What made this occasion different was how I reacted to it. If
I played this wrong, I would re-write my place in his future.
An echo of Julia calmly dealing with one of Lacey's many
scrapes came to mind. *'You can't wrap your kids in cotton wool,
it suffocates them.'* It would have exactly the same effect on
the man I loved.

'The shower was really good,' I announced, crossing
over to the fire and extending my hands to its warmth. Ben
came to stand beside me, and slid his arm around my waist,
drawing me closer. I laid my head on his shoulder and sighed
softly, still sad that his illness had been such an efficient
stalker, tracking us down, even here. The calling card it
had left behind was an unnecessary reminder that we could
never outrun it.

I allowed myself just one tiny acknowledgement of what
had happened. As we stood at the cottage door, dressed

warmly in coats and scarves, I stood on tiptoe and reached up to press a feather-light kiss on the small injury. Ben's eyes met mine, but no words were spoken. They weren't necessary.

The wind was a bully, pummelling us with invisible fists as we headed along the beach. It whipped strands free from the ponytail my hair was now long enough to be tied up in, and flicked sand against our exposed skin. I snuggled closer to Ben's side, using him as a highly effective wind-break. The swell was high, and not surprisingly there were no boats braving the water, although Ben had said this area was popular with local fishermen. We walked just close enough to the water's edge to leave booted footprints in the wet sand, yet far enough in to avoid all but the boldest of incoming waves.

We walked slowly, pausing frequently as I stooped down to pick up tiny shells or pebbles with interesting markings. I dropped them into the pockets of my coat, until they could hold no more.

'If a wave comes in and washes you off your feet, you're going to sink straight to the bottom with that much ballast,' Ben teased.

I shrugged, which was actually quite hard to do, given the weight of my stone collection. 'I'm not worried,' I said confidently, coming to a stop and smiling up at him. 'You'll save me. It's what you do.' I brushed an annoying strand of hair from my face, and Ben captured my raised hand, turning it over and looking at the pink scar on my inner wrist. He ran his thumb slowly across the healed skin, and I shivered.

'For as long as I can,' he promised.

We walked hand-in-hand along the length of the beach, never once seeing another person, never once wanting to. Eventually Ben led us away from the water's edge to a small headland, bordered by tall grasses and deep sand dunes. It was a welcome relief to escape the bite of the wind, and I happily dropped down to sit beside him. Walking across the beach had been a challenge, with the undulating sand suck-ing hungrily on our feet, making each step a tug of war. My leg muscles were twitching and trembling from the effort and I suspected Ben's felt even worse, from the way he kept rubbing and kneading his thigh.

I inched closer to him, hoping he understood what the nudge of my shoulder against his actually meant: *I'm sorry that you're hurting. I'm with you. I'm here for you.* He turned and smiled so warmly at me, I think maybe he did.

'This was the spot where I used to spend hours of every holiday looking out for seals,' he said, raising a hand and holding it like a visor above his eyes as he scanned the undu-lating grey waves.

'Did you ever see any?'

'Only from a distance,' he said, probably unaware there was still a note of lingering regret in his voice. 'I always hoped I'd find one on that inlet over there.' He pointed over to a section of the shoreline, where the sand gave way to a narrow pebbled bank. 'But I never did.' I swivelled to look at the spot he'd indicated. If this was a book, if this was a film, a seal would be there now, fulfilling Ben's wish after all these years. But real life isn't like that. I'd worked that one out a very long time ago. Desperately wanting something isn't enough to make it happen. The dead can't come back, however much you miss them, illnesses can't suddenly be cured, and seals are sometimes as elusive unicorns.

I would never have been the one to give up first, but thankfully Ben called time on our nature watch before I turned into a human ice sculpture.

'I'm sorry,' he said, holding out his hand and pulling me to my feet. 'You should have said you were cold.'

'I'm f . . . fine,' I said through chattering teeth. Ben's eyebrows rose, but he allowed me the lie.

He paused for a long moment before we set off. 'We should come back here again.'

I nodded, already trying to work out how many more jumpers I would need to wear to keep out the February wind. 'Tomorrow,' I agreed.

He shook his head. 'No, not tomorrow. In the summer. When it's warm enough for us to stand by the shore and let the waves break over our feet. When the sun's so bright the glare on the sea will dazzle us.' He pulled me close and kissed me. 'When I can lie on a blanket, hold you in my arms, and watch the sun move across a clear blue sky. *That's* when we'll come back.'

'When the seals are here,' I added, so lost in the picture he'd painted it no longer mattered that I couldn't feel my toes any more.

Ben looked out at the water one last time and nodded, as though a deal had been struck.

I stood by the car, ignoring the wind that tried to force me into the vehicle's warm interior, to steal one last snapshot memory. Ben crouched down beside a planter on the deck to replace the cottage key from where we'd found it, before walking towards me. A sudden gust ran invisible fingers through his hair, and I wanted so badly to do the same that I rammed my hands deep into the pockets of my coat until I was certain they could be trusted to behave. Ben's body was a map that I'd explored with slow and delicious care, as he had mine. We'd discovered pathways and secrets and had followed them like lost explorers, until they led us somewhere neither of us had been expecting.

'That's everything, I think,' said Ben, stowing the final bag in the boot and sounding almost as reluctant to leave as I was. I tried to ignore the small worried voice that wondered if we'd be able to transport the magic of this place back home with us, or if we'd only find it again when we returned in the summer.

'It still seems a very dodgy place to leave a door key,' I muttered. 'I'm sure it's the first spot any self-respecting burglar would look.'

'Self-respecting criminals? Are they a thing?' Ben queried

with a grin, as he pulled me against him for a brief hard hug. It was impossible to explain my misplaced feelings of protectiveness for a property that wasn't even mine. Except something had happened to me here, something which I already knew had changed the path of my future. Ben had wanted to come here because it had been a significant part of his past, and there was a feeling of rightness and serendipity that it had now become part of ours too.

I had loved everything about our time here: every long frozen walk, every warming fireside thaw had been perfect. We'd sat side-by-side at the water's edge, watching the sun slip slowly into the grey waves, before walking hand-in-hand across the beach, like the last two survivors at the end of the world. We had no internet, no phone signal and yet I'd felt more connected to everything around me than ever before.

There wasn't a single moment that I'd have changed, I confided, while lying in Ben's arms on our final morning, my skin still damp and tingling from celebrating the end of our stay.

'Not even losing Scrabble, *every single time?*' Ben teased.

I kissed the hollow of his shoulder. 'Not even that, although I *still* think you were cheating.'

'Or the boiler that cut out in the middle of every shower?'

'Nothing wrong with a cold shower,' I replied sassily.

Ben's hands tightened on my hips, taking me by surprise as he effortlessly pulled me back on top of him. 'Hmm . . . per-haps I should have one,' he suggested. His eyes were dark, the pupils dilated like huge drops of black ink in molten caramel.

'Perhaps not,' I replied. My cheeks were flushed, but my eyes held his as I took the lead, pushing him back against the pillows to make one more last memory.

I swivelled like a child in my seat as he drove back along the dirt track, keeping the cottage in sight until the bend in the road robbed it from view.

'It will be even better when we come back,' Ben promised. I smiled and nodded, even though I knew he was wrong; nothing could *ever* be better than this.

Chapter 14

March

Two falls, but one of them was my fault because I left my shoes in the middle of the floor.

I bought one of those rubber slip mats and put it in Ben's shower. It looked ugly.

He put the slip mat in the bin. I took it out again. It's still in the shower.

He uses the banister more than he used to when climbing the stairs.

Still on the drug trial.

Chapter 15

April

I deliberately walk a little slower when we're out together. I don't think Ben has noticed.

He has.

Two trips outside the house, but the kerb is much higher on that section of pavement than it should be. Someone should write to the council.

One dropped mug. But it was the one with the silly handle, which is ridiculously difficult to hold on to, so that was probably why.

He types out notes, rather than writing them by hand. But why not? The computer is right there, and you can never find a pen when you need one.

Someone couldn't understand what he said on the phone the other day. But it was a bad line. I should probably get BT to check it.

The hospital gave Ben a walking stick. He threw it in the cupboard. It's still there.

Still on the drug trial.

Chapter 16

May

I finish every meal before he does. I should really learn to chew more. What do they say? Thirty times before you swallow a mouthful? Sounds ridiculous, but I'm going to try.

Four falls.

I drive more than Ben these days. But I *love* driving his car. He teases me about my parking.

One dropped casserole dish. But those oven gloves are rubbish. I'm going to get some new ones. We got a Chinese takeaway instead. We didn't bother with chopsticks.

Someone asked Ben if he'd been drinking. For fuck's sake, it was ten o'clock in the morning. People are so dumb.

Julia couldn't understand something he said when we were round there for dinner. We all laughed.

Still on the drug trial.

Chapter 17

June

I caught a cold. A summer cold, although it doesn't feel much like summer yet.

It took me ages to shake it off.

Ben caught my cold.

Still on the drug trial.

Chapter 18

I don't believe in telepathy. When one of the girls at uni said she'd known her twin had broken her leg before she ever got the message, we all thought she was making it up. I certainly never had any inkling that Scott had been in danger on the night the car ploughed into his bike, and we were just about as close as two siblings could possibly be.

And yet I'd woken that morning with a prescient feeling of approaching danger. Despite having looked forward to it for days, I suddenly didn't want to have lunch at the fancy restaurant I'd booked to celebrate Julia's birthday with her. I didn't want to go anywhere: not out of the house; out of this bed; or out of Ben's arms. But the alarm clock was no respecter of my sudden change of heart, and rang mercilessly until I was forced to turn over and thump it belligerently into silence.

Amazingly it didn't appear to have woken Ben, and for that I was especially glad. He'd been awake for half the night coughing, and as a result neither of us had slept well. The morning light wasn't particularly conducive in tempting me to emerge from the marshmallow depths of the duvet. 'Flaming June' had yet to put in an appearance, and 'grey and damp June', her considerably less appealing sister, was still holding centre stage. A fine sheen of drizzle clung to the surface of the window, like condensation in a greenhouse.

I swung my feet out of bed, and like a pair of blind moles they began searching for my slippers. They'd just found them when Ben's hand reached across the mattress and circled my wrist.

'Are you getting up already?' He sounded disappointed, and the temptation to wriggle back under the covers and curl myself around him once more was hard to resist. I glanced at the clock, ran through everything I needed to do before I met Julia in town, and sighed regretfully.

'I have to. But *you* should go back to sleep,' I suggested. 'I'm just going to jump in the shower downstairs.' Strangely, although we shared Ben's bed each night, I still preferred to use my own bathroom in the basement flat, rather than his. Perhaps I wasn't quite ready for the total dissolution of the mystique so early in our relationship. Or it could just be because Ben took such a surprisingly long time in the bathroom that I got fed up waiting for my turn. *'You're worse than a girl,'* I'd teased, remembering with a small secret smile how he'd proceeding to demonstrate – very effectively – how very *un-girly* he was capable of being.

'No, I'll get up, if you are,' Ben said, sitting up and throwing aside the covers. Four months was nowhere near long enough for me to become immune. I still stared at his naked body as though I'd never seen it before . . . every single time. The hours he spent at the gym, or doing endless lengths of the local pool, as though preparing for a cross-Channel swim, were clearly visible. The irony, that Ben was in the best physical shape of his life, because of MND, wasn't lost on either of us.

He caught me staring and smiled, but the moment was ruined by yet another paroxysm of coughing. My eyes clouded in concern. 'You're coughing well.'

'Been up half the night practising,' he countered, which would have been an awful lot funnier if it hadn't been true.

'I wish you'd see a doctor about it.'

'I see enough doctors. It's just a cold.'

I didn't want to argue with him, especially if I was going out and leaving him alone for the day, but I felt another frisson of alarm as he got to his feet *(one hand on the bedside table for support; that was new)* and headed towards his bathroom.

The restaurant was busy. Apart from Julia and me, everyone appeared to be dressed in a suit. It was as though they'd sent out a dress code memo that hadn't reached either of us. Business, in one form or another, looked to be taking place at practically every table around us. At our white-linen-covered table, with its gleaming silver cutlery, the only item on today's agenda was the celebration of a birthday.

Julia snorted loudly, sounding genuinely porcine as she read my – admittedly rude – card. 'Well, that one can't go on the shelf with the others,' she said, stuffing it hurriedly back into its envelope as our waiter approached carrying two oversized menus. 'I have no intention of explaining to my daughter what *any* of those words mean!'

I smiled, waited until we were alone and then passed her a small box, almost hidden beneath its decoration of trailing corkscrew ribbons. The silver earrings I'd chosen were a big hit, and she immediately slipped them on. 'Very nice,' I said, glancing discreetly down at my watch while she examined her gift in a tiny mirror pulled from her bag. I thought she hadn't noticed, but I should have known better.

'Is something wrong? That's the fifth time you've checked either your watch or your phone since we sat down.'

'I'm sorry,' I said, pulling down the sleeve of my dress to cover my watch, just in case I was tempted to take one last peek. 'I'm just a bit worried about Den, that's all.'

'Has he fallen again?'

I shook my head, knowing how much he would hate hearing us discuss his condition like this. 'No, it's just that damn cough that he can't seem to get rid of.'

I closed my eyes for a moment, remembering the waxy pallor of his face and the tiny beads of perspiration on his upper lip as he kissed me goodbye.

'Do you want to call him?' Julia asked, her pretty face creasing in concern.

'Nah. He'll be fine,' I said, not sure which one of us I was trying to convince, because if it was *me*, it wasn't working. 'Anyway I think they confiscate your mobile if you get it out in fancy joints like this.'

'I *knew* we should have gone to McDonald's,' joked Julia, picking up her menu and blowing out a low whistle of amazement. 'My God, the selection on here is huge. It's going to take me at least an hour to choose what I want to order.'

I really hope not, I thought silently, and then felt instantly guilty. With two young children, this kind of daytime outing was a real treat for my best friend. By the time she'd organised child care, and got dressed in something that wasn't covered in Play Doh or baby sick, she deserved to enjoy her celebration at leisure, without her clock-watching companion ruining it for her.

'Anyway, Carla is calling round later this afternoon, as she's got some business documents she wants Ben to look over for her, so it's not as if he's going to be alone for long.'

Julia lowered her menu and looked at me, the amusement gone from her face. 'You're really worried about him, aren't you?'

For some stupid reason I felt my eyes begin to well up with tears. I reached for the serviette, ignoring a hovering waiter's look of dismay, and dabbed at my eyes before there was mascara everywhere. 'Don't mind me,' I said, aware the waiter was still eyeing me cautiously as though I might now be intending to blow my nose on the tablecloth. A small devilish part of me wanted to do it, just to see his face. That, at least, made me smile.

'I'm sorry, Jules. I'm just being ridiculous. I woke up this morning with a bad feeling, and I appear to have brought it out with us. Just ignore me. Now, what do you fancy ordering?'

Julia looked at me for a long moment, before glancing back at her menu. 'Well, I *was* thinking of suggesting the beef thing they have for two, but they say to allow an extra thirty minutes for preparation time ...' As much as I tried to immobilise my features, I don't think I could have been terribly successful, because she quickly amended her choice. 'But actually, the fish sounds delicious, so I think I'm going to go with that.'

It was the sort of restaurant where they didn't hurry you. It was the sort of place where a three-hour business lunch was par for the course. And I felt so guilty that I'd shown how anxious I was to go home that I went totally the other way. I ordered us a bottle of wine, instead of just a glass each, and only flinched a little when Julia sent the waiter away, saying she needed a little bit longer to make up her mind. However, she did have one sensible piece of advice. 'You have Carla's number, right?'

'I do.'

'Well, why don't you send her a text and ask her to try and convince Ben to go to the GP. You said they're good friends, so perhaps he'll listen to her.'

It was a good plan, and one I should have been able to

come up with myself, if only I hadn't been so busy mentally running around like a headless chicken. Under cover of the voluminous serviette, I rattled off a quick text to Carla and then purposefully switched off the ringer on my phone and dropped it back into my handbag.

The meal was every bit as delicious as the review guides had promised, and for most of the time I really enjoyed myself. It was as much of a treat for me as it was for Julia to have a chance for us to spend time together, somewhere we could relax, without having to wipe a single runny nose or change a nappy.

Of course my anxiety – like my phone – was only on silent; it hadn't actually been switched off. I knew that for certain by the way my stomach plummeted several hours later, as though a part of me had already known this was coming. Julia had just disappeared to the Ladies, and was still weaving her way through the tables when I plucked my phone from the depths of my bag, like a heron finding a fish.

Three missed calls. All from Ben. He knew today was all about Julia, and wouldn't have tried to contact me while we were out unless there was some kind of emergency. I was already ringing his number by the time Julia returned to the table.

'I *knew* you'd cave as soon as my back was turned,' she said with a laugh, which died almost instantly when she saw the look on my face. 'Sophie, what is it?'

I swallowed noisily several times before I could speak.

'Ben tried to call me several times, but now he's not answering either his mobile or the home phone.'

Julia slid back into her seat, going instantly into calming mummy mode. 'Right, first thing: don't panic. There are a million and one reasons why he's not picking up. Don't automatically opt for the one that has him lying in a pool of blood on the floor.'

I swear the colour drained from my face at her words. That would be reason one million and two, because I hadn't even considered that dreadful possibility.

'He could be out in the garden.'

'It's still raining,' I countered, glancing out of the restaurant window to confirm it was true.

'Or he could have popped out on an errand and left his phone behind.'

'He never does that.'

'Or he could be tied up with one of the other people from his group.'

The group. Of course. If someone had called round, and was going through some awful crisis, Ben would be there for them. I'd seen him do exactly that several times over the last few months. He could hardly break off in the middle of someone's emergency to chat to his paranoid girlfriend.

'Couldn't you ask Carla if she could get there earlier?' suggested Julia, still firing on far more cylinders than I was. 'If only to put your mind at rest.'

My mind felt like it would never know a single moment's

rest again until I held Ben safely in my arms, but I swallowed down the bitter lump of panic, as though it was an unpalatable pill, and nodded.

'*This person's phone is switched off.*' I don't think I've ever hated six words as much as I did those as I repeatedly dialled Carla's number.

'Could I interest you in some coffee, ladies?' I looked at the waiter blankly, as though he was speaking Martian.

'Just the bill, please,' said Julia smoothly.

'No, have a coffee, Jules,' I said, still trying to pretend that my world wasn't falling apart, because I still had no real proof that it was, apart from this stupid sixth sense that wouldn't stop screaming at me to leave. *Right now.* Possibly even before paying the bill.

The waiter hovered, looking uncertain. I got to my feet, suddenly decisive. 'Please could you bring my friend a coffee and me the bill,' I instructed. Julia was shaking her head, but I laid a hand on her shoulder, pushing her gently back down in her chair. 'Sit down and finish your meal properly,' I told her, already rummaging in my bag for my purse.

'Just go,' she urged. 'I'll get this.'

'Absolutely not. This was my treat for your birthday,' I said, beginning to panic when my purse remained obstinately elusive. Uncaring of whether or not it was appropriate, I upended my bag, covering the recently cleared and swept table top with my personal belongings. I plucked my purse from the pile of handbag miscellanea and pulled out a handful of notes, thrusting them at the waiter who was approaching us, ceremoniously carrying a small silver platter on which was our bill.

I swept down, kissed Julia briefly on the cheek and hastily began stuffing everything back into my bag.

'Let me know how he is, as soon as you get back,' Julia urged.

'I will,' I said, already racing for the door, aware I was being followed by many curious glances from my fellow diners. Admittedly it wasn't the type of establishment where patrons customarily legged it for the exit. I threw open the door and dived out into the rainy afternoon, my arms already windmilling like sails as I spotted an approaching cab with its light on. It pulled up in a puddle, soaking my feet, and I scarcely even noticed.

'Is there another way we could go?' I asked, fidgeting so much on the seat of the cab, the driver probably thought I had some sort of nervous affliction. But despite the genuine nausea that churned within me, *I* wasn't the one who was ill. That was Ben.

'Sorry, love. There's no way around these roadworks,' he apologised with a shrug. 'We shouldn't be delayed for more than a couple of minutes.'

I sat back on the bench seat, plucking nervously at the fabric of my dress. We weren't even halfway there yet, and I felt trapped within the stationary vehicle. My hand kept fluttering towards the door handle, as though at any moment

I would throw caution to the wind, fling it open and run through the rain-splattered streets to get home.

I reached into my bag for my phone, wondering how many degrees of stupid I was going to feel if Ben answered on the first ring. It was something I never got a chance to find out, because my phone wasn't there. For the second time in less than half an hour I tipped my bag upside down, and watched its contents spill out onto the back seat of the cab. Anything that could roll quickly found its way onto the floor as the traffic finally began to move, but despite vigorously shaking the bag, as though gravity might somehow be playing tricks on me, no phone tumbled from it. I bit my lip, trying to remember picking up the device from the restaurant table, but the memory had been washed away by the tide of panic I was currently surfing.

I leant forward and knocked anxiously on the reinforced glass partition separating the driver from his more eccentric passengers; a category I was rapidly falling into.

'My phone? You want to use my phone?' He sounded almost amused and my fraying nerves shredded a little more at the delay. I could see now why the partition between us was a good idea – for him at least.

'I think I've left mine at the restaurant,' I said. The driver flicked on his indicator, as though preparing to pull over to the kerb.

'Do you want to go back for it?'

'Yes. No. I don't know. No, I want to go home. But I really need to borrow your phone.' His eyes met mine in his rear-view mirror. He looked as though he was trying to decide if I was the most unreasonable fare he'd had all week, or just plain crazy. And then I started to cry, and his face instantly softened. 'Please,' I added, and even I could hear the desperation in my voice.

He reached into his pocket, undid the lock on the partition, and passed me his phone. I tried Ben's mobile first, and then the house phone. When neither was answered, I dialled my own number.

'You left your phone,' Julia said, instead of 'hello'.

'I know. Has Ben tried to call me again?'

'No, hon. Not yet. Are you nearly there?'

'Almost,' I said, glancing out through the rain-spattered window at the major intersection just ahead. 'About another five minutes or so.'

'Okay. Shall I come round after I've picked up Lacey and Noah?'

There was a time when my knee-jerk answer would have been yes, but I was stronger now. Ben had made me stronger. I just had to hope that the 'new and improved Sophie' was better equipped to deal with whatever lay ahead than the old version would have been.

'No. I'll be fine. I'll call if I need you.'

I passed the phone back to its rightful owner, and was still thanking him when my words were drowned out by the sound of an approaching siren. I bolted upright, as though electrocuted. My blood cooled and my pulse rose as the strident two-tone notes grew louder and louder. The lights were on green in our favour, but no one moved as they waited for the emergency vehicle to cross the junction.

Police car, be a police car. Or a fire engine, rescuing some stupid cat from a tree.

I didn't know I was holding my breath until the tightness in my chest forced me to expel it, on a long and shaky gasp. The ambulance shot past us at speed, a blur of white vehicle and flashing blue lights.

'That ambulance . . . can you follow it?' The driver's eyes flew to his mirror, and from the look in them I knew I'd tipped all the way back into 'crazy' again, as far as he was concerned.

'You want me to follow the ambulance? And *not* go to the address you gave me?' He spoke slowly, over-enunciating every word.

The road ahead was now clear, and from the queued traffic behind the cab, an impatient motorist tooted their horn. My driver paid no attention, but swivelled in his seat to face me.

'I don't know.' My torment was obviously visible.

He looked as confused as I felt, and the driver behind us, who now appeared to be leaning on his horn, wasn't helping matters.

'Left to follow the ambulance, or right to go to the address?'

Time seemed to be suspended for a very long moment before I eventually gave him my answer. 'Right. Go right.'

*

This Love

I almost fell getting out of the cab, but that's what happens when you try to leap from a vehicle before it's come to a complete stop. I didn't even look at the meter, I just thrust a balled-up note into the driver's hand and ran – without looking – across the fortunately empty road.

Ben's car was still parked on the drive, so my list of possible reasons why I couldn't reach him was rapidly revised as I ran towards his front door. I leant heavily on the door bell, with about as much patience as the irate motorist behind us on the road had had. I didn't have a key to Ben's home, I'd never needed one. But now that oversight seemed like an act of colossal stupidity. In the morning we would go and get one cut, I told myself, as though planning a mundane chore for tomorrow would have the power to prevent anything bad from happening today.

Ben walked slowly these days; it was a fact we both knew, although neither of us had ever acknowledged it. Even so, he should have answered the door by now . . . if he could. *Don't automatically assume the worst,* said Scott's voice in my ear. For once there was no comfort in his imagined advice. My dead brother was hardly in a position to tell me that people's worst fears don't always come true.

I rummaged in my bag for my own door key and ran around the front of the building towards the flat's entrance. I saw the broken glass first. Long dangerous shards of it were pooled on the path. I rocked on my feet, slow and stupid with shock, before lifting my head to the large window beside my front door, or rather the place where the window

395

had been. Who knew a single pane could disintegrate in quite so many pieces, I found myself thinking randomly. Seeing the glass on the pathway had been just an appetiser, a small *amuse-bouche* for the panic I now felt. There were only a few pieces of jagged glass still attached to the frame; the rest of it was on the floor of the hallway beside my front door.

Burglary was my first thought, and instead of running to a neighbour's home to call the police, as any sensible person would have done, I fumbled to insert my key into the door lock. If someone had broken in . . . If Ben had been hurt trying to defend his home from intruders . . . Suddenly the thought of him lying in a pool of blood didn't sound like a ridiculous suggestion after all; it sounded more like a premonition.

The door swung open, and although I wanted to call out his name, I forced my lips to remain locked. Small pieces of glass crunched beneath my feet, sounding horribly loud in the silence of the building. I looked down, and for the first time noticed something truly bizarre. The glass wasn't scattered across the floor of the hallway as it should have been. Instead it was gathered together in a neat and shiny glittering mountain. Propped up against the wall was the broom from my kitchen. What sort of burglar smashes their way into a building and then sweeps up the broken glass behind them?

'Sophie, thank goodness!'

I jumped what felt like a foot in the air and turned to

face Carla, who was coming towards me with a dustpan and brush in her hand. She dropped them to the floor and threw her arms around me. I struggled to get out of her embrace, but for a small woman she was surprisingly strong, and she wasn't letting go.

'Where's Ben? What's happened? Did someone break in?'

'Yes. *I* did. I broke in,' Carla said, as though smashing her way into someone's home was a new and interesting hobby she'd recently taken up.

'What?' I pulled out of her hold and this time she let me go. 'Why?' I shook my head as though I didn't care why, and if truth be told, I really didn't. There was a far more important question that she still hadn't answered. 'Where's Ben?'

Carla's eyes were soft and full of sympathy as she reached for my hand before replying. 'He's on his way to hospital. The ambulance left about ten minutes ago.'

I knew it. Or rather I had known it. There'd been absolutely no reason for me to suspect that Ben was the patient being hurried to hospital in that ambulance, and yet my initial instinct to follow the speeding vehicle had been uncannily correct. The strength of the connection between us had always surprised me, but now it felt like a real and tangible entity. A living organism that bound his life to mine.

'What happened?' I asked shakily. Weirdly, I was now sitting down on my settee, although I had no idea of how I'd got there.

'Ben called to cancel our meeting earlier today. He said he wasn't feeling well.'

'He has a cold. I gave him a cold,' I said, my voice heavy with guilt, as though I'd done it on purpose. I struggled to get to my feet, but once again Carla's forceful personality, coupled with a pretty solidly built forearm, stopped me. 'You're not going anywhere until you've finished that,' she said firmly.

I looked down and bizarrely saw a cup of tea in my hand. Where had that come from?

'Drink,' she commanded. I took a sip and winced at the sweetness. 'It's for the shock,' she continued, although I wasn't sure that statement held any medical validity. 'I'm not driving you to the hospital until I'm certain you're not about to pass out on me.'

I took another huge mouthful, my need to get to Ben far more important than my own physical well-being.

'There was something in his voice that worried me. I kept trying to put it to the back of my mind, but it wouldn't let me,' Carla admitted. I nodded vigorously. To a lesser extent, she too had known something was wrong, that Ben was in trouble. 'So I shut the salon and drove over. I knew he was home because of his car, but he didn't come to the door. And then I saw—' She shook her head as though regretting her words. 'Anyway, that was when I knew I had to get in here.'

'What did you see?' I questioned, ignoring the tea and getting to my feet. With or without her, I was leaving right now for the hospital.

Carla nodded, perhaps realising that this time there would be no restraining me. 'I could see that Ben had collapsed in his lounge. So I phoned for an ambulance and then ...' She shrugged her plump shoulders helplessly, and it was only then that her face crumpled. 'And then I smashed my way in here so I could get to him.'

Time seemed to keep escaping from me. I was losing worrying chunks of it. Somehow I was now in Carla's car and we were driving through the rush-hour traffic towards the hospital. Carla was keeping up an endless stream of chatter, most of which I simply didn't hear. It was as though she was speaking on a different frequency to the one I was tuned in to. I caught only random snatches of conversation here and there.

'So you don't have to worry about the window. One of my clients is married to a glazier. It will be replaced by the time you get back home.'

Window? What window? My memory provided me with a prompt. The sound of glass crunching on a wooden floor. Oh yes, the window.

'And I've shut your cat in Ben's part of the house, so he can't get out. And put down some fresh food and water.'

I looked at her blankly for a moment as though I had no idea what she was talking about, and then I nodded. Fred. I hadn't even given him a thought. I was a terrible owner, forgetting my own pet; I was a terrible girlfriend, giving the man I loved a cold that had made him collapse. I thought motor neurone was the worst thing that could happen to Ben, but it turned out that *I was.*

I stood by impatiently as Carla fumbled in her purse for change for the hospital car park, knowing if the car had been mine I simply wouldn't have bothered, and would have worried about the fine later. After what seemed like an eternity, we were crossing the vast parking area and heading for the hospital's main entrance. My legs were longer than Carla's, my need to reach Ben more urgent than hers, but I forced myself to slow down for her. Sometimes, because she seemed so full of life and vitality, it was easy to forget that she too was sick.

'My boyfriend was brought in by ambulance. He collapsed at home. Please can you tell me where he's been taken?'

The receptionist looked up, and there was a sympathy on her face that I didn't want to acknowledge. I knew and remembered that look only too well from the past.

'Name?' she prompted.

'Sophie Winter,' I replied, my feet twitching with my need to go, to move, to keep on moving until they took me to Ben's side.

'Not yours. His.'

'Oh. Ben. His name is Ben.'

'Stevens,' added Carla usefully, reaching for my hand and giving it a squeeze. 'His name is Ben Stevens.'

They asked us to take a seat in the waiting room, and the time that I'd been losing in segments was suddenly returned to me in one huge immovable block. I must have gone back to the reception desk at least ten times, asking for news or an update, or when we'd be allowed to go to wherever Ben had been taken.

'He's still being assessed,' I said tightly, as I sat back beside Carla on the uncomfortable hospital chairs. On the table before us was a row of empty plastic cups from the vending machine, lined up like sentries. They marked the passage of time that we'd been waiting. If they kept us here much longer, we were going to need a bigger table.

Finally the swing doors — through which we'd seen countless people disappear — were opened and a young nurse emerged. 'Are the family or friends of Ben Stevens here?' she called out to the waiting room. I jumped to my feet as though I was at an auction and worried someone else would put in a higher bid and claim Ben before I could.

'Yes, here,' I said, rushing towards her. She smiled, and I could see a kindness behind the professional demeanour, and that frightened me. They were always kind just before they broke the really bad news.

'How is he?' I held my breath.

I'm afraid Scott's injuries are extremely severe. We've done all that we can, but . . .

'He's more comfortable now. The doctors are still with him, but I can take you up to the ward now. They'll be able to tell you more.'

By the time the lift had carried us up to the sixth floor, I'd managed to ask the nurse a further three times how

Ben was *really* doing, as if I was incapable of trusting her first answer. Her reply was unswerving: Ben's condition was stable, although I could tell she didn't think the same could be said about my state of mind. I didn't care. My treatment, my cure, would come only when I saw that Ben was alright.

Every second of delay was a torture. The trolley being wheeled through the door ahead of us was pushed too slowly; the disinfectant we squirted onto our hands took too long to rub in, and the wait at the nurses' station to be told Ben's room number just added to my anxiety. Finally we were directed to his room. The doctors must have been and gone already, because apart from the occupant of the hospital bed, the room was empty.

'I'll wait out here,' Carla said, hanging back to allow us some privacy. I smiled, and nodded, but my attention was already only on the room, and the man within it.

Dusk had fallen, and the room was a kaleidoscope of shadows. The man in the bed had his head turned away from the door. There was an oxygen mask covering the lower half of his face, and he appeared to be asleep. I shut the door as quietly as I could, but the sound alerted him, and his head turned slowly towards me.

For one dreadful moment I thought they'd sent me to the wrong room. That wasn't Ben. Ben's skin wasn't that weird alabaster colour, nor was it stretched drumskin-tight over his cheekbones like that. Yet the man had Ben's hair. And when his eyes flickered open to look at me, they were the colour of warm caramel. My knees wanted to buckle, but I wouldn't let them. I don't remember crossing the room to reach him, just finding myself suddenly there as though I'd been bewitched by a spell. The same spell I'd been under since the night I met him, I realised.

There were wires attached to electrodes on his chest, there was a drip in one arm, and the oxygen mask was yet another hazard to negotiate, but my arms slid over and under every obstacle to reach him. His torso was bare, and felt hot. Although an electric fan blew noisily from a table beside the bed, Ben's temperature was still sky high. He reached for my hand, and his grip felt so much weaker than ever before.

I folded down onto a chair positioned beside the bed, and even though it was right next to the mattress, I still felt nowhere near close enough.

'Just a cold, huh?'

Through the mask I could see a watered-down version of his familiar smile. But his voice sounded strange, shot through with a wheezy gasp. 'You get one "I told you so", just one. Use it wisely,' he advised.

I nodded fiercely, determined not to cry, because I knew that would make him feel even worse.

'They say you have pneumonia,' I told him. '*Double* pneumonia,' I added for emphasis, although I had no idea what that actually meant.

'I don't like doing things by halves,' he wheezed, his eyes searching my face as though looking for fault lines in something that could very easily break. He knew me even better than I realised. This *could* fracture me, but I wasn't going to let it do so in front of him.

I reached up and smoothed the hair back from the dampness of his brow, my fingertips skimming over furrows and creases that I'd never noticed before. There were huge smudged shadows beneath his eyes, making him look like a panda – a panda that hadn't slept in about a month. He was the man I'd woken up beside that morning, and yet he looked nothing like him.

'What did the doctors say?'

His eyes flickered, and if I hadn't been watching him so closely, I might not have realised that he wasn't telling me the truth.

'They say I'm going to be fine.'

A soft knock on the door interrupted us, and when I turned towards it, Carla's head – which was swathed in yet another of her colourful turbans – squeezed through the opening. 'I just wanted to let you know the nurse said the doctors are coming back to speak to you in a few minutes.'

Ben's arm rose weakly from the mattress and beckoned her into the room. 'They told me in the ambulance that you broke into my house and climbed in through a window?'

It didn't matter how many times I heard it, I still had trouble imagining the small plump hairdresser performing that stunt.

'It was just one more thing I'd been meaning to cross off my bucket list,' Carla said blithely.

But Ben wasn't letting her off that lightly. 'I owe you, Carla.' Their eyes locked and held, and although they weren't related, there was a mother's love on Carla's face as she looked at Ben.

'What you owe me,' she replied pertly, 'is a new blouse.' She held up one arm to show him a long jagged rip running from the elbow to the cuff of her bright pink top that had been ruined during her breaking and entering escapade.

'I'll buy you a whole wardrobe full of blouses when I get out of here,' Ben promised.

Everyone has a trigger, everyone has a tipping point, and that was Carla's. She burst into the kind of noisy tears that come from a place so deep within you there's no way of staunching them, you just have to let them flow. 'Just hurry up and get out of here, and go back home to this lovely girl of yours,' Carla said, uncaring of the colourful rivulets of eyeshadow and mascara coursing down her cheeks.

I think we were all rather grateful for the distraction provided by the arrival of the team of doctors. Led by a tall, grey-haired physician with a stoop, and a neat Brillo-pad moustache, they gave a peremptory knock and filed into Ben's room.

'Dr Fisher,' introduced the senior medic, extending his hand to me. 'As I explained to Mr Stevens earlier, my team and I will be looking after him during his stay with us.' He made it sound as though Ben had just checked into a rather nice boutique hotel. I released my hand from his as soon as it was polite to do so, and reclaimed Ben's.

'Your husband's pneumonia is not uncommon in patients suffering from MND.' I glanced down at Ben, waiting for him to correct the doctor, but he said nothing. Although the fingers that were tightly curled around mine squeezed a little bit harder. 'We hope that by treating it aggressively with antibiotics we'll be able to make him a great deal more comfortable over the next forty-eight hours.' It was less of a guarantee than I'd been hoping to hear. 'In the meantime, we've asked for his records to be sent over from the clinic.'

Something flickered in Ben's eyes, something I couldn't read.

'Have you been aware of any significant changes in your condition recently?' Dr Fisher enquired.

There was a moment of silence, which eventually I chose to fill. 'Actually Ben's been on an experimental drug trial for the last three months.' The doctor's pale blue eyes met mine. The man should play poker, because they gave nothing away. 'We're really hopeful that it's working.'

No one said a thing, not even Ben or Carla. I looked at them all in turn: the doctors, the nurses, my friend, the man I loved, and they were all wearing the same expression. It wasn't exactly pity, more of a reluctant sadness, as though they all shared a secret that no one had yet found the courage to tell me.

'Well, that's good,' said Dr Fisher with a bluster to his voice that hadn't been there before. 'I'm sure that will all be there in his notes.'

Ben's hand broke free of mine to push his oxygen mask aside. A nurse swooped in like a diving seagull to replace it, but he motioned her away. 'It's getting worse,' he said, looking not at the doctor or the nurse, but at me. I shook my head, as though none of it would be true as long as I kept on denying it. 'Sophie, we can pretend to each other as much as we like, but we both know what's happening here.'

'I'm sorry. I couldn't quite make that out,' said the doctor gently.

'You'll need to explain how it really is,' said Ben, his eyes incredibly sad.

Something was wrong here. Something I couldn't quite understand.

The doctor was looking at me expectantly. 'Ben trips up now and again and he's fallen a few times ... and he's dropped a couple of things,' I admitted reluctantly, feeling like I was betraying him to the enemy.

'More than a few times,' corrected Carla quietly from the corner of the room. I turned on her angrily. Whose side was she on?

'This isn't something we can cover up, Sophie. The doctors need to know how bad things have been getting.' Ben's voice sounded weaker, and he reached for the oxygen mask himself, holding it over his nose and inhaling deeply, like an addict taking a fix.

'And your speech, the dysarthria – slurring – how long has that been a problem for you?'

I swivelled to stare at the doctor, my confidence in his ability to diagnose suddenly gone. 'Ben's speech is fine. It hasn't been affected at all, and he certainly doesn't slur.' I glanced across to Carla for confirmation, and saw she was crying again. 'What?' I challenged her, angry when I had no right to be.

Carla crossed to the bed and lifted Ben's hand into hers, as though the sting of her words could be lessened by her touch. 'It's been getting worse for a while now,' she said quietly.

Ben smiled sadly at her and nodded.

I paced the corridor, trying to outrun both the scene in Ben's room and Carla at my side. I failed on both counts.

'I can understand everything Ben says. Every single word. How do you explain that then, huh?'

Carla took hold of my shoulders and brought me to an abrupt stop, so effectively she could probably moonlight as a nightclub bouncer if she ever wanted. 'You understand him, because you love him. You hear him differently than we do. The rest of us listen with our ears, but you listen with your heart.' Anatomically her answer made no sense whatsoever, but a small part of me found some comfort in the sentiment.

I looked over her head towards the closed door of Ben's room with genuine longing. When one of the nurses had arrived with Ben's clinic notes, he'd asked if he could speak privately with the doctor. I felt shut out, and the longer I spent pacing the corridor, the more my imagination went into overdrive. After what felt like an eternity, the door opened and the doctors filed out, followed by the nurse. 'He wants to speak to you, but he really needs to get some rest, so please be brief.'

Chastened, I hurried back to Ben's bedside. Once again he pushed aside the oxygen mask to talk to me.

'How are you doing?' he asked wheezily.

'That's supposed to be my line.'

He smiled and beckoned me closer. I was probably breaking every hospital rule in the book when I climbed onto the bed to lie down beside him. But I didn't care. The sharp edge of an electrode pressed uncomfortably against my temple, but nothing mattered as long I was being held in his arms again.

'I'm so sorry, Sophie. I never wanted this to happen.'

I breathed in deeply, inhaling him as though stockpiling a memory. 'I don't suppose anyone ever does.'

'I don't just mean about today, although I *am* sorry I ruined Julia's birthday.'

'She'll have plenty more,' I said stupidly, realising almost in shock that the same might no longer be true for Ben.

I raised my head slowly to look into his eyes as he spoke. 'The last thing I ever wanted to do was to make you sit by another hospital bedside,' he said with a sigh. 'But sometimes things spiral out of our control and we can't stop them from happening. This love was one of those things.'

We lay quietly for a moment before he tensed up beside me. 'I need you to do something for me.'

'Anything,' I assured him, my heart in my eyes. A spasm of pain crossed his face, fleeting like a shooting star, and something inside me started to feel very, very afraid.

'I need you to bring something to the hospital for me.'

'Okaaaay.' I drew the word out, already sensing we were talking about something far more important than clean pyjamas or toiletries.

'There's a briefcase at the back of my wardrobe. Inside it you'll find a file containing an envelope with my solicitor's name on it. I need you to bring it here tomorrow.'

'This all sounds very *Mission Impossible,*' I said, trying to make him smile. He didn't, and alarm bells started going off in my head. 'What's in the envelope, Ben?'

'It's something the doctors need for my medical records.'

'I thought they had everything they need. And why was your solicitor involved?' I could hear the fear seeping into my voice. It was like I already knew. 'What's in the envelope, Ben?' I asked again.

'It's something they drew up for me a long time ago. Before you and me. I'm not actioning it, I just want to have it here, on my records.'

'What's in the envelope?' Three times I'd asked; three times he'd avoided answering.

'It's a living will,' he said solemnly. 'It gives me the right to refuse medical intervention, if I wish to do so.'

'You knew about this, didn't you?'

Carla took her time replying. She appeared to be

concentrating far harder than necessary on checking the empty road in front was clear, before pulling out.

'I did,' she admitted at last.

'And you're okay with this? You think it's acceptable for Ben to give up, to just stop fighting?'

Carla took her eyes off the road to look at me, suddenly far less concerned about road safety than she'd been a minute ago. 'Ben is *not* giving up. Not yet. He's going to keep on fighting to stay alive – to stay with you – for as long as he can. But this piece of paper will give him the dignity to say "Enough now" when the people around him can't make that decision, and when *he's* no longer able to put it into words. It's his way of protecting not just himself, but also everyone he cares about.'

I stared at her for a long moment. 'You've got one too, haven't you?'

Her smile was wintry, as she slowly nodded her head. 'Quite a few of us in the group do.'

I told myself I simply wouldn't do it. Then I told myself I would tell him that *I had* looked, but couldn't find it. And finally I told myself what I'd known all along: I would do what Ben had asked. I would take him his damn envelope with his Advance Decision to refuse treatment. But then I was going to use every means of persuasion known to man to make him tear it up into a thousand tiny pieces.

You do know I'd have pulled the plug on me too, if anyone had offered me the chance. I was already spooked, creeping through

Ben's darkened house in the early hours of the morning, so I certainly could have done without hearing Scott's voice in my head right then. I was already unsettled by how frequently I'd been hearing him – more than I'd done in years – so having him take Ben's side on this, instead of mine, seemed unacceptably disloyal.

He doesn't want to have a machine breathing for him, said Scott as I flicked on every light switch I passed, until the house was lit up like a power station. *He doesn't want that any more than I did.* The annoying thing about hearing voices in your head, the kind of voices that pretend to be ghosts, is that they don't have the decency to slip away into the shadows the way an honest-to-goodness spectre would do when you've flooded the place with light.

I hadn't wanted to sleep in Ben's bed, not without him. So for the first time in ages I had returned to my own bedroom in the basement, a room Fred had claimed by default in my absence. But the bed that had once seemed so comfortable felt rigid and unyielding. I twisted and turned, throwing the covers off, only to drag them back over me moments later. I thumped the pillows viciously, as though the feathers within them were personally responsible for my tortured conscience. Eventually, after watching the numbers on my clock tick over into a new hour, I threw off the covers one last time and reached for my dressing gown.

I had paused for a moment at the threshold to Ben's bedroom, hating the sight of the neatly made bed, because he should have been in it. With me.

Do what you came here to do, and then go back to bed. You'll sleep then, Scott advised. He was wrong, of course, very, very wrong, but neither of us knew that then.

Ben's wardrobe was custom-built and covered the length of an entire wall. Somewhere within it, behind one of its many doors, was a single piece of paper which would instruct the doctors *not* to put a tube down Ben's throat to help him breathe. It was his own death warrant, and I still couldn't believe that he'd signed it and now wanted me to deliver it to him. He might just as well have given me a loaded gun, and asked me to shoot him.

There are people who are meticulous in throwing away paperwork they no longer need. I am not one of those people. I need a ravaging house fire before I'm forced to part with documents and memorabilia from my past. Ben and I were compatible in this, except he'd not had the benefit of a fire to eliminate the papers he no longer needed. The wardrobes were deeper and more cavernous than I'd realised. They were easily able to accommodate the large number of neatly stacked storage boxes, and still allow plenty of space for Ben's clothes.

On the plus side, most of the boxes were neatly labelled. The majority of them appeared to contain files and docu-ments relating to the business he had owned and then sold after receiving his diagnosis. But there were others that went back even further into Ben's past.

My search wasn't particularly organised. I kept pulling out boxes, rifling through their contents and then moving on to the next one, without bothering to clear away the mess I'd left behind. I was working in chaos, and that wasn't like me at all.

Despite my very best efforts to sabotage my search, I eventually found the briefcase Ben had spoken of at the back of the last section of the wardrobe. I withdrew the leather folio slowly, as though defusing an explosive device. My fingers hovered over the small gold catch, but hesitated before sliding it open. *Cut the green wire or the red?* Suddenly bomb disposal sounded like a breeze. At least it gave you a fifty-fifty chance of survival. The piece of paper drawn up by Ben's solicitors made those odds appealing, because once his Advance Decision had been implemented, it would give him zero chance.

I held the envelope in my hands for a long time, turning it over and over as though suddenly I would be able to understand why he had done this thing. Why, even now, when I was part of his life, he *still* wanted to do it. I got to my feet, weary and clumsy with exhaustion. It was very late and it had been an incredibly long and stressful day. What I needed more than anything was the oblivion of sleep. I began putting the contents of his wardrobe back, stacking things haphazardly, and promising myself I would tidy them up properly tomorrow.

I shoved a box, and something slipped out from behind it. A folder. It was bright yellow, but that wasn't what caught my eye. It was Ben's handwriting printed on the top right-hand corner. Just one word, but that one word stopped me from straightening it up and shutting the wardrobe doors, because it wasn't just a word, it was also a name. *My name. 'WINTER'.*

I sat back down on the floor and drew the folder out of the wardrobe. It was heavy and bound shut with several thick elastic bands. He'd wrapped them horizontally and vertically around the folder, like ribbon around a parcel. It looked very secure. It looked as though he'd not wanted anything in this wallet to accidentally slip out. The room was warm, but suddenly I was shivering.

I ran my finger over the six handwritten letters, as though reading Braille. This folder didn't have to be anything to do with me, I knew that. My name was also a season. This folder could just as easily contain instructions for how the garden should be maintained during that time of year. I leapt up and looked once more in the wardrobe, searching for three similar folders with the other seasons' names upon them. But they weren't there. And somehow I'd known all along that they wouldn't be.

I slid my finger beneath the first elastic band.

Don't do that, sis. Put it back where you found it.

I looked up and imagined I saw Scott, standing beside the wardrobe door, an expression of disapproval on his face. The rubber band pinged off and landed somewhere in the corner of the room. I reached for the second one.

Seriously, this is his private stuff you're going through. You shouldn't be doing this.

Ping. And there went the second band. The folder expanded slightly in my hands, like the welcome release of a zip after a big meal. The flap has risen slightly, a bit like a mouth, smiling, inviting me in.

Don't say I didn't warn you. I think this is a colossally bad idea. It was probably the wisest thing Scott had ever said, alive or dead.

The first thing that fell from the folder was the newspaper cutting. I recognised it instantly. I had read it so many times I could probably recite it verbatim. Ben's copy was yellowed and faded. It looked as though it had been opened and folded a great many times. How many times had he read it? I wondered. As many as me? The photograph was still hard to look at. The mangled wreckage of the bike, the crumpled car . . . there would never be enough years that passed for that image not to affect me.

I slid my hand inside the folder and pulled out a further handful of papers. Most of them were about me, and those that weren't were about my parents. There was a report from a private investigator, with information about my life that made my own CV look sketchy and incomplete. Ben knew everything about my past. He knew the grades I got for my GCSEs and A levels. He knew the name of my hall of residence at university. He knew where I'd worked and the dates of my employment. I flicked through the dossier, already numb with shock. There was a list of my friends – even the names of the men I had briefly dated, some of whom *I* would have struggled to remember. On a separate sheet were details about Julia and Gary: where they lived, their occupations, and the names of their children. That was when I became angry – no, more than angry – I was livid with rage. Ben had pretended not to know them; he'd held out his hand as though he was some charmingly polite stranger, and all the time he had this ... this thing ... this stalker's handbook, tucked away in his wardrobe.

I didn't realise I was crying until the paper in my hands was speckled from my falling tears. I picked up the transcript of the inquest held after Scott's accident. How had Ben got hold of this? Come to that, how – and why – had he also got a copy of the police report? I picked up the document, gripping it tightly for a very long time before I opened it. I'd never seen it before – and I didn't believe my parents had either. I didn't want to open it. I didn't want to read it. But I knew I would, because there was a reason for it being here. There was a reason why my life, and my parents' lives, had been detailed and documented and then hidden away like a shameful secret among Ben's possessions.

I flipped open the first page. My eye scanned it quickly. It stated the date of the accident, the name of the victim, the make and model of Scott's bike and also that of the car that hit him. I turned the page and there it was. The thing I never wanted to see. The thing that would change everything.

The driver of the car was Sam Jacobson. He was eighteen years of age at the time of the accident. Almost the same age as Scott had been. These were facts I already knew, even though his name had never been spoken in our house. He had never been charged or prosecuted, although why that was, I'd never known or understood.

And there was something else I had never known, something no one had ever told me in the sixteen years since the night of the accident. Sam Jacobson wasn't the only person in the car that killed Scott. There had been two other passengers. Their names had been excluded from any reports because they were still juveniles. But they were there in the police report. They were there on the page right in front of me. One I didn't know; the other I did. Benjamin Stevens.

Chapter 19

'I'm sorry, visiting isn't until two o'clock this afternoon.' The nurse smiled to soften her refusal, although she looked firm and unyielding. But then so did I.

'I really won't stay long – just a few minutes,' I assured her. 'Mr Stevens – Ben – asked me to bring a very important document in this morning. He needs to give it to his doctors.'

The nurse looked at me, and I wondered what she could see. Did she see a woman who hadn't slept at all the night before? Did she see someone so torn down the middle with conflicting emotions, everything within her was in danger of slowly seeping away? Did she see a woman who could love and hate a man at the same time?

'If it's medical information, then I'd be happy to take it and pass it on to the team for you.'

She held out her hand, and my arm instinctively tightened, securing the yellow folder more firmly against my side. For a crazy moment I imagined her trying to wrest the portfolio from my grip in an ugly tug-of-war. I wished her good luck with that. This folder was staying with me until I saw Ben face to face.

'I'm sorry. I don't want to be difficult, but it's a very important legal document, a living will. And obviously if it should go astray . . .' I left the rest of that sentence hanging in the air, allowing her time to consider the implications. Her gaze dropped to the yellow folder, only this time I could see she was wavering. 'I'll be quick,' I promised, nudging her subtly along. She glanced at the nurses' station behind her. The desk was empty. She made her decision swiftly.

'Okay then. But if anyone asks, you snuck in by yourself. I never saw you.'

I didn't want to get anyone into trouble, and I wasn't entirely comfortable with my methods, but the possibility of leaving without speaking to Ben wasn't even a consideration. The eight hours that had passed since I found the damning evidence had been hard enough. I really didn't think my shattered nerves could take any further delay.

I marched with purpose towards Ben's room – hoping my false bravado would stop anyone from challenging me. A cleaner pushing a laden trolley muttered something to me in Portuguese as I passed, and then looked genuinely shocked when I answered in her own language. Instead of questioning my right to be there, she just smiled broadly and wished me a pleasant morning. Somehow I really didn't think I was destined to have one of those.

It wasn't as though I'd lied to the nurse. As Ben had requested, I *had* brought his Advance Decision document to the hospital, which I'm sure he was going to be very pleased to see. The same probably couldn't be said for the other documents in the yellow folder.

I stopped outside his room, making sure I couldn't be seen through the glass insert. I had written, rehearsed, and then re-written what I had to say to him so many times as I waited for dawn to finally break that the words were now a jumble of accusations, spinning like a centrifuge in my head.

My heart was hammering so loudly in my chest I felt sure Ben would have heard it before I entered the room. I suppose if you are about to have a stress-induced heart attack, a hospital is probably the best place to do it.

Despite every incriminating piece of evidence; despite having to admit that everything I'd believed to be true over the last eight months was probably a lie, I still couldn't help my feelings when I opened the door. My heart stopped thundering long enough to twist painfully in my chest at the sight of Ben lying in his hospital bed. He looked a little better than he'd done the night before, and despite everything, I was grateful for that. Love isn't like a tap. You can't simply turn it off when everything goes wrong. It continues to keep flowing when someone you love dies ... or when someone you love has betrayed you.

Ben's smile was so broad, so genuinely pleased to see me, that I only just managed to stop myself from instinctively smiling back.

'Hello, you. This is a lovely surprise. I didn't think I'd be seeing you until—' His words were severed like a falling guillotine, as he saw the yellow folder beneath my arm.

He wasn't using the oxygen mask this morning, although perhaps he should have been, because the sound of ragged breathing filled the room. It took a moment or two before I realised it was coming from me and not him.

Ben's eyes were glued to the folder as I took a step closer and dropped it onto the bed. 'I brought your Advance Decision.'

'Sophie.'

'So you can give it to your doctors. Or not.'

'Sophie.'

'At least you get to choose if you live or die.'

'Sophie.'

'Which was more than my brother could.'

I started to cry. And that hadn't been in my script at all. I was ad-libbing now, everything I had so carefully prepared just a distant memory. 'Why, Ben? Just tell me that. What kind of sick and twisted game have you been playing with me for the last eight months?'

He reached out his arm, the one with the IV drip still attached. It was an unnecessary reminder that he was still sick and that perhaps I shouldn't be doing this. I knew I ought to stop, only I didn't know how.

'My brother died . . . and you were involved in that accident. That alone is enough to make me want to have nothing to do with you. You should have told me everything on the night we first met.'

'We were kind of preoccupied, if you remember,' he said, lashing out at me in a way I wasn't expecting.

'You're asking me to believe there hasn't been a single moment in all these months when you could have come clean about who you really are?'

'You know who I am.'

'I do now,' I said bitterly. 'You're the man who helped kill my brother.'

Ben's face twisted.

He wasn't driving the sodding car, Sophie. He was just a kid. Give him a break. Of all the advocates to speak up for Ben, Scott was the most surprising.

I looked down at the folder with disgust, as though it was a rodent sitting on his bed. 'And this, this dossier you have on us. What the hell is that about? Have you been stalking us since the accident?' Tears ran down my face as he reached for the folder and the newspaper cutting fell onto the blanket. I could see the grainy image of the mangled bike.

'No, it's nothing like that. I used to live near Cotterham.'

Another lie, I thought bitterly. He'd pretended not to know the area at all, when clearly he must have done. How was it possible to trust anything he'd ever said, not just about his past, but about us too?

'There were people I knew who went to your school. After the accident they used to let me know how you were doing.'

'Wonderful,' I said bitterly. 'I can't tell you how comforting it is to know that you've been spying on me for practically half my life.'

'I felt responsible,' said Ben in explanation.

'Because you bloody well were,' I said, staggering back as though from a blow. 'I don't know what you thought *this* would do,' I said, touching the folder with real disgust. 'But hiring a private investigator goes beyond being just concerned – it's fucking creepy.'

'I wanted to know how you and your family were doing after I'd moved away from the area.'

'Not very well. But I imagine you know that already, I believe page twenty-four of your investigator's report covers my counselling sessions.'

Ben flopped back on the pillows, his face pale, and for a moment I panicked that I'd gone too far. I wanted to run from the room and never see him again, and at the same time I still wanted to go to him and hold him tightly against me. Both courses of action had the potential to destroy me.

'I will never forgive myself for what happened that night,' Ben said brokenly. His eyes were glittering brightly. 'I'd fallen in with a crowd of guys I shouldn't have been hanging about with. They were older than me. That night we were driving back from a party. We were all mucking around, being idiots. And then—'

'I don't want to hear this. I *can't* hear this. I need to get out of here,' I said, leaping away from the bed as though it was suddenly writhing with snakes.

I spun on my heel to leave, but Ben's voice stopped me. 'Are you coming back?'

I turned slowly to face him. 'I have no idea. The way I feel right now, it doesn't seem likely.'

I didn't tell them I was coming. I didn't want to have to give my reasons over the phone. I packed a bag without noticing or caring what was thrown inside it. I would have to come back later for the rest of my things, but for now I just needed to get out from under Ben's roof, and there was only one place I wanted to go.

I was lucky; despite the short notice, the cattery could take Fred for a few days. It was less luxurious accommodation than he'd been used to when staying with Alice, but severing myself from Ben's life was a bit like a divorce. And naturally he was the one who'd get custody of his friends, for whatever time they had left with each other. I was going to miss them, though. I was going to miss— I cut that thought off before it was formed, as though cauterising a wound.

The station was busy, loud and impersonal. I bought a sandwich to eat on the journey and then threw it away unopened when I got to the other end. I decided to hail a taxi rather than phoning home for a lift, hoping that somehow in the twenty-minute drive I would magically summon up the words I needed to explain everything to my parents. I wasn't hopeful, because after three hours on the train, I'd still come up dry.

My parents were both in the garden when I arrived. I could see them through the kitchen window, sitting side by side on deck chairs, enjoying a glass of wine in the early evening sunshine. Perhaps I'd made a mistake in coming home. Perhaps they *didn't* need to be told about any of this. Why open up the old wounds all over again? My parents didn't need to feel the way I was now feeling, I could at least spare them from that.

I glanced back over my shoulder at the front door, but before I could begin creeping silently towards it, my mum turned around and saw me. Her mouth formed a tiny O of surprise and she said something to my dad, who appeared equally astounded to find me looking back at them through the window.

The setting sun shifted across the lawn as I haltingly began to explain to them why I was there. The shadows were short, squat spectres when I started to speak, and elongated wraiths when I was done.

'I'm sorry. I'm so very, very sorry,' I said, reaching first for my mother's hand, and then my father's, as though we were about to conduct an alfresco séance.

My mother looked paler than she'd been when I had first joined them in the garden. 'What are you sorry for? None of this is *your* fault.'

I glanced up at my father, who so far hadn't said a word. He was studying a nearby rose bush with close attention, as though garden surveillance was a new and absorbing hobby.

'It *is* my fault,' I contradicted. 'I brought Ben into this house. I introduced you to one of the last people on earth you would ever want to meet. I invited him to share our family Christmas. For Christ's sake, he even sat in Scott's chair at the table.'

My father turned away from his examination of the foliage. 'But it *isn't* Scott's chair, sweetheart. Not any more. It hasn't been for a very long time.'

His eyes travelled from me to my mum, and something inside me broke just a little bit more to see him crying.

'I don't know what Ben was trying to accomplish. I thought I knew him, I thought I could trust him, and now I don't know how I could ever look at him again without being reminded of what he did to this family; what he did to Scott.'

My mum raised her eyes to my father, who shook his head infinitesimally. They both looked sad, but strangely nowhere near as surprised as I'd been expecting. The penny dropped slowly, the sound of its falling was almost audible in my head.

'You knew, didn't you? You knew about Ben?'

My mum reached over and took my hand in hers. They were identical in shape, and it shocked me that I'd never noticed that before. The skin on hers was wrinkled, speckled with brown spots, as though she'd been painting clumsily in sepia.

'No, Sophie. We didn't know that Ben was one of the youngsters in the car.'

'But you knew there *were* other passengers?' She nodded slowly. 'Why didn't you ever say anything to me? Why did you let me carry on thinking there was just one drunk driver who was responsible?'

'Because the other people were irrelevant,' said my father brusquely, getting to his feet. 'It only needed *one* drunk driver to cause the accident that night.'

'Are you going to phone the hospital to see how Ben is doing?' I shook my head, taking the pile of clean laundry for my bed from her outstretched arms.

'I can't, Mum. I just can't.'

She nodded, as though she understood. But how could she, when I didn't even understand myself.

'He must be in a lot of pain.'

'I'm sure they've given him medication.'

My mum shook her head at me, the way she used to do when Scott and I were children. 'Not that kind of pain, Sophie.'

I didn't want to hear this and if my arms hadn't been full of clean sheets and a duvet cover, I might well have put my hands over my ears, like the recalcitrant child I seemed to be changing back into.

'I can't condone Ben's actions, for deceiving you – for deceiving all of us. But I also can't forget how happy you've been with him for the last six months.'

My sigh sounded broken. 'But none of it was true. Ben wasn't some random stranger who fate had put in my life. He orchestrated all of this, and I still don't understand why.'

'Then perhaps you should have asked him to explain.'

'I was too angry. I was too hurt.'

My mum put her arms around me, in a real cuddle, the

428

type I could scarcely remember receiving from her for a very long time. 'Don't leave anything unsaid or unresolved between you and Ben. Time is precious with the people you love. You never know when your last goodbye is your last goodbye.'

Somehow I didn't think we were still talking about Ben.

She kissed my forehead gently. 'However bad you're feeling tonight, I'm sure Ben is feeling exactly the same.'

I should have fallen asleep the moment my head touched the pillow; I was certainly exhausted enough. But there was something wrong and strangely off-kilter about my parents' reaction to Ben's involvement in my brother's death that kept me awake. It was like having a hard and uncomfortable pea beneath my mattress, refusing to let me rest. I saw the change of every hour on the clock until the birds outside my window began serenading in the new day.

'Breakfast?' asked my dad as I stumbled like a zombie into the kitchen. I shook my head.

'Just coffee, please, Dad.'

My mother came in from the garden, a watering can in her hand. She and my father wore matching dark circles beneath their eyes, which didn't surprise me. I'd got up twice in the night, and had seen the revealing sliver of light shining from beneath their bedroom door. Their whispered murmurings had been indistinct, but something had clearly kept them awake.

They waited until I had finished my second coffee and had

placed my cup in the dishwasher. My mum raised an eyebrow and my dad nodded. 'Sophie, will you sit down for a minute. Your dad and I want to talk to you.'

I had a sudden flashback to exactly the same words, which had preceded a hugely excruciating talk covering the facts of life. 'If it's about the birds and the bees, I think I've figured it all out by now.' It wasn't a great joke, but it didn't even raise a smile on either of them. I sat back down on the seat I had only recently vacated.

'There's no easy way of saying this . . .' began my father, and then fell silent.

'We know it's going to be a shock,' completed my mother, as though the conversation was a relay race and they were passing the baton to each other.

A sudden sick lurching feeling twisted my stomach. One of them was ill. That was it. What else could account for the serious expressions on their faces?

'There's something we should have told you a very long time ago.'

I ran through a mental checklist of possibilities, each more bizarre than the last: I was adopted; they were bankrupt; they'd won the lottery; they were getting divorced. They would all have shocked me, but nowhere near as much as the truth did.

'The reason why your mother and I don't blame Ben for his involvement in the car accident is . . .'

My father paused, and I leapt in to help him out. ' . . . is because he was only a passenger?'

He shook his head sadly. 'It's because their car wasn't the one at fault.'

'Then who was?' I questioned, pivoting in my seat to direct the question to my mother.

Her lips twisted into a parody of a smile, which looked odd as the tears began to course down her cheeks. 'Scott was. *He* was the driver who drove through a red light, not the car. And . . .' She really struggled with the next revelation, because once you've put someone you love on a pedestal, knocking them down from it is always going to hurt. 'And he'd been drinking – he was over twice the legal limit.'

The air in the room felt suddenly heavy with the weight of old secrets. 'What? No, that's not right. What's this all about?'

My parents looked at each other, actors in a play who knew their lines . . . they just didn't want to deliver them.

'No one could have loved a son more than we loved your brother,' began my dad falteringly, 'but he wasn't perfect.'

'I know that,' I said, remembering the lovable hothead who pushed at every boundary that had ever been set. 'But he didn't drink when he was driving his bike. He wasn't that stupid.'

I looked at them in turn, and then allowed my eye to travel to the empty space beside the door. I imagined Scott standing there, a sheepish look on his face, the kind he used to wear when he'd been caught out in a lie.

'Scott was drunk?' This time I didn't sound so disbelieving.

They nodded, practically in unison. 'There were witnesses who came forward after the crash to say he'd been driving erratically. There were a couple of near misses before he reached the junction.' My father swallowed noisily, his voice thick and gruff. 'The car – the one with Ben and his friends in it – was crossing the junction. They were travelling a little too fast, and the driver was young and inexperienced, but that wasn't what caused the accident. Scott drove straight through a red light and into the side of their vehicle. There was nothing they could have done to avoid it, well, at least that's what the police told us.'

Everything I thought I knew was suddenly wrong. North was now south and I was lost, completely and utterly lost. 'Why did you never tell me this? Why am I only hearing this *now*, sixteen years later?'

Beats me, volunteered imaginary Scott with an artless shrug.

'Because you were struggling so much to cope after losing him. Scott was your hero, he always had been. You'd idolised him since you were a tiny toddler trailing behind him everywhere. Losing him so tragically was bad enough, we didn't think you'd be able to deal with knowing *he* was the one responsible. We wanted to keep his memory perfect for you. So – rightly or wrongly – we made the decision not to tell you. We couldn't see there was any harm in letting you believe the accident was caused by the other car. Except—'

'Except for the fact that I've blamed the only man I've ever been in love with for something that wasn't his fault,' I completed sadly.

*

'Are you through yet?'

'They've still got me on hold.' My father pulled a suitably sympathetic face, and patted me on the shoulder as he walked past me in the hallway. I was using their landline phone, which didn't offer me as much privacy as I would have preferred, but mobile reception here was so unreliable, and this was *one* call I really didn't want to put off making.

'Sorry,' came a disembodied voice, from hundreds of miles away. 'Which ward were you holding for?'

I tried not to sound agitated. It wasn't the telephonist's fault that I'd already been waiting for over ten minutes, and was still no closer to speaking to Ben.

'Winchester,' I said, my voice quivering with tension. I was really hoping the nurses would be able to take the phone to Ben's room so I could speak to him in person. There'd already been more than enough misunderstanding between us, and leaving a message with a third party – especially a message as important as this – would just feel wrong. Ben's own mobile was either switched off, out of battery, or not even at the hospital with him, and the frustration of not being able to reach him instantly made me feel as though I'd slipped back several decades into the past.

After what felt like an eternity, a different voice sounded in my ear. 'Winchester Ward. Can I help you?'

My own voice sounded choked with relief as I spoke hurriedly into the receiver. 'I'm sorry to bother you, but I'd really like to speak to one of the patients on the ward, Ben Stevens, if that's possible?'

The line was bad; it sounded as though someone was frying eggs at the other end, and I had to press the handset close to my ear to hear anything at all. Even then, I could only manage to decipher every other word: ' . . . not now . . . doing rounds . . . an hour . . .'

I reassembled the snippets into a cohesive sentence and gave a small disappointed sigh. 'Could I leave a message for him then?' I asked, hoping the ward clerk at the end of the phone was able to hear me better than I could her. There was a mumble and several words I couldn't catch. I decided to assume they were, *'Of course. What would you like to say?'*

'Can you please tell him that Sophie called? Can you say that I'm sorry, and that I was wrong. And that I'm coming back right now and will see him later this afternoon.'

There was a long moment of crackling and then silence, during which I convinced myself we'd lost the connection. But then the line cleared momentarily and the voice came back, sounding younger than I'd first thought, and more than a little harassed.

'Sure, will do. I'll see that message gets to Steven for you.' *Steven?*

'It's for Ben. Ben Stevens.' The line erupted into the sound of crackling popcorn.

'Sorry. Len Stephenson. I got it. I'll pass the message on to one of the nurses for you.'

They hung up and I was left staring at the phone in a mixture of dismay and irritation. I glanced at my watch. Should

I call back and risk missing the next train, or just wait until I was finally able to speak to Ben in person?

'Dad, can you get me to the station in time to catch the twelve forty-five train?'

My father, who prided himself on fifty years of driving with an unblemished licence; who thought going at thirty-two miles an hour made you a speed fiend; and who had a very compelling reason to never want another member of our family involved in any kind of accident, surprised me totally with his reply.

'I'll have to put my foot down, but if we leave right now we should just about make it.'

So many things nearly stopped me from getting to the hospital that day, it was almost as though the universe was deliberately trying to keep me from reaching Ben. First my dad's car, which he assured me had only been serviced the week before, wouldn't start. I hopped anxiously from foot to foot as he tinkered with the battery, grumbling under his breath about cowboy mechanics. I must have looked at my watch fifty times before the engine finally roared back to life. My dad gave me a huge 'thumbs up' and I dropped a swift kiss on my mum's cheek before jumping into the passenger seat.

'Can we still make it?' I asked worriedly.

'Probably. Yes. Maybe,' he replied ambiguously.

I kept one eye on the clock on the dashboard and the other on the speedometer for the entire journey. One was going way too quickly, and the other nowhere near fast enough.

'I daren't drive any quicker on these roads, they're too narrow,' my father apologised as we both watched the clock inching closer to the time when the train was due at the local station. If I missed that one there wouldn't be another for a further three hours, and I couldn't bear the thought of Ben having to go through a second day believing I wanted nothing more to do with him.

It seemed like an omen – a bad omen – when a tractor pulled out in front of us, causing our speed to drop so low I might just as well have got out and walked. I watched the digital display on the clock flicker and change to my departure time. We were still three miles from the station.

'Well, that's that then,' I said, flopping back in the passenger seat. 'We may as well turn back, Dad.'

He slowed down momentarily, but then with a grim set to his lips he pressed his foot back down on the accelerator. I leant over and laid my hand gently on his arm. 'There's no point. I'm too late. I've missed the train.'

'I'm being a fatalist,' he said, not sounding at all like my pragmatic father. 'If you're meant to get to Ben today, if there's any meaning or purpose in all the bad things that have happened to us ... and to him, then fate is going to be on your side.'

'How, exactly?'

'The train will still be there, waiting for you,' he declared.

He'd sounded so positive, I'm not sure which of us was the most disappointed when we pulled up at the station to see the level crossing barriers pointing straight up towards the

436

cloudless blue sky, like accusatory fingers. The train had been and gone. And if this *was* a message from fate . . . it wasn't a very encouraging one.

'I'm sorry, sweetheart, I really thought that—' My dad broke off suddenly as a familiar deafening claxon sounded right beside us. Very slowly the level crossing barriers began to descend.

I was all fingers and thumbs as I fumbled for the door handle, hauled my bag from the back seat, and ran like hell through the ticket office towards the platform. It was nothing short of a miracle that I caught the train. I collapsed noisily into a vacant seat in the carriage, red-faced and more breathless than Ben had sounded when he'd needed his oxygen mask.

I glanced at the passengers around me. Directly opposite sat a middle-aged woman who had lowered her paperback, and was looking at me curiously. Beside her were a mother and child, busily absorbed in a game they were playing on her tablet. The woman gave me a fleeting smile, while her son inched shyly against her side, hiding his face from me.

I waited until I'd regained my breath, before reaching into my bag for my phone, knowing I was about to become the person I would least want to be sitting beside on a three-hour journey. Perhaps I was turning into a grumpy old woman way before my time, but people who conducted private conversations on their mobiles in public places were my pet peeve. But today I was willing to risk annoying every single passenger in the carriage, in order to make sure Ben knew I was on my way.

It was a different voice, older and more authoritative, who picked up the phone on Winchester Ward this time.

'Would it be possible to speak to one of your patients, please? Mr Ben Stevens.'

The line was perfectly clear this time, so I had no trouble at all hearing the slight clearing of her throat before she answered me. 'Can I ask if you're a family member?'

Stupidly I answered her honestly. 'No, I'm not.'

'I'm sorry,' she replied, and there was something in her voice that alarmed me. 'I'm afraid we can only give out information to the direct family.'

I hadn't asked for information, only to speak to him. Something was wrong here. Something had happened.

'He's my partner,' I said, my voice rising enough to probably qualify me as a nuisance passenger. 'Please, can't you just tell me if he's alright?'

'Why's that lady shouting, Mummy?' asked the little boy guilelessly, looking up from his game.

'Hush now,' said his mother, and I wasn't sure whether the comment was directed at her young son or me.

I tried lowering my voice. It was important to remain calm, even if I already felt like a planet spinning off its axis. 'Would you be able to let him know that I'm on the phone? Perhaps if I could just talk to him for a minute?'

The nurse paused and I held my breath, waiting for her response. 'I'm afraid that won't be possible. Mr Stevens is no longer here.'

Relief flooded through me as I flopped back against my

seat. 'He's been discharged?' I hadn't expected that. I had imagined Ben's stay in hospital to be longer than this. Had he caught a taxi home, or had Carla driven him? I should have been there, I thought, overwhelmed by guilt.

The nurse's correcting comment cut through me like a surgeon's scalpel. 'Actually Mr Stevens was moved to a different ward this morning.'

'Which ward?' My voice was suddenly too loud, too strained, too panicked. The only thing it didn't sound was surprised, because deep down some part of me had known that this was what fate had been planning all along. Life was a carousel, forever turning, and now it was taking me right back to the place I'd never wanted to see again.

'Mr Stevens has been moved to our Intensive Care Unit,' she confirmed. And my nightmare was complete.

They couldn't transfer the call, so I had to go through the whole agony of redialling and going back through the switchboard all over again. The passengers around me had stopped pretending that they weren't listening in to my conversation. The middle-aged woman lowered her book to her lap, and I could no longer hear the subtle beep of the child's computer game. I could feel many pairs of eyes on me as I asked the operator to connect me to the ICU.

If I'd thought the nurse on the previous ward had been cagey and reluctant to share information, *this one* could have withstood a full-on CIA interrogation without cracking.

'Can you at least tell me what happened to him?' I

begged. It wasn't just for my sake; the passengers in the seats around me looked like they needed to know almost as much as I did.

'Mr Stevens was transferred to the unit a short while ago because of respiratory difficulties.' My hand went to my throat, as though I was the one who was unable to breathe, and not Ben.

'Can you tell me how he's doing now? Has he needed to be intubated?' The medical term flowed off my tongue all too easily. There are some words or phrases you never forget. I closed my eyes, as I realised that wasn't the question I should be asking anyway. There was another far more important one. 'Has the Advance Decision been put into place? Can you check his notes and tell me if he did that?'

'I'm afraid a patient's notes are confidential, as is their treatment. There really is nothing more I can tell you over the telephone.'

'I need him to know that I'm on my way. I need him to know that he has to keep on fighting; that whatever happens, we'll face it together. He needs to tell the doctors that he's changed his mind about the Advance Decision. He wants to live, I know he does.'

'Just get here as soon as you can,' advised the nurse, and for the first time I heard a kindness in her voice. I think that worried me most of all.

I disconnected the call and stared blankly ahead, not seeing anyone or anything. I wasn't even aware that I was crying until the lady opposite leant forward and pressed a folded tissue into my palm. Her eyes were warm and sympathetic as she patted my arm comfortingly.

Beside her the young boy began fidgeting in his seat, trying to extract something from his mother's bag. Without asking for her approval, he pulled out an open bag of jelly babies and thrust them towards me.

'When I'm sad, Mummy always gives me one of these,' he said hesitantly. He flinched, but only a little, when his generosity made me cry even harder. 'The red ones are the best,' he whispered shyly.

I smiled and forced the tears to stop, because I didn't want to scare him, and dipped my hand into the bag, pulling out a soft crimson sweet. 'Thank you,' I said quietly.

People say that commuters can be cold; that travelling on public transport dehumanises us and transforms us into unfeeling robots. I categorically disagree with that statement. I was scared for every minute of that train journey, but I never felt alone. There were nameless strangers who went through every agonising minute of it with me. When the train finally pulled into the station, someone took my bag and placed it in my hands, someone else passed me my jacket, and a man who hadn't even said a word to me asked if I needed money for a taxi. I jumped down from the train with the sound of their good wishes still ringing in my ears.

The Intensive Care Unit was on the fourth floor, but I couldn't wait for the lift. After jabbing repeatedly on the button to call it down to the foyer, I never even waited to see if it arrived. I headed for the stairwell, still compelled by the need to remain constantly in motion. My feet were noisy on the linoleum of the staircase, as though the sound of my sandals on the treads could drown out the questions that kept screaming in my head. Had Ben instructed the doctors not to intervene if his breathing worsened? Had he decided that this would be the last round in a fight he could never win? And how much of that decision was down to what had happened twenty-four hours earlier? Was our first argument also going to be our last?

I burst through the double doors onto the fourth floor, winded and terrified. I probably looked far less healthy than some of the patients on the ward as I anxiously approached the nurse at the desk.

'Ben Stevens,' I gasped, leaning against the counter for support.

'His bed is just around the corner,' she said, gesturing which way I needed to go. The need for speed was gone, and suddenly becalmed, I took slow and faltering steps as I walked towards the bay. I turned the corner and found him.

My legs felt boneless, without the strength to power me across the floor to reach him. This was, I realised sadly, something Ben could easily understand. I swayed, and gripped tightly onto the bed frame for support. A nurse was standing beside Ben's bed, a chart in her hands. She looked concerned when she saw me. 'Hello. Are you okay? Are you here for Mr Stevens?' I nodded, my voice trapped behind the huge lump in my throat. 'You look like you need to sit down,' she said, slipping a chair behind my legs. I sank onto it and reached for Ben's hand.

'I know this all looks very scary when you first walk in, but don't let any of it worry you.'

'It doesn't worry me,' I said, tears of relief rolling down my face and landing like raindrops on Ben's unmoving hand. 'I honestly don't think anything has ever made me happier.'

The nurse actually took a small step backwards, clearly thrown by my words. I could hardly blame her, I'm sure it wasn't the normal reaction from a patient's loved one. 'Would you like me to explain what all the equipment is, what it's doing?'

I laid my hand lightly on Ben's bare chest, feeling its rhythmic rise and fall, powered not by him, but by the machine working quietly beside his bed. Even the plastic tubing the doctors had inserted into his airway didn't scare me. It was a lifeline thrown out to him ... and also to me.

'I know what it's doing,' I said quietly, my lips trembling as they curved into a grateful smile. 'It's bringing him back to me.'

I wouldn't leave, and after a while they stopped asking me to go. Someone brought me a drink and then later a tray of hospital food, which I discovered tastes just as unpalatable when you're well as it does when you're sick.

My head was on the mattress, beside Ben's hand, when I felt the lightest of touches on my shoulder. I bolted upright, my eyes going first to Ben, before I turned to see who had woken me. I blinked at the nurse standing before me, wondering why she looked familiar.

'I'm sorry, I didn't mean to startle you,' she apologised, 'but are you Sophie?'

I came all the way awake at her question, because I had suddenly placed her. She was one of the nurses on Winchester Ward.

'I am.'

She nodded, and her eyes went briefly to Ben. 'Then I have a message for you.' I wondered who had managed to track me down here, but before I could ask, she added, 'It's from Ben.' My heart started thudding in my chest as I nodded, urging her to deliver it. 'He said to check your emails.'

'Huh?' I'm not sure what I was hoping or expecting to hear: *I forgive you for running away from me? I never want to see you again? Can we please start over?* Those I knew how to respond to. His concern about my inbox was harder to understand.

'Was he delirious? His temperature had been really high.'

'No. He was making perfect sense.' She turned to look at Ben in his drug-induced coma and smiled, and I could see in that moment that she liked him. Her face was kind as she turned back to me and once again placed her hand on my shoulder, patting it gently.

'Check your emails,' she said softly and then slipped away into the shadows of the ward.

*

It was almost 9 p.m., but the sky still bore a few lingering stains of daylight. I'd come outside the hospital to use my phone, because I still wasn't sure about the rules of using it on the ward. I walked past a cluster of patients, some in wheelchairs, who were gathered around the entrance in their dressing gowns, like Colditz prisoners planning their great escape.

I kept walking until I found a small garden area with a duck pond and a couple of wooden benches. When I sat down, I noticed a small brass plaque fixed to the topmost slat. Someone named Doris had liked to sit on this very spot and watch the ducks. I felt a single stray tear slither down my cheek. Was I crying for Doris, or in fear that somewhere out there another bench was waiting to hold the name of the man I loved in the Intensive Care Unit?

I took a deep and steadying breath and withdrew my phone from my bag. Not surprisingly I hadn't bothered checking my emails that day. If I *had* done, I would have seen the one from Den, which curiously had been sent at exactly the same time he'd been in the operating theatre, being intubated.

My fingers trembled so much, it took three attempts before I successfully managed to open the message.

> I'm hoping you don't get to read this email. I'm hoping that when I wake up tomorrow, I'm going to see you sitting beside my bed, and that I get the chance to say all of this to you in person. But there are things I

don't know, and things I'm not sure of, and some of them scare me more than this disease I've got has ever done.

My biggest fear? That one is easy. I'm afraid you won't be coming back. And I can't blame you if you don't. How can you trust me now, when I've kept so much from you? I don't deserve your trust, but I pray there's still enough between us that you'll give me a chance to try to explain. I hope you'll listen, even if you're still as mad at me as you have every right to be.

If I hadn't been so scared of losing you, I would have told you all of this a very long time ago. Believe it or not, that was always my intention.

There are things I never thought I'd end up being. Some of them aren't that great: a liar, a stalker, or a patient with an incurable disease. The first two bother me far more than the last, because they affect how *you* feel about me. In my defence, I've never lied to you, except by omission, which I *do know* is just a technicality and not an excuse. Hiring an over-zealous private investigator, who dug far deeper than I'd asked him to do, hopefully only makes me a borderline stalker (if that's a thing?).

Oh, and there's something else I never thought I'd end up being . . . and that's so completely in love with you that I can face all the shit life wants to throw at me, because it also gave me you.

And now I probably don't have you any more, and

for that I've got no one to blame but myself. But if you've got this far without hitting the delete key, I hope you'll carry on reading while I try to explain.

The accident which took Scott's life will always be my biggest regret. It's the one thing, if I could turn back time, that I'd alter. How it affected you and your parents' lives breaks my heart just as much now as it did sixteen years ago. I've come so close to telling you the truth, but whenever you spoke about his death, I could hear how much you blamed the other vehicle, and I was terrified that I'd lose you forever if I admitted I was there on that night.

It was late and we were coming back from a party. Sam – the driver – was sober, but the rest of us had been drinking. We were mucking around, being rowdy and stupid the way kids do. Sam was getting really pissed off with us. I remember him yelling for us to shut up because he couldn't concentrate and then . . . and then there was this almighty bang.

We blamed ourselves, even though the police said it wasn't our fault. I wanted to make amends, but there was nothing I could say or do to make things better. But I couldn't let go of what we'd done to you and your family. Eventually I lost contact with everyone I knew in Cotterham, and I kidded myself that time would have healed your wounds. It was a lie I told myself for a very long time.

I pushed what had happened deep down, and yet

when I got my diagnosis the first thing I thought of was Scott, and how you can't outrun karma. The doctors tell you to 'put your house in order' and for me that meant only one thing. I needed to make sure you were all okay, that you'd been able to move on.

Your parents were easy to track down, but I had no idea how to find you, so I hired an investigator, who ended up giving me far more information than I'd asked or bargained for. That's when I knew I had to try to find a way to fix things. To fix *you*, because it was my fault you were broken.

You once asked me what was on my bucket list. *You*. You were my bucket list. You were what I needed to put right before I died.

After I moved here I always intended to tell you that I'd been in the car Scott had driven into. But finding the nerve to do it was so much harder than I'd ever imagined. I don't know how many times I almost knocked on your door, only to bail out at the last moment. And then last October I told myself I was finally going to do it. Except when I got there, the flat below yours was having a party. I sat in my car for hours, waiting for the noise to die down, but eventually it got too late, so I gave up and drove away. Something made me look back in my mirror, and that's when I saw the flames. Well . . . you know the rest.

I thought being your friend would be enough, but I soon realised that I wanted so much more. I should have walked away, because I knew the last person in the world you'd ever want to be close to was the man who helped destroy your life. But it was too late by then, because I already loved you. Right from that first night, I loved you.

If I could change the past I would: I'd never have gone to that party; I'd never have been in that car; and Scott would never have been on that bike. But the one thing I won't wish for, is that I'd never fallen in love with you. Because you saved me, in a way that goes far beyond what I did on the night of the fire. I can die knowing that you loved me. I just can't live knowing that you don't.

I wish things could have been different for us. There's so much I would have wanted to give you: a ring, a promise of a future, my name. But I can't. And that makes me sadder than anything else. I tore up the Advance Decision, because if there's even just the smallest chance of making things right with you, I have to take it.

I'm going to ask one of the nurses to send this email to you, in case something happens and I can't send it myself. I know it's too much to hope that you'll still feel the same way about me after this, but I'm going to fight to stay alive long enough to know if you can ever forgive me.

I love you, Sophie, and I always will.

Ben x

Ben had many visitors over the next forty-eight hours, none of whom he got to see. Carla came and then left; Alice, Henry, Charlie and Jacqueline all came, and then left. Even Julia and Gary stopped by, although possibly more to see me than Ben. Every one of them tried to persuade me to go home and get some rest, but I only smiled and shook my head. Once I'd refused to go anywhere near a hospital, now I was refusing to leave.

I was there when the doctors decided the infection was finally responding to the antibiotics; I was there when they wheeled Ben down to theatre to remove the tube from his throat, and I was still there when they wheeled him back up again.

And when he finally woke up, when he lifted his head from the pillow and his eyes searched the room looking for me, I was there.

Because beside him was where I belonged.

Chapter 20

September

Even though the air con was turned up to its maximum setting, it still felt hot inside the car. I took one hand off the wheel and wafted the fabric of my sleeveless top away from my neckline to create a temporary draught.

I turned to Ben on the passenger seat. 'You'd *so* better not be trying to look down my top,' I said teasingly. He didn't reply, but he didn't have to. He would *definitely* have been looking.

It had been a long drive and my legs felt tired and cramped. It made me wonder how he'd been able to do it without complaint back in February, when we'd first come to this place. Now Ben didn't drive at all. He'd stopped a couple of months ago, and I knew how hard it must have been on the day when he'd wordlessly passed me the car keys after that final journey. 'Just try not to scratch it too many times,' was all he'd said, and then had grinned when I'd stuck my tongue out at him.

'Very mature, Mrs Stevens,' he'd answered. And I had smiled, the way I still did whenever I heard my new name.

I tilted my left hand slightly, still keeping it on the wheel as I examined the circlet of diamonds on my third finger. The stones caught and reflected the September sun slanting through the windscreen, filling the car with dancing shards of light. I turned to Ben's seat and smiled, remembering the night he'd slipped the ring unexpectedly on my finger. It was the one I'd have chosen for myself, if I'd had a considerably healthier bank balance. 'You didn't need to buy me a ring,' I'd protested, already so in love with it, I knew I was never going to take it off.

He'd kissed me slowly and very thoroughly. 'Well, I thought *one* of us should,' he'd teased, pulling me tightly against him as he gave a small tut of disapproval. 'I still can't believe you proposed to me and never even bought me a ring.'

I snuggled against his neck, my cheeks a little warm with a blush I didn't want him to see. 'I still can't believe I *proposed*.'

His chuckle reverberated through his chest wall to mine. 'I don't think anyone on the ward could either.'

I hadn't planned it, and yet as the words were forming and falling from my lips, I knew without a single doubt that I was making the best decision of my life. The doctors had just told Ben that he would be discharged the following day, and that he could then resume the drug trial. It felt like an appropriate moment to embrace and celebrate the future.

'Most people would have just gone out and bought a bottle of champagne,' Ben said, lifting the hand with its new band of diamonds to his lips, and kissing my palm.

'I'm not most people.'

His eyes had softened, and suddenly there was another new favourite memory that I would treasure for the rest of my life. 'No, you're not.'

We had always said that we would return to the beach in the summer, and for a time I had worried that Ben wouldn't be well enough to do so, or that we had left it too late and the cottage would be fully booked up. But fortunately because we had waited until September, the cottage was vacant and was ours for as long as we wanted it.

This time *I* was the one who phoned the owner to make the booking. Ben's speech had suffered from the intubation, just as the doctors had warned us it might. I still had no trouble understanding him, nor did Carla and several of his other close friends. '*Because we listen with our hearts,*' I'd reminded Carla, quoting her own words back to her. She had smiled, even though she was crying. However, it was impossible not to be aware that Ben chose to speak far less frequently as the summer progressed.

August had been an uncommonly dark and gloomy month, but September had undergone a change of heart, and although the evenings were beginning to grow cooler, the days were still filled with warmth and sunshine.

'The turning for that store is just up ahead,' I said,

peering at the Sat Nav that Ben hadn't needed to use on our last journey. The car park was surprisingly crowded, even though the holiday season was technically over by now. At first I thought I wouldn't be able to find a space. I knew Ben was watching me with amusement as I drove past several gaps that I deemed too tricky to manoeuvre into. I also knew that had *he* been driving, he'd have slipped effortlessly into one of them.

'Stop harassing me,' I said to him, even though he hadn't said a word. 'I'll find one that I like eventually.' I did. But I see-sawed his car in and out of the bay so many times that small beads of perspiration were trickling between my shoulder blades when I eventually pulled on the handbrake and switched off the engine. It hadn't helped that a couple of guys had been standing and chatting at the edge of the car park, clearly watching my efforts. 'Everyone's a parking critic,' I muttered, knowing without even turning my head that Ben would be smiling.

'Why don't I just dash in and pick up a few provisions for our stay?' I suggested, plucking up my handbag from the passenger footwell. 'Will it be okay if you stay in the car?' My eye went to the space behind his seat, where a collapsible walking frame was wedged. He'd never taken to using it, preferring a single stick, which admittedly he coped with really well.

I reached over and rested my hand lightly on him, and I knew he understood all the things I wanted to say, and also the things I never did.

I was surprised to see the same shop assistant sitting at the till inside the store, and even more astounded when she remembered me. 'You're the newlyweds who were here at the beginning of the year, aren't you?' she asked, as I lifted my wire basket onto the counter. I smiled, because now I could legitimately claim that title.

'Well, I'm one half of them,' I said as I began loading my purchases into several bags.

'So where's that lovely handsome husband of yours?' It didn't surprise me at all that she had remembered Ben. He wasn't someone who was easily forgotten.

'He's waiting in the car,' I said, hoping she wouldn't ask me why. And luckily she didn't.

'No free bottle of wine this time,' I said, stowing the shopping bags on the back seat and giving Ben a rueful shrug.

I didn't panic when the Sat Nav lost the road we were travelling on, because it was already starting to look familiar to me. Admittedly the roadside foliage was a lot more abundant than it had been in February, and the weeds in the middle of the road were staking their claim even more boldly after a summer's growth.

I glanced over at Ben when the cottage finally came into view. 'We're back,' I said, and just like that, I started to cry. I brushed the tears away with the back of my hand and turned to him in apology. 'Sorry, I think I always knew I was going to do that.'

The property had clearly benefited from some care and

attention, and the new layers of paint had yet to suffer a harsh Welsh winter. In a way I think I actually preferred how it had been before. Ben was obviously no longer able to carry our bags from the car, and it made me sad to realise just how much had slipped away from him, from us, in the last seven months. I could feel his eyes watching me as I retrieved the key from beneath the planter and directed an amused shrug towards the car, which I hoped he saw. It still didn't seem like a very secure hiding place.

The cottage looked the same when we went inside, and I was pleased about that. When so much had changed, what I really wanted was continuity. I cooked pasta for dinner, remembering that was what I had prepared on our very first visit. It was impossible to be here, to sit at the same dinner table and not think back to that night. Although our wedding had been in the summer, our honeymoon had been here several months earlier, and for that reason alone this place would always be special to both of us.

After dinner we moved by unspoken agreement to the settee. The room was cool, and if things had been different Ben would probably have lit us a fire in the neatly swept grate. Instead I just shook out the Aztec-patterned throw and draped it over us. I snuggled down beneath the warm cover, enjoying the tranquillity of the cottage as it creaked towards night-time. I thought I'd remembered everything about our last stay here, but I'd forgotten the peaceful percussion of the settling timbers. The sound was interrupted by an incoming text from my phone.

I drew it from my pocket, surprised to find I had signal, and then smiled at the screen. 'It's Julia,' I informed Ben, clicking on her message. "'*Hey hon. Just wanted to make sure you got there without any problems*,'" I read out loud. I glanced over at Ben and gave a wry smile. 'Someone *else* who questions my driving skills,' I said lightly, knowing perfectly well that wasn't why my friend had messaged me.

'*The journey down was fine*,' I tapped out on my keypad, sounding out the words as I typed them, for Ben's benefit. I could easily imagine Julia, sitting in her lounge, her long legs tucked beneath her and her phone clutched anxiously in hand, waiting for my reply.

'*I was just worried about you.*'

'*There's no need. Relax. Everything's good here*,' I rattled in, smiling across at Ben, knowing he was unlikely to be surprised by her concern, particularly as she and Gary were no longer just *my* friends, they now belonged to both of us. *Mine* was now *ours*; *me* had become *we*; and that alchemy of his soul with mine still felt magical and wonderful; I suspected it always would. Ben and I were united long before we had a piece of paper to prove it. We were already soldiers standing shoulder to shoulder facing a cruel and heartless adversary. There was a comfort in knowing that whatever life threw into the ring, we'd both keep coming out punching. Together we were stronger.

I turned the slim black phone over and over in my hand, like a magician about to perform a card trick, and for once managed to resist the urge to press the tiny camera icon on the screen.

'How many times have you watched that video now?' Ben had asked only a few weeks earlier, making me jump as he walked up silently behind me. I slapped down the lid of my laptop as though I'd been caught watching porn. He'd chuckled softly and walked carefully around the sofa to lower himself beside me. I heaved a tiny silent sigh of relief when the manoeuvre was complete. Ben rarely used his stick inside the house, but it meant I spent more time than I cared to admit anxiously holding my breath. He pretended not to notice, but I knew that he did.

'That wouldn't be a certain wedding video you were watching *again*, would it?' he teased, reaching over to lift the lid of my laptop. The screen was frozen, and the faces of our guests were all turned towards the camera positioned at the end of the aisle. Gary had done an excellent job as our unofficial videographer, but I think even *he* would have been surprised to discover just how many times I had watched the footage.

I turned towards Ben. 'Want to watch it with me?'

He shook his head, but he was grinning and even though the light of day was beginning to fade, the room seemed to brighten with his smile. 'I've seen this one before,' he assured me, lifting one arm and inviting me to cuddle up beside him. 'I already know how it ends.'

For just a moment a dark cloud scudded across his eyes, and then mine. 'And how's that?' I asked, my voice just a little too overly bright and chipper.

Ben lowered his face to mine, until we were forehead to

forehead, eyelashes brushing together in feather-light strokes. 'And they all lived happily ever after,' he said, his breath on mine. I wanted to inhale, to draw him inside me, and keep him there forever.

'How did you get on at the hospital today?' I asked, my voice a whisper, as though nothing bad could ever be spoken or heard, as long as we kept it *sotto voce*.

'Same old, same old,' he said, giving a small shrug that travelled from his skeleton through to mine, like a ricochet. Ben still insisted on attending his regular appointments alone, and although I respected his decision, I often wondered if I was only receiving an edited version of the outcome.

I suspected there was something he was holding back, when he tried to divert me by leaning over and pressing the play icon on the screen. 'I just want to see this next bit, because some beautiful girl in a long white dress is about to come in, and then that guy at the front there,' he reached over and touched his own frozen image on the screen, 'is going to smile and then lose it totally and start crying like a complete idiot.'

As though waking up from a witch's spell, every figure on the screen suddenly came to life. Ben wasn't the only one who was overcome with emotion. Carla was openly weeping as she stood beside Alice and Henry, and even though the camera hadn't caught it, I clearly remembered two large fat tear drops slowly travelling down my dad's ruddy cheeks as he'd walked me down the aisle.

Ben murmured something, but I didn't turn my head

because I was focusing intently on the screen of my laptop, on his face to be precise, because for me the next few seconds were the very best part of the entire recording. Each time I watched it, I felt my breath catch in my throat, exactly as it had done on the day, when Ben's eyes had met and held mine as I walked slowly towards him. The joy, the love and the tenderness on his face lost none of their potency, however many times I watched the video. There were things I wished I could change; things I wished had never happened, but that look ... that expression ... the one that confirmed I was exactly where I was supposed to be in the universe ... *that* I would never change.

We watched the video all the way to the end, of course we did, all fifty-six minutes of it. And even though I knew every word of Ben's speech, when he told our guests that despite what they might think, he really *was* the luckiest man in the world, and that finding me had saved him, I still cried like I was hearing it for the very first time.

He had a tissue ready and waiting as the final shot of us, swaying gently in each other's arms on the small dance floor, faded away to black. 'I'm seriously considering not letting you watch this again. I can't afford the Kleenex.'

I burrowed my face into his neck and felt his arms tighten around me. We sat like that for a long time, until my arm went numb with pins and needles and the evening shadows stopped teasing and taunting the dusk, and filled every corner of the room with darkness.

'We should go away,' Ben said, breathing the words into

the parted hair at the nape of my neck. I shivered in his arms, despite the warmth of the room.

'Away? Away where?'

'To the beach. We always said we'd go back in the summer. I think we should go now. Soon.'

I raised my head and the movement felt awkward and cumbersome, as though it was suddenly too heavy for my neck muscles to support. 'Why right now, Ben? What's the rush?'

His heart thudded just a little bit faster; I felt it resonate down my ribcage. My own inexplicably joined in, as though both organs were engaged in a private race.

'There's no rush. I just think that now would be a good time to go, that's all.'

It wasn't all. I knew that. And more importantly, he *knew* that I knew it. The question I really wanted to ask, the one I was far too scared to voice, would have given me the answer. All I had to do was open my mouth and set the words free. *'Was something said at the hospital today? Is that why you're bringing this up now?'*

My lips parted, I turned to him, and saw the look in his eyes and the question remained forever unasked, because I already had my answer.

'We should come back here every year,' I told Ben as I pulled the bed covers up and switched off the light. The sound of the waves breaking on the beach was just as restful as I remembered, and I was more than half asleep when I

461

felt Ben's arms reach out and draw me back against him. 'I love you, Sophie,' Ben whispered into my ear, and I had no trouble understanding him at all.

I decided that breakfast could wait when I flung open the windows and felt the warmth of the sunshine on my arms. There were a lot of things that we'd planned to do that morning, and the weather looked so glorious, I didn't want to waste a single moment.

I packed a very quick impromptu breakfast picnic. 'Yes, that *is* a real thing,' I assured Ben, as I placed the foil-wrapped food into a bag, along with a tartan-patterned blanket.

I was worried how we would manage crossing the sand, but actually the surface had been much more difficult to walk on in February. By unspoken agreement we were making for the headland, to the place where a much younger Ben had once spent so many hours looking for seals. My legs were aching slightly when we got there, and even though I was only dressed in shorts and a T-shirt, I felt incredibly hot.

I unfolded the blanket and laid it on the sand before holding tightly on to Ben and picking out a pathway among the washed-up seaweed to the water's edge. The waves felt like ice water and I gasped as they broke over my feet. 'Definitely no skinny-dipping in this water,' I told him teasingly, before he even thought about suggesting it. The sea might have been too cool for bathing, but the sun was certainly bright enough to dazzle me as it bounced over the water's surface. I pulled my sunglasses down from the top of my head, where they'd been doubling up as a hairband,

and stared out to sea for a very long time, with Ben at my side. This was what we'd come here for, and it filled me with mixed emotions.

Eventually, when my feet were practically numb, we returned to the blanket. I flopped down on the sun-warmed fabric and stared up at the cloudless sky. 'You were right about this place,' I said eventually. 'It's absolutely beautiful in the summer. I'm so glad we came back.' Ben was lying on the blanket, but I eased myself up into a sitting position and looked down at the small pebbled bank by the water's edge. I blinked, because for a moment I didn't actually believe what I was seeing. I looked away and then back again, not sure if my brain was conjuring up the thing I most wanted Ben to see, but when I looked back it was still there. A solitary seal sat on the pebbles, his skin gleaming like black oil in the sun. His eyes were soulful, enormous dark pools that held mine with a knowledge that defied all logic or reason.

'Ben, Ben,' I whispered, anxious not to spook the creature he had waited over twenty years to see. 'Look, Ben, look. It's a seal.'

The seal looked our way for a considerable time, as though silently communicating his apology for having made us wait for so long before he finally appeared.

It felt like a sign.

It is a sign, came Scott's voice in my head, startling me, because I hadn't heard it for a while.

'Is it?' I said out loud. 'Is it time?' I rarely spoke to my brother in actual words, but today it didn't sound odd doing so.

'*Yes, it is,*' replied Ben, almost as though he too had been able to hear Scott.

'I don't think I can do this,' I said brokenly, beginning to cry.

'*Yes, you can,*' assured Ben beside me. '*You know now that you can do anything.*'

'But not this. It's just too much.'

I felt his hand in mine, I felt it with every single fibre of my being. I closed my eyes so he wouldn't see my tears, but they kept on falling anyway. When I opened my eyes and looked down, my hand was empty.

'Loving you was the easiest thing in the world,' I whispered to the empty beach, 'and letting you go is going to be the hardest.'

'*I'm always going to be here,*' Ben promised. '*I'll whisper your name in the wind. I'll be with you at every sunrise and every sunset. Look for me in every cloud, and every rainbow. That's where I'll be.*'

I got shakily to my feet and reached for Ben one last time.

'Look after him for me, Scott.'

Of course I will, my brother said, more clearly than I'd ever heard him before.

One kiss, one final touch of my lips on him. It would have to last me for a very long time.

'*I love you, Sophie. Remember that. I will always love you.*'

I nodded because now speech was beyond me. Very carefully I undid the lid and lifted the container above my head, and scattered Ben's ashes to the wind.

Afterlife

I'll be setting with the sunset,
I'll be falling with the rain.
And when the wind blows fiercely;
I'll be whispering your name.

I'll be lingering with the shadows,
I'll be floating in the snow.
And when you stop believing;
I'll be all you need to know.

I'll be soaring with the clouds,
I'll be the sparkle in the star.
And when you feel that you're alone;
I'll be there where you are.

I'll be splashing in your teardrops,
I'll be dancing all day long.
And when you only hear the silence;
I'll be the music to our song.

You must not cry, for life gone by:
Choose the path that lies ahead.
For I'll be stepping in the moonlight
Where the angels fear to tread.

KA

Acknowledgements

As ever, I would like to thank the incredible team at Simon & Schuster, who consistently take my ramblings and magically turn them into something we can all be proud of. Particular thanks go to my amazing editor Jo Dickinson who 'gets' where I'm coming from – perhaps even better than I do! Thanks also to Emma Capron, Sara-Jade Virtue and everyone at S&S for their overwhelming enthusiasm and expertise.

A heartfelt thank you goes to my incredible agent Kate Burke, for her wisdom, sharp mind, eagle-eye and unfailing Sherpa duties whenever we have to journey anywhere together! I feel extremely fortunate to be represented by the dedicated and caring team at Diane Banks Associates. Thank you for all your hard work on my behalf.

I've made many new author friends over the past few years, and without them the process would be a great deal lonelier and more confusing. I'm sure one day we'll figure out what we're doing, but until then a big thank you goes to Kate Thompson, Ella Harper and Kate Riordan for being there, on email or in person, with a glass in hand and a funny story to tell!

This Love was, at times, a difficult and emotional book to write. Motor Neurone Disease (MND) is a cruel and arbitrary opponent, affecting up to 5,000 adults in the UK at any one time. Every day in this country six people will receive a diagnosis that will literally change, and sadly shorten, their lives. But I didn't want this to be a book without hope. To quote Ben's own words (yes, I do know they're really mine), 'They *will* find a cure, I'm sure of it. But they might not find it in time for me.'

One person who sadly did not get to see that cure was Cath Dolan, whose husband Joe Ross spent time telling me with bravery and honesty how devastating it had been when MND infiltrated their lives. I learnt more from listening to Joe than I could have found out from a hundred internet searches or books. I'd like to thank the entire Ross family for allowing me a glimpse into the reality they lived through. I wish I could have met and known Cath, who faced and challenged death in the same feisty way she did life. I'd like to think we could have been friends had we been given the chance.

Friends and family can help get you through anything – including writing a book. And so I'd like to say a special thank you to Debbie and Hazel (my first readers), and also to Kim and Sheila for their continued cheerleading support (minus the pom-poms, of course), Christine (thank you for introducing me to Joe), and lastly to Barb, who has proved it's never too late to make a new friend for life.

Without my family, I simply couldn't do this. Ralph, Kimberley and Luke, thank you for supporting and listening, while I ping-pong from jubilation when the writing is going well, to despair when it isn't, and for always loving me, whether the words come out right or not.

BANYAN TREE
~ VABBINFARU ~

WIN A HOLIDAY OF A LIFETIME AT
BANYAN TREE VABBINFARU IN THE MALDIVES!

Included in the prize:

- A seven night stay at Banyan Tree Vabbinfaru in a Beachfront Pool villa for two people
- Full board basis, incl. soft drinks, excl. alcohol
- Return transfers from Male to Banyan Tree Vabbinfaru
- Two × return economy flights from London to Male up to a value of £700 per person
- Trip to be taken between 1 November 2017 and 30 April 2018 Blackout dates include 27 December 2017 – 5 January 2018

To enter the competition visit the website
www.simonandschuster.co.uk

Entrants must be resident in the UK only